NAYANTARA SAHGAL

The author is a novelist and political journalist who has published two volumes of autobiography, PRISON AND CHOCOLATE CAKE and FROM FEAR SET FREE, and six novels – A TIME TO BE HAPPY, THIS TIME OF MORNING, STORM IN CHANDI-GARH, THE DAY IN SHADOW, A SITUATION IN NEW DELHI, RICH LIKE US and PLANS FOR DEPARTURE. She has also written INDIRA GANDHI: HER ROAD TO POWER, a study of Mrs Gandhi's political style. Nayantara Sahgal lives in Dehra Dun, India. Her chief involvement outside writing is with the civil liberties movement launched during the Emergency.

Nayantara Sahgal

RICH LIKE US

First published in Great Britain in 1985 by William Heinemann Ltd.

Sceptre edition 1987

Sceptre is an imprint of Hodder and Stoughton Paperbacks, a division of Hodder and Stoughton Ltd

British Library C.I.P.

Sahgal, Nayantara
   Rich like us.
   I. Title
   823[F]   PR9499.3.S154

   ISBN 0-340-40432-9

Printed and bound in Great Britain for Hodder and Stoughton Paperbacks, a division of Hodder and Stoughton Ltd., Mill Road, Dunton Green, Sevenoaks, Kent (Editorial Office: 47 Bedford Square, London, WC1B 3DP) by Richard Clay Ltd., Bungay, Suffolk. Photoset by Rowland Phototypesetting Ltd., Bury St Edmunds, Suffolk.

To
The Indo-British Experience
and what its sharers have
learned from each other

ACKNOWLEDGEMENTS

The author would like to thank the following for granting permission to quote from their works:

On page 255 quotation from Edward Fitzgerald, *Rubaiyat of Omar Khayyám*, B. K. Khanna and Bros, 158 Harrison Road, Calcutta (no date), page 50.

On pages 125 and 202, the quotations are from 'La Figlia Che Piange' taken from T. S. Elliot, *Collected Poems 1909–1935*, Faber & Faber Ltd, London, 1958, page 34.

On page 130, the quotation is from 'The Puckle Circular', an original document.

On pages 137–139 the quotations are from original documents with National Archives of India, Janpath, New Delhi.

On page 219, the quotation is from the song 'Why Was I Born?' from *Sweet Adeline*, words by Oscar Hammerstein, music by Jerome Kern, published in 1929.

On page 265, the two quotations are from Percival Spear, *India, A Modern History*, Ann Arbor: The University of Michigan Press, 1961, pages 138 and 146.

ONE

The richer the host, the later dinner was served. Dining late was a status symbol, like Scotch whisky, five times the price of the Indian, and the imported car, a particularly costly luxury, that had brought him here from his hotel. 'The first thing those local elites do – not to mention their presidents or generals or whoever's at the top – is to get themselves the biggest, latest model foreign cars,' he had been told in his briefing before this trip, 'and why not? We like the way we live. We can't blame them for wanting to live like us. Besides, it's what makes them ready to buy what we have to sell.'

'Won't you have another drink, Mr Neuman?' his hostess offered.

'I still have some, thank you.'

'It's Scotch.'

He raised his hand in polite refusal. The room was remarkable for its total anonymity. No echo of time past or things to come. Roses stood stiff and upright on display in a blinding array of surgically cut, bulk-bought crystal, to judge by the profusion of vases, ashtrays and bowls all over the room. His host, who had left the room to answer the telephone, returned, a cherubic face on a prematurely elderly frame.

'Another drink, Mr Neuman?'

'Not yet, thanks.'

'It's Scotch.'

'A little later,' he said.

His hostess was curled up on the sofa, tiny and elegant in her airy cotton sari, with decanters and bottles lined up on a trolley at her elbow. Ignoring his refusal she lifted a hand to press a bell near her, the bright cluster on her wrist glinting in the lamplight, and an old white-coated servant hobbled slowly across yards of floor to refill his glass and present it to him.

'So you see,' his host took up the tale where he had left it, 'this emergency is just what we needed. The troublemakers are in jail. An opposition is something we never needed. The way the country's being run now, with one person giving the orders, and no one being allowed to make a fuss about it in the Cabinet or in Parliament, means things can go full steam ahead without delays and weighing pros and cons for ever. Strikes are banned. It's going to be very good for business.'

Neuman had seen huge posters of the Prime Minister's stern unsmiling face, and hoardings proclaiming the nation's support for the emergency declared a month earlier, all over the city. They had made no special impression on him. The walls outside the cool, controlled climate of his hotel room, wherever it happened to be, in a republic, a sheikhdom, or a monarchy, had erupted with predictable regularity into the violent poster paint and purple prose of announcement and celebration, hailing a coup, the return of an old prophet, or the rise of a new messiah. Almost any shoot-out was labelled revolution, even if all it changed was the clique at the top for another clique at the top. Political convulsions left him cold and political clichés bored him. He had no trouble avoiding controversy in the host country as he had been told to do. If the bosses, whoever they were, made their shambling bureaucracies easier to handle, it was all he asked. And this, his host told him, had been taken care of. Neuman was a traveller on his way in or out. He had no interest in prolonging his stay, tempted only occasionally by a fragment from the past, some wondrous bit of broken stone, or a jewel of a temple, the work of stonemasons, not architects, connoisseurs' items for men with time and a different calling. His knowledge of history and archaeology, once his great fascination, had fallen into disuse like other once compelling interests he had discarded because they did not contribute to the financial basis of his happiness. Now that his work here was done, he was impatient to leave. Tomorrow morning he had an appointment in the Ministry of Industry and it would take no longer than ten minutes to confirm the collaboration already agreed on.

Tomorrow midnight he would be on his way home. 'The welcome to foreign firms hasn't been exactly enthusiastic in the past,' the India expert had briefed him. 'They're touchy about their resources and terms for collaboration. Applications take forever to process, even joint-venture proposals. Since the crackdown things are a lot easier. And whatever the changes mean over there, as far as we're concerned their attitude is less doctrinaire about Indian controls and ownership. Partnership still isn't quite on the terms we want it, but it's getting us further than we used to. Look at it this way, there's a vast consumer market out there. If even two out of one hundred Indians use what we manufacture, that's a bigger market than a medium-sized European country.'

A woman in a sleeveless print dress, her hair dyed a peremptory scarlet, was coming ponderously, heavy-treaded into the room.

'Mr Neuman, this is my mother-in-law,' said his hostess.

He got up to greet her and sat down again.

'I was upstairs with my husband,' she said, settling her weight laboriously into a chair.

The drink-serving pantomime was played out again, but this time the old servant bent his head to have a whispered conversation with mother-in-law that lengthened into minutes, so it could not have been a ritual enquiry about when to serve dinner. In any case she was not the mistress of the house, the light and airy creature on the sofa was, and dinner could be hours away. His host cut short the exchange with a curt order to the servant for more ice.

'My husband's lying ill upstairs, Mr Neuman,' said mother-in-law, transferring a bewildered blue-eyed gaze to him. 'He can't move a muscle since his stroke. The doctor says Ram could get well or he could be like this for the rest of his life.'

Neuman was no expert at shades of English, but this broad accent, even with its aitches in place, was Cockney. She drank deeply from her glass before setting it down at last to light a cigarette.

His host cleared his throat and continued, 'We're realizing business is business. The PM's son is in business himself –'

'He's making a people's car,' spoke light and bright from the sofa.

'– and now that you've seen the Minister, our project will get started very soon. Your visit to the Ministry tomorrow is just a formality.'

'You're here on business then, Mr Neuman?' mother-in-law inquired.

'Yes ma'am, I am.'

'Well who says business is business? Never was. It's that and so many other things. Know what I mean?'

If it wasn't actually the difference between peace and opium wars any more, or flags of empire planted and unfurled continents away, it was other dreams of dominion. And after the land there was the sea. But mother-in-law apparently had something else in mind.

'My husband understood business. He started two from scratch, one when he was young, but that one got wiped out by the partition –'

'She means the partition of the country in 1947,' his host explained.

'– and then he started all over again with a different one. Took some doing, let me tell you. And *his* father started off with a mule caravan.' She looked meditatively into her glass. 'Makes you think, doesn't it? Took mules carrying salt all the way to the border, and brought back wool. It was months coming and going. But the money from those mule trains got him started, and that's what educated my husband and set him up in his own business, an' then he comes to England, and meets me, an' –'

'The Tibetan border,' his host interrupted. 'That's a long long time ago, Mummy, and we've come a long way since mules.'

'Don't long-time-ago me. What you call enter-prenner-ship now, or however you pronounce it, is one minute you're nothing and the next minute you're an enter-prenner and a bloomin' millionaire. Where's all the money come from all of a sudden, I'd like to know? I like maharajas better.'

'Really, Mummy, what's the connection?'

'Least you knew where the loot came from.' She got back doggedly to her starting point. 'Business isn't only business. I

learned that standing at the till in my husband's shop in Lahore
that *he'd* set up from scratch –'

Neuman lost the rest of the sentence imagining the electric
effect of her unquenchable hair and whiteness, all red, white and
blue of her – a veritable Union Jack – at the till of the shop in
Lahore. The recollection had brought a flash to her eyes and a
smile to her lips, and suddenly he could see her smooth and
young, an improbable advertisement for a business that owed
its start to a mule caravan winding around roadless mountainsides
to Tibet.

'Mummy's right,' said the sofa voice, high-flying under the
heavy artillery of the Cockney. 'She's talking about public
relations and they're ever so important.'

'I'm not talking about public bloody relations. I'm talking about
human beings. Know what I mean, Mr –'

'Neuman,' he supplied.

'Human beings. Like there don't seem to be any more.' She
looked pointedly at the two who were her family, and her aitches
took flight. 'Take my father-in-law. 'E never saw a contract in
'is life. Couldn't speak a word of English. Wouldn't even have
chairs and tables in 'is part of the 'ouse. 'E was a villager, that's
wot 'e was, and that's wot 'e stayed till 'is dying day. Anyone
wanted to do business with 'im came and sat on the floor, English
people an' all, and did it 'is way. They knew who they were
dealing with, a proper business man down to 'is toes, who knew
everything there was to know about whatever 'e was 'andling,
not like nowadays when the business is minding itself and you're
sitting pretty with the loot. And there's some businesses more
like the 'at trick. Before you can say bob's your uncle, there
they are, out of a 'at.'

Neuman filled the awkward pause. 'Then after the salt trade
he went into other lines?'

Her surprising laughter relieved the tension, unveiling a young
woman again. 'Oh dear me, yes. 'E became quite a power on
the stock exchange. And with no education to speak of. 'E told
me 'e taught 'imself to read by the light of a kerosene lantern in
the room behind the little shack where 'e sold kerosene and
matches and string and things. Funny when you think of all the

money 'e made, it didn't change 'im one little scrap. 'E always hated the city, any city. Said it was a false place. 'E could be a 'ard man all right, didn't stand any nonsense. That's wot made it so odd about 'im and me getting along, but 'e came round to it, 'e did. 'E knew the genuine article. People did business with 'im on trust, you know, nothing in writing, and 'e never made a mistake. 'E'd put in the work, see? *That's* an enter-prenner. Used 'is head and started from scratch.'

'You come from a business family yourself?' Neuman asked in the long pause no one else cared to fill.

"Not me. My father was a working man, spent 'is life working in a bottle factory, and then in the 'ard times after the war, the First War that is, 'e didn't have a job for ages. Always planning for the future, my parents were, we'll be able to afford this next year or the year after, and we'll put this by for a rainy day, and most of the time it was raining, know what I mean, and they were putting it by for even 'arder times.' A clock struck nine and she said, ''Ere, wot about dinner? Mr Neuman must be 'ungry. I know I am.'

The silence stirred. 'We're waiting for Ravi. He's going to tie up some ends for Mr Neuman.'

'Oh 'im. Take 'im all night getting here. I never saw *'im* in a 'urry. Might as well 'ave another gin then, wot about you, Mr Neuman?'

A twitter and flutter from the sofa endorsed the invitation. After the servant had come in and poured drinks, mother-in-law lifted herself with an effort out of her chair in response to some urgent signal from him and went out of the room taking her glass with her. It was another half-hour before the late guest arrived and they sat down to a vast amount of food that Neuman was no longer hungry enough to enjoy. He wondered about the seed he had sown so that giant wheels could turn several thousand miles away, controlled by men in skyscrapers whom those around this table would never see. Across the table from him sat the latecomer, a bureaucrat of importance in the current set-up, Neuman had been told, and part of the conveyor belt that had delivered the cash to the Minister for Industry, relatively minor graft in terms of a big investment and the returns expected from it. Experience had taught Neuman that key figures were never to be underestimated. They had to excel at something, if only the fine art of survival through changing times, directing the beheading of queens, the guillotining of aristocrats and entire revolutions, and when the pendulum swung, ushering in imperial pomp and dynasty with the same superb savoir-faire. This one had a narrow build, brilliant grey eyes in a pale chiselled face, and his uses of speech gave an air of distinction to anything he said. Neuman had known actors like that whose mastery of inflexion made Yes, it's a nice day, sound like a grave and wise observation.

'You've got a perfect piece of land here for your factory,' the bureaucrat remarked.

'Then this is your own land?' Neuman asked his host.

'It was a rural belt, requisitioned from the villagers,' the bureaucrat replied instead, 'with compensation paid, of course. And it will mean jobs for them.'

'Jobs is all very well. What about their 'omes?' came from mother-in-law.

'They have been given compensation,' repeated the host, testily.

'And I suppose it would be all the same to you if a bulldozer came along and levelled this 'ouse and you were given com-peng-say-tion. Compengsaytion! 'Ow do we know if it was enough compengsaytion?'

The bureaucrat rescued the conversation with exemplary tact, turning the talk to his hostess's recent trip to London.

When Neuman came out on to the front verandah with his host, the humidity clasped him in its hot, damp embrace, pasting his shirt and trousers to his skin, creeping down his forehead into his eyes from prickling points in his scalp. Long tongue-like leaves of creeper, black in this light, hung down from the portico, mesmerised and motionless. Nothing stirred. The trees skirting the circular drive drooped like haggard corpses nailed to invisible masts. But overhead a pale, candlelit sky showed signs of life. Stray stabs of feeble lightning and a premonition of thunder promised rain. Rain level during the next hundred days would decide whether the subcontinent's cattle, crops and men lived

16 NAYANTARA SAHGAL

or died. His host's plump cheeks and plump outstretched hand looked unreal against a climate cruel to life. He shook the offered hand, slid thankfully into the car's cool quilted leather interior and leaned back to savour his release from the stifling night and the long drawn out evening. He could hardly see the outline of the medieval tomb across the way. The setting sun had been going down in glory behind it when he had arrived hours earlier, kindling the blackened, rusted stone, suffusing its rough stony hollows with an unearthly light. Stories to tell, more rewarding by far than the contacts he encountered in the life he had chosen. But this monument, like so many others, would go its way to slow, surreptitious ruin unexplored by him, decaying peacefully under the summer sun, sweating out the monsoon with a peculiarly human resignation. As the car turned out of the gate its headlights captured a sight that jerked Neuman forward. Only the face was still a face, tilted sideways at the car, on a neck no thicker than a stalk. Where the stumps, once arms, joined the body, were archways of bone. Altogether a great bone arch, more insect than animal, inching diagonally across the road on its knees. A monster ant, but for the eyes gleaming with intelligence in a face angled enquiringly towards the car. Obviously not a candidate for a job when construction labourers' shanties sprouted, portable slums of thatch and cloth with swarms of ragged children in and out of them. Neuman leaned back and closed his eyes. If they'd do like we do, they'd be rich like us, his briefing had suggested. Eleven thousand miles distant it sounded the way his host's cheeks looked, fat, sleek and unbelievable in the monstrous heat.

Dev started to fume about Rose's behaviour when he came in after seeing Mr Neuman and Ravi off, but Nishi reminded him Rose always talked too much when she drank, and the evening had gone well all the same, thanks to Ravi. The foundation stone would be laid in two months' time and then at last Dev would come into his own. Nishi could understand his wanting to be head of a proper company, and not just running his father's garment business. The new venture was ideal for Dev. With the main equipment coming lock, stock and barrel from abroad he would be saved all the big headaches. It would be almost as simple as pressing a button. She searched sleepily for the phrase Ravi had given her, not press-button, but turn-key. You turned a key and there it all was without the bother of starting an industry from scratch, which Rose had gone on and on about so tiresomely. A key turned, unlocking secrets of ownership, control, importance, all ready-made. Poor Devikins, it was time he had a break. The word forced its way through her drowsiness.

Dev was saying, 'One of these days I'll break her neck.'

'Now Devikins, what a way to talk,' Nishi mumbled into her pillow.

Why did he bother about Rose, wasting his time when there were other things to attend to. He said he didn't know what had happened to the garment business his father had expanded abroad in the last ten years, but how could he *not* know why it tottered and fell, and why the boutiques in London and New York had closed and suppliers had stopped orders?

'The seams weren't even straight on the last batch, Devikins,' she had sighed when he got angry about Mr Goldfinkel's letter. "It was done in too much of a hurry.'

'Don't be stupid. They don't sit down and examine every seam. The garment has got to hold together, that's all. What do they expect when they want seven thousand of them?'

Nishi, who had sewn her own clothes till she got married, and understood the rigorous requirements of the 'hand-made' label, had been ashamed to despatch that particular consignment. Sending it off had endangered their only remaining supply channel, Mr Goldfinkel. The more ambitious projects started by Daddy-ji had already folded up. The fancy French designer had been quite dumbfounded on his last trip, his speech frozen between his teeth. Nishi could tell he was profoundly shocked. It was the greatest of pities, he had said at last, that since the illness of Monsieur, the standards had so regretfully disappeared. A little attention paid perhaps. A little regard for execution. The integrity of the design was of the utmost. And Frederick Graham the Third, though outwardly genial, had lost even less time in ending the association with them when he saw what was happening, even though he had drawn up plans with

Daddy-ji to launch an India Week at all his stores throughout the
United States. Daddy-ji's irreplaceable contacts had dissolved
like ice cubes. Mention of his father did not please Dev, but
Nishi felt obliged to mention his name now and then. He *was*
the head of the family, even though he was lying useless and
paralysed in bed.

'It's your fault,' Dev had said to her about the last disastrous
consignment to Mr Goldfinkel. 'You aren't making those bastards
work.'

Of course workers had to be kept in their place but Dev didn't
know what work was. It meant proper hours and holidays and
nowadays a little politeness, or else they'd start throwing their
weight around, talking back and being cheeky and so forth.
Yesterday when the tailors had asked for time off, Dev had
pushed past her and started yelling at them and it had taken
Nishi the better part of an hour to placate them. They had
gathered in a mutinous knot under the mango tree with swarms
of midges buzzing above their heads around a mango gnawed
open earlier by a parrot. The Tailor Master swore by all nine
Gurus he had threaded his last needle in this compound. Years
of fine needlework, thick-lensed glasses and a white beard gave
him a venerable look and Nishi would have hesitated to talk
rudely to him if only because he was so old. And Dev pouring
mother-sister abuse on to the empty verandah didn't realize
tailors couldn't be treated like cooks and bearers. She wheedled
and coaxed between him and the poised battalion to no avail
until the Tailor Master after conferring with his band promised
to take the matter up with the union, a word that slit through
the argument like acid and put an end to it. Tailors were just
workers, of course, and not a class, but if even they were
starting unions there was no telling what hurdles lay ahead and
her advice to Dev was they'd get more consignments off if he
kept his temper. Later the emergency solved that problem but
by then they weren't in the garment business any more.

With the tantrums and temperament she and the tailors got
from Dev the starch had gone out of the establishment, and
certainly the style. RamRose Fashions had gone from elegance
and quality to sausage production, and misshapen sausages at

that. Even the humble assembly line had its standards and had to conform to accurate specifications, though it was a far cry from the exquisite superior fashions Daddy-ji had begun to acquaint the foreign market with. And somehow he had taken the business smoothly ahead, with just medium-sized bribes to deal with, and most problems at the Indian end solved in a friendly way with bottles of Scotch and five star hotel dinners. Now they were down to a forest of red tape, bogged down in a hierarchical network of bribes to get consignments loaded for the outward journey, or they would lie rotting in warehouses for weeks, and bribes to customs when samples came in, to get them released. Dev was in a temper from morning till night when he need never had got into this situation at all. 'We need a contact in political circles,' he kept saying, when Daddy-ji had managed quite well without one. And if Dev needed a political contact, why didn't he have one, when he'd been to school with so many high-ups?

When Mr Goldfinkel came to India she had a feeling it would be his last trip, or his last as far as they were concerned, though he was altogether more human and understanding than the frozen French perfectionist or Frederick Graham the Third with his genial double face. Yet Dev showed no interest at all in trying to make the evening a success when they invited Mr Goldfinkel and his companion to dinner at his hotel ostensibly to discuss the samples Nishi had shown him that afternoon. Nishi knew the evening would decide the future of the business one way or the other.

'That fancy blouse is gonna cost too much with all that special Indian embroidery and mirrorwork. Don't get me wrong. I got nothing against Indian embroidery. Lucy, here, loves it, don't you, sweetie? And I know you don't have to worry about what it costs you to make it, you've got the cheap labour and you're the boss – do you have any idea what it would cost to make it in the USA? But you've got all those tailors sitting right there on the porch, what a set-up! But *we* got to worry how we're gonna price it because if it's too expensive, the public we're lookin' for isn't gonna buy it.'

'But Mr Goldfinkel –' Nishi began.

'Call me Herb.'

It really was so sweet of Mr Goldfinkel but it was dreadfully awkward calling him Herb if she had only this evening left to call him Herb in.

'Without the embroidery,' said Nishi, 'it'll be a pointless blouse. It won't catch the eye and no one will want it anyway.'

'Who sez so? Once you're sure of your article, you gotta make people want it. Who wants half the things they buy? That's why the supermarkets got music. Even after you've done your shopping you keep on lookin' because you're listenin' to *Yes sir that's my baby*. And you come home with about six different items you didn't want in the first place.'

'I've never been in a supermarket,' said Nishi.

'Hear that, Lucy? She's never bin in a supermarket. When we get them over you gotta take her round the supermarkets.'

There he was again, making it sound like a long, long relationship, bringing a lump to Nishi's throat.

'The public we're lookin' for,' Mr Goldfinkel said to Dev, 'is the budget-minded public. I know your father had a different approach, and he was making high style fashions, exclusive you might say, but that's not what you're after and this is how you can do better is all I'm sayin'.'

Dev, hardly disguising his boredom, said, 'But how long is this demand for Indian readymades going to last?'

'Who cares how long it lasts? Look at it this way, by the time it's over you can go out of business, you've made plenty of money. There used to be the gold rush way back when, now it's ready-to-wear. You make 'em, we'll sell 'em. And Nishi and Lucy, here, will get all the pin money they want, how about that, sweetie?'

Lucy gave Mr Goldfinkel a limpid, fabulashed, moisturized look, and Nishi felt rather moist-eyed herself, he was ever so kind and friendly. Not in a thousand years would pedigreed Frederick Graham the Third have lingered so long after a disastrous consignment. He hadn't even waited till one. But Dev said coolly, 'I don't call that money.'

'Oh I know you're worried about quotas,' Mr Goldfinkel went on, 'but you can't spend time worryin' about quotas. It's a waste of time when you can be gettin' the stuff off before the quotas get less than they are now.'

'Quotas is important, honey,' said Lucy.

'Okay, so quotas is important. And while we're sittin' here talkin' about it, they're gettin' less not more. But let someone else beat his head against walls worryin' about them. Let's you and me cash in. And right now this business has got a turnover you can't beat. Step in and make your fortune.'

It did seem that if you could make a fortune by not much more than producing straight seams, Dev would get down to it and make one, since all that magic money was rolling around for the asking. It wasn't even as if he had any of the work to do. She bought the material and supervised the tailors. But he brooded around while the French designer and Mr Graham the Third did the disappearing trick and a wonderful opportunity painstakingly built by Daddy-ji vanished with them. Mr Goldfinkel and Dev had Scotch after Scotch, Nishi had a sherry, and Lucy two glasses of mineral water, no ice, and one lemon juice, sugarless, before dinner arrived. With every dish on the menu costing so much of Daddy-ji's money, all to get this deal out of danger, Dev could at least have listened to Mr Goldfinkel's suggestions and contributed some comment of his own.

'I just love this,' said Lucy with a sharp intake of breath, staring fascinated at the object on her fork. 'What is it?'

'That? Oh it's just a piece of cucumber,' said Nishi, 'in yogurt – *raita*.'

'I just love it,' said Lucy, radiant.

'Lucy loves yogurt,' said Mr Goldfinkel lovingly. 'Anyone wants to lose weight, they can lose ten pounds before you can say blackstrap molasses if they follow Lucy's diet. Look, it comes to makin' up your mind what you want to do and doin' it. Your father belonged to the smart school, one of every model, hotkootoor like the French say, or like Neiman Marcus, that's a store back home. I seen *one*, just one, fur coat in a room in their store in Dallas. It's a great idea if you got that much floor space and oil men's wives for clients, but we're runnin' a whole different showbiz. And we got plenty of competition.'

'I got to go to the ladies', honey,' said Lucy two minutes after

Dev had gone to the men's, leaving Nishi with Mr Goldfinkel.

'What do you pay those tailors you got workin' for you on your porch?'

Nishi told him.

'What a set-up! You could have a night shift going, pay them extra, double your turnover. Seems like your husband isn't really interested.'

'What makes you say so, Mr Goldfinkel? He's very interested, really he is. It's just that he gets discouraged. We've got so many restrictions here, and then the quotas at your end.'

'Government is a pain in the fanny,' he said. 'Governments could well be the invention of the devil, you can say that again,' though she had not said it before. Mr Goldfinkel leaned towards her across his chicken tandoori. 'But I don't know if this is a problem with the government you got or a business problem you got, or another sort of problem. I think it's a personality problem you got with your husband. Now don't misunderstand me, I feel like we're old friends. And I think you got a personality problem on your hands.'

'What kind?' she asked, anxiously watching business prospects recede.

'I don't wanna step on your culture or anything like that, but you got an ego trip on your hands.'

'What's that?' she asked faintly.

'The message I get is he isn't interested. Maybe he'd rather fly planes, who knows, or do some other kind of business. In this one he's gotta do better. Now you know what a competitive line we're in.'

'I know, and that consignment –'

'Forget about those crooked seams. I came here tellin' myself where there's crooked seams there can be straight ones, provided the party is interested, but you and me got to face the fact he isn't.'

Nishi looked dejectedly at the zigzag orange lightning bolt on Mr Goldfinkel's purple tie.

'The kind of competition there is back in the States, these days the cosmetic surgeons are putting aggressive chins on people.'

'Putting chins?' repeated Nishi, startled.

'It used to be nose jobs, now it's chins. Some fellow comes along with a receding chin and he isn't going to make any impression on the customers so he gets himself another chin. But what I'm tellin' you and I'm tellin' you before your husband comes back from the men's is this isn't his line. If it was he'd be out there thinking up ways to do better. For instance there's companies back home that package store design and there's one that designed meandering aisles so customers won't march straight through but will kind of get stuck and have to notice what's on the shelves.'

'Meandering isles?' echoed Nishi, baffled.

'Yeah, and that's just one of the ways to sell more. When I look at the tailors you got out on your porch you could really be going places, but it isn't what your husband wants, now maybe *you* know what he wants, but it isn't this. I feel like you're my daughter so I'm tellin' you you got an ego trip on your hands.'

And before this fascinating colloquialism could be explained Dev and Lucy were back, and everyone stood up to leave, Lucy towering over Mr Goldfinkel. Dev and Nishi saw them to their room in the hotel and went home, with Dev in a filthy mood all the way home, when all he had been given was some kind advice. They would lose this collaboration too.

'It'll be such a blow to Daddy-ji, if he recovers, losing the French designer and Mr Graham.'

'He's not going to recover so he isn't going to know about it.'

'No, I suppose not.' Her father-in-law had made such a fine impression on her family with his looks and his manners. Such a gentleman, so good to her, so thoughtful of her relatives.

'If he hadn't had a stroke he'd be dying soon anyway. He's getting on.'

'Oh, Devikins.'

'That's what's wrong with this country. Too many old fogies running it.'

'I don't think you should talk about your father like that.'

'Why not? What did he ever do but chase white women, pull out chairs for them, hand them out of cars and screw them behind bushes?'

'Devikins!' she said, shocked. 'He gave you everything you've got.'

'Who else would he give it to? He's only got me. And he probably feels guilty as hell about me. Or did before his stroke.'

It was not for them to judge their elders, thought Nishi silently. The liking of Daddy-ji for European ways was well known, but it was too much to accuse him as Dev did. She thanked heaven the boys were at boarding school, away from this kind of talk. At home she went to Daddy-ji's room to check if the nurse was on duty as she should be. The gooseneck lamp on the desk craned over the nurse's film magazine, casting a ferocious white light on Rekha's latest romance. The figure on the bed was unconscious or asleep. Nishi could not get the scene of his collapse out of her mind. He was not a man who raised his voice much in anger, yet the raging quarrel had reached Nishi's ears as she sat in her own room doing household accounts. She had run into this very room, once his study, to find him and Dev confronting each other, Daddy-ji's face distorted with fury. He staggered back, slowly lowered himself on to the edge of the chair behind him, sagging off it in a heap on the carpet. His last words had been too strangled for her to catch. She had cried out and flown to him, trying futilely to raise the heavy body, then putting a cushion under his head and loosening his tie.

'Stop behaving like a headless chicken. Leave him alone,' Dev commanded. 'I'll ring for a doctor.'

Rose came into the room while he was on the telephone.

'How did this happen?' She sank to the carpet beside Ram.

Dev put the telephone down. 'He had some kind of fit.'

Rose's composure was frightening. 'He didn't have no fit,' she said, hard and level, not taking her eyes off Dev, 'it's you brought this on. I heard you quarrelling from my room. Ram never shouted like that, never in his life.'

Dev, thank goodness, walked out of the room, because when he was in a temper he said rude and terrible things. Nishi stayed with Rose, her mother-in-law after all, until the doctor came. Days afterwards Nishi found, pushed to the back of her own desk, a sheet of paper with rows of m's and r's running along it, and underneath, rows of signatures, Ram L. Surya. The last few had the square-cornered letters of Ram's handwriting and his m's like u's. Only why would Daddy-ji be practising his own handwriting and was this what had started the quarrel? She meant to take it up with Dev but when the boys came home from school for their holidays she couldn't risk any unpleasantness in the house, and after they went back to school it seemed better to let well alone.

Mr Goldfinkel had said goodbye in his own nice goldfinkly way, and not until after his return to New York. His voice crossed the Atlantic and Indian Oceans late one night like a long swimming sigh. 'I could have done business with you, Nishi, but not with your husband. Like I told you, he's not interested.'

TWO

It is uncanny what a bare month of censorship can do, exactly the opposite of what I would have expected of a news blackout. I have heard from people who have lived under it all their lives that censorship really does kill and bury curiosity. What you don't have you stop missing after a while. But one month is just long enough for an artificial silence to start exploding. The facts it is trying to conceal shriek out to be noticed. Since June 26th officially all was well, but it was impossible not to be aware of the sullenness building up along New Delhi's heavily policed roads, and news travelled from the old city of rioting when tenements were torn from under slum dwellers and they were packed off out of sight to distant locations. It did not need much imagination to sense the hate and fear inside the vans with iron-barred windows, like the ones used for collecting stray dogs for drowning, that now roamed the streets picking up citizens for vasectomy. I saw one ahead of me one night, the threatening twinkle of its tail light longer lived than its body disappearing into the dark void. We knew there had been hunger strikes and a breakout of political prisoners from Tihar Jail because the government had printed a denial. The ban on more than five people getting together in a public place did not work in the teeming bazaars of the old city but I had seen a group of seven or eight broken up by the police outside a coffee house in Connaught Place and hustled towards a waiting van. One of the young men had flung the policeman's hand off his shoulder and been kicked from behind for his pains. As he was dragged struggling and shouting to the van his glasses had fallen off. With the unmistakable apparatus of modern authoritarianism all about us, if we could be certain of one fact, it was that everything was not all right. Yet my colleagues and I, passing each other on the stairs and in the corridors of the Ministry, with vague smiles and nods, never stopped to ask each other why we were carrying on as though nothing had happened. Industry was an important Ministry and had to show results.

Once upon a time we had thought of the civil service as 'we' and politicians as 'they', two different sides of the coin. 'We' were bound by more than a discipline. We partook of a mystique. Our job was to stay free of the political circus. We were successors to the ICS, the 'steel frame' the British had ruled India with, but with more on our hands since independence than the steel frame had had in two hundred years. And we had a new tradition to create, our own independent worth to prove. Papa, a member of the ICS himself, had said with a pride I was used to hearing in his voice, 'Sonali, people like you, especially women like you, are going to Indianize India.' It was the day my name had topped the list in the competitive examination for the civil service. He was an emotional man and that day, fifteen years ago, there had been tears in his eyes with the achievement – his as much as mine – of having passed on to me, and only to me of his two daughters, a precious responsibility he had carried, and his firm faith that huge historical change could be peaceful. And though the fires and fevers of my belief were different from his, it touched us both with its magic, this passage from British-trained to Indian-trained machine accomplished without a creak. Papa's work had been his life. His memories of it had been my inheritance. Where had the tradition we were trying to build gone wrong? The distinction between politics and the service had become so badly blurred over the last few years it had all but disappeared. The two sides were hopelessly mixed, with politicians meddling in administration, and favourites like Kachru, the prime example, playing politics as if his life depended on it. His career certainly did. From the three-on-ten general rating most of us now gave him, suddenly he was indispensable, here, there and everywhere, the right hand and left leg of the Prime Minister and her household. And only partly because he was a Kashmiri and next door to being her kith and kin. He was that ineffable blend of mediocrity and respectful response embroidered with manners that counted with the political bosses.

But how much better were the rest of us, pretending the emergency was an emergency, when civil servants should know what a real emergency is? They've dealt with all kinds, partition, famine, war, refugees on a scale so monumental it made refugees of all disasters till then and many after look like minor migrations. We knew this was no emergency. If it had been, the priorities would have been quite different. We were all taking part in a thinly disguised masquerade, preparing the stage for family rule. And we were involved in a conspiracy of silence, which is why we were careful not to do more than say hello when we passed each other in the building, and not to talk about our work after hours, which made after-hours sessions very silent indeed. No one wanted trouble. So long as it didn't touch us, we played along, pretending the Empress's new clothes were beautiful. To put it charitably, we were being realistic. We knew we were up against a power we couldn't handle, individually or collectively. Though I am sure the true explanation is that we are blind from birth, born of parents blind from birth. We do not see what we do not want to, and when we cannot avoid a nasty sight it still can't do much to hurt us. I was superbly insulated by the centuries against that sight in Connaught Place. I, after all, had never been kicked, pushed or slapped, never been threatened with jail. It didn't upset more than five minutes of my day. And then, in spite of the fact that our profession now divided as much as it united us, as the civil service elite we were closer than a class. We were a club, and we knew we would survive the blasts outside only if we pretended they weren't happening. So we pretended, and went on and up the stairs and into our offices without unnecessary talk. Instructions were that files had to move fast and on that morning, one month after June 26th, I wrote a brief rejection in the wide margin of the proposal on my desk. I had had plenty of time to study it and there was no other decision I could make. It was a preposterous proposal, requiring the import of more or less an entire factory. Policy did not allow foreign collaboration in industry except under a complicated set of regulations, although essential items the economy needed that we couldn't produce for ourselves were exempt from the list. There were a number of those but a fizzy drink called Happyola wasn't one of them. When the visiting representative of the company came into my office, I told him so.

Facing me across my desk, he looked taken aback.

'I understood there were changes in policy.'

'There are,' I assured him, 'but they don't apply in this particular case.'

He seemed about to say something, then thought better of it. He didn't get up to go either. He looked absolutely staggered. I waited, wondering what I could add to my rejection.

'I have had an interview with the Minister,' he said, 'and he gave me to understand the project would be considered.'

Something odd there, but since the Minister, new to his portfolio, spent the worst of the heat on official tours in more salubrious climates abroad, and since the only Minister who counted was the Prime Minister, it did not seem a point worth taking up. If the Minister had seen him before he left for Vienna, he must have given him no special assurance, just the usual friendly formula, leaving the details to his department to work out.

'It's a good product,' urged my visitor, 'and we're expanding in Asia.'

My training had taught me to review good harmless products with care and the sellers of wares as the world's most relentless people. What they sold could turn out to be as harmless as radiation, and the new breed of salesmen high technology had spawned were not greatly worried about the fallout from their wares on distant shores. Or they could be really harmless and totally unnecessary. I love choices as much as the next person, but beyond a point variety is for Ali Baba's cave and not this country. There isn't enough money around to buy all the tempting goodies. I was about to explain to my visitor that Asia was one of those mosaics where every few hundred miles there's another sort of regime and regimen, and our own policies had been designed towards self-reliance, producing un-fancy goods but ours, when I stopped myself. It was the sort of statement one could not comfortably make since June 26th. The emergency had given all kinds of new twists and turns to policy and the world's largest democracy was looking like nothing so much as one of the two-bit dictatorships we had loftily looked down upon. The things that had set us apart were not very clear to me any more.

I said, 'We have plenty of soft drinks here to choose from.'

'But you do go in for competition.'

I pointed out the rules again. I got up, we shook hands, and seeing that there was no more to be said, he left. The file moved up to the Minister. And the next morning, one month and one day after June 26th, Kachru came into my room. We are the same age, thirty-eight, and we belong to the same batch in the service. I had watched him chair an international seminar in Delhi last winter. Kachru has the current socio-economic jargon at his fingertips, those tongue-twisters that have banished simple sentences for ever and made experts in one field incomprehensible to all others, and certainly to the public at large. Fluent phrases had rolled off his tongue like choicest silk. He radiated sincerity. His voice and manner conveyed earnestness and commitment. And if one stopped to think what he had said at the end of it all, one was almost persuaded that the reason he hadn't said anything specific or profound was that he was striving to simplify, to tie together a bunch of enormously complex issues for delegates from all over the world. Judging by the bouquets he got he was a raging success, which made me come away with the disturbing suspicion that everyone else there must have been a bit of a fraud too. Kachru, of course, would get through any charade with finesse. It was the realities that floored him. But whatever else I thought of him, he had the social graces befitting a courtier, a man who made a ceremony of everything from lighting a cigarette to opening a conversation, and I was surprised he had just barged in. I looked up to find him there, telling me with the harassed look of a good gynaecologist who can't explain the freak he's delivered, that he didn't know why, but he was to replace me immediately as Joint Secretary in the Ministry of Industry. He waited for me to say something, and when I didn't utter a word, he spread his hands in an apologetic gesture, turned round and walked out. If he had sneaked in and shot me I could not have been more dazed. Yet I remember thinking with a shaft of painful clarity that the kind of automatons we of the civil service have become are not expected to reply. They are expected to obey. Ten minutes later a phone call informed me I was to go back to a posting in my State where, I already knew, and the Union government certainly knew, there was no vacancy at my level. I hadn't merely been transferred without warning, I had been demoted, punished, and humiliated, and I had no inkling why.

I opened the left-hand drawer of my desk for the sake of something to do and my hand shook. I put my right hand over it to stop the tremor. And suddenly I felt as shocked and shaken right through as if I had been physically assaulted. I had no idea what I was supposed to do. Leave, and get the office cleared of my belongings later? Call my personal assistant in and give him instructions about work pending? Let the whole world know what had happened, or say nothing? In this service there is no preparation for instant dismissal. I did nothing at all. An immense fatigue immobilized me. I sat looking at the decrepit office furniture, the beige-brown unevenly hung curtains, the air conditioner thrumming anciently. This shabby sixteen by twenty foot area I had never bothered to refurnish, so the grant had lapsed, was more to me than home. It was my share of what we were trying to build. The window opened on to a segment of Lutyens' orderly mathematical New Delhi, a well-conducted world where things happened according to plan, not whim. Beyond my line of vision was Parliament, circular, colonnaded, serene. The July sky, a boiling grey, was the unbroken sky of a subcontinent, but this bit of it was peculiarly, patiently Indian. The alienness of what had just happened, the midnight knock at midday, for no reason I could understand, paralysed me, until I realized that nothing new or shattering had happened after all. No malign fate had singled me out for punishment. The logic of June 26th had simply caught up with me. The same soundless nudge that landed me in the ditch had carted thousands off to jail, swept hundreds more out of sight to distant 'colonies' to live, herded as many like animals to sterilization centres.

When the telephone rang an hour later at my house it was Rose's warm kind voice. 'Sonali, you're home! I was going to leave a message with your cook to ring me when you got back. What're you doing back at this time of day? But I'm glad I got you. Can you come and see me tomorrow?'

I interrupted the flow of Cockney, unleavened by forty-odd years of being a memsahib in India. 'I can't, Rose, I'm not feeling at all well.'

'You don't sound it. I *am* sorry, love. Ring me when you're better then. I've got to talk to you.'

'What's the matter?' I managed to ask weakly.

'It'll wait till you're better, love. Do you need anything? Shall I come and see you?'

I said no. I couldn't face anyone even as loving as Rose yet. Papa had been friends with her husband, but I liked her for herself. As for the difference in our ages, though she was sixty-three there were times when I felt she was the younger of us. There was such an air of vitality and expectation about Rose, or had been until recently when Uncle Ram had a stroke. She must have been irresistible as a girl. I said I would get in touch with her as soon as I could. When I put down the receiver I felt feverish and I knew I was, quite literally, ill. Kachru, and what the doctor later told me was hepatitis, struck on the same day. In good health I would have got on with routine matters, wound up my affairs at the office, tried to make plans, but illness threw me back on myself. I lay in bed with orders not to leave it unless I had to – a caution I did not need since even talking was an effort. The liver fortunately regenerates itself, given a chance, said the doctor. Just as well, he grumbled, since hepatitis this year was as common as colds and coughs, with the sewage spill into the Jumna making Delhi's dirty water supply more dangerous than ever.

'God knows why we survive at all,' he said, 'with a sun that shines to kill, rains that flood us out, or if it isn't flood, it's drought.'

He put the syringe with my blood in it carefully into his case, went into the bathroom to wash his hands, and stood drying them on his handkerchief.

'No, you're not to get up even to get me a towel,' he said. 'We're a callous people, Sonali, or we'd have remedied many things by now.'

'Stopped the sun from shining?'

'Administration, my dear girl, administration. What's become of it? Why can't we keep the city's water supply clean? Now be a good girl and realize you are very ill.'

He drew the curtain across the window to keep out the sun and said, 'I am sorry about what has happened, my dear. I heard.' Irrelevantly he added, 'When I was a child, I remember my mother getting up at 4 a.m. to walk with the other women to the well to fetch water. Then she got down to the housework, grinding spices and the rest. She had seven children, unassisted. Three of them died before they were a year old. I remember her after one of her pregnancies, leaning out of her bed to stir the *dal* on the stove. The kind of life that makes for courage.'

I felt rigid with the strain of keeping the tears from my eyes, for myself, not womankind.

I had nothing to do but think and that was far from restful, because nothing I had believed in made sense to me any more. Nothing anywhere made sense, since in a moral universe either everything must have meaning or nothing. Memory dragged me backward to reports I had read with momentary shock and then deliberately pushed away because they were too terrible to remember. Appalling images marched through my mind. The bride burnt to death by her in-laws not more than two miles from where I lived because her family could not satisfy their greedy demands for more dowry. She was one of three hundred such women burnt during one year in this our capital city. Criminals blinded by the police with needles dipped in acid to cure them once and for all of crime. Sharecroppers murdered for demanding their share of the harvest. I must have been mad, or so obsessed with my work, that I could push accounts like these from my mind and forget them. In my fever I saw the boy in Connaught Place again and again, stumbling half-blind towards his glasses while the policeman wrenched him in the opposite direction. The boy at least had shouted, fought to free himself, while I, I had walked on. I could see his glasses lying there, cheap black hornrims for the next passerby to pick up or crush underfoot. If human feeling failed me then, had my professional training failed me too? What must an administrator do who sees a citizen kicked and cuffed and arrested for standing on the pavement talking? And if I had never before seen power and authority so nakedly displayed on the pavement, wasn't something very wrong the day it was?

A philosopher I admire wrote that a coward is not a coward 'on account of a cowardly heart or lungs or cerebrum . . . he is like that because he has made himself into a coward by his actions . . . A coward is defined by the deed he has done'. I would wake up sweating, throw off my sheet, and stare into the hot, empty darkness. What if there was a collective will to cowardice, when men and women in their millions, a whole nationful, did cowardly deeds? Was there a way out of that? And how naive the cast-iron idealism I had been brought up with, believing we were moderate, tolerant people, steeped in civilized ways. I should have been differently taught, told how casual we are about cruelty, depravity. I had grown to adulthood nourished on monumental lies. By the end of my illness I had sloughed off my upbringing, the orgy of idealism I had been fed, the second skin of it I wore. It was a relief to tell myself in the dark on one of those interminable nights, 'In many ways we are barbarians. All the evidence says so.' I wished I could throw everything I had been taught away in one grand symbolic gesture, like renouncing my religion, but I couldn't because religion was one thing I had never been taught. There was a holy arrogance about not teaching it, too, the casual assumption that there is no need to pass Hinduism on. It does that itself like the seasons. Nothing on earth can challenge or upset it. So I had no text or scripture to hurl out of the window, but I knew there was no fundamental truth to believe in any more because there *is* no fundamental truth. If anything surprised me, it was only that I had sat at my desk and worked, believing change for the better would come while I sat there, so long as I handled my files properly and made the right recommendations. All would be well because there was a building outside my office called Parliament. Yet an epoch had come to an end in ways we did not recognize. The continuity in affairs that Papa so highly prized had been neatly lifted and tucked like the hem of a garment, while Parliament still stood, the same people met inside it, the surface of Delhi remained unrocked, the sky above cloudless. I had been obsessed with symbols. Well, the symbols were still there. I knew I was getting better when instead of wanting to strangle the sycophancy out of Kachru, my fury spread wider. The emergency had finished my career, but suddenly I didn't want a career in the crumbling unprofessionalism that bowed and scraped to a bogus emergency.

Being well turned out to be another kind of disease. I was a different person, twelve pounds lighter, my clothes hanging on me, with a beginning to make in a situation where there was not so much as a toehold for anyone cast out of official favour. Not one of my colleagues had rung to say hello. Quite likely mine was a case of news not having travelled, but I knew in my heart the Indian Administrative Service had decided by common unspoken consent that I had wilfully disappeared through a trapdoor in my office one July morning without leaving a trace. I didn't even have the sympathy of my nearest and dearest. My sister came to see me, flawless as ever, the discreet lustre of a pearl about her. She was horrified at my predicament, much less concerned about my thin, wan, wasting looks, except to comment on the way my glasses kept slipping off my nose.

'You'd better get contact lenses.'

'Why should I pretend I don't wear glasses when I do?' I said irritably.

'Isn't it awful?' Kiran kept saying, genuinely distressed, but meaning I was suddenly nobody and nothing, not the way I had been treated. 'Surely, Sonali, there's some misunderstanding. You should go right to the top, get an appointment with the PM and explain the whole thing.'

There is a queer idea in Delhi's social circles that 'the top' is a rational, intelligent, humane place, and all the cunning and callousness is conceived at lower levels, behind 'the top's' back. Kiran stubbornly believes that power makes for deity. I much prefer Rose's attitude. She is quite candid about not understanding 'poly-ticks' but that never prevents her from delivering judgements very close to the bone.

'It's no use going to "the top",' I explained wearily. 'The order obviously came from the top. You know perfectly well everything is controlled by one and a half people. Any other kind of decision-making went to pot ages ago. Long before this ridiculous emergency.'

Kiran looked uneasily around though there was no one else in the room. 'Oh, d'you think so?' she said dubiously. 'Well, then you could apologize and get reinstated or something. But surely, Sonali, a transfer back to your State isn't the same thing as a dismissal?'

'It's either humiliation or dismissal, whichever I prefer. There's no vacancy in Uttar Pradesh. I would have to be in a junior post, one I served in before coming to Delhi.'

'Well, at least it would be something. And you could get back into favour later.'

'Oh my God,' I said.

My expression must have stopped her saying any more on the subject. She looked away and sighed, 'There's no need to be so fierce about it. I wish Papa were alive. He was the only one who understood you.'

But Papa had been dead for weeks, and ashes don't even leave a grave to weep over. And what on earth was there to 'understand' about not wanting to grovel and beg favours and act like a worm instead of a person on whom a family's love and pride and a good education and years of training have been lavished?

Kiran got up to go. 'I don't want to tire you. You must move over to the house as soon as the doctor lets you.'

The house was the one Papa had built. He and Mama had shared it with Kiran and her family and meant me to share it after I retired. I would move in, but if I was going to live at peace with myself, every step I took after I left the sick room would have to be away from lives like Kiran and Neel's. Six weeks later, when I could move around without getting exhausted, I started the process of severing my connections with my official past. I had to go back to my office for a final look round.

Briefly I sat down at my desk for the last time, and a train
of thought abruptly severed started again. Even a greenhorn
administrator knew the vital outlines of policy. Its slant and
substance were ingrained into us like multiplication tables from
the day we entered the service. Twice ten can never make fifty.
And Happyola cannot by any standards be a national necessity.
There had to be production, yes. But of what, and for whom?
We had decided long ago that though world markets might
be controlled by other countries, though we were a nothing
currency, expected to sell cheap and buy dear, nevertheless we
were going to do things our way, produce everything ourselves,
and get help on our terms when we wanted it. They keep telling
us, of course, that markets don't work that way, you have to
obey bigger outer laws, it's an interdependent world, and you're
the dependent so you'd better do as you're told. Those might
be the facts, but when did facts make history all by themselves?
And making history was what we were after, nothing less.

From my desk in the office I rang Rose, the first long personal
chat I had had in weeks, and I felt much more human afterwards.

'I do want your advice,' she said, 'but tomorrow morning is
the Happyola foundation stone ceremony. You could come after
it.'

'I'll come to it with you,' I said, surprising myself.

THREE

Rose's bedroom held ghostly spirals of cigarette smoke, gin and cologne essences like treasures replenished when they threatened to disperse. Morning light streamed in but Rose lay half asleep, one open palm cradling a cheek. She had pushed the soft pink blanket down to the foot of the double bed when she had stopped the air conditioner and opened the window some time during the night. The room might have been an island off the mainland of the house, so little had it to do with the cubes and rectangles, chrome and shine, black and white sophistication of the rest of it. Hers had the flowered chintz, frills and flounces, pastel blues and baby pinks she had admired in magazines when she was a girl. It was a room that looked like a room, to live what was left of her life in. Or what was left of Ram's life, for their two lives had never been so vitally linked, even though he lay speechless after his stroke, his study next door converted into a hospital room with a drip machine, a bedpan and a nurse on duty. And though the only communication between her and Ram now was the flicker of recognition his eyes sometimes had, that feeble flicker, more vital than the rest of the household put together, spoke volumes, telling her their need was mutual, that each would live only as long as the other. Was this why they had met in a chocolate shop in London forty-three years ago, and why, obeying an invisible summons, pulled on strings, she had left her home and country without a backward glance? Was this then the meaning of Rose and Ram – or were these only sickroom fancies that muddled and confused her as she sat by his bed every evening?

These days all her imaginings took her back to the past, to her mother's voice, high-pitched with anxiety, calling her a fool, saying, 'I don't know wot's got into you, Rose, 'ere you was,

engaged to Freddie, I am disgusted and so is your Dad.' Poor
Mum, all gone to pieces, not over Rose's broken engagement,
but because Ram whom she was going out with was 'black'.
Rose, just as anxious to be accurate as to soothe and pacify,
had said, ''E's not black, you know, 'e's brown. I mean you *seen*
'im, Mum.' 'I don't care wot shade of black 'e may be, and nor does
your Dad.' Men like that with all that money to throw around were
bounders anyway and then a black one on top of it was what she
meant. 'No good will come of it, Rose, and 'e's still black whatever
kind of gentleman 'e looks like now, taking you out to fine places
your own boyfriend can't afford and the Lord knows wot else.' But
Mum was wrong about 'the Lord knows wot else'. The barrage of
amorous attention her daughter's arresting looks had received for
years had given Rose a vast experience by the age of twenty at
dealing with the male of the species, and Rose had remained virgin
by choice. Ram treated this as a personal affront. Once he had
angrily stalked out of a restaurant, after paying the bill, leaving
her to find her own way home. But he had not been able to coax,
bully or trick her into bed. It was a lovely restaurant, too, an
orchestra playing on one side of the room like in the pictures,
flowers on the table, him and her and the flowers reflected in the
curly-framed mirror panel beside their table. The waiter had just
put their Cherries Jubilee in front of them when Ram had
suggested they go to his flat after dinner. It was no impulse, she
was sure, it had been in his mind all evening right through watching
Jean Harlow in *Red Dust*.

'I don't get your meaning, Mr Ram N. Surya,' Rose had said
very succinctly. Putting down the spoon halfway to her mouth
with a cherry jubilee in it, she had placed her arms squarely on
the table and looked him straight in the eye. 'I was minding my
own business, weighing 'alf a pound of chocolates, coffee cream
and 'ard centres, for a good steady customer, Mr Butterworth,
who comes in regular every Monday –'

'Regularly,' Ram corrected.

'Don't you go teaching me English,' she said, furious at the
interruption. 'Who do you think you are? And who *do* you think
you are, just because you popped up out of the blue one fine
day and took me out to lunch and dinner a few times?'

In the face of righteous anger Ram retreated to his cherries, rolling them disinterestedly around in their bowl. Instead of going in search of easier quarry he was determined to have her, tantalized that a girl he had picked up without much effort was in virtual control of the situation, a chocolate shop pick-up talking to him like a social equal. The accidental meeting had lengthened his trip. His father's two cables summoning him home remained unanswered, and the enormity of the omission did not worry him. Yet Rose showed not the slightest sign of relenting, though she knew perfectly well who he was. He was a man. He was rich. He was abroad. What more did she need to know? The fuss she was making about her silly virginity was quite preposterous. She would never have seen a smart expensive London with her Freddie of the bottle factory.

'Very well,' he said icily, abruptly pushing his chair back and getting up, 'there's no reason for us to meet again.'

He had not expected her scandalized attack. 'You mean that's the only reason you been taking me out? And 'ere I was thinking you liked me. You're bloody right there's no reason to meet again.'

That was when he put down the money for the bill and walked out, ignoring her ''Ere, what about your cherries?' So had she walked out, with as much dignity as she could muster, after finishing her Cherries Jubilee, and then finishing his, no sense in wasting them. Two mornings later he had come to the shop and said, stiff and formal, not to her but to the other girl, Vi, who was serving at the other end of the counter, he wanted the biggest box of assorted chocolates she had, for 'a young lady' he knew. Rose had caught his eye and giggled and he had come over to her, leaned on the counter and said softly so that Vi did not hear, 'I see I'll have to court you properly.'

''Ow d'you mean, court me proper?'

'-ly,' he corrected.

'Oh you, teaching me my own language. What'll you be teaching me next?'

'Lots and lots of things,' he promised, looking intensely desirous and desirable.

She had never seen such speaking eyes, with the power to

open doorways to other worlds, and she shivered in anticipation, but unwary still, since Destiny didn't visit chocolate shops. And now Ram's deliberate talk took the place of her cheerful aimless chatter during their outings.

'Wot's he 'anging around 'ere for?' her mother, more resigned than irate, demanded as his stay lengthened. ''Asn't 'e got a 'ome of 'is own to go back to?'

'Course 'e 'as, Mum. 'E's buying things. It's to do with 'is business at 'ome.'

'You ought to know more about 'is business in all this time.'

'We been talking about ever such a lot of things.'

They were going on more walks, and to fewer restaurants and cinemas, Ram's talk erecting a world around her, drawing her deep into it, the door shutting, Rose inside.

'My father's a genius in his own way,' said Ram. 'If he hadn't had a genius for making money, he would have become the prophet of some terrible, flesh-mortifying order. He goes all out for whatever he does.'

'Sounds frightening to me.'

'I suppose he is. He used to take the stick to me when I was a child. That's why I finally rebelled. Too much discipline.'

'How d'you mean rebelled when you're living in the same house with him?' She was making a special effort to get her speech right. It wasn't easy, with the imagery his words conjured. She didn't have the words to meet it.

'Well, inwardly rebelled. I don't let him arrange my life any more. I go my own way. That's probably why my morals aren't all they should be.'

'There's nothing wrong with your morals,' she said loyally, 'so long as you keep them in check,' and she had hastily got off that dangerous subject.

'But I haven't kept them in check. Also, I drink. My father thinks drink is evil.' They were strolling in the grounds of Hampton Court after a picnic lunch and Ram, who had been telling her about the short unhappy reign of Anne Boleyn as though it was his country's history and not hers, said, 'My father would not have approved of Henry VIII if he'd heard of him. He'd think him a savage.'

'An Englishman a savage?'

'People who drink and sit in their own bath water, not to mention Henry's table manners and womanizing and executing his wives and robbing the monasteries and breaking with the Church. If the force of my father's feeling could have driven the British out of India there wouldn't be an Englishman left in India.'

Rose had looked at him amazed. 'Why doesn't he like the English?'

'He doesn't see why Indian cotton should be sold back to us at enormous prices as English cloth. And when we have trees loaded with citrus fruit why should we have only Cooper's marmalade in the shops? My father's a businessman.'

But the real reason, Rose discovered, was the order passed in his town when he was a boy that Indians had to crawl on their bellies if they wanted to pass a white person on that particular stretch of road. It was where an English missionary called Miss Sherwood had been dragged off her cycle and beaten up in 1919. So a whipping frame had been set up there and six boys had been tied to it and flogged, and Ram's father, who refused to crawl, had been whipped too. Rose was appalled, though Ram lay with leafy patterns on his face, no more bothered than he'd been about Anne Boleyn's beheading.

'Don't you *care?*' she insisted.

'Why get into a lather about what you can't undo?' And one afternoon he told her, in a natural everyday voice, that he had a wife and an infant child. Her shock was so great she couldn't speak. But after some seconds' silence she had begun asking questions about them in what she hoped was *her* natural voice, while her brain grappled with this new turmoil, and a man who could talk about a courtship with her when he was already married and a father.

'How old is your child?'

'He was born last month. My father cabled the news of his birth.'

'Then you haven't even seen him!'

By that time there was no need for a courtship. She had entered an emotional labyrinth and she was drawn magnetically on, with Ram doing no more than holding her hand for the entire

two weeks before he asked her, a victim of casual unthinking
sorcery, to marry him. And it was a sign of the distance she had
travelled that all she could say in a small crushed voice was,
'How can we get married when you're married?'

'My religion lets a man have more than one wife.'

The tart response she would once have made died unspoken
on her tongue. She was out in strange territory and had lost her
way home. She had to marry him, as sane a desire, she knew,
as walking blindfolded off a gangplank into the deep blue sea.
When she got her voice back it was to ask, 'But what about your
father?' And for once Ram had no reply.

Her mother, waiting for the glad news of Ram's departure,
had been distraught at Rose's decision to go with him.

''E's left you no choice quite likely –'

'Oh Mum, it isn't like that at all.'

''Ow can you marry a man that's married? 'E's going to throw
you out when he gets tired of you, 'e's not even a Christian.
And wot's going to protect you out there?'

Poor Mum, religion and everything mixed up in it, and having
to say it twice as loud because Dad was too sad and puzzled to
say anything, especially after getting Freddie work at the bottle
factory so he'd have a nice steady job and everything. Rose was
as distraught as her mother, as baffled as her father, and she
couldn't explain what she was doing. She didn't know herself
any more. Leaving her parents was the only deliberately cruel
thing she had ever done. Their future of security, of plenty,
never seemed to arrive, and now she was deserting them too,
the only tangible future they had disappearing out of their sight.
Rose wept bitterly as she said goodbye, yet her resolve to go
was quite weirdly unimpaired. It had been easier taking leave of
Freddie, the only person who recognized her fateful encounter
with Ram – Ram himself didn't recognize it. Her guilt was
absolved when he said wistfully, 'I knew from the start you
wasn't for me, Rosie, a girl looking like you, and then this bloke
comes along, well it was like you was waiting for it to happen.'

She and Ram had sailed for India together, and spent the first
few days quarrelling when he tried to make love to her. He was
moody and bad-tempered, staring out at the ocean for hours

until one night he had taken her face in his hands as he left her at the door of her cabin and said, 'I do understand, Rose, I do.' She had cried, 'Oh darling, do you?' and had flung herself gratefully, passionately, into his arms and then drawn hastily back, because two bodies were two bodies and warmth was warmth, and she loved him very much.

A ruffled white curtain trembled and billowed inwards at the window near Rose's bed. The breeze on her face woke her but she drifted back to half-sleep, reluctant to face the present. Funny, when she thought about holding Ram off like that until they were married, because in the end they never did have a marriage she or her parents would have called legal, him having a wife already. But holding him off had had very little to do with guarding her virginity. It was the only way she could show him she had a mind and feelings of her own. There were plenty of times in the years afterward – Ram being a man who appreciated female flesh – when her mother's dire prophecies might have come true if he had not learned to respect her for the individual she was. And funny how she had stopped caring about their marriage not being Christian-legal. The sanctity of hoary tradition had not kept Ram attached to his first wife. He had described his elaborate wedding to Rose, hours long, starting at the carefully chosen hour of 1 a.m. of a sweltering May night. Priests poring over horoscopes had picked the date and the hour. Every detail of it had been planned to suit the stars, the sacrament complete with incense, flowers, rice, butter, priests chanting scripture, steps around the fire, hundreds of guests as witnesses. If all that hadn't been proof against failure, what good was it anyway? Rose had anchored her future in what she trusted most, her instincts, and they had not let her down. She had believed in romantic love and it had come true, only never as she had imagined it, no married life beginning with herself in white lace, holding a bouquet of spring flowers, saying, 'I, Rose, take thee, Ram.' The reality was herself in a sari she could hardly keep on, her legs cramped under her, pins and needles torturing her feet, the fire, into which the priest stopped his nasal chanting to throw bits of this and that, stinging her face, her ears filled with foreign talk she couldn't understand, and finally, when she was almost hysterical with fatigue, wifehood. And if none of it had been as she had imagined it, nor was a single other thing afterwards, except Ram's father.

They had arrived tired but exhilarated at the house after a long dusty train journey from Bombay where the ship had docked. They had gone straight to his father's room. A white sheet covered part of the straw matting. He sat cross-legged on it at a low table, turning the pages of what looked like an exercise book containing columns of figures. He glanced up, eyes bleak in his gaunt face, said without raising his voice, 'Take that woman out of my sight,' and went back to his figures.

She and Mona, Ram's wife, lived on different floors, but the sounds, how the sounds carried! The first one Rose remembered was the elaborate prayer chanted in thanksgiving by Mona's priest for Ram's safe return. And then Mona's voice instructing servants hurrying between kitchen and backyard, directing the feeding of beggars once a week, the voice of the mistress of the house, whoever else might be in it. The week had another day when the mistress fasted for her husband's long life and prosperity. And apart from Mona's fasts and prayers, there were Mona's loud insistent tears.

Sonali parked her car under a tree and walked up the stairs and down the corridor to Rose's room, thinking of the ravishing red-and-whiteness of Rose as she had first seen her, and how, even now, powder and paint, so ageing on another woman, seemed to dramatize an innocence no one should have at Rose's age. Hardly anyone looking at the bulky woman past middle age could help being incongruously and instantly aware of her vanished slenderness and youth. It took no more than a smile for a young, decorative, sparkling Rose to materialize for the unsuspecting stranger. Not even her talk, nowadays garrulous and repetitive after the extra gin, spoilt the effect of a whole nature preserved against the corruption of time. Rose had become a legend and not because English wives were rare.

Sonali knocked on the door, turned the handle noiselessly and went in. It gave her a small shock to look at Rose asleep. Only a little over two months since they had met but the remembered radiance belonged to longer ago. This was a woman nearly old, making Sonali realize how much of her own life had passed. At sixty-three not much lies ahead, but at thirty-eight still less. She rescued the pink blanket slipping off the bed and Rose stirred and woke. She sat up and held her arms out to Sonali.

'Look at you, ducks, I thought you said you were well. You're a bag of bones.'

Maternal warmth reached out palpably to enclose Sonali in a little cocoon of concern.

'It's late, Rose, hurry, the foundation stone ceremony will be starting soon,' Sonali told her.

Sonali had not seen the Minister since he had left for his trip abroad, but it was like seeing him for the first time. His long grey hair and long nose giving him an air of mournful erudition were familiar enough. He was reputed to be pious, steeped in religion and culture, patron of priests and astrologers, giver of alms to the poor. In the daily durbar at his house people touched his feet, a greeting he approved of. All this she knew, yet she had seen him, an individual in his office, behind a desk, not as she saw him now, a politician in the full resplendence of public acclaim. Welcome arches had been erected for him along the route and school children carrying banners saying 'She Stood Between Order and Chaos' had been brought in trucks from New Delhi to sing a song in praise of the emergency as the Minister stepped out of his car on to the carpet that extended all the way to the dais. Sonali had been at foundation stone laying ceremonies before, but half-looking and half-listening while she flitted about attending to arrangements. There was time to look at the performers now. The human corridor lining the carpet had its palms glued together, its eyes fastened on the Minister, but some enthusiasts broke ranks to scramble forward to touch his feet, jostling each other in the short scuffle that ensued. Confusion reigned as his entourage stumbled out of cars just behind his. One of them would have tripped and sprawled had a security man behind him not caught him by the back of his *kurta* and restored him expertly to balance. For seconds the chaos the emergency had halted threatened to overtake the scene until security men, pockets bulging with revolvers, pushed forward to clear a passage, while the corridor sighed with relief and muttered thank God that's under control, these days you never knew, enemies of the people lurked waiting. The Minister emerged from the jumble with a beatific smile and, piloted by Dev, started his dignified progress to the dais. Heads swung into profile as he passed, a single immense Egyptian frieze in rapt contemplation, before snapping back to centre again. The breeze of adulation accompanied him as far as the potted plants on the platform where a restrained but approving applause rewarded his arrival. Across the road, dark against the sun, construction workers scooped up their crawling infants, swung their accordion-pleated skirts around their anklets and walked away. Only Rose's handless beggar was left.

'You'd think butter wouldn't melt in his mouth,' whispered Rose as the Minister greeted Nishi and the others on the dais before sitting down. 'He can turn his thoughts to God all right, now that he's got the money safely stashed away in Vienna or wherever he's been.'

'He's just back from Vienna,' Sonali agreed, 'but I thought Switzerland was where ill-gotten gains were kept.'

'Well, wherever it is, I don't know. Wait a minute, I heard them talking about it. It's Venice – no, Venezuela, that's it.'

'The Minister didn't go to Venezuela.'

'He went to Vienna, but it was all arranged about the money being put in an account in Venezuela.'

'He's a fund collector for his party. It's well known.'

'If 'e was collecting it for 'is party, wot's it doing in Venice – Venezuela?' Rose retorted.

Kachru in the first row on the dais looked in excellent spiritual condition, in the right place at the right time, the order of events exactly as anticipated by him. His survivor's skills had never been so evident, thought Sonali, making him appear a spectator to what must surely have been of his own designing. There was no other explanation for him, and not someone else, knocking her off her perch. Dev got up to welcome the Minister and say how grateful he was to have the Happyola foundation stone laid by no other than a person synonymous with religion, tradition and moral values, but he would hasten to add with the modern world, too, as evinced by his fatherly love and unceasing concern for the Happyola project without which this happy day might never have dawned. Dev took out a handkerchief and blew his nose. In the absence of his own father, who lay seriously ill, and of whose life also this would have been the happiest day, he therefore extended a welcome doubly warm, emotional and filial to the Honourable Minister. The Minister spoke next in mellifluous Hindi about the Vedas, the undimmed glory of India's heritage, the high place of selflessness and sacrifice in her tradition and the brightness of the future assured by the emergency. He would not take much of the audience's time, going back only to 1917 when he had first seen the Mahatma in Champaran, Bihar, organizing the great Champaran Satyagraha among the indigo workers. The Mahatma had inspired him to shed his profession, the law, and the luxuries of life, to follow, a humble disciple, in his footsteps. A humble follower of Gandhi was what he still remained though the journey had taken him and the country from Mahatma to Madam. He was but a speck of dust at her feet as he had been of the other. The Minister then laid the decades of his discipleship before them, rejoicing in the service he had been called upon to render his motherland as a Cabinet Minister and, God and Madam willing, he would continue in the Cabinet till the day he died. But a word about the emergency so tenderly portrayed in song as he arrived. Now that it had ended bonded labour and brought other social evils to an end a new era of opportunity and plenty awaited the weaker sections. The Minister's gaze wandered over the audience. When he looked around him, he said, he saw people much better fed and better dressed than ever before. His travels around the country confirmed this. But let it not be forgotten that the weak and the poor, the oppressed, the repressed and the suppressed were the first concern of the government. Radical change was the order of the day and a country united under one party and one Leader would help to bring it about. He ended on the warning note that vested interests had not been entirely vanquished. Left adventurists and Right reactionaries waited to seize their next opportunity to create chaos but the Leader who had never failed to vanquish the enemies of the

people was alert, and with these words it gave him great pleasure
to lay the Happyola foundation stone, augury of the country's
bright future.

'Bright future for him more likely,' muttered Rose while he
laid it.

Escorts flapped and swooped around the VIPs as they
descended from the dais and made their way to the pavilion
where coffee was being served.

'I'm sure to say something wrong in that gathering,' said
Rose. 'We'll go back to the house.'

'It's no secret he collects money,' said Sonali, settled with
a cup of coffee in Rose's room, 'but I don't know about
Venezuela.'

'His daughter-in-law is the collector. Dev's been to her with
a suitcase full of it. I heard him telling about it. She doesn't even
count it. She knows exactly how much it is by tossing it up and
down in her hand. The safe is in her bedroom and sitting right
there on her bed she threw those bundles of notes one by one
into her safe. Good aim she must have with all the practice she's
had.'

'Dev told you?'

'Dev wouldn't tell me anything. I heard him start telling about
it as I was leaving the room to feed the beggar the night the
Happyola man came to dinner, and they were still talking about
it when I got back. But that's not the whole story. After she'd
tossed that lot into her safe, sitting there cross-legged, looking
religious, and it was exactly the amount she'd asked for, *then*
she tells him it isn't enough and the rest will have to be put away
abroad *if* he wants Happyola.'

'And did Dev raise more?'

'It's Ram's money he's been raising, he's never earned a bean,
you know that. But the new lot came from the Happyola man,
Mr Neuman. It's chicken feed for Happyola so everybody's
happy, Dev and Neuman and Shirimutty-sitting-on-her-charpoy
bouncing bundles of money.'

'How did you manage to hear all this?'

'They talk about these things all the time. I can't help hearing.
The talk that goes on at Dev's parties – and why should car

parts and engines be arriving for the Happyola factory? I heard Dev telling one of his cronies.'

It at least explained Happyola, a child of the emergency, with a blanket import licence that would store underground hidden wares for car manufacture, while machines produced a fizzy brown drink above.

'What's worrying me,' said Rose, 'is I don't know what my legal rights are if anything happens to Ram. He never made a will. We're a joint family and Dev is already helping himself to Ram's money.'

'Have you consulted a lawyer?'

'There's the family lawyer, I couldn't talk frankly to him about Dev. Come to that, who *can* one consult nowadays? It's different from the old days. The other night the new doctor Dev's got hold of was here to examine Ram, and Dev asked him to stay on for dinner. It was a party and they were all well away, and the doctor was talking about some patient of his, about his liver or lungs or kidneys or something, as if they were meat in a butcher's shop. It gave me the nastiest feeling.'

Sonali, still recovering from the jolt of Happyola fizzing above car parts, felt her heart beat faster at the thought of the doctor dulled into a society beast by the whisky, in some ghastly way even his medical opinion mixed up with the drink inside him, and Rose watching, listening.

'We used to drink,' said Rose, 'but we talked too, proper talk. Dev's crowd drinks and shouts. I wanted to tell the doctor to stop talking like that. Not that he was shouting more than anyone else, you *had* to shout to be heard, but he *was* shouting, and all about some poor patient of his. It sounded more as if he was trying to kill the man than cure him. He said it would be quite possible to finish him off, yes that's what he said, finish him off with salt tablets, ordinary salt, instead of his medicine, because plain salt in big enough doses could kill a man in that condition. Sonali, why are you looking at me like that?'

'Who were they talking about, Rose?'

'I don't know, there was such a mob, they got on to poly-ticks and this came up.'

But had they turned around and seen Rose's eyes on them,

known she was listening to a doctor-butcher prescribe an appallingly simple prescription for death behind bars, to be followed by two days' national mourning for an old and misguided freedom fighter who had, regrettably, died of old age in prison?

Sonali said with a sense of urgency, 'I'll consult a lawyer for you as quickly as possible. Neel is sure to know one.'

'Ravi was there that night,' Rose remembered.

'He's everywhere. He's indispensable.'

'Not enough red blood in his veins, that's his trouble. You were sensible not to marry him,' said Rose.

And as Sonali got up to leave, Rose said, 'Can't we get artificial hands for the beggar, Sonali? He can't do any work without them.'

FOUR

I wanted my part of the house to look as different as possible
from Kiran and Neel's though it was bound to since I didn't have
their income. I would have been happier with more to spend. A
journalist had told me after he had been to interview the Defence
Minister at his house, 'Such a simple man. He lives like any
other lower middle class family man.' Too many of the simple
men and women who rule us, along with their sons and daughters
and in-laws and best friends, have cured the rest of us of
simplicity for ever. In any case, poverty and simplicity are for
the satiated. Indians are reaching for their share of the goods
of the earth. All I wanted was my own kind of rooms. I hated a
'show'. I think one reason why I never married was the weddings
I saw as a child. I'll never forget Bimmie's, who was only sixteen
and still in the tenth standard of the convent Kiran and I, much
younger than her, attended. On our way to her wedding that
September night with our parents our car got wedged in the
winding motorcade of the bridegroom's party because of our
late start. We were moving with suffocating slowness, halting
every few minutes, parallel with the hired band in red uniforms
with braid and trimmings, and on its other side men carrying
gas lanterns slung from poles on their shoulders. Trees stepped
into the spotlight and retreated into darkness as we passed,
and percussion instruments shone in the theatrical daylight of
acetylene flares. If I had put my hand out I could have touched
the blown-out cheek of a trumpeter. I could see the sweat
beading his face and the stain of hair oil at the rim of his cap.
His trumpet brayed in monotonous spasms above the discord of
cymbal and drum further up the road, all the tuneless dissonance
imprisoned in hot bright fluorescence. Volleys of errant notes
broke loose and splintered the outer air, colliding and crashing

in a confusion of noise so deafening, I had to cover my ears. It was a relief when we managed to manoeuvre out of the motorcade and find our way down another road to the bride's house.

'What a racket! They *will* overdo things,' my mother complained as we drove through the gates into the overdone rainbow lighting of the garden. 'Punjabis have no taste.'

Kiran and I followed her into the room where the bride waited, looking like a tent. I couldn't see her face under the crimson and gold sari pulled so low over her forehead, but in any case my eyes were riveted to the backs of her hands cobwebbed with fine gold chains, a regular cat's cradle of them attached to the rings on her fingers. A busybody relative drew Bimmie's sari aside from her face to show my mother tiers of gold chains below the red and green stones flashing at her throat. I did not identify anything so red, so green and so big as rubies and emeralds, and asked the busybody if that's what those whacking great stones were, and she said 'Isn't she the clever one' to my furious mother. 'Sonali, behave yourself!' But I was hypnotized by Bimmie's nose ring, the sandalpaste dots on her face, eyes downcast, and those manacled hands resting submissively in her red silk lap. This was never Bimmie. 'Hey, Bimmie!' I hissed. She looked up and it was her in the tent and the chains and the dots, nobody else. Wails welled up in me, erupting like claps of thunder into the room. 'You'll get a good thrashing when I get you home, Sonali, I don't know what's come over you.' The busybody bustled up, 'Your turn will come, little darling, never worry,' while other busybodies fussed around Bimmie, tilting her head, fiddling with her bangles and chains, stroking her cheek, praising her sweet, docile nature, which made it clear they knew nothing about Bimmie and had captured and tented her by mistake. My wailing protest did nothing to keep Bimmie's future at bay. I could hear it approaching to trumpet and drums through the frightful noise I was making. A trumpet blast announced its arrival and everyone tumbled out excitedly to the front steps to receive it, though a few stayed behind to take Bimmie out, walking as slowly as if she'd grown old, her head hanging and her sari pulled down over her face. Bimmie! My heart felt like a stone.

'Kiran's wedding won't be like that, will it, will it?' I harried my mother on the way home.

'Certainly not, we're not Punjabis. Nor will yours.'

'What are we?'

'You know perfectly well what we are, don't ask silly questions.'

The home was my mother's and my mother's culture prevailed in it, so we were Kashmiris, and Kashminess is the more powerful for inhabiting a territory of the imagination. The three-hundred-year-old migration from the Kashmir Valley to the Moghul court at Agra might have been three minutes. Our customs, food and complexions might have been plucked fresh today from the Valley. All the delicacies of Papa's Maharashtra passed us by, and it would have been a silly question to ask why, because which Kashmiri in his right mind would eat any but Kashmiri food? It must have been high caste – all Kashmiri Hindus are Brahmins – and their usefulness as administrators to the marauders, that saved them from slaughter or conversion by the Afghan invaders of Kashmir. Survival knit them tightly together, made profit and loss terms of power and position, and gave one of the world's oldest aristocracies its air of regal condescension toward the inhabitants of the Indian plains. And then Kashmiris had ruled India since independence so they, I mean *we*, were entitled to feel smug and special. But Kashmiri or no Kashmiri, there was no getting away from marriage. It was what life was about, from Kabul to the sea.

'A boy for Sonali' sent me into tantrums in my early teens. 'Really Sonali, there's no need to start screaming and shouting like a *jungli* whenever marriage is mentioned. Nobody's forcing you.' Nobody was forcing me. They were just waiting to catch me like flying fish are caught when they leap up out of the waves, like Bimmie had been caught in midair tossing a basketball into a net, waiting to say Ha! Got you! and turn you into a sweet and docile nature. And when Kachru became 'the boy' I was caught and pinned like a butterfly by his mother's fond looks as I passed through a room. Bhabi-jān, as Kachru and all of us called her, cuddled me with a future-settled knowingness, her smile serene in a face to preside over pregnancies.

Taking me to her Mata-ji was my mother's way of settling me down, as though I were abnormally risen dough to be patted down into shape by the saintly presence.

'What did she do to become a saint?'

'She didn't do anything. Saints are saints because they are good and holy. They pray and they think of God. And don't ask silly questions.'

So far I only knew the convent saints, arrows stuck into their bleeding bodies, eyes rolling heavenward in agony, their plaster statues surrounded by terra cotta angels. They were fishermen and tax collectors who had ended up saints. They'd earned their halos. I stared at the blob who was my mother's saint, who neither ate nor drank nor moved, and hardly spoke, much less earned her keep. Her disciples fed morsels into the big bland frame, dressed and undressed her, took her to the bathroom, stuffed or starved her as they pleased. Another inanimate object like approaching marriage had made Bimmie. Outside, shaven-headed little girls wrapped in grimy saris, girls younger than me, waited for leftover food to be thrown to them from the saint's kitchen, their susurrating, overlapping voices cut off to a sibilance softer than bats' wings. My mother stopped me staring and we hurried past them. Child widows. Their karma. Nothing to be done. And repeated visits to the saint did nothing for me. Just the same, it's good for her to be in the Presence, it has a soothing effect, my mother told Papa, don't go ruining it now, when I hung around his neck and muttered, Do I have to go to the saint again?

The saint unsettled me once and for all. Kachru and I fled our different ways, he to college in Delhi, I in Lucknow, while our mothers schemed and waited for us to cross the degree hurdle. And then! A marriage joined from top to bottom by caste, community and background, *koftas* and *mitha bhatta*, was the best, they said, both forgetting in their tribal plotting that Papa was a Maharashtrian. You're wrong, Sonali, my mother said, his people came from Kashmir too. The Sarasvat Brahmins all came originally from Kashmir. Most of us settled in the north, but some went south. Not south, she amended hastily, more southwest, but they were really northerners who went a little

further afield, that's all. But there's nothing Kashmiri about
them, I pointed out. I mean Papa's not what you'd call *fair*.
Mama's look silenced that line of argument. Your father's complexion is a good colour for a man. But what about them eating
coconut and garlic and fish for three hundred years instead of
kofta and *mitha bhatta* and *chaman*, and three hundred years of
facing the Arabian Sea outward to other continents and thinking
seaward thoughts, and what about their language being Marathi,
what about all that? Quite touching the way the girl is attached
to her father, said Bhabi-jān, impaling me on a loving glance.

Papa, I told him in panic, I am going abroad after my BA. I
don't care if you didn't send Kiran, I'm not Kiran. I love coconut
and garlic, Marathi, Gujerati and Malayali food. And Konkani
fish curry. This country is three-quarters surrounded by water
so there have to be hundreds of ways to cook fish and Tamil is
the world's oldest language. And why would you have given me
a Bengali name if there wasn't a rest of India? Papa looked up
from the book he was reading, made a long mental journey
northward from the Deccan plateau, outward from tempestuous
waters I knew nothing of but sensed in his dark/not light-skinned
face and smiled his sweetest smile. It will depend upon your
performance in your BA, Sonali. If you think universities abroad
take third-rate students, you can think again. And that is probably
what drove me to frantic competition, to stardom in my studies,
to deliverance from suitable 'boys' and marriage, abroad. And
to everything afterwards, from a career of my own to not
wearing contact lenses and wanting my living room to look my
own.

My luggage arrived from the government accommodation I
had lived in and most of it was books. In another corner of what
was going to be my living room were two trunks of Papa's papers
Kiran had taken out of the godown now that I would have time
to sort them out. I sat down on one of my book crates, my
glasses beside me, so I did not immediately recognize the man
who came in as Kachru.

'May I help?'

I picked up my glasses and put them on.

'I hope I'm not intruding,' he said.

He came into the room convivial and chatty.

'I didn't know you'd been ill,' he continued, 'I'm sorry. I had no idea. And the day of the Happyola ceremony when Dev and Nishi told me, you disappeared before I could get to you.'

I took my glasses off and put them beside me on the crate again. Even after 'You Tarzan, me Jane' there is something to say, a warm physical purpose to pursue, if no other, but what reality could there be between Kachru and me any more? The tensions between us were nearly as old and wrinkled as the pond water at the bottom of his garden looked years ago, just before the monsoon unwrinkled and rejuvenated it again, the first intoxicating downpour we used to rush out to sing and dance in. He sat down on a crate facing me.

'You have every right to be annoyed, Sonali. I'm sorry they picked me to replace you, and I know how you feel about the emergency, but all any of us have been doing is our jobs.'

The conscientiousness of civil servants knows no bounds. Austerlitz and Dachau, emergencies and genocides are on record to prove it. But I couldn't just keep taking off and putting on my glasses. Nor was there any need to ask, Would you be so enthusiastic about the emergency and a royal family if the family came from south of the Vindhyas, if it had a dark skin and spoke Tamil or Telegu, if its name was Venkataraman or Balasubramaniam? I knew very well that Kachru's sun had to rise in the north, on the banks of the Jhelum in Kashmir, and sink into the horizon no further south than the Gangetic Plain. What I wanted to ask was how had he, of all people, made the journey from the Communist Manifesto to royalist? Didn't he see somewhere inside him the absurdity of it?

But what was the use, oh what was the use of anything any more? The past was finished, and when I thought of the future I saw only as far ahead as a lawyer for Rose and hands for the beggar.

FIVE

Rose had been wretched after her arrival in India, with a rebellious active misery quite different from the creeping uneasiness she felt now, more than forty years later. It wasn't only this house, though the small flat she and Ram had had in Delhi after the Partition had been so much nicer as well as being within reach of friends, and the house in Lahore had eventually become home, with its high ceilings, rooms opening into other rooms, acres of sparsely furnished space and no privacy at all. A bed was a bed, not like the bed she had now, consisting of eight inches of coils, springs and fibre on eight more inches of wooden base. The *nivar* beds they had used in Lahore had looked austere but were cool and comfortable. They were taken down into the garden once a month for the cloth bands to be rewoven tighter on their wooden frames, carried in and out of the house with ease and lightly up the narrow curving stair to the roof terrace, degrees cooler than the rest of the house, where she and Ram slept during the hot weather under mosquito nets. Food was cooked on wood and coal. Electric lighting had come to Lahore seven years earlier but there was no fridge, and until Ram had the bathrooms redesigned, no flush toilet. Ram's wife, Mona, and his father, lived on the ground floor with infant Dev, and if they were hostile, it was a natural enough reaction to an intruder, a usurper. The undeclared war around her now was harder to understand.

Ram should have taken another house in Lahore, but she had stopped arguing about it when he said lives and assets could not be so easily separated, the Hindu Undivided Family was a legal entity under laws and laws apart, flesh and blood bonds could not be broken. And though he didn't say it, whoever heard of a man moving away from his new-born son? She wondered what

had possessed her to imagine against all the evidence herself
and Ram living in a house of their own surrounded by a garden
with English flowers in it, a blessed English privacy enclosing
them? Whatever had possessed her to imagine just herself and
Ram?

Mona's protest was far from silent. Calling upon the Almighty
to spell out what she had done in this or past lives to deserve
such outrageous treatment, she had wept with vigour. Rose,
who had not set eyes on her, only heard her loud, unnerving
lamentations. Some nights she got so carried away that Ram,
tossing and grumbling in his bed, would finally get up and go
down and Mona would reclaim her husband for a few minutes,
an hour or a night. Stars glimmered through the mosquito net
as Rose lay on her back wide awake, counting them, listening
to Mona's accusations die down and the leisurely murmur of
two voices take their place. Sounds she could not distinguish
travelled up from Mona's room overlooking the garden. She
woke much later to Ram's step on the stair. The luminous
dial of her bedside clock told her not much of the night was
left.

'I don't think I can take much more of this, Ram.'

'Of what?' he had the temerity to ask.

'You living with two wives.'

He was stretched out on his bed, too good-humoured and too
lazy to quarrel. 'Lord Krishna had three hundred.'

'Oh, 'e did, did 'e? And what did 'e do for the other sixty-five
days of the year?'

Ram laughed and admitted a certain amount of duplication
must have become necessary.

'I can't go on like this.'

Ram crossed his arms under his head, contemplating a different sky, another universe. 'How does it hurt us, Rose, to live
upstairs and let Mona live downstairs? There must be cases like
ours in this very city, though perhaps not so much on display.
I know a man who keeps his first wife and five children in his
village and lives here in town with his second wife, but everyone
knows about the arrangement, so what's the point of hiding
it?'

'I'm not a case,' said Rose.

'Of course not, my dearest Rose. But there's no divorce. Hindu marriage is not a contract, it's a sacrament.'

'It's no good using all those long words at me. You know as well as I do that this is ridiculous.'

'King Dasrath, Rama's father, had four wives,' he went on amiably.

'I thought it was Mohammedans who had four wives.'

'Muslims can have *only* four, at a time. We are more adventurous, even polyandrous. In the Mahabharata a woman marries five brothers, in a charming accidental sort of way. One of the brothers goes to their mother, who is blind, and says, "Mother, we have found something precious." And she replies, "Then share it among you, my sons."'

'Why didn't they tell her it was a woman they'd found and not a thing?'

'They did put it rather ambiguously, so Draupadi married all five brothers.'

'I call it disgusting, this poly-whichever it is.'

'It's not Christian,' he admitted, 'and much good it did her having five husbands. They gambled her away in a game of dice after they'd lost everything else they owned.'

'Charming chaps,' said Rose.

'Mythology is like that, human behaviour in the raw. Look at the Greeks.'

'I don't know anything about the Greeks, but it seems to me, if you want to behave all right, you do, and if you don't want to, you blame it on what your mother made you do, or on the Greeks.'

'My good Christian Rose,' said Ram, delighted and amused.

Should she be bursting her sides laughing too, at Mona down there suckling the infant whose arrival had been announced by cable when Ram was courting Rose and behaving like King Henry VIII he was telling her about? What was so funny about infant cries floating up in the night and early morning, at Mona still milk-burdened and practically under their beds? If only they had a house of their own. The stars disappeared, the sky grew pale, a bird sang somewhere in the garden. The kitchen door opened and shut with a bang. It would be Kumar getting the fire going to boil a kettle for tea. They heard him on the stair bringing their tray. He set it down quietly and went away. Rose got out of bed and sat in one of the two hard wooden chairs kept on the terrace for their morning tea. Her back felt very straight. Her nerves were steady. She had survived the shocks of the first weeks of adjustment. She and Ram no longer quarrelled, they conversed, like two reasonable middle-aged people with their tempests behind them. Rose felt angry, bitter, wronged. She could ask Ram to book her a passage back to England and he would. He was generous with his money and there was plenty of it. But she didn't want to go home, leaving him here to console and comfort Mona in her weeping fits, solicitous when summoned in the night to watch Mona breast-feed their baby, a man who flourished in intimacy, who unlike other men seemed to become more and more interested and involved with his women. But even otherwise, Rose could no more have abandoned her marriage than an exploration of the Antarctic in mid-ocean, or a story mid-story, never knowing what was going to happen next and next. Whatever the reason she was good and stuck. The Christian ceremony she'd never had put it in a nutshell. For better or for worse. She poured a cup of tea and handed it to Ram.

'Suppose a woman married five brothers today?'

'If it had worked out well, it would still be going on. It does, of course, in some communities in a few remote places, but nowhere else.'

There was no getting the better of Ram, he could talk the hind leg off the Devil. She had only one dull old argument, that this was a lunatic way for a married couple to live in the year 1932.

'Is tea finished, memsahib?' Kumar stood by her chair, as young as herself, a sympathetic and approving spirit in an alien household. 'Was it all right?'

'Yes, Kumar, lovely tea.'

Soaping her hands in the basin later reminded Rose of her mother's arms elbow-deep in the steam and carbolic soap of the week's washing, hanging clothes to dry on the line outside if there was sun, more often stringing them above the kitchen stove. Dad's arm timidly encircling Mum's waist and Mum sighing, more weary than cross, 'Ow, get away with you, Alf, just because you're laid off doesn't mean I 'aven't got my work to do.' Tired sex at night, fear of more mouths to feed. The timid tentative flight that had produced Rose must have got grounded for fear of accident, and loving each other had fallen into disuse. Had she ever seen them looking at each other, and not at kitchen sinks and washing tubs and dirt shovels? Had they ever seen themselves reflected in each other's eyes long enough to read each other's thoughts? There was none of that in other parents' eyes either. Down the road identical houses mirrored identical disappointments and defeats, though it was a monotony broken, unlike her parents', with gaggles of children. The adult world around Mum talked of nothing but remedy. Broths and brews, prayers and knitting needles, scissors and gin, hope-against-hope that might abort a pregnancy. Miscarriages were better than nothing, but in the end you were back to full-term deliveries, your bruised and battered body returned, a loose empty sack to fill up again. She heard women telling her mother, 'You don't know how lucky you are.' And here was Rose, lucky too, her life enough of a muddle without a child added to it. The women down the road of her childhood would have told her, quick as they were to see the signs or their lack, that she should have been expecting by now if she was ever going to. Chance had brought Rose to another meadow. She would have said Ram had the rare sensitivity of the blind and the deaf if he had not had such a thorough acquaintance with the pleasures of the senses, a voluptuary's delight in everything his hands and eyes touched, the treasures in the gift shop he had opened, the special editions he kept there in a private alcove, with illustrations of court ladies and their lovers, peacocks and lotuses, books of Persian and English poetry and, of course, Rose herself. It was his world, from roof terrace to alcove, and she an idle guest, housed, feasted and invited to enjoy herself. A life like this, with all its silver nutmegs and golden pears, no cares, no responsibilities, had to be paid for somewhere, didn't it?

* * *

'It's no way for a married couple to live, Rose, I don't know how you put up with it. Dick says you're a heroine the way you put up with it.'

'Oh, I don't know about that, Minnie.'

'I can't think of a soul who would. Put the tray down here, Boy.'

Boy had a grey beard and side whiskers, Rose observed.

'What's his name?' she asked when he had gone.

'I haven't got a clue,' said Minnie. 'We always call the bearer Boy and the cook Ahmed. Dick had a cook called Ahmed before he married me and after that there's been so many I can't remember their names. Here, try one of these cheese tarts. Our new Ahmed's learned how to make them. But how does it work out, Rose? It must be grim for you.'

''E can't very well turn 'er out, can 'e? It would be 'eartless,' said Rose.

'That's what I mean, you're so generous.' Minnie poured hot milk into Rose's coffee. 'But it must get on your nerves, you should come over more often.'

'But I do come every Tuesday, Minnie.'

'What's every Tuesday when you're so far from home? Why don't you come up to Simla with Dick and me, that's if Ram isn't taking you?'

But I want to be with Ram, and this *is* my home, I'm not far from home, she wanted to say. But explaining was an endless tug-of-war with herself. She was at both ends pulling. When she won, she also lost. Whatever happened, she lost.

'I forgot to tell you, Dick rang when he got to the office to say there's going to be a procession starting in about half an hour's time and there's bound to be trouble in the streets. Why don't you stay to lunch and let Dick drop you home later?'

'I promised I'd be back. Ram's got a friend to lunch. If I leave now I won't get caught.'

'You don't understand, Rose. These will be rowdies out to make trouble, not our kind of Indians. It's too risky. Ram wouldn't like it at all.'

And Rose, insisting on leaving, found herself at the heart of the procession in a thoroughfare dense with humanity. The crowd surging forward on either side the car with the frenzy of a bursting dam convinced her it would blast a tunnel right through this obstructive piece of toy machinery if it could. It converged in front of the car to spread broad and hard as frozen flood waters, touching other crowds at the edges, shopkeepers who stood, arms folded across chests, outside their shops, with garlanded balconies of people above them. She looked back through the rear window on a mass as solid and unbreakable. What had the driver been thinking of, coming straight into this? Unknown, impenetrable faces encircled her and far ahead she could seen a man swing round, walk backward a few steps, throw his arms into the air and empty his lungs into the skies. The human river roared the words after him, a hoarse ecstasy reverberating up and down the road.

'What are they shouting?' she asked the driver.

'Inquilab Zindabad.'

He did not translate it for her or turn round to look at her when he replied, though the car was almost stationary and his hands rested idly on the wheel. He was joined to the spectacle outside, behind the wheel against his will, nothing but crushable metal between him and the mob. If the car dissolved and disappeared he would become one of them, the same strange cry of *Inquila-a-b* issuing from his throat. Crowds thumped and bumped against the car, hands smeared the window glass she had rolled up in a sudden panicky need for protection. But she felt no safer between glass windows a stone could easily smash, and the dirty hand marks on them were as insulting as blows on her cheeks. The driver, usually so careful with the car, did not even order hands off the glass. Fright convulsed Rose. She shrank back against the seat, gripping her handbag, remembering Miss Sherwood at the mercy of a mob, dragged off her bicycle and beaten, her body left trampled on the street. And here though she was in a car, what protection was a car if they smelled the blood of an Englishwoman? But the mob was thinning, at last the car was moving, the procession was marching rapidly ahead, and then it was gone.

Rose sat up, feeling curiously abandoned, wondering if it had happened at all, so quickly had all signs of it vanished. The street was back to normal, shopkeepers behind their counters. The marchers had gone, not so much as glancing at her. Their tumult was taking them somewhere else. They had no emotion to spare for her, not even hate. She was of no importance to anybody. She felt calm and listless, certain she would leave the country. It would never be hers and Ram would never make it easier for her to live in it. Why after all was she hurrying to him? After the driver had delivered her to the doorstep and driven the car away to the garage at the back of the compound near the kitchen, she lingered on the verandah in front of the old mirrored umbrella stand to look at a strained unfamiliar face, small and white against the heated purple bougainvillaea bordering the red-gravelled drive behind her. I've got to get away from things I don't understand. How can anyone live two lives, be on two sides, without going mad? The hall was cool and empty but she heard a man's excited voice in the drawing room say there had never been civil disobedience on this scale before with thousands of women arrested, too. Lord Willingdon had made the worst miscalculation, arresting Gandhi when he arrived home after the Round Table Conference. It was the beginning of the end of British rule.

'Rose, are you all right?' Ram came forward to put a protective arm around her and a glass of lemonade in her hand. 'How did you get through? Keshav wants us to believe it's the beginning of the end of empire. British rule is always about to end according to him. If it ends quickly enough he won't have to join the ICS.'

You must be joking, she wanted to say, empires don't end like that. The procession had passed her by. No one had stoned the car or smashed a window or so much as looked at her. But she wasn't clever, how would she know about history and politics?

'What is your opinion?' Keshav asked her.

'Mine?' she was astonished. 'I don't know anything about poly-ticks.'

'Ram said you came through the procession. What was your impression?'

'It didn't look like real trouble to me, not like if the army turned against the government or anything like that. That *would* be the end.'

Another Mutiny, they laughed, what next! If that was the prescription, the sun would never set on the British Empire.

'And I'm afraid it's government service for you,' said Ram.

'It will be in any case,' agreed Keshav, 'because we keep becoming what our parents want us to be.'

Rose, too curious to contain herself, asked, 'But why are you joining the ICS if you want British rule to end? Whose side are you on anyway?'

Afterwards she couldn't remember the exact words of his reply, only that she had understood it in her very bones, and the bits of dancing disorder her own days were made of had come to rest as he described himself – though it could have been her he was describing – as two people, at home and in exile, ecstatic and wretched, Indian and British, saved and doomed.

'Doom is getting a bit melodramatic,' Ram had objected.

'We're doomed for reasons like Rama's cruelty. We revere the Ramayana and worship a man who turned his wife out alone and pregnant into the forest. Not even ordeal by fire, proving her purity, saved her. How am I supposed to know what's right for me to do – whose "side" I'm on, as Rose says – if even what we worship needs second thoughts?'

'Myths and legends,' said Rose's Ram tolerantly. 'Keshav comes from a family of feminists, Rose. His father marched in a suffragette procession in London, probably the only man there. And Keshav must be the only person on earth to tie himself up in knots about Sita who died about 2,000 years ago if she lived at all.'

'What's the Ramayana?' asked Rose.

'A short poem of 24,000 couplets arranged in seven books,' said Keshav.

Rose asked weakly, 'How d'you mean short?'

'Compared with the Mahabharata which is about 100,000 couplets.'

'I don't know what's in all those thousands of couplets,' said Rose, 'but I wouldn't say you're exactly doomed, I'd say you're more like on a seesaw going up and down and that's enough to drive one crazy if it goes on and on.'

Keshav, studying her attentively, earnestly, thinking, she

supposed of Mahatma Gandhi, Lord Willingdon and the ICS, said yes, that was exactly it, a seesaw was what he was on, and it was definitely driving him crazy.

'How's our Marcella?' asked Rose.

They giggled about Marcella over coffee on Tuesdays. Rose and Minnie had first seen her at the bridge room and bar called the Green Room in Simla last summer with the men buzzing around her like flies around a honey pot after the performance of *Lady Windermere's Fan* attended by the Governor.

'It's never a good sign, not that many,' Minnie had informed Rose as they sat by themselves with the gimlets Dick had brought them when he returned to his friends at the bar.

'Why ever not?'

'If she's a husband-hunter like we know she is, then it puts her too much in demand. And looking like Marlene Dietrich is bound to ruin her chances. Simla's not Hollywood. You'll see, she won't find anyone in a hurry. Did you ever meet Florence Mason who got a husband her first season out though she looked as much like a boiled gooseberry as makes no difference? Dick said what in the world does the man see in her, but men are the last to know what they see in anyone. 'Course, anyone new makes a stir because they're new.'

Rose followed her glance across the room to Marcella's extreme newness, from the neat gold braids round her head to silver-sandalled feet under the fragile chiffon of her frock.

'Funny of her to do her hair that old-fashioned way,' Rose remarked. 'Doesn't seem to go with the rest of her, does it?'

'All that eye-shadow looks tarty,' Minnie pronounced.

'I don't see any eye-shadow,' said Rose, fascinated.

'You and I wouldn't, we're not tall enough. But Dick did when he was dancing with her last night. He was doing a dreamy foxtrot when the band switched to a Paul Jones and he got Mrs Mulligan who weighs two hundred pounds. But he said Marcella's lids were pure poison green. You should have seen him turning his eyes up to the ceiling, sort of signalling me about it. I nearly died laughing. But let me tell you, Rose my girl, if he saw that stuff on me, he wouldn't be rolling his eyes, he'd be raising the rafters.'

Rose thought that entirely likely judging from Ram's explosive reaction whenever she used the barest extra make-up.

'Don't you think my cheekbones are high?' demanded Minnie.

She lifted her chin and moved her small pointed face from side to side in the lamp light of the Green Room. Rose scrutinized her bones as carefully as she could.

'Quite high,' she agreed. 'Not as high as some, of course.'

'No, well I was practising putting some black stuff on my eyes to give me a mysterious look and make my cheek bones look a bit higher, when Dick comes home and sees me sitting at the dressing table – I was just experimenting, mind – and he yells, "Who do you think you are, Anna May Wong gone wrong? Wipe that muck off, it looks horrible." I can't think why men get so worked up about make-up, can you?'

'Isn't that the Governor's ADC?' asked Rose, referring to one of the flies buzzing around Marcella.

'It most certainly is. Government House is taking a lot of notice of her. He might have been put on duty with her to escort her ladyship around. Two legs and a Government House rickshaw at her disposal isn't enough. Oh dear me no. She's very well connected, is our Marcella.'

'To some Lord you mean?'

'So I've heard. And that's another thing, who's she going to find for a husband? There's Willie Leonard who's Number Two in Wilcox and Kings. He's got a family tree. But Dick says he'll never be Number One, he's as tight as a tick by nine o'clock every night with his bearer putting him to bed. They'll have to get someone else out from England when McCavity retires next year.'

'They could make the Indian who's under Willie the next head,' said Rose.

'They wouldn't do that. Dick says an Indian wouldn't know how to manage critical situations like breakdowns in production and any serious trouble on the production side. Oh, I *am* sorry, Rose, I didn't mean anything, really.'

'Don't worry, Minnie, I know you didn't.'

'Anyway, Marcella couldn't marry *him*, could she – Rose, I could kick myself,' said Minnie, frustrated, 'I don't know what's got into me.'

'Not to worry, Minnie,' said Rose mechanically. 'What were you saying about Marcella?'

'I was saying Willie's the best-connected bachelor but he's blotto every evening, and if you count him out there's Percy Harwell. His father's Sir Somebody, just for his lifetime mind, no title to pass on. But can you imagine Marcella marrying Percy? I don't see her with anyone who tells the same three jokes every evening even if he's got a walloping bank account. If I have to listen one more time to what Aunt Matilda said to the duck on the duck's wedding day I'll drown Percy in his *chota peg*, I don't care if he *is* a big shot and Dick isn't. Not Marcella's type at all.'

'No,' said Rose slowly. 'No, he's not.'

Marcella brought to mind pictures in fairy tales of princesses disguised as goose-girls, princesses in high pointed gauzy head-dresses and tiny-waisted flowing gowns, feeding swans in front of turreted castles. Snow queens and ice princesses.

Somewhere in the house a child was growing, his clothes and nappies hung out to dry on a line in the back garden. Dev, turning himself over in his cot, crawling around in it, pulling himself up by its bars, rising sturdily to his feet and arriving in the garden, was suddenly visible for the first time since he had left the womb. The flesh and blood of him gave Rose quite a shock. Then it was true they had this child, while she hadn't even conceived, which might have made things easier, made her, however resentfully, acceptable, since a woman is a vehicle for the next generation, and it would need a breakdown of the existing world order to change that. But she hadn't performed the service for which women are intended, and meanwhile Dev was the only sign here of a man and woman's union.

From the roof terrace she could see him toddling around the garden early in the morning, trailed by his ayah holding a glass of milk in her hand, setting it down on the verandah step to give chase like the prow of a Viking ship in full sail, her beaky nose pointing the direction, her *dupatta* floating out behind her.

'What is she saying?' Rose asked Kumar.

'She is calling baba slice of her liver, rows of pearls and other sweet names to call children,' Kumar informed her.

The rows of pearls crashed through the chrysanthemums and sprinted around a hibiscus hedge, deaf to all entreaty.

'This evening I have to take baba to birthday party,' said Kumar.

'You can't. You know we're having people here for drinks.'

Kumar looked down at his bare toes in embarrassment.

'Why can't Dev's ayah take him?'

'We both must go. Orders.'

Orders came from Mona who knew her husband was having a party and that Rose relied on Kumar. The other servants would report to Mona what was eaten, drunk and said, little whorls and spirals of unimportant intrigue to spice up life on the ground floor and infuriate Rose upstairs. Without a child of her own Rose would never be mistress of the house, not even her half of it. She would pass through this family, this frightening unshakeable permanence, leaving not the shadowiest imprint of her own on it. She was less than mist, there wouldn't be a trace left of her dreams or her nightmares, no one to regret her going, not a tear to mark her passage, while Mona's son grew and Mona's war trickled down to become a Hindu–Muslim riot in the kitchen where the Muslim cook for English food and the Hindu cook for Indian food became embattled belligerents over wood and coal, oil, rice, tea, sugar and chains of command.

The dining room was common and plates hastily removed for other plates and menus made the discord even more obvious. When Rose complained of the waste to Ram he said the fires in a kitchen never went out, *chappati* dough was always ready, meals waited to be served to unexpected arrivals, so it was all right. But of course it wasn't. Voices carried irritation all over the house, Mona's own voice dispelling early on Rose's idea of frail, shy timidity inhabiting the downstairs. And Mona hardly needed spies at the party. Zafar Khan's uninhibited booming 'How's the rosebud today?' and his boisterous exchanges with Ram, telling him a man needed a wife for every season of his life, while he looked Rose over approvingly like a prime cut of

meat on sale, were wafted to the garden's very end and vibrated
there in the branches of old trees for passersby to carry away,
and burrowed through ancient roots into the old soil for generations of earthworms to digest and remember. Jokes frayed with
happy retelling bound him and Ram together in the old deep
complicity of a labyrinthine past. Rose at the party sometimes
felt as isolated as Mona in her room, worse, because Begum
Zafar's eyes rested black and unblinking on her, her vigil fuelled
by quarts of fruit juice and platefuls of kababs, while Zafar
bellowed, 'Bring the rosebud to tennis, Ram,' or 'Are you taking
the rosebud to Kashmir or Simla this summer?'

'You have the path to heaven all paved for you,' Zafar congratu-
lated Ram on arrival that evening, 'with a cocktail party upstairs
and a prayer meeting downstairs.' And they had embraced and
back-slapped and slipped into their exuberant bilingual conversation, a hem-stitched language, in and out of English. Rose
remembered it was one of Mona's religious evenings, the pundit
reciting from the Ramayana, her women friends gathered around
her in staunch militant support. After a while Begum Zafar,
satisfied that no irreparable damage to her conjugal status could
take place within the next half hour, would unglue her eyes from
Rose to rustle and billow downstairs to Mona's *kirtan* and
commiserate with her in audible whispers between the shorter
stanzas.

Rose looked at Ram and Zafar across the room. She didn't
understand all the uproar about religion these days and
the shouts in the streets of *'Hindu–Muslim ek ho,'* telling the
communities to be one when they were one already, like the
plaster on the wall if Ram and Zafar were any indication. What
could possibly pry them apart? They could be blood brothers,
she thought, tall and aquiline, unhurried, unhurriable, handsome,
conceited, lovable and insufferable in all the same ways. You
couldn't put a grain of rice between them, they were that alike.
If Ram was a Muslimized Hindu, Zafar was a Hinduized Muslim.
So what was all the shouting about? If she knew anything about
either of them, they both looked forward to a heavenful of houris
when they'd left their earthful behind, and home for both of
them was this patch of earth and no other. You two look like

brothers, Rose told them, to which Zafar, coming over to her, replied, 'We are, the rosebud, we are. Our grandfather's great-grandfather two thousand years removed was Alexander the Great's ambassador to the Punjab.'

The Greeks again. 'You mean you're descended from the Greeks?'

'And the Afghans, the Turks, the Mongols and the Persians, not necessarily in that order. The two civilized specimens you see before you are the end result of I don't know how many criss-crossing caravans, migrations and invading hordes.'

'Then what's all this about Muslims being different from Hindus and wanting their own country, and where's it going to be anyway?'

'Ah, Pakistan!' said Zafar, and choked on his drink.

'Is that what they want to call it?'

But Zafar and Ram were falling about with merriment at the joke of the century and incapable of coherence. It was then that Begum Zafar, who distrusted male camaraderie on principle, found a suitable time for departure, and bestowing one last glare on the company, took herself down to Mona.

'You've had one too many I'd say,' scolded Rose, 'and after swearing to the begum you wouldn't.'

'I swore – but was I sober when I swore?' Zafar appealed to the room, giving Rose the impression he was quoting, but with that kind of nonsense you never could tell. And the talk turned to Pakistan, Cythera and other mythical places.

'Where is Cythera?' Rose asked Zafar, greatly relieved by his begum's departure.

'Nowhere. Everywhere. Like Pakistan,' said Zafar. 'It's in your dreams, the rosebud. Cythera is where you embarked for when you left your native shores.'

How could you try to make sense of their talk, especially when they weren't very sober, Rose thought, sitting down beside an army major with a ferocious moustache and a more predictable turn of phrase. But there was no making sense of anything with Mona's religion rushing in and occupying all the pauses in conversation. The pundit's voice rose and fell melodiously, compellingly at the window behind them reciting mys-

teries as complete as those around Rose upstairs, invoking
Ishvar again and again in his explanations between readings.
And winding in and out of the rhythm of the Ramayana were
Begum Zafar's *'Oof toba, toba'* and *'Hai, hai!'* and her own
muttered invocations to Allah for a better deal for Mona. Ishvar
and Allah, two separate sovereign deities, presiding over temple
and mosque, and Hindu Water and Muslin Water at railway
stations, not to be confused until the day years later when Rose
heard their names joined Ishvar-Allah in a hymn of a different
kind.

After the party she hunted in Ram's dictionary. Cytherea,
epithet of Venus–Aphrodite fr. Gk. Kythereia, fr. Kythera
Cythera, Greek island associated with Aphrodite. Southern-
most and eastern-most of the Ionian Islands, off southern coast
of Peloponnesus. Cytherean – a votary of Aphródite. Well,
anyway it was an island, a real place (not like Pakistan at all),
but it was unreal too, an island for believers in love. Embarked
for Cythera, did I, she wondered, going through rooms ghostly
after midnight, all traces of cocktail party and *kirtan* vanished,
the household sound asleep. She sat in the middle of the sofa
vacated by the ferocious moustache, her crisp nightie beginning
to wilt in the room's warmth. Against one wall black ink calligraphy fragile as filigree sprang like gazelles across a page burnished
by moonlight, within wide borders decorated with gold leaves
and flowers. Fancy putting a frame around handwriting! And
such a lot of daytime muddles got sorted out in Rose's nocturnal
wanderings, breaking the night up into manageable pieces.
Serenely sectioned by bars of moonlight on the sofa she could
answer questions that were questions no more, Keshav joining
government service to the music of *Inquila-a-a-b*, Rose and
Mona both wrenched from sleep to Dev's imperious cries for
milk in the night, Rose and Mona seeing each other's face
in mirrors, bound by never-to-be-broken sacraments, Rose in
India, in Cythera, her exile, her home. Her spirit came alive in
the night to other spirits long before the walls of these rooms,
before the city, endlessly before, until she heard the cries of
newborn twins in a forest hermitage. And don't think that was
the end of the story, Keshav had said. In the very end when life

became too much even for the long-suffering Sita, she prayed
for the earth, her mother, to open up and receive her, which
the earth did; i.e., Ram had remarked, reaching for a second
helping of mutton curry, she died. Or was murdered by society,
corrected Keshav, for how voluntary are voluntary deaths, and
was it bliss hereafter or earthly hell that drove *satis* to climb
their husbands' funeral pyres and be burned alive? Why would
a lovely princess cry out for the earth to swallow her if life hadn't
become a wilderness?

If that's what happens to princesses, what about ordinary
people? Rose kept the thought in mind, but it was years before
another story as horrifying came her way when the beggar told
her about the Ganges and the hundreds of brick kilns along it
that open and swallow up women. How? Still? Are you making
it up, she asked. People who had been through as much as he
had did make up things, their judgements got all twisted. I don't
have to make it up, he said, and her head swam with their
names, Muzzafarpur, Samastipur, Bhojpur, Beguserai,
Monghyr, Purnea, Gaya, Patna, Chapra, along the holiest of
rivers where now, not in centuries BC, women labourers disappeared into the kilns where they worked and the pigholes where
they lived, sometimes never to return, used, he said, by the
kiln masters and their men when they had finished carrying
brickloads for the day. Some came back to the village when they
were hard and old to recruit young girls for the kilns. How do
you know all this? she asked. Because my wife was swallowed
such, he replied. And the beggar was a sight to match the story,
a man who couldn't wipe away his own tears.

SIX

Nishi could take the credit for bringing Ravi into their lives. She had met him at ten o'clock in the morning on Air India's daylight inaugural flight to London. Dev would never have accepted him as a person Daddy-ji and Rose already knew, especially Rose. From her window seat in the cabin Nishi was watching other passengers cross the tarmac from the VIP lounge to the plane when a man was ushered to the seat beside her. She guessed she was sitting next to the most important man in the administration when champagne arrived shaking and shuddering in a precariously balanced glass before the plane finished taxiing and rose into the air. Anything was possible sitting level with sunlit clouds instead of normal windowpane landscape and providence works in strange ways. It had whisked her without a dowry from a family of eight, sharing beds and wearing each other's clothes, and a father who had never recovered the money, position or illusions Partition had ripped off him, to the luxury of Daddy-ji's home. It seated her opposite Ravi at the airline's lunch at the Post Office Tower restaurant in London, as unreal as the plane, this meeting, with the barely perceptible jerk of the revolving tower and the changing view reminding them they were eating and drinking far above the city. Countries like Sweden were quite neurotic about human rights, she heard him telling his neighbour, incredible the questions the Swedes asked about a mere fifty or a hundred thousand arrests. Apart from them his mission in Europe had been reasonably easy. When the table had been cleared for dessert, Air India's regional manager said, 'We have with us today' and Ravi had made a little thank-you speech on behalf of all the passengers. Over the raspberry soufflé, talking to his neighbour of the Prime Minister not taking a single step without popular support – her party being, if anything, an obstruction in her direct appeal to the people and the changes she wanted to make to serve the needs of the masses – he recognized Nishi and smiled cordially at her. Warmed by wine she leaned forward and said breathlessly, 'Like changing the Constitution, to make herself President for life.' It was common talk after all.

He said abruptly, 'Where did you hear that?'

Nishi hastily withdrew. 'Oh nowhere. So many rumours float around, one should pay no attention.'

But he came obligingly to her rescue, saying it had to be changed but not till a climate had been created for it, which was what the emergency was for, and that was where people like herself came in. Entrusted with the gravity of changing a climate Nishi began to protest her incompetence when he spoke of setting up lawyers', teachers', entrepreneurs' forums to provide solid public support for constitutional change to strengthen the Prime Minister's hands, asking her suddenly, 'Would your husband be interested in joining one?' Nishi swallowed iced water to clear her brain and reached out gratefully to grasp one more gift of providence.

She had been away only five days but the house was crackling with tensions when she got back and she longed for Daddy-ji to recover, though there was no sign of it, and be in control again. On her first evening home after saying goodnight to Rose she said to Dev in their bedroom, 'Devikins, Mummy wants some money.'

'Well, give it to her.'

'What you gave me to give her is already finished.'

Dev made an impatient sound. He would attend to it tomorrow, he said, but he must have forgotten, he was so busy with three men in his study, one with a dagger in his belt and two with pistols. She went to Rose's room in the evening after waiting all day for him to remember. Rose's bed linen had been aired and Kumar was walking carefully around the bed tucking in sheets printed with ferns and flowers. Shoes had been dusted and stood in neat rows against the wall waiting to be put away. Clothes lay across chairs. Cupboard doors were open to dispel monsoon damp and snapshots smiled up from glass-topped tables. A picture postcard was clipped to the dressing-table mirror of pink and white ladies in powdered wigs and ball gowns reclining languidly on a grass slope beside a river, with sailing ships at anchor nearby. The room was full of light and memory. Nishi sat down in a chintz-covered chair, closed her eyes and inhaled the Yardley's English Lavender scent of Rose's cosy, cushiony, powdery room. Earlier Rose had been in Daddy-ji's room where she spent a fixed hour every evening, not only to give the nurse a rest. There were servants to do that. Once Nishi had gone in and seen her looking intensely at Daddy-ji's face as though the power of her looking would make him stir, smile, speak.

Kumar did not have to say, 'Memsahib is out walking.' They both knew where she was. He pointed his chin in the direction of the window, Nishi went to it and there was Rose as always, walking up down, up down beside the tomb, her gait queerly resembling Kumar's as he tucked her sheets in up here. The ugly tomb squatted hunch-backed in the dusk, and Nishi turned from it quickly to face the room's lighted interior. Going to the dressing table she picked up the swan's-down puff from Rose's lucite powder box and pressed it passionately to her nose, then ran down the stairs, out of the house, calling Mummy, Mummy when she sighted Rose. To Rose it seemed a child ran across the uncut grass towards her in the twilight, stumbling over small stones littering the uneven ground. Nishi came up breathless and caught her hand, swinging it as they walked, chattering, Mummy, you shouldn't be alone so much, why didn't you call me, I'd have come walking with you, it's bad to be alone so much, in an onrush of affection minus sympathy suited to the limbo Rose inhabited, neither wife nor widow. She kept turning eagerly to Rose as a child will, or a frisky puppy that romps ahead and looks back invitingly, head on one side. A face as clear-cut as if it had been snipped out of paper with a sharp and shining pair of scissors. No flesh to make folds or shadows on that face. Rose's own when young had been softly rounded, getting fuller, fleshier with age, a travesty of what it had once been. Nishi, with nothing to spare, would stay this way, look a child, go on behaving like a child, a kind of protection perhaps, even at thirty-five. Yet those winsome ways and quick, light movements were oddly disturbing.

'It's a pretty sunset, isn't it?' said Rose, at a loss for words to describe it.

Darkness, so long coming, arrived, and to Nishi's surprise the hideous hunched up tomb she hated looked old and reliable at close quarters, a dreaming, gently brooding mound and the house, with its lighted windows looked new-sprung, sharp and alien. Even before she had seen their personalities cross and confuse in this peculiar way, she had, impelled by nothing she could name, run down the stairs and away from the house. And now, she and Rose by common unspoken consent were still out in the deepening dark, unwilling to feel those unknowable floors underfoot before they had to.

'What's this fencing they're putting up?' asked Rose.

'It's to mark out a compound for the youth camp drill and activities, archery and target practice and so on. Dev's organizing it. You see there're going to be several youth camps one after another, as soon as the rains are over.'

'Is that what those toughs with pistols have been coming about?'

'Must be,' said Nishi absently.

'Forty if they're a day,' said Rose. 'If they're youths, I'm Wee Willie Winkie.'

Nishi yelped with laughter. 'You're so funny, Mummy.'

'I thought they were supposed to be planting trees, not doing target practice.'

When they reached the front door, Nishi said, 'I'll tell you what, Mummy, make me a list. I'll go into town tomorrow and get you what you need.'

There was a sudden gleam in Rose's eye and she said, 'If you're driving into town, I'll come along with you.'

'Yes, of course,' agreed Nishi, why hadn't she thought of it herself, and found Dev in the entrance blocking the way.

'I need the car tomorrow,' he said.

'All right, Devikins, we'll go another time.'

Not since her school days at the convent had things fallen so satisfyingly into place. There was a serenity about the geometric flower beds of the convent garden, the scrubbed wimple-framed faces of the nuns, bells chiming for angelus at noon, heaven and hell, angels and devil, each in its proper place unlike the noise and confusion of home where her mother's children, born one after another, came to stay once the nursing home expelled them. The convent was the only place, until the emergency made the country as comforting, where Nishi had not been in doubt about anything. The country had been in a mess, people screaming for more wages or bonus, or just screaming, too many political parties, so humiliating to explain to foreigners. And then overnight a magical calm had descended like in Taiwan or Singapore. The idea of a Leader, someone to look up to, made her pulse beat faster, fulfilled a yearning for tidiness, and a woman in command put at least one woman beyond the furies all others face. And then the emergency was so popular. You could tell by the delegations of teachers, lawyers, schoolchildren and so on and so forth who went every day to congratulate the Prime Minister for declaring it. They were stopped at the gate and searched, and directed to waiting rooms after being sorted out by an official inside. The general public were taken to the lawn; people like herself were shown into an oval anteroom. She took a chair and sat looking at the wall above the heads of those facing her. When their glances met they smiled mistily, wordlessly at each other before glancing away again. She was sure they, like her, were not thinking about anything special while they waited. There wasn't time before an audience with the Leader to think about anything because at any minute the door might open and the next person be asked to go in. But they shared the mystical glow of people doing the right patriotic thing, or pilgrims who had journeyed far and hazardously to kiss the big toe already worn out with pilgrim kisses.

Uplifted by her two minutes in the Leader's presence, she went to see her father. She asked the driver to park the shining white Mercedes around the corner out of sight though the alley around that corner was full of potholes and he didn't like doing it. Her father's shop in Connaught Circus was in worse confusion than she had ever known it. Bolts of shower curtain material cluttered the entrance. She had to edge around them, and his clumsy servant, coming around the shower curtain mountain in blue striped night pyjamas and a dirty shirt with an armful of polythene buckets of various colours, which for some reason her father chose to display on the pavement outside the shop, blundered into her.

'Idiot!' she said angrily while the oaf apologized energetically, making the top layer of buckets wobble and fall on her toes. More polythene pails and mugs and soap dishes, floor brushes and brooms and other bathroom paraphernalia stood on the floor of the shop, and the shelves usually crammed with detergents and toilet paper were bare. She wondered irritably why her father had to sell bathroom equipment instead of some more dignified commodity. He was not at his place at the desk but in a corner at one of the shelves. He looked over his steel-rimmed bifocals at her.

'Oh, it's you. And about time. Your mother has been pestering me to get you over.'

He turned back to the shelf. Nishi suppressed her annoyance. 'I've brought some fruit and chocolates for her.'

He grunted, not asking her to sit down. It was his oaf of a servant who ambled round and brought her a rickety chair. Her father might have been to Government College in Lahore but he didn't look as if he had been anywhere in his life except in this ratty old shop in Connaught Circus. He had once remarked that after paying the dowry to marry off four daughters (not including her) he felt he had spent his entire life in this shop. Which he had, more or less, since the Partition had torn the ground, ancestral, emotional and actual, from under his feet and flung him into space with scarcely a *paisa* to his name just because a skeletal old fanatic who couldn't speak his own language, hardly ever wore any but English clothes, and wasn't even an orthodox Muslim, had decided he wanted a Muslim homeland and had raised hell and preached damnation till he got it. Her father had never had any religious beliefs but since Partition he had been a Hindu for voting purposes, and it seemed to give him a bitter childish pleasure to wear a long red *tilak* on his forehead now to proclaim his allegiance to the Jan Sangh though at home he was forever upsetting her mother with his atheism. It was

positively dangerous since the emergency had marked his political party out for surveillance and put all its leaders and crowds
of its workers in jail, and she was going to speak to Ravi to
protect him if she had to, but meanwhile she would try to make
him see reason. It was never easy coping with his obstinacy and
more disturbing coping with the thirty-five-year-old adult she
became only in his presence, her voice changing its timbre, her
adult self omniscient with things to come that could not be
dispersed like fluffy chickens with her usual chatter.

'What are you doing, cleaning up the shop?' she asked.

He turned from the shelf, his hands on his hips, a withered
wisp of a man. 'No, I am not cleaning out the shelves. Those
bullies have been and wrecked everything, pulling things apart
and throwing everything around.'

'Oh, hush, you mean the police?'

'Who else is strutting around like the Nawab of I-don't-give-a-
damn these days?'

'Please don't talk like that,' she begged, 'they're only doing
their duty. But what did they come in here for?'

'To see if I had the price tag on every item I was selling. But
since I haven't had the price tag on anything I have sold in this
shop since the year 1948, which is twenty-seven years ago, and
since the price of everything is here on this list on the wall
where they didn't have the sense to look, and that has been a
perfectly satisfactory arrangement for my customers for
twenty-seven years, why am I supposed to have the price tag
on every item now?'

'Oh, hush, if anybody hears you – and if it's the rule now, why
not just do it?'

'Well, what do you think I'm doing?'

'Oh, I see.' She was gratified that he was doing what he had
been told to do. Perhaps everything would be all right. But to
insure his safety she asked, 'Would you come along with a group
of people, businessmen like yourself –'

'Come along where?' he interrupted.

He had not come to the house since Daddy-ji's illness. He
was rude about Dev and called his friends morons instead of
being grateful that she at least of his daughters had not cost him

a dowry. Her mother was right, gratitude to God was not part of his nature.

'To the Prime Minister's House,' she said.

'What're you trying to quick-march me over there for?'

'Because everyone is going,' she said patiently, 'you must have seen it in the papers, to say congratulations.'

'For clapping a whole lot of people into jail? They nearly clapped me into jail for not having prices marked on items. They don't need a good reason. Just quick march off to jail. If that's a matter for congratulation, you need your head examined.'

The oaf without asking her had ambled off to the shop next door and brought a frosty bottle of some sickly looking drink which she detested on sight, and she was forced to take a sip or two for politeness' sake before putting it down.

'They've got so jail-happy, there're ten prisoners in cells where one used to be, stinking clogged toilets, and not a drop of water.'

'That's not true. They said on TV prisoners are being well treated, and how would you know anyway?'

'They said on TV JP's a raving conspirator. They need their heads examined. Of course I know. With the entire Sanskrit department of the university in jail, word trickles out.'

She knew he had friends at Delhi University and she was aghast at the implication of his involvement.

'I hope you're not in touch with any of those people.'

'How could I be, even their relations aren't, though the TV told you they're being so tenderly treated. But news trickles out.'

'I don't believe it. I know someone very high up in the administration who says prisoners are being very well looked after. JP's not even in jail, he's in hospital.'

'After they've finished with him he'll be ready for his grave. Hospital's where they'd keep him, wouldn't they? It's more convenient for bumping him off, with all that hospital care around him. They'll say he was old and ill –'

'He *is* old and ill.'

'So would I be in no time flat if they were looking after me. Then they'll slip him out the back way dead as a doornail. With this lot in power it's happened once too often already, even before your precious emergency.'

'I don't know what makes you talk like this.'

'They can't stand the sight of anyone so clean, makes them look even more disgusting than they are.'

'Look, I didn't come here to talk about politics. This group of businessmen is going to get together and make suggestions to the Prime Minister about business policies, how to deal with workers, and become more like Taiwan and Singapore, and set up new industries and lots of other things that could be of concern to you.'

'One suggestion they can make is to stop ruining the businesses that are already set up.'

'Dev says you should apply for an agency for Madam's son's car and throw out all this bathroom equipment. It isn't dignified.'

'I suppose it's more dignified to be an agent for a non-existent car. And where am I supposed to get the money to buy an agency? Madam's son's agencies don't come cheap from what I've heard.'

'Dev will provide the money.'

'And who'll provide the car? Or will Dev pull it out of a hat?'

He was in one of his tiresome moods and her patience snapped.

'Why can't you just do as I say?' she cried. 'Why didn't you and Mama come to the foundation stone ceremony? Why can't you be *sensible?*'

And there he was, suddenly old and ill before her eyes and a perfect silent accord between them. Anger fought with misery in her breast at policemen throwing his Saniflush and Odonil and mops and pails around, when it should have been his books and papers, private researches on whatever he would have researched if this country had not been hacked in two when she was seven years old and, with five brothers and sisters still waiting to be born, and four dowry lumps of cancer at the end of eight educations. Some missed buses could never be caught again.

'The chocolate and fruit for Mama,' said Nishi quietly, putting the basket she had brought on his desk.

Around the corner on cracked peeling walls plastered and replastered with posters, a brand new one of the Leader smiled at her, a brand new gleaming wet moustache adorning her smile, and though Nishi looked quickly from side to side she saw no trace of a vanishing miscreant or a drop of spilled paint. The white Mercedes looked like a dollop of cream miraculously intact at the edge of a blocked drain.

Ravi had arranged for the meeting to be held in a suite of the Intercontinental as her own home was too far away for the other New Entrepreneur wives' convenience. The response had been heartening and the management was providing coffee and snacks. As she took the lift up to the fifth floor she found she had forgotten to bring the Twenty Point Programme with her. She would have to do her best without it and it was the spirit of the thing that mattered, getting the wives to pool their energies and ideas to popularize the emergency more and more. There was so much they could do, take groups to congratulate the Prime Minister, plant trees and prevent their servants from having children. They were already talking about it when she arrived. The room was full of the dyed hair, imported skin fragrances and solid flesh of women long past forty whose summer saris, delicate as eggshells, seemed to have nothing whatever to do with their bulging midriffs and sons in Gulf Oil and the World Bank. Nishi felt young, small and skimpy.

'Isolated threats don't get any results,' Leila was saying from the security of menopause. 'I've threatened my ayah with dismissal more than once if she produces another child but she goes on popping brats. This is her fourth. I tell you it's a nightmare.'

'Get her tubes tied.'

Leila was going to get her tubes tied the last time but the brat had come three weeks early or the wretched woman had told a deliberate lie about the date but there it was, out before they could get her to the hospital after all the trouble Pritam had taken to make arrangements.

Nishi went to the table at the end of the room with a bowl of azaleas on it, a pad and a pencil, a jug and a glass, and hesitantly tinkled a spoon in a glass for attention. After that she couldn't find her voice. She cleared her throat discreetly and began.

'I know how concerned you all are about the Twenty Points. That's why you're all here.'

Cake and sandwich crumbs littered the sideboard. A waiter came in with hot coffee and fresh fragrant *samosas*. The company looked expectantly at Nishi.

'I forgot to bring the Twenty Points with me,' she apologized, 'but I know how concerned you all are. Well, so I thought why don't we informally discuss ways and means to popularize the Twenty Points, or – since I don't have them with me – ways to make the emergency more successful – than it already is of course.'

Middle age looked portentously at her across the room and Nishi thought she detected the faintest trace of complacency and irony at her inexperience, which she still might have carried off if she hadn't been so skimpy and small, though thank goodness she was fair.

'So,' she cleared her throat again, 'if you have any suggestions about popularizing the points – or any other suggestions – do say so.'

She smiled nervously, waiting for hands to go up. Instead Leila's voice took the floor without asking permission of the chair.

'It's perfectly obvious what our priority should be. I was saying so before you arrived. Birth control. We've got to take our cue from the government. I have it on reliable authority school teachers are being dismissed if they can't certify that they've had five people sterilized. Of course they've got to get themselves sterilized first. That's the kind of businesslike programme we've got to start for domestic servants and no nonsense about it.'

A no-nonsense burst of applause greeted her businesslike announcement. Nishi craned her neck over the top of the azaleas at Leila and moved them a fraction to one side, but the meeting had trundled away from her and Leila was monitoring the flood of comment and bringing it to order with more information she had on reliable authority. It was not to be repeated because bad news had to be suppressed, it sapped the morale, but there had been riots against vasectomy, Muslim sentiment being opposed to it, and it would be the height of folly to start sterilizing Muslim servants. They could decide what to do about them later when the Hindus had been vasectomized, Pritam was quite clear about that, though of course he did warn that this raised questions of the Muslim population rate going up and a possible Hindu backlash, but they needn't go into all that this minute.

'How about the Christians?' someone wanted to know while the chair waited to be consulted. 'My ayah is a Catholic. She'll never agree and I can't dismiss her, I'd have the children on my hands, but what about the Protestants?'

No one knew the Protestant view, and anyway, said Leila, there aren't that many Protestant servants, you leave them to me. Nishi moved the azaleas further to the right and bravely seized the pause. 'If we only sterilize the Hindus, the Hindus won't like it. We shouldn't worry about whose religion is what.'

'Quite right,' Leila supported her, 'it's a secular state. But let's get started with the Hindus. Let's just get on with the job to show we mean business, and arrange for one of those vans and have a vasectomy centre set up and get all our servants taken there on the same day. It's a question of management and organization, Pritam says. If we give him the signal he'll get us a van. They've got so many at the biscuit factory. He's sure one could be spared, and the trip needn't be wasted. It could do a biscuit delivery at the same time.'

Pritam's assistance was welcomed and thanks conveyed in advance, but they were not to mention it, said Leila, Pritam would be pleased as punch. Women involved in the work of the nation had his wholehearted support, proper constructive work, not like shouting for women's rights.

'That's settled then,' said Nishi with a sigh. 'Any other suggestions?'

The most creative one was a flower decoration week explaining the Twenty Points in Ikebana. And talking of flowers, said the Austrian wife who had made the suggestion, so desolate she was going up to Mussoorie last weekend and noticing the hillsides how they looked bald, never to grow a blade of grass again, and happy it was making her to hear about a so marvellous movement called Chipko in the tradition of Mahatma Gandhi's satyagraha where the people were embracing the trees when the contractors' men came to axe them –

'Mrs Mathur, Mrs Mathur –' Nishi agitated softly, trying to stem the torrent, remembering that the contracts for felling had been given by the Minister for Industry himself, and that satyagraha was jailable and the hotel room might be bugged. But Mrs Gerda Mathur's eloquent espousal of the so marvellous Chipko movement took its course. And if it had been recorded on hidden tape for the censor in charge of the electronic media, Ravi would have to help them out, but first of all Mrs Gerda Mathur could go and congratulate the Prime Minister on the emergency and sign the congratulations book.

The next thing was to get the servants rounded up at home, which didn't take long – there were no Muslims or Protestants to complicate matters and the Hindus immediately understood it was either vasectomy or dismissal – until it came to Kumar, obdurate as only an old servant can be. Rose, who never left her room until after her breakfast, came out in her dressing gown when she heard Nishi arguing with Kumar in the corridor, her childish treble flying higher and petulantly higher.

'There's nothing wrong with vasectomy, Mummy,' she piped at Rose.

'This man,' said Rose, 'is your father's age. Would you drag your father off to a vasectomy camp?'

Nishi's face bleached and a shiver went through her. Never in her life had she quarrelled with Rose, but just then, inexplicably, she would have struck her, not Rose, of course, whom she liked, but the spectre she had raised, the dreaded tormenting fear that had gripped Nishi since the emergency began that someone might lay a finger on her father. It was the reason why, apart from getting Dev ahead, the emergency had to be supported. How dare you, how dare you, she wanted to shriek insanely, he's been through too much already. How dare you mention his name, someone might hear. Rose, seeing her narrowed pupils, those of a cat's poised to kill, said no more. Kumar was safe enough but Nishi, rushing through the house collecting servants, hustling a voiceless parade of them into the biscuit factory's van, doubling her energies to make up for the loss of one body in the count, suddenly alighted on the beggar and pounced. A struggle ensued, between strange forms of life before life on earth became human. Rose looked down on the scene in horror. What had happened to the girl, was she losing her mind? Nishi, beside the van with Custard Cream Crunchies for Tea painted in pink on it, masterminding the operation of capture, had the set fanatic look of torturers as the cook's crooked-faced one-eyed boy fought with the truncated torso of the beggar and the beggar thrashed about, handless and crippled, cleverly flinging himself out of reach each time the other thought he had him in a secure grip. It was still going on when Rose reached the last step of the staircase, bore down on Nishi and physically restrained her, breaking the fanatical link of command between her and the cook's boy. Rose shook her gently and Nishi's eyes focused with difficulty on her.

'It's no use taking him,' said Rose, 'he's not even a whole man. He won't count.'

Nishi nodded and went into the house after ordering the van's driver to take his passengers to their destination and bring them back vasectomized after making his biscuit deliveries. The panting beggar, regaining his breath after combat, raised one stump of an arm in a shaky salute to Rose who was steadying herself against the verandah wall. It looked, that arm, like the end result of another violent struggle. She made up her mind to ask him about it some time. The handless salute left her thinking about his hands, and the struggle about his humanness. Whenever she saw him afterwards from her bedroom window, looking no bigger than a beetle at that distance as he moved about near the tomb, she could picture him healed and whole, walking upright, running and leaping, and each nightfall becoming exultantly whole once again by the light of the stars.

SEVEN

Neel's lawyer friend came to dinner, and late as I always am catching up with the facts of life I didn't realize till I walked into the drawing room that a dinner party would not be the best time to get advice for Rose, with two professors and an editor there too besides the lawyer couple. But it wasn't the party so much as what parties had become. There must be something about a desk job – reading and writing substituting for living – that prevents one from connecting with what's right under one's nose. Not that I connected much at dinner. Kiran had insisted I leave off my glasses ('No one can see your beautiful eyes') and I got rather a dim picture of the opinion-makers of our society.

Conversation was a lake, milky and mild, the leisurely exchange of people on the winning side who don't have to lose their tempers in argument. The dictatorship around us was one of nature's marvels, not man-made, not 'made' at all. It had the naturalness, the mother-and-child-ness of a crop and was as cultivable. Or, in another variation, it had been unearthed, a brilliant archaeological find, evidence of the early blossoms of our culture, institutions that had endured, proof that family counted. What was wrong with a son succeeding his mother in this particular republic? And which mother anywhere in the world wouldn't move heaven and earth for her son?

'Especially when he's shown such organizational talent,' said the chief editor of an important daily newspaper.

You had to start somewhere, he expounded wittily, and Madam's son had, vasectomizing the lower classes, blowing up tenements and scattering slum-dwellers to beautify Delhi, setting up youth camps with drop-outs in command, loafers and ruffians who would otherwise have been no more than loafers and ruffians. With his ill-wishers out of the way now, a patriotic, hand-spun, hand-woven car, every nut and bolt of it made in India, would soon be on the road. Look at the way he'd sprung full-blown, up and doing, into the power structure, while grandpa had had to spend years in jail and mummy had led doll processions before making it to the executive suite. The editor made ripples in the lake. He was the jolly, fun-loving type. It was permitted to be laughingly critical of either or, but not both, mother and son, and everyone knew the son had made him chief editor after dismissing his annoying predecessor who had reported that The Car had fallen into a ditch during trials and never been heard of since. When prodded, the Communist professor from Delhi University who was pro-mother but anti-son had to agree it had taken the son to persuade her to crack down. Catching the President in his pyjamas, added the editor, and the Cabinet in its underpants, which would teach that bunch of stooges who was boss. Decision was the thing, not like grandpa with his view-sharing and soul-searching, his to-be-or-not-to-be and comrades-all in the struggle.

'And now Madam can go ahead with her plans for the poor,' said Kiran sentimentally.

She was sitting beside the lawyer's wife in a pose considered classically feminine after feminity had been downgraded from matriarchy to madonna, from goddess to wife, daughter or mother of god. The professor's wife, a professor herself, at least had views and postures of her own.

The men seemed anxious to record statements though there was no tape recorder in the room, and it was the lawyer's turn. 'It's perfectly natural,' he began. 'Is there a mother in the country who would not have –' when I interrupted to ask him about the Hindu Code Bill, and like an informal relay race the editor obligingly took up the naturalness of the hereditary principle in democracy.

'The Hindu Code Bill, you say,' the lawyer frowned, but he quickly recovered his good humour – it was only a quarter to eight and he could record his statement later – and told me that since 1957 a widow had equal rights to property and assets along with other members of the family. I said the person concerned was Rose and there were tensions in the family.

'But Dev is doing splendidly, isn't he?' the lawyer turned to Neel for confirmation. 'Quite a place he's got out there.'

'It's his father's place,' I said. 'Would you act for Rose? Uncle Ram is not going to recover and may not have long to live. She wants an arrangement drawn up that will protect her rights.'

'There's no need. She's entitled to a share according to the law.'

'She'll never get it. And she won't have the means to go to court.'

'I wouldn't advise it either. Litigation takes years. It would be better if she came to an understanding with Dev. What's the problem? He's doing so well.'

'He's a dunce,' I said bluntly, 'and here he is heading this enormous enterprise.'

'Oh come, come,' said the lawyer genially, weighing my beautiful eyes in the balance with my gaucherie, eyes winning. 'A worldwide company wouldn't go into collaboration with anyone who doesn't know his job. The first thing they would do is check up on the person.'

'Then they must know he's a dunce.'

He laughed cheerily. 'Neel, your sister-in-law is being very hard on poor Dev. He wouldn't be chairman of the New Entrepreneurs if he didn't know his job.'

'Is that what he is now!'

He nodded and turned to Neel again, 'Have you joined it?'

'Not yet, but I will. There's an advantage to being part and parcel of an organization and presenting industry's views in a unified way.'

But what were the chambers of commerce for, and how could Neel join anything with a dunce at the head of it, him of all people with his experience and training? Neel brushed my remarks good-naturedly aside. I hadn't heard but if lawyers were becoming New Lawyers I would never find one willing to have a confrontation with Dev. I glanced around for Kiran and saw her deep in shared motherhood with the lawyer's wife.

'We've known Dev since we were children,' I said. 'Would you call him reliable?'

'He's Chairman of the New Entrepreneurs,' she assured me.

'There you are, my dear,' said the lawyer affably, 'I've known the family for years myself. I wouldn't like to upset Dev. And why wouldn't he look after his stepmother's interests? He's doing so well. Look at the way his factory is coming up. Did you ever see anything coming up so fast?'

I never had. It took other businessmen months to get cement released. Nor had I ever seen a rural zone converted with the speed of lightning into an industrial zone, and only for one industry, after the Delhi planners had decided to leave that land free for rural development.

Kiran invited us in to dinner, prettily explaining what was in the casserole, the flavours in the fish sauce and the ingredients of the salad. More feminine charm was trained on the chutneys and pickles. And then the capital's professional elite gave a demonstration of what the Third World's upper crust talks about when its country's democratic institutions have just been engulfed by a tidal wave. The Establishment professor, whose wife was ably defending Madam's recent actions further down the table, described the clinic in the Soviet Union where he had had eight months' free treatment for arthritis. The editor outlined tomorrow's editorial, in which he would say Madam had in good faith thought it her constitutional duty to override the Constitution, and while he would regret the suspension of liberty and the right to life, he would reluctantly conclude there had been no alternative. And the lawyer summed it all up when he gave his professional opinion that the Constitution would have to be drastically amended, if not rewritten, to give Madam powers to fight disruptive forces and crush the vested interests she had been battling against since infancy. Delhi had always been an imperial city, hadn't it? When had it not been the fief of absolute rulers who believed God and the angels were on their side, so what was so new about special powers and hereditary rule? In the mellow interval before the final course was served, Kiran daintily described the pudding.

The room should have swooped and spun with contradictions. We were living in confusing times. Marxists and Hindus were fraternizing in jail, Establishment Communists were cheering monarchy, and the millennium had arrived disguised as an emergency headed by a Mother Tsar whose ignorant little peasants were quite happy with mother's blessing. But the chairs and tables stayed put and the meal moved peacefully on till Kiran's guests had laid democracy as comfortably to rest as her fish sauce now lay buried in the juices of their capitalist and communist stomachs. If the Constitution and laws had become such a nuisance, where was I going to find a lawyer for Rose? After they had gone I felt so completely confused I went to my room to put on my glasses and think about it. I put on my glasses and thought. Why blame Prime Ministers and emergencies? There were mixed-up people all down the line just because, as Rose would put it, Simon says thumbs up so it's thumbs up. I rang Rose.

'Neel's lawyer friend came to dinner tonight,' I said. 'I spoke to him about you but he won't help. He was like the doctor you told me about.'

'Damn and blast,' said Rose, understanding at once. For a person who's supposed to be fuddled in the evenings she's quicker than most to grasp a situation. 'What was his name?'

'His name?'

I burrowed back into the introductions but I couldn't remember, or the chief editor's, or the two professors'. They were The Lawyer, The Editor, The Professors.

'Well, if that isn't the limit,' Rose chuckled. 'But what difference does it make if he won't help? It's doctor, lawyer, merchant, chief, like cherry stones on a plate, not like people.'

That seemed to sum up the evening, and the morning of the next day as the Bible says, as well as what we could see of the rest of our lives. The professors were on this plate too, so it was obviously time for a new jingle to fit them in where the tinkers and tailors had been, because the makers and menders of things as far as we knew were still behaving like people, not cherry stones. I smiled for the first time that evening and at a telephone of all things.

I got into bed and thought about Rose and her jingles and nursery rhymes. And along with them, or because of them, her unerring clarity regardless of gin and lime. Evidently the world's sorrows and disasters were much nearer and clearer if you had felt sorry for Bo-peep and shared the terrors of Miss Muffet. Rose had remained young and raw. She bled when wounded. She was not a great reader unless you counted *Woman and Home* and snippets about the British royal family. She didn't need to be. I had seen the great readers at dinner today. It had taken an illiterate Akbar to hold dialogues on religious doctrine with Jesuit priests and build a Fatehpuri Sikri to extol the oneness of religions.

EIGHT

One of Rose's more foolish fancies had been that everything would work out all right if Mona were dead. If only she'd be dead, dead, dead, she had hammered out the thought night after night after night. It is wicked to think such thoughts, Rose, she has done you no harm and it isn't her fault. The night hung endlessly about. She lay watched by the eye of a vertical staring moon, listening to the singing needle-and-thread sound of mosquitoes celebrating their life and times around the mosquito netting. Ram had told her if you can hear them singing they are not malaria mosquitoes. Still, they bit. A swarm hovered over her, twanging like a tuning fork in the confined space of her bathroom when she undressed, narrowing to needles as it travelled in a halo above her head up the stairs to the roof terrace. She went to bed smelling of citronella, with the lemon grass oil all over her sheets and pillows as well. Outside the net, insects that whirred like propellers and opened like umbrellas and swung in arcs up to lights heralded the monsoon's advance up the coast and across the plain. When the lights went out, so did they, but not the mosquitoes. In the night dogs lost their common sense and barked with a stupid persistence, on and on, while in the further distance a maniac's bloodcurdling cry pierced the air. The jackal started shrill and solo, slid down the descending scale then rose again and again to hysterical heights, joined by the pack until the demented disjointed chorus made her feel it was she who was losing her reason. Be sensible, Rose, you're up here on the terrace, they're down there, miles away at the edge of the city, you heard what Ram said. Think they're coming towards you, walking miles and miles, lunging up the stairs right through a door that stays locked till Kumar opens it in the morning? The door is shut and that's that and that maniacs' army isn't marching anywhere, it's driving you crazy from right where it is miles away. But she heard panting animal breath, smelled fur. Her mind's eye saw their eyes, their rabid lolling tongues. Rose sat up shocked and sweating, her heart pounding. She pulled her torch out from under her pillow and shone it round the terrace. Vacant darkness showed through the net. Ram was asleep, he'd sleep through the second coming. Only sounds from Mona's bedroom woke him. She buried her face in her pillow blocking out the jackals. Mona was only two years older than herself, she wouldn't die for years. The three of them would live and die together, an impossible situation that entered the realm of possibility every morning when she went down the stairs into the household and tried to discover ways to make it work. She tried to win Dev. It was unhealthy how that child clung to his mother all the time, how the servants followed him around with food and toys when he wouldn't eat, and just followed him around. He was the centre of a houseful of adorers and Ram spoiled him rotten too. He couldn't dress or undress himself and he backed away from her whenever she approached. His mother must have told him to, children aren't unfriendly on their own. The occupants of the ground floor were rigidly against her, yet every day she got up breathing hope, and a painful, problem-filled happiness carried her through the hours.

The shop was easier because it was not one iota Mona's. She and Ram had it to themselves. It was centrally located, their friends could drop in for a chat and she liked being in the busy cosmopolitan section of town, close to cinemas and where she had her hair done. With the kind of fancy imports Ram stocked, she had wondered if they would be able to sell much, but they had a steady clientele for fine bone china from England, Belgian lace, Chinese jade, Austrian petit-point handbags and Irish doily sets. Rose was unpacking a set of Sèvres coffee cups with the salesman's help when she saw Marcella in the doorway. Back again then. Sunlight outside and the tangle of traffic moving past on the road behind her gave Marcella's silhouette a look of deep dark permanence but for the nimbus of light gilding her head.

'May I help you?' Ram was at her side, unselfconscious as usual about looking after his customers.

Marcella's eyebrows rose infinitesimally. She said, 'I'm not sure that I want anything. I'm just looking around.'

'How delightful.'

And since that was not what a salesman would say, she took another look at his impeccable clothes, recalled his impeccable accent, and, thought Rose from behind the Sèvres, her ladyship air relaxed into slightly more ordinary though still Marcella-like behaviour. Ram brought her to Rose.

'I believe we met at the Green Room in Simla when you were here before,' said Rose.

'Yes, of course,' said Marcella, clearly not remembering.

She strolled around the room with Ram, exclaiming over new Chinese brocade and a goddess of white jade, while Ram told her their histories. She picked up a parchment lying on the counter, not for sale but for framing and hanging in the drawing room at home.

'This looks like a Hindu god,' she said, 'I thought this was a Moghul painting.'

'It is an illustration from the life of Krishna. Akbar the Great had the Hindu epics translated and illustrated. He was very interested in the land he ruled.'

'It's beautiful,' she said, holding it up, saying the red, blue, gold mosaic looked as detailed as embroidery, and that cluster of pale blue cows in the corner lifting their faces to a crescent moon looked as trusting as medieval madonnas. It must have been horrendously expensive.

'It's a reproduction but a Moghul one,' said Ram. 'The Moghul emperors had copies made of paintings they liked and gave them away as presents to guests who admired them. My father found this one in a wooden house on Hawa Kadal Bridge in Srinagar in the 1920s, and bought it for a few rupees. It was being used to paper over the cracks on the window to keep out the cold.'

'I can't believe it,' she said, 'how absolutely enthralling. I hadn't intended to shop, but now I can't decide what to leave behind, I want to take everything away with me.'

'Come and have a cup of coffee next door while you make up your mind,' said Ram. 'Rose, will you join us?'

'In a minute, when I've finished here.'

Usually they sent for their coffee and drank it in the shop. Of course Ram knew a good customer when he saw one and he was always the gentleman, quite as attentive when her friends came, but Rose fought with uncomfortable feelings. Who built the Suez Canal? Darned fool whoever it was. These husband hunters wouldn't have arrived by the shipload if ships had had to go round the Cape of Good Hope. She'd already had a go at hunting so why was she back?

Ram and Marcella were at a corner table. Rose could see, you had to be blind not to see how handsome they looked together, tall, slim, elegant. But it was more than that. The word she wanted eluded her. It was the way they sat, their limbs arranged that way by centuries of being in command of situations. It was their grammar, yet it didn't matter what they were talking about or if they were talking at all. They matched, fatally, without the slightest effort. There was something terribly horribly right about them. Why on earth should Marcella bother with drunken Willie or Percy with Sir Something for a father or anybody else when there was Ram? Then she cleared her head of imaginary nonsense and went up to their table. And nonsense it was, just because Ram and Marlene Dietrich were having a cup of coffee together before she went back to her shopping and the high seas and home. Ram got up to hold out Rose's chair for her and suddenly the atmosphere was transposed to a different key, to accommodate the wife Rose, the child Rose, pretty common little Rose. Above her head the grown-ups talked, indulgently helping her to snatches of explanation.

'The extraordinary clarity of her voice,' Marcella was saying. She turned to Rose, 'Didn't you think so? In a room as small as that one and with those quite appalling acoustics, I should have thought everything would be one loud noise. But her extraordinary clarity –'

They were talking about *Lady Windermere's Fan*, Simla's Green Room production of Marcella's earlier visit, and Rose did think the leading actress's voice had been nice and clear, she didn't know about ex-straw-nry cla-rity. Marcella's upper-class accent had spent quite ten minutes ballet-dancing around two words when all she was saying was that the girl who had played

Lady Windermere had a nice voice. A regular hullaballoo around syllables, making such a production out of pronunciation.

'I adore India,' Marcella was saying, 'I simply couldn't wait to get back and then when the Craiks asked me to come and stay –'

Rose listened to descriptions of Government House and what Their Exes were doing about redecoration, and Her Ex's simply marvellous taste, utter darlings that they were, being much too kind.

'You were not very gracious, my dear,' Ram said regretfully when they were back in the shop and Marcella had left with her purchases. 'You hardly said a word.'

'With her being so gracious, two of us being gracious would have been too much.' Rose put her handbag down below the counter, picked it up again, fidgeted with its clasp and said for no rhyme or reason, it wasn't the day for it, 'I think I'll go and get my hair done.'

Ram was surprised but said yes, do, he'd be at the shop.

She added cattily, unable to help herself, 'How does she go about adoring India from Government House?'

'It's just a manner of speaking,' said Ram.

A manner of speaking was an unscalable wall of steel and concrete between half the world and the other half. At Claudette's, no bigger than a sectioned corridor, Rose greeted Mr Parameshwar Singh who was Claudette, and to whom she was white and classless, with extra affection. He kept her brush, comb and bobby pins wrapped in a clean cloth in a dirty drawer marked with her name. He never gave her an oil massage. 'It will darken the hair, Madam, like our Indian ladies.' He attended to her from start to finish himself, banishing his assistant to the doorway where the boy lounged, one hip jutting, watching the world go by. She bent her head forward into the basin, the soapy shampoo Mr Singh used trickling into her eyes, down her chin, soaking into the neck of her smock. Mr Singh's speciality was hair-cutting, not hair-washing, but his assistant was worse. He towelled it with vigour, twirled strands of it into pincurls flat against her scalp and baked it brick-dry under a fiercely hot dryer. She emerged dazed from under it. 'I trust you have heard from your family in London, Madam.' 'Yes thanks, Mr Singh.' 'I trust they are well.' 'Yes thanks, they are very well.' Mr Singh's accent and hers could, though not the least alike, sit down comfortably for a chat, Marcella's kept her standing. 'No doubt you and sir will be going to London shortly.' 'Well, not too shortly.' 'No doubt sir is busy with many business matters not to mention many family matters.' 'No doubt.' Though there was no bloody doubt that sir had been busy doing damn all this morning, unless you call entertaining Marcellas with Moghul chit-chat and coffee doing something. Mr Singh took out the clips, stroked her corkscrew curls with lightly brilliantined palms, brushed out the red frizz and manoeuvred it with skilful fingers. He beamed fondly at her mirror image, trusting she liked it no doubt. It had looked like the last word – it *was* the last word, she and Minnie had found it together in Minnie's latest *Woman & Beauty* and had tried it on each other – until Marcella had come along with her severe gold storybook braids.

'D'you like my hair this way?' she asked Ram.

'Isn't it the same as before?'

'Yes, it is. D'you like it?'

'Of course.' He seemed surprised.

But the implacable, eternal, unchangeable hair of Marcella troubled her dreams. Rapunzel, Rapunzel, let down your hair. Down fell the flaxen ropes, flax-hair spun from enchanted spindles, and whoever had been standing beneath that high window in the tower had grasped them like a lifeline and journeyed to the source of all mystery, magic and joy. I don't mind Marcella one bit, she argued with herself, I mind her hair. Batty, that's what you are, Rose.

She brought up the subject one morning at Minnie's.

'What, Marcella's hair?' trilled Minnie. 'But she hasn't *got* a hairstyle, I mean not what you'd call a *hairstyle*.'

'No,' said Rose doubtfully.

'Then what are you going on about?'

She was blessed if she knew.

'Odd, isn't it,' said Minnie, 'coming out of the top drawer and her clothes just so, and then her hair. It might have looked all right twenty years ago.'

Or a hundred, or two hundred or any timeless time ago or to come. A few nights after Marcella's visit to the shop Dev fell ill. Mona sent the ayah up to the roof terrace to wake Ram and he went down in the middle of the night to phone the doctor. Rose hardly noticed the summons. Mona's had become a phantom presence in the house, remote, unimportant.

'I wonder if you and your husband would be free to come to dinner next Wednesday,' it was Marcella on the telephone. 'Just a small party Lady Craik insists on having for me.'

Invitations followed their acceptance. Peculiar the way the nobs behaved. First they found out if someone could come, then they sent the invitation, instead of sending it to find out if they were coming or not. There they were at Marcella's utter darlings' party for her, under a chandelier, a legion of servants in scarlet cummerbunds and turbans to match lined up against the walls, another legion each holding an olive or an oyster or something that had travelled leagues from a high mountain or the deep sea to end its days on a massive silver salver. His Excellency and Her Excellency inclining their heads this way and that just like His Majesty whose representatives they were and never letting anyone forget it. And of course there were the ADCs, the Number One boxwallahs, so Minnie and Dick didn't qualify, and local gentry, prize hothouse blooms one and all, and not one ordinary mortal but herself among them. The Empire's pomp and circumstance laid out on an intimate little scale for a small dinner party for Marcella. Ram looked like a fish in water and Marcella a mermaid in sinuous green. Tinkling fountains of talk and trimmed cypresses of laughter. In the great mirror between two scarlet-turbanned sentinels Rose saw Rose start as a gong announced dinner and the second act began. As the stately procession glided past her into the dining room, its huge doors held open by more liveried attendants, she stood transfixed at the sight of her hectic red hair, her cheeks feverish in a white face, as though hard accidental sunlight had strayed into the salon and chosen to settle cruelly on her.

She was seated next to the fly that had buzzed around Marcella in the Green Room, and he looked like a film star in his lovely uniform and all, but not very bright, was he? Didn't seem to know horses cost money and how could she have learned to ride on a factory worker's income? But I could tell you a lot about chocolates, she offered, and could you really, he laughed uproariously and went on to the season's plays in London and Noël Coward's madly successful new hit. But it was not till the third act when the dancing began that Rose understood the treachery of the world's waterways, and knew with a dull and chilly instinct why the Suez Canal had been built. Ram and Marcella were waltzing. It would have to be a Viennese waltz, with them like twin pillars flared outward at the waist, a regal formality ushering in an epoch of fearful beauty and grandeur. In England when Rose had gone to church on Sundays she had listened to organ music swell and soar up the stained glass windows into the vaulted ceiling and stop there, with just this sense of fear and awe, momentous as the struggle for breath. The music filling the church to bursting had nowhere to go, a perfect unbearable rightness to be where it was. Nothing was the same again after the waltz.

Ram rode and played tennis with Marcella and her friends, and there had been no real communication between Rose and him for weeks when he came home one night, with no attempt at subterfuge, his footfall open and normal on the stair at three a.m. He lay down and she knew by his uneven breathing he was not asleep. Five hours later when she was up and dressed, he was not awake. Day and night changed places in his timetable. Her anguish and rage fought for an outlet and gathered like a gale inside her without a word said, organ music threatening to burst but not bursting. What word was there to say? Who was to blame? The enchantress in the fairy tale had let down her hair, and the candidate for bewitchment had grasped the golden rope and climbed up into the tower to live haunted for ever after. There was nothing, nothing to be done about it. She did not have even everyday words to pick and choose from, much less words to break spells.

Now the moonlit rooms were more than ever her domain, bold ink calligraphy and cows trusting as madonnas familiar companions in the sleepless dark. Sights became less strange, hers, just by looking. Moonlight lay solid on upholstery, liquid on glass. It cut her into stripes as she flitted through rooms shuttered against night-flying creatures. She touched diamonds of it with the soles of her bare feet. Memories of things said, names heard during the day, came back to her. Complicated cadences, jumbled tongues became clear language, no longer foreign, in her night wandering. Words never spoken had actually been said, 'I, Rose, take thee, Ram' in an English chapel, springtime outside. A breeze at the drawing room window lifted Rose's red curls, cooled her hot damp face and neck, went away, and in the utter stillness the thin sobbing sound of pure grief no one was meant to hear, froze Mona's tears in Rose's eyes.

Years later – though when she counted it, it was actually only four months – when Rose was old and experienced in suffering, Marcella left. Ram went with her to the station, saw her off on the train to Bombay, where she would set sail for England, and came back to find Rose. That's how he'll look when he's old, thought Rose, as he crossed the lawn towards her, a bit stooped, and not at all impeccable, as if everything's behind him now. Close up he looked invalided as with the crippling of some organ that would function poorly from now on, dark holes for his eyes. And Rose, with an idiot's flair for saying the wrong thing, at long last broke the silence between them, blurting out, 'You loved her dreadfully, my darling, and now she's gone,' and burst into helpless weeping, shedding the tears he couldn't.

King Edward's romance had been making news all over the Empire. Rose and Minnie, listening to the abdication speech together over the wireless, sighed over the King's sacrifice of his crown for a woman neither of them liked the look of. 'Hard as nails she looks,' said Minnie. 'Nothing good will come of it.' Ram hadn't renounced anything, it was Marcella who had renounced him. Or it was geography that had intervened, putting an ocean between them. Rose was never to know, and the war creeping up on their thriving business without their realizing it gave her something else to worry about. Only the summer before the war Rose and Ram had been to England and seen

Mum and Dad and made them promise they would come to India next year, but no one could travel now. And Ram still wasn't himself. Unlike the King he had got nothing in return for a sacrifice.

NINE

When did one 'first' meet a person one has known all one's life?
We were born only four months apart in the same room of the
same hospital and our mothers and their mothers had known
each other before that. In the communal eating only Kashmiri
Hindus among all Indians have, because we're all Brahmins and
there's no danger of contamination, Ravi Kachru and I had often
shared a *thali* at his house or mine, Kiran sharing one with his
sister. Ravi had a way of helping himself to the juiciest morsels
out of each *katori* while he kept me talking, whipping the rice
into little hills and polishing them off while I looked out of the
window, and getting to the marrow bone and the fat pieces of
chaman before me. We met regularly during the holidays though
we went to different schools and colleges, and after our BAs we
both found ourselves at Oxford. My first two terms were a
struggle with the weather, my studies and my homesickness.
Then one day at the end of the spring term I found a message
from Ravi at my college saying he would pick me up the next
day, and we would have lunch together. We took the bus to the
Trout Inn where weeping willows bowed graciously over a rustic
bridge across the Isis. We had driven past green pasture and
low hills and the sun was the most wonderful sight I had ever
seen. I had been afraid I would never see it again as I shivered
through the winter at Oxford. Ravi fetched smoked salmon
sandwiches and glasses of wine from the inn to one of the
benches along the river. Putting them down he straightened up
and with his hand fluttering on his heart sang Happy Birthday,
parodying the liquid outpouring of Italian opera so comically that
people around us smiled and clapped. I prevented him from
launching into an enthusiastic encore by dragging him down
beside me on the bench.

'You remembered!'

'I didn't get you a present,' he warned. 'Enough is enough and I'm broke.'

'What more could I want? *This* is my present – and look at the *sun*!'

'And the moon and the stars,' he offered, magnanimous. 'What I love about you, Sonali, is you're so happy with un-haveable things.'

We were both happier at Oxford than we had ever been before. The un-haveables, intangibles, had us in their thrall. Does the world exist because we believe it does, or would it anyway? Do Ideas have a capital I and are they immutable and unchanging? Not quite how many angels can dance on the head of a pin, since neither of us was theologically inclined, but other projections as fascinating. We inhabited all the centuries with their insoluble intangibles laid out for our inspection, as pristinely pure and glitteringly fresh as if generations had not handled them already and wouldn't in future. They were ours. I, more than Ravi, had a sense of new-found freedom. I had escaped my sari and my two long plaits. I was wearing a skirt and blouse, and my hair flopped as it liked to my shoulders. But freedom crystallized that day in the weather, an agent of exhilaration and rapture, not an enemy to be battled with. We had so much to catch up on as we lay in the grass with more wine, eagerly exchanging notes about our terms.

'I should be more "motivated", as an American friend of mine puts it,' said Ravi.

'Towards what?'

'Towards the next thing, whatever it is, the a-b-c of life, rat-a-tat-tat. The Americans plan their lives as remorselessly as the Russians plan their economy. Everything ticking away like a clock, or a computer. By the way, does a computer tick?'

I still don't know if a computer ticks, but this was 1959 and I didn't even know what a computer was. Ravi held his wine glass up to watch the sun glint through it and cheerfully agreed we were hopelessly ignorant about that sort of thing. We would leave Motivation to the ideologues and the consumers of shredded wheat and vitamins, who having built up all that energy and

drive were quite naturally at the mercy of it for the rest of their
lives. As for us, the Isis! Which the Thames became merely by
flowing through Oxford, and if some of that magic rubbed off on
us, what more could anyone want? That afternoon the magical
river hardly flowed. Summer arrived and stood still. The day
was a day in the garden of Eden. Ravi and I idled it away,
blissfully complacent, truly Victorian in our belief in India's
inevitable progress, in peaceful change, in democracy everlast-
ing. We would study for ever and go home stuffed with useless
knowledge, having sorted out If I don't think, will I cease to be?
And why Shelley addressing a skylark said Bird thou never wert.
Independence was twelve years old and we could bask in it. The
abstract would absorb our energies. It was all comfortably
settled when we parted that day, and it came unstuck like bad
glue with the first blast that blew through our unsuspecting souls
as soon as we had squared our account with our curriculums and
the weather, and I had got used to my emancipated hair and my
skirts and blouses. This was not the England that had educated
and trained our fathers and grandfathers, a country we knew
only by hearsay. The liberal heyday of the Indo-English, Hindu-
Christian mind and the flowers it had produced of reform, was
over. We heard and responded to the siren song of Marxism.

I wonder what would have happened to us if we had been at
an American university. Would the shredded wheat have got to
us there, marched us burning with a different purpose to other
meetings, made us reverential joggers, Zen Buddhists and
saviours of whales? And at home would we have stumbled on
anything at all to stir us out of our high caste complacency? We
were hit instead by European winds, though language will ravish
anywhere if it is real and you are ready for it. The meek shall
inherit the earth. Long years ago we made a tryst with destiny.
And now, like an elixir, you have nothing to lose but your chains.
I wrote that sentence in large capitals in one of my notebooks
to keep its lilting promise before me (reminding me not only of
Marx but of my liberated hair and my skirt and blouse). There
it was, the aim of all endeavour, the reason for living, the goad
we needed to bring our privileged Indian blood to a boil. Why
had nobody, nobody at all, put those words together in exactly

this eight-word formation before? Then there was Expropriate the expropriators. Did any phrase in any scripture pack more power? There is no doubt Ravi and I were seduced partly by the language. But not only. It unlocked a small high window in my mind, an unused attic window, and air rushed in to swirl old scraps and particles around in a blizzard of dust, settling them after the storm in strange new configurations. I could see distinct images surfacing from that meaningless accumulation in the attic. Gnarled old hands at work on ancient occupations, epics handed on by word of mouth through social structures still intact. Still intact too the child at the back of a mud-walled village classroom, sitting the width of six rows from the last row in the class, his drinking water in a separate vessel outside the classroom. A sightless beggar reflected in the glass show window of a shop displaying high-heeled snakeskin shoes. Baby brides taking their dolls with them to their husbands' homes. My attic window gave me an anguished awareness I would never have had, though all that I became aware of at one stroke had been as if for ever present in my consciousness.

Mine was no romance with Marxism. Ravi's was. Our hearts beat quite differently over our discovery of it, his for humanity, mine for small actual conscience-pricking images, giving me a scratchy inner lining of anxiety. The Marxist sequence that would change mankind gave me trouble from the start: step one, the workers overthrow the government by force. Step two, they expropriate the expropriators, and establish the dictatorship of the proletariat. Step three is the classless society. And step four the State withers away. Only in actual examples the new commissars became a new class, and the State instead of withering away remained a national State. And what about that sub-proletariat of fifteen million Stalin had short-changed Marx with when he assembled it to build the great industrial space-age USSR? But it's still a better answer in our conditions, Ravi insisted, and we have to commit ourselves to it. So we abandoned the banks of the Isis and fell into an organizing fever, setting up a tiny radical group to discuss Indian problems. Ravi roped in every similarly smitten student and professor he could find to lead our discussions and every suitably radical visiting dignitary from India. It wasn't easy. Most of them belonged to Papa's capitalist ilk and the pale pink dilly-dally liberals among them were our least favourite. The Communist Party that Ravi wanted us to throw in our lot with had cooked its goose when it supported the British war effort instead of Quit India, and though the proletariat at home was getting organized, there was no great proletarian surge towards the Communist Party. The first trade union in the textile industry had been the work of Mahatma Gandhi and he'd kept throwing a spanner in the works of the proletarian uprising by just being around. 'My life is my message,' he'd told a reporter requesting one, and since *egalité* has to be lived, not talked about, the message had come across loud and clear. Even with him dead and gone long since, the revolution had got itself preserved in pickle and it was no good expecting the true red voices at our gatherings to tell us why, because they didn't seem to be making much political headway and obviously didn't have the answers. By comparison Gandhi's non-violence had worked like a streak of forked lightning.

Could it be that five hundred million anarchists found him more believable? I said to Ravi. You and your five hundred million anarchists, he exploded. What kind of argument is that? And if it's true, it's all the more reason for someone to crack a whip and lick them into shape. In the middle of whatever I was organizing at the time that little verbal flick of the whip, come and gone like a blink, stopped me in my tracks. I loathed regimentation. Since Bimmie and the saint I had made a lifestyle of asymmetry, my bedspread hanging lower on one side than the other, checking to see that it was, my slippers never side by side. Sonali, my well-groomed friends told me, you can't let your hair flop around, get a hairstyle. But how would a hairstyle be different from marriages, saints and goose-stepping regiments with six curls having to bounce backward and three forward and the front shorter than the back? I would as soon have joined the army. I felt well and happy with a little disorder around me, insurance that we were human beings, not sardines. The perfect neatness of Ravi's room unnerved me so much that we began to get together more often in mine.

If we had only had Soviet Communism to reckon with we

might have had fewer arguments. But it was 1959, three years since a part of the Communist world had risen against Communist practice, and if we were going to express our solidarity with anyone, I said, it should be with that lot. Maybe, I kept saying, Communism can no more be perfectly realized than anything else, and until it works out the way it's supposed to, why treat it as gospel? Let's keep its possibilities in our heads like grand symphonic harmonies, so that we never fall into somnambulism again. We were never meant to toe a laid down line, especially now that there were so many interpretations of it coming out of Europe's universities where thinkers, too dangerous for actual societies, had been driven. We were meant to argue and criticize. After all, thousands of British Communists, people we admire among them, had walked out of their party because of Hungary. But that only strengthens the Other Side, objected Ravi, and the way to keep Our Side strong is to stick to doctrine.

I think he said that because he was a man. He had never fought a battle for freedom, never been patted down firmly when his sap was rising, never had a sari throttling his legs, making walking in the wind and running to catch a bus a threat to life and limb, never had his mother set up a howl when he went and got a haircut. He had no idea what the simplest subjugations were all about. I, who did, had no intention of chaining myself to any doctrine when I had just lost some of my chains. Besides, I said, sitting on my rumpled bed, munching an apple, a heavenly disarray of books and papers around me, I don't like dictatorships, not even of the proletariat, not even as a passing phase because who knows the phase might get stuck and never pass. You are grossly muddled, Ravi told me, look at the state of this room! You aren't willing to think straight and take the consequences. You've got to commit yourself like me. You'll never become effective till you do.

Naturally I was muddled. So was he. Why wouldn't we be? We had had the West coming at us since our great grandfathers' time, while all we knew of our own culture were the droplets that had managed to seep in through osmosis, not ideas we had been taught and examined in. Even the Christianity we knew was what it had become after it left Galilee and fell into Western hands.

'If we aren't mixed up, I don't know who is.'

'Who's we?' he demanded.

'The tiny wee handful whose uncles and aunts all know each other and who are in charge of everything without a notion of what "everything" really is.'

'All the more reason to have a commitment,' said Ravi.

I did admire and envy his commitment, it was so cloudless. But I couldn't understand why we had to keep cutting and pasting Western concepts together and tying ourselves to them for ever as if Europe were the centre of the universe, and the Bible and Marx were the last word on mankind. Wasn't it time after all these centuries to produce a thought of our own and wasn't that what Gandhi had done, pack off an empire with an antique idea instead of an atom bomb? And half naked in his middle-class middle-caste skin he'd taken human rights a hundred years ahead in two decades without a glimmer of class war. It wasn't the end of the story, but didn't it deserve good marks for a start?

'Oh yes, Gandhi. I'm glad you mentioned Gandhi,' said Ravi, 'God's gift to the capitalists if ever there was one, to make sure there'd be no revolution for the next thousand years.'

But I was thinking once again of the beauty of words and of their power to inspire, and the new vocabulary which had. 'Daridranarayan', God of the poor. 'For the hungry, God is a loaf of bread.' And 'Harijan'. Words that had existed in no Indian language. This was the language of a new epic, invented by Gandhi. The man had used his brains, and what we needed now was a like inventiveness to suit our own conditions.

Wayward disciples must be educated and Ravi did his best with me, never swerving from straight and narrow doctrine. Even when we did not agree with him, he was the inspiration of all us radicals, and we never did understand why instead of throwing in his lot with the Communists after Oxford he changed his mind and joined the civil service, as I, in search of another kind of involvement, had already decided to do.

There was nothing out of the ordinary in our being in and out of each other's rooms. We had been practically sister and brother since birth. When I imagined adventures in love, they took place on trains hurtling through a lunar landscape. A total stranger and I would meet and make violent extraordinary love without a word said. Early next morning he would leave the train thank goodness and we would never meet again. A low sex drive, some would call it, but I was quite happy and I don't know why sex or any other drive has to be high. My room at Oxford with my familiar books and familiar dishevelment and the familiar presence of Ravi who had hogged all the juicy morsels from our common *thali* was the last setting I had imagined for love. Yet the day we lay down together on my bed we were doing little more than rejoicing in our long familiarity, our continuing brother-and-sisterhood. Like our predecessors the royal children of ancient Egypt must have been, we were as childishly inept at this as we were at technology. It made no difference that our generation all over the Western world had figured out computers and mastered arrays and varieties of techniques. Ravi and I, unprogrammed Isis people who had charged ourselves with the responsibility of changing the world, had not a technique or a guile or a shadow of sexual sophistication between us. We knew we could kiss without bumping noses and that was about all. From there we invented the making of love for ourselves, and it was the enriching of an acquaintance begun from the womb, my flutters and kicks and laboured descent, my first cry in the world, my first ounces and pounds compared and contrasted with his. We lay brain to brain as much as body to body, with a completeness of loving old and practised lovers would have envied. It was because of this – because even when we were discussing the Communist Manifesto, it was love we were making – that the path was so rocky. Only the perfect relationship can be utterly destroyed the moment one fine hairlike crack appears in the structure, when betrayal becomes a matter of one person ordering fish and chips for dinner instead of the stew agreed on, and a chapter read separately out of a book two were reading together.

TEN

Even a little bit of education gives you a few answers, Rose said to herself, such as, it isn't the sun going down behind the tomb, or going anywhere. The sun is in its place in the heavens and the earth is turning around away from it, bringing darkness to us here. A proper education, the sort she'd never had, might have given her other more complicated answers, like what became of past events and conversations, loving and hating and collections of emotions? Where was the evidence, except for people's memories, to show they had happened, and did they get wiped out for ever when people died? She couldn't accept an explanation so wasteful. There had to be places, spaces, where they remained for transmission later, so that in a hundred or so years some clever discovery would lift out of the ether an entire chat between herself and Minnie, for example, or the Ramayana chanted in the house in Lahore, or any one of the thousands upon thousands of words people had spoken since speaking began. The whole of time past was probably there waiting to be tuned into. Entire lifetimes couldn't disappear without a trace. What, in any case, does 'disappear' mean, only that we can't see it any more, but it must be there, turned transparent till it's recalled. Her power of recall since Ram's illness astonished her. Not that she thought about the past when she lay in bed or walked about near the tomb. *It* was catching up with *her* all the time, with an air of wait-for-me-I'm-coming, did-you-think-I'd-gone, convincing her nothing was ever lost, only held in a larger than human memory. No good or evil deed, nothing wonderful or disappointing, great or small, was ever wiped out; not even the dreary days after the Marcella affair.

Mourning for Marcella had taken its course though she was

presumably alive and fighting fit across the ocean. They were condemned to mourn her jointly because the geographical conclusion of a love affair that otherwise wouldn't have ended is bound to drive three people batty, not two. Rose was resigned to being part of a threesome, even when the third person wasn't there any more, like Marcella, or didn't matter any more, like Mona. Marcella's absence rang with the chords of Marcella's presence. She had walked into their life with the effortless, guiltless ease of the ruling class, and occupied it. She and Ram had behaved like the rightful lovers, making her, Rose, the outsider. And if they had been the married pair, then Rose would have been only the cuddly fling, while Ram's wife would have been his enthroned, abiding love. The matter of who belonged in the charmed circle and who didn't had been settled centuries ago and was a barrier people like her would never cross.

Ram sank into melancholy and became impassioned about his Dresden china shepherdesses and his Wedgwood plates. He was lost for hours in contemplation of the beauty of jade, the width and shine of taffeta, the substitute softness of silk. When he was not brooding over left-over imported treasures, he was closeted in his screened-off alcove of office space with Moghul miniatures, English poetry and Persian mysticism. There wasn't a thing to do in the shop, no consignments to check, no orders to place and not a customer in sight. With a war blocking the seaways Ram's business of imported luxuries had ground to a halt and he hardly seemed aware of the fact, brooding deeply, darkly in his alcove. His father's business, Indian cotton and wool from his own mills, was jauntily expanding, and all his outlets were booming. No point me standing around here waiting for Ram to snap out of it, thought Rose, and taking her courage in her hands, set out for the bazaar shop where the old gentleman chose to keep his headquarters. The worst that could happen would be the brush-off from him, and after the Marcella affair she doubted it would make a scrap of difference to her sanity. Getting into a *tonga* that Ram was too submerged in the Moghul empire to forbid her to take, she felt revived even before she reached his father's shop. He was there, sitting like an astute and alert Buddha, no flies on him, watching her step down gingerly from the *tonga*, count out coins for the driver and come uncertainly towards him. He waved his assistants away and gestured her to the floor facing him. Rose rapidly calculated the distance between her knees and the floor and lowered herself cautiously as she had seen others do. A gong should have sounded to mark the occasion. She had never exchanged more than the briefest formal greeting with him if they happened to meet in the house.

'Yes,' he said, quite a concession coming from him.

'I'm ever so sorry to disturb you,' Rose apologized, 'but I don't know who to ask, see, about where to look for the better shops for Indian saris and other things.'

'You wish to shop.'

'Not for myself.' In seconds the words poured out of her in a long despairing recital about Ram's shop, Ram ignoring a world at war and not stocking what was available in India. She'd seen such fabulous colours out shopping with Minnie, a rich ripe plum silk looking as if all the plums in creation had been squashed into it. English cloth was not – gorgeous – like that. It looked ever so tame, all right you know for tea-and-tennis frocks and English children's party frocks, but – at a loss for description Rose gestured sweepingly in the direction of Madras and Travancore, Benares and Gwalior, taking in the romance and colour of a subcontinent, her body as alive and aglow with enthusiasm as her knees and ankles were dead and done for. She'd like to throw out all the foreign stuff, she said, and get in Indian things. Ram didn't seem to understand that the business was going to pot, and she was worried sick about the business, because if the business got on its feet again then of course so would Ram. She wavered and stopped. Well, at least she could walk away feeling lighter if she ever walked again. His eyes did not leave her face as he waited for the eloquent silence between them to complete what she had left unsaid. He sent for two of his assistants and gave them instructions and Rose was somehow up on her feet again, being escorted through lanes and alleys over banana skins, stray dogs and dung, past beggars and cows to treasures Ram's shop should have been handling for years, and all a few banana skins instead of oceans away. Her next weeks were a whirlwind of thrilling investigation and shopping. Between them she and Ram's father restocked Ram's shelves and sent orders out for materials to Benares, Bangalore, and other weaving centres where the looms were. At her insistence Ram began to travel in search of Indian craftsmanship, leaving Rose in charge of the shop. Apart, they grew together in the nearest approach to an equal relationship they had ever known. And Rose took to dropping in on Ram's father at the bazaar shop, asking his advice, and talking easily now that pure business and not matters of sentiment were involved. It was too late to start calling him anything personal so he became Lalaji to her as he was to everyone else and she found she'd become Lalaji's *Angrezi bahu*. Ram was away in the south and Rose was beside the till in the shop when she saw a British tommy come in. She gave a little shriek of joy.

'Freddie! Fred-die!'

'Rosie!' He picked her up by the waist and whirled her around, not letting her get a proper look at him until he put her down. No wonder he looked different, it was the uniform, one of the flood arriving.

'In 'is Majesty's armed forces,' said Freddie, saluting smartly, ''ere to fight a war, but really to see you, Rosie.'

'Oh Freddie, it's really you!'

'I 'aven't got much time, two days is all, so wot can we do to beat it up, Rosie?'

Rose rang Minnie who was good at organizing.

'I know what, Rose. We'll go to the dinner dance at Stiffle's tonight, the four of us. It's packed nowadays so Dick will have to book a table. They've got a new cabaret, Robert and his Danish Beauties. What are you going to wear?'

When they had settled that Rose took Freddie to lunch. Ram would never have heard of Freddie paying.

'They told us not to mix with the Wogs,' he said, 'but I told them I'd come 'ere to mix with the Wog who's married to our Rosie.'

'I wish Ram was here, Freddie, but he isn't going to be back till tomorrow.'

'But 'ow's everything? You're 'appy, aren't you?'

'You can't be happy all the time. Sometimes I am and some-times I'm not.'

'Well, you look a treat. Done you good your marriage 'as.'

'You know how it was with me, Freddie, when I came out here. It wasn't me making up my mind. It was outside me, bigger. If I was a Hindu and believed in other lives, I'd say I must've been here before and wanted to come back.'

'You *'ave* changed, Rosie, become more serious-like.'

'Well, we won't be serious any more. Tell me about home and what's going on.'

Freddie could have had anything on the lunch menu. The restaurant had chops and steaks and fish. But he chose Madras curry and ate it determinedly, mopping his forehead and blowing his nose.

'If it's that hot,' worried Rose, 'I hope it isn't going to upset you.'

'Give some of this stuff to the Japs and we won't need guns and ammunition to deal with them,' said Freddie fervently, wiping his plate clean and asking for more.

'No more. I'm not going to have you falling ill with the beating it up we've got to do tonight.'

They had a drink first at Dick and Minnie's and went in their car to Stiffle's.

'Ooh, you really feel there's a war on,' said Minnie with an excited little shiver.

The room was full of uniforms. Red, white and blue crêpe paper streamers decorated doorways and balloons hung from lights. Behind the band a poster the length of the dais proclaimed Loose Lips Sink Ships. With a war on even a regular dance evening at Stiffle's became a little special but there was no need for McCavity to get up and go to the mike and make a little speech welcoming our boys.

'Likes his own importance, doesn't he?' said Minnie, not obliged to be respectful in Freddie's presence to someone else's, not Dick's, boss. But Dick, yearning for a uniform, was not pleased.

'The management must've asked him to,' he said reprovingly. 'You've got to remember, Minnie, there's a war on.'

'It's only just begun. You'll have a chance to get into it later on and that's soon enough,' Minnie's voice broke and she sniffled into her hanky.

'Now, now, wot's all this?' said Freddie. 'Come along, Minnie. Let's show 'em the Lambeth Walk,' and he had her up in no time, promenading and 'oi-ing' with the rest of them on a floor where you couldn't budge without bumping ten other people, it was packed that solid. Rose could hear 'Oi' being yelled lustily all over the hall as she and Dick sat it out to finish their drinks. But by the time the band had swung into the Beer Barrel Polka the voices raised in unison were so rousing, and even two-hundred pounders like Mrs Mulligan were kicking up their heels, that she and Dick abandoned their drinks to join the dancers.

'We rolled out the barrel all right,' said Freddie, flushed and triumphant, returning to the table.

'Da-da-da barrel of fun,' sang Minnie, tripping around the table before sitting down.

And then the band went into war songs from the First War. Pack up your troubles, Wish me luck as you wave me goodbye, and others Rose had not heard since she was a child. They had walked in, four people out for an evening's relaxation, when the tensions of battles, past and present, closed around them. War stretched into the future as far as the eye could see, and ran like an electric current through their collective consciousness, jungle war, desert war and their own London war, Mum and Dad's war as Freddie was describing the Blitz. They sat around their table straining to catch his words above trombone and saxophone while the dance floor heaved and creaked to Tipperary, and a simultaneous release sent them slumping thankfully in their chairs when Freddie concluded authoritatively, 'But Britain can't lose!' A statement too obvious to question, coming from a soldier who knew what was what, the talisman they needed to relieve unbearable fears and imaginings.

The band struck a fanfare. 'Ladies – and gentlemen. Robert,' the drum stammered a tattoo, 'and' – the stutter again – 'his adorable – incomparable – Danish' a longer tattoo, 'Beauties'. Robert in black tie and tails, black hair cemented to his scalp, strode militarily on to the floor, followed by four bare-legged bleached ageing blondes, and a thunderous applause meant for Allied battlefields made do with the cabaret at Stiffle's. Robert, rigid as etiquette, twirled and sidestepped stiffly to the music, extending his iron bar of an arm now and then to let a Danish Beauty exercise her incredibly elastic vertebrae backward over it. The audience concentrated feverishly, as people will on something they are waiting with bated breath to be done with. The music became silky, the spotlight softened to blue dissolving into green. Robert and the Danish Beauties now flowing like cool lava over his arm might have been one black and four silvery fish darting and gliding around in an aquarium, or flashes of marine life leagues below the surface of the sea, while the audience waited far above on firm ground in an agony like hiccups held in check. As soon as Robert had bowed his final bow and a burst of confetti had descended on his head, the lights came on and the company was on its feet dancing compulsively again.

'Do you know the Siegfried Line?' Freddie cupped his mouth and called to the band leader from below the dais.

'No, sir.'

'Bring your 'ead down a bit then,' said Freddie and sang a few bars.

The band leader recognized the tune and led the musicians into it. Before you could say Bob's your uncle, Rose thought, they were all singing it and Freddie had bounded up to the dais to conduct the band, dragging her by the hand, and she, Rose, was singing away into the mike:

'Whether the weather may be wet or fine,
We'll just scrub along without a care,
We're going to hang out our washing on the Siegfried Line
If the Siegfried Line's still there.'

It was a treat watching Freddie conduct the band with one arm, and the other round her, the ballroom full of dancers standing and swaying with their arms around each other's shoulders, while the dance floor groaned beneath their feet, balloons popped, and everyone went into the next number led by Freddie:

> *'Adolf,*
> *You've bitten off*
> *Much more than you can chew.'*

Voices rose in enthusiastic chorus: 'We're all fed up with you, cor blimey,'

> *'Adolf,*
> *You'll topple off*
> *And all your Narzees too,*
> *Or you may get something to remind you*
> *Of the old red, white and blue.'*

'After all his conducting Freddie needs champagne,' said Dick.

'We all do,' said Minnie, 'but isn't he the life and soul!'

Drinking was slurring their speech but it wasn't making them drunk, and when they stood up to the stirring strains of God Save the King, it was not the routine anthem singing that ended a dance evening. It sounded like a battle hymn with 'Send him victorious' battering defiantly through the walls of Stiffle's ballroom into the parking lot where chauffeurs were snoring behind the wheels of cars.

Rose and Ram slept in their bedroom on the upper floor because of blackout regulations. Rose walked in, doing a brisk foxtrot to the Siegfried Line, her arms around an imaginary Freddie, and bumped into the wooden stand with the goblet of drinking water on it, sending it clattering and crashing to the ground.

'Where the devil have you been?' came from Ram's bed.

'Oops,' said Rose walking unsteadily to her bed, laying her evening bag on it and sitting down to remove her shoes. 'When did you get back? I've been 'anging out the washing on the Siegfried Line at Stiffle's.'

'Till half-past two? I've been back for four hours. You know I don't mind your going out with friends when I'm away, but making a spectacle of yourself till all hours in public places is another matter.'

Rose held up one shoe and peered at it critically.

'Worn down it's got, past wearing now, and past repairing too, 'ow's that for a rhyme?'

'Who were you out with?'

'Minnie and Dick and Freddie.'

'Who's Freddie?'

'You know Freddie – from 'ome.'

Ram sat bolt upright. 'What do you mean by cavorting with Freddie till all hours?'

'I wasn't cavorting with Freddie till all hours. Part of the time I was conducting the band with 'im. Freddie's in uniform. And 'e's on leave. And in case you 'adn't 'eard, there's a war on.' She got up and twirled on one bare foot in imitation of a Danish Beauty and collapsed on her bed.

'Is that supposed to be an excuse for all kinds of behaviour? This Freddie individual has only got to arrive and you start dropping your aitches, while my country is being bled for the damned war.'

'All this bleeding nationalism is news coming from you,' said Rose matter-of-factly, sitting up and putting her shoes neatly side by side, 'and never you mind my aitches, they 'aven't gone anywhere they can't come back from.' Meaning, she thought vaguely, that Marcella had and good riddance.

Trust him to lie awake thinking about aitches with a war on. But why would Ram worry about the war, her war, when he had never worried about his own people's battles? Let his countrymen shout themselves hoarse in their processions, let his friend Keshav get worked up about what was happening on the streets and who was getting arrested and why Mahatma Gandhi had gone on a fast, let Keshav have pangs of conscience about it on his seesaw. Ram didn't know what a pang or a seesaw was. Only Marcella had ever got through to him and she had reduced him to a dazed jelly for years, which was different, oh, very different from pangs and seesaws. Otherwise Ram was immune. Tornadoes in which other people lost their lives and limbs and sanity left him bright as a button and fresh as a daisy. For the first time she pitied him. He was the outsider, not her. He was an outsider to bellyfuls of laughter and tears. She'd had a bellyful of both this evening, and of dancing and singing and drinking and saving 'is Majesty the King, and in Freddie's arms she'd been back in the good old British Isles. London had never seemed dearer than as he had described it. The Hun bombs were flattening beloved parts of it, yet people were picking themselves up out of crumbled heaps of masonry, out of death and destruction, and going about their work. Mum and Dad and their neighbours were sticking in London not just because of jobs but because they wouldn't have dreamed of leaving it. 'No 'eroics, mind you,' Freddie had said of her parents, 'but they're 'eroes just the same, same as mine and all the others.' Freddie was dead right, Britain can't lose.

'I've never heard of a dance at Stiffle's lasting this long,' said Ram when she came out of the bathroom.

'Oh, you 'aven't? Well, why – don't – you – just – go – back – to – sleep?' Rose chose her words with infinite kindness and care.

Surprisingly he did. And the next morning no more was said about her evening out, and Freddie was asked to spend the whole of his last day with them. With the almost feminine intuition Ram could display when it was most needed, he sent a long cable to her parents and from that day he made a point of listening to the war news on the wireless with her, taking the trouble to explain the war to her quite thoroughly with maps, as it followed its terrible course. She wouldn't have understood otherwise how the German armour cut through five hundred miles of French countryside like knives through grease, or why any question there might have been of hanging out the washing on the Siegfried Line had become a terrifying joke as massive fortifications kept springing up along the Rhineland. Ram, with the map between them, sombrely cataloguing defeats and retreats, glanced up to see her face crumpled with tears and said, deserting the map and holding her to him, 'No tears, Rose, it's going to be a long war and you must be brave.' Out of such war discourses and dry dialogues about Germany's military might is love reborn. And now he kept vigil with her as the Germans bombarded London, and soothed her in the night when she started out of sleep with visions of houses in flames.

And, as ever, there was no subterfuge about Ram. Rose

found a page of a letter to Marcella lying in his drawer when she
went to look for stamps.

the agony you have all been through, and how much grimmer
since the fall of France. Mahatma Gandhi has recently said,
'We must look at the world with calm eyes, though the eyes
of the world may be bloodshot.' Treason to you, Marcella,
but he is not anti-British. He is pro-British and pro-Allies. He
says, and I see the logic of it, that India must be guaranteed
her freedom if she is to fight a war for freedom on the Allies'
side. She is fighting now but as an imperial possession, her
resources and men used as the Government sees fit. But
think what a much bigger effort it could be, involving millions
more people, if we had a government of our own choosing.
There is no time to lose. We are in danger ourselves with the
Japanese advance. It is time for an understanding, not between
a colony and its imperial master, but between two civilized
countries. I'm convinced an understanding could be worked
out, like the lines from T. S. Eliot I showed you:

'Some way incomparably light and deft,
Some way we both should understand . . .'

Only I am afraid in the fever of war it may not happen.

No, there was no subterfuge about Ram and never had been
unless his whole personality was subterfuge, three-quarters
hidden. This grain of new concern for India was the last thing
she would have expected of him. Nor would she have expected
a letter to Marcella to read like this. How had it begun, my
darling Marcella, my own, my beloved? She sat down at Ram's
table and re-read the letter, and knew without a doubt that it
must have begun 'Marcella' and would end 'Ram'. Those two
words would say it all. In this one instance he had been left
stripped and scarred and naked as the day that he was born.
Every letter he wrote Marcella was a love letter even if it was
only about the fall of France and the Japanese, for love, Rose
had discovered, was like that, touching the oddest subjects with

a tender warmth. But the understanding he had written to Marcella about never did take place. What took place was confrontation. Ram read Mahatma Gandhi's speech on 8 August 1942 to the enormous gathering in Bombay aloud to her from next morning's paper:

> Here is the *mantra*, a short one, that I give you. You may imprint it on your hearts and let every breath of yours give expression to it. The *mantra* is: 'Do or die.' We shall either free India or die in the attempt. If the Government keep me free, I will spare you the trouble of filling the jails. I will not put on the Government the strain of maintaining a large number of prisoners at a time when it is in trouble . . . Take a pledge, with God and your own conscience as witness, that you will no longer rest till freedom is achieved and will be prepared to lay down your lives in the attempt to achieve it . . .

A few hours later he and thousands were in jail, bridges were being burnt and trains derailed in protest and it was said, calls were going out from underground leaders to steel workers to strike, stopping production for the war effort. The new wave of nationalism resurrected a militant personality in the house. Ram's father, incensed by the British Government's action, said he was through with British hypocrisy, and with a violence Rose had never suspected in his weedy frame, Lalaji threw every item of British manufacture, including Chivers Orange Marmalade and an unopened tin of Scottish shortbread Rose had been hoarding, out of the house. 'For God's sake,' said Ram, exasperated, 'it's too late for all that. Bonfires of British goods were made in the 1920s. There's no call for them now.' But the old gentleman was picking up where he had left off in 1919 when they had untied him stunned but defiant from the flogging frame. 'There was not one British thing in this house,' he told Ram, his eyes blazing, 'until you filled it up with foreign rubbish.' Rose, wondering if she would be seized and hurled over the hedge or otherwise nastily disposed of, then heard him say, 'It took Rose to even make you see sense in your business. But for her you would be mooning over Brussels lace even now.' And he ordered the astonished servants to rip the antimacassars off the drawing-room chairs and never let them cross his path again.

He started holding prayer meetings at the house, patterned after the Mahatma's, with readings from the Gita, the Koran and the Bible, and ending with the Mahatma's own hymn to Hindu–Muslim unity:

Ishvar-Allah tērē nām
Sab ko sammati de bhagvan

But how could those two, presiders over Hindu water and Muslim water, the god of Hinduism and the god of Islam, be joined together in one hymn, Rose asked, and Lalaji replied grimly, The British have conquered us, they have divided and ruled, and they will divide and quit one day, on the day and the hour it suits them to do so, leaving us torn in pieces, unless we learn the two are one and the same god. *They*, he said to Rose, not your people, for she, Rose, was sitting with others at the prayer meeting, her ankles killing her, listening to the stirring prayer sung around her, and then to the little sermon afterwards when one of Gandhi's disciples said that violence feeds on the victim's fear. If all the mice in the world stopped running away and stood their ground, cats would stop killing them, an intriguing idea she later told Minnie about. Cats and mice indeed, said Minnie indignantly, they're preaching sedition, that's what it is. You can wrap it up in cats and mice if you like but what they're wanting, can you beat it? is for us to get out. Violence or non-violence makes no difference, it's all sedition against the King. Don't tell me you go and sit with all those Indians who have nothing in common with us. And Minnie in her stout-hearted patriotism couldn't be made to understand that they were, if you thought about it, more like us, if 'us' meant Rose and Minnie, than the Indian nobs were. My Dad works in a bottle factory, Minnie. He might be working in a bottle factory in England, but if he came out here he'd be English, said Minnie with finality.

The crowd at the prayer meeting grew, made up of people

Rose recognized from the bazaar mixing with Lalaji's well-dressed friends, but indistinguishable from Lalaji, since he looked quite scruffy himself in his rumpled *pyjama-kurta*. There were more bazaar people than well-dressed ones, many of the tinkers, tailors and tradesmen familiar to her since her delve into materials and handicrafts for Ram's gift shop. No soldiers and sailors here since they were quite properly in His Majesty's armed forces, but rich men, poor men, beggarmen – the beggars Mona fed on Tuesdays now turned up to take part in the prayer meeting – and for all she knew, even thieves, all sorts and classes of Hindus and Muslims collected daily in a brown and white blur. It's the first time since I've come to India, no the first time in my life, amended Rose, that I've seen people high and low mixed up like this. They were watching her as avidly as she was watching them, sitting on her tortured English legs in their midst, and there was nothing ingratiating about their salaams and smiles when they met her afterwards stepping over banana skins in bazaar lanes and alleys. It was as if Gandhi, sitting in jail himself, had introduced them by magic to each other.

You are in good company, Rose, Lalaji told her animatedly, fondly recalling English names that had become as good as Indian, C. F. Andrews, college professor and friend of the Mahatma, editor B. G. Horniman who had taken off his English suit, put on a *pyjama-kurta* and joined the civil disobedience marchers in the streets of Bombay, and the English admiral's daughter, now Miraben, who had given up an admiral's daughter's life for an ashram and a spinning wheel. Ram, uneasy with his father's animation, and already seeing him with the tinkers, tailors and untouchables in the street, said, I hope you're not planning to join the Quit India movement. Lalaji gave his son a pitying look. I had already joined it before it was called Quit India, and long before you were conceived.

The service of India, said Gandhi's disciple, speaking after the hymn-singing, means wiping the tear from every eye, a phrase Rose forgot until the handless beggar who couldn't wipe his own tears brought it back to her. Till then she had more or less taken it for granted that tears were something one wiped away for oneself.

ELEVEN

No one mentions a person once he's dead. Perhaps they think it kinder not to. To me it seemed a cruelty. I longed to talk about Papa to someone who had known him. I was out of the official social circuit where I would have met his younger colleagues, and Kiran would have thought me morbid and tried to divert me to other topics if I had tried recalling Papa with her. What did we actually know about him, firmly planted as we were on my mother's home ground, among her people? Papa must have felt a little isolated in the sparklingly self-assured, softly contoured Kashmiri world we inhabited. His assurance had been of another kind. He had yielded much and constantly on the surface, little surrenders hiding a hard inner structure that didn't yield at all. Once Kiran and I had gone to wheedle him into taking us to the cinema, each pulling at a hand as we tried to drag him out of his chair. He had got up unresisting, but said in an aloof tone I had never heard from him, 'You can drag my body where you like but my heart is in my old home today.' While Kiran ran off to tell my mother we were going out, I clung to his hand with an urgent need to bring him back to me from far away.

'What are you thinking of, Papa?'

His eyes lost their shadowed look and, back in the present, he said, 'I was thinking that this is the day my father died, nineteen years ago. I was about your age.'

The cinema was a treat seldom allowed but that day it made no impression on me. I was obsessed by the body of Papa beside me and his heart in his home somewhere else, the division in his soul that split him, his life, his job in two, starting me on the quest of 'tell me about you when you were small' and 'where did you come from' and learning a plateau history about guerilla warfare in harsh boulder-strewn terrain, table-topped hills with jutting triangular peaks, ideal for hill fortresses and their defence, and Shivaji, that match-for-the-Moghuls who had so brilliantly defended them against Aurangzeb's elephantine armies. We knew little enough about Papa's plateau, where his family had moved from the coast, and less about how the drama of civil disobedience had affected a civil servant with a conscience whose body had served the sovereign power and his heart and mind, *satyagraha*. I had started the work of going through his papers and letters with a sense of anticipation that I'm sure Kiran would have found ghoulish, and had become absorbed in it. Accounts of shillings and pence spent during his student days in England, bundles of letters from a German girl testifying to a long relationship, playbills, personal and official correspondence helped me to reconstruct segments of a life I knew nothing about, tips of icebergs intact out of sight, but even the tips told me more than I had ever known about him, especially the two-ness spawned by government service in British India among those who had breakable hearts.

Here was a printed circular headed 'Secret Instructions issued by Sir Frederick Puckle, Secretary to the Government of India' dated 17 July 1942, less than a month before the last national convulsion, the Quit India movement, began. The Puckle Circular read:

We have three weeks until the meeting of the All India Congress Committee at Bombay on August 7th. During this time the matter is mainly a problem of propaganda to mobilize opinion against the concrete proposals contained in the Congress resolution and the threat with which the resolution concludes, described by Gandhi as 'open rebellion'. We have to encourage those on whose support we can depend, win over the waverers, and avoid stiffening the determination of the Congress; with the object either of putting pressure on the Congress to withdraw from its position, or if action has to be taken against the Congress, to secure that such action has the support of public opinion inside and outside India . . .

Pinned to the Puckle Circular was a newspaper clipping of
Mahatma Gandhi's comment that friends had brought him news
of it. 'Let the public know,' he said, 'that these circulars are an
additional reason for the cry of Quit India, which comes not from
the lips, but the aching hearts of millions. Let the masses know
that there are many other ways of earning a living than betraying
the national interests . . .' Papa had underlined the last few
words in red pencil, but he had remained on the seesaw all his
working life till Independence.

At the bottom of a trunk I found a small manuscript marked,
in Papa's hand, 'Written by my father in 1915'. I turned over
the pages of strong, legible script written in red ink with a relief
nib. I took it to bed with me that night and read:

There is a war on and they will soon come recruiting again
for the army. Each raw recruit gets blades of grass tied to
one ankle and a bunch of leaves to the other, and learns to
march to the order of '*ghās-patta, ghās-patta*' instead of left,
right. Wars change worlds. But can even war cause greater
upheavals than those a new language and its legacies have
brought to our shores in the past hundred years, and which
will in time become part of what future Indians will call
heritage? I write in English and that is a sign of it, but the
changes go deeper than language. My father was a student
of law and his own imagination was most stirred by the
Regulation abolishing *sati* in Bengal twenty-six years before
he was born, and the law passed a year after his birth,
permitting widows to remarry so that society would have no
excuse to immolate widows alive any more. The first legal
act against *sati* had caused a sensation and the Governor
General, Lord William Cavendish Bentinck, who had put his
signature to the statute, must have gone back to England with
the praise of our countrymen ringing in his ears, but my father
held the view that this was a wishful reform and would not be
worth the paper it was written on. 'If the British government
wants to abolish *sati*, then abolition must be absolute.' The
people who visited our house said a beginning had been made.
In some parts of the country it was punishable in criminal

courts. But did violent acts of ancient origin, rooted in mythology, stop because Lord Bentinck sitting in Fort William,
Calcutta, signed a statute, or because the reformers among
us wished them to, my father demanded. 'The custom of *sati*
was old,' I heard him say, 'when the first century was in the
distant future. In that reckoning Calcutta is a speck on our
map, and British rule a speck in our history.' An odd statement
for him to have made in the 1890s. Great Britain's rule is as
strong and stable as ever today. After the Queen's long reign,
her son came to the throne, and now her grandson, George
V, is King Emperor. Four years ago he and his Empress held
a durbar on this soil, probably the grandest state occasion this
country will see for a long time to come, and surely a sign
that the Empire and Pax Britannica stretch much further than
we, the living, can see. But my father thought otherwise.
And he insisted that the abolition of *sati* had done little but
salve the Government's conscience. If a custom so atrocious
were to be stopped in every part of British India, as well as
the states ruled by the princes, in one of which we then lived,
it must be ruthlessly prevented and publicly punished. Those
who perpetrated it must be hanged in the marketplace, or it
would go on into the next century. Wasn't it still going on,
openly or clandestinely, in parts of the country?

   As a lawyer such cases came to his ears. I never knew him
to waste words or exaggerate. Excess of any kind was foreign
to his nature. He was frugal and spartan, and his mind was a
blaze of purpose. It lifted him to high achievement in his
education at Wilson College in Bombay and made an English-
speaking lawyer of him with a successful practice, far-flung
for that time, in some of the princely states around us. He
had clients who paid him in every coinage, from goats and live
chickens to gold, all of which he received with equal pleasure,
sometimes the goats with more pleasure than the gold. He
lived in far too interesting times, with too much absorbing
work and intellectual challenge, to be greatly taken with the
pursuit of money. He would have considered it a waste of
time and a foolish diversion from the proper business of living.
His passion was reform and in this he reflected the spirit of

his generation, the heady winds that were sweeping our peninsula from east to west, and churning up a tidal wave in Hinduism. The Hindu Reformation was rightly named. It was an organized movement, a united endeavour, an awakening in the true sense. Mighty echoes of it are still with us in the remembered eloquence of the young monk, Vivekananda, the swami who thundered against the abuses of Hinduism from Kashmir to Cape Comorin and across the seas, saying it had become a religion of cooking pots. But it was in full flower in my father's youth, urging a clean sweep of the cruel and corrupt practices that were making a mockery of true religion. The burning of widows was the most barbarous of these.

My father's friend, the British resident in our state, Mr Timmons, maintained that if Raja Ram Mohan Roy had left the Hindu fold and embraced Christianity as had once seemed likely, a Christian wave would have swept the country instead of a Hindu Reformation. My father did not think so and nor do I. How far could a landowner, however enlightened or respected, influence the ways of the masses far from the cities? But apart from this there was the nature of Hinduism itself, a religion of immense antiquity with no traceable beginning, without a founder, a prophet or a church, with no single bible or commandments, no judgment day, no heaven and no hell, and therefore no conceivable way to pack it up and dispense with it. Hinduism is not taught, nor does it seek converts. It simply is. What welds us together? What carries it on? Ram Mohan Roy recognized not only his own dilemma but the dilemma of his age when he saw it must be unified from within, for it could never be dislodged, never replaced by simpler, later substitutions, by a Holy Trinity or the Son of God or No God but God. He was greatly attracted to Christianity, and he respected all religions, but he understood there are beliefs that cannot be conquered because they do not go to war. They have a life of their own, as the sea has a life of its own, or as encrustation upon encrustation of rock grows more durable, because of the material it is made of and not because it is ancient. The most ancient forms of worship – animism, paganism – have all but disappeared from the earth. It is metaphysics that time cannot vanquish. If the divine is everywhere, for ever, and part of everything, how shall we escape it either in time or in thought? At what stage of evolution can we get up one morning and say, Now we have outgrown this, we must move on to something else? So Hinduism remains, as uplifting as salvation, as destructive as slavery, and we must reckon with it. And this the Reformation tried to do.

Of course the abolition of *sati* was a landmark and my father made a study of the historical practice and the effects of the law. He had in his files the editorial of the *Calcutta Gazette* on 7 December 1829, expressing 'supreme pleasure' on the passage of the Regulation abolishing the 'horrid rite of suttee' and saying it was 'the glory of Lord William Bentinck's administration to have carried into effect' this reform by ending 'a system demoralizing in its effects on the living, a revolting system of suicide and murder'. He and Mr Timmons talked about this and so many other subjects sitting in the only room in our house an Englishman would have found comfortable, though it had no carpet and only plain utilitarian furniture, my father's desk, some upright chairs and a bench along one wall. It was where my father received his clients and spent hours reading and writing. It was better lit than the rest of the house, though my father's *shikar* trophies stared glassily at each other from their shadows on the walls. I sat on the bench doing my homework near a two-wick kerosene lamp, where I could not see the hairy bison head on the wall above my head. I did not mind the smooth straight-horned stags on the opposite wall. The hunt, like tennis, was a bond my father and Mr Timmons shared, though talk, I think, was their biggest bond. In those days talking was a regular pastime, much more than it is now.

Horror stories become diluted when they are told in normal surroundings. My father's voice and presence, Mr Timmons' broad back to me as I sat on the bench, the quiet rhythm of the household around us made it seem like fantasy when he said that seven ranis of the raja of a neighbouring state had been forcibly dragged to the raja's funeral pyre and burned there at half past two in the morning.

'Even if *sati* were not illegal, murder is illegal, but the Government will not lift a finger against those murderers,' said my father.

'It is not British territory,' Mr Timmons pointed out.

'No, it is not. Neither was the kingdom of Oudh British territory when Lord Dalhousie marched his troops in to annex it for no reason other than to extend British dominion. You are not paralysed by the legalities when it suits you to set them aside.'

Mr Timmons' view of history was that it had happened. By having happened it had become inevitable. In any case it was over. It was time to get on with the firm present. But for my father it was nothing of the kind and need never have happened at all if people had behaved differently at the time. And if, as sometimes, it was a network of error, then the present was by no means terra firma. So he resented British domination, but he admired the British and the law was a symbol of his admiration. He had set his heart on sending me to England for my higher education and training for the Bar. And if he railed at the inadequacies of the law it was because he had given his life to it and felt it should be a weapon and not a piece of paper.

'Some day,' he told Mr Timmons, 'there will be a law against untouchability. Do you think that alone will wipe it out? I hear of cases of *sati* still because there are ways of getting around abolition outside the major towns. They give intoxicating drinks and sedatives to the poor wretched women and drag them to the funeral. There are not even screams to mark the event.'

'Evil is evil. Can you eradicate it with legislation?'

'Then what good is legislation?' my father demanded.

'The Government has to be careful where religious senti-ments are touched. Any foreign government would have to be in a populace of this size. Did the Moghuls interfere with *sati*?'

'They were not on a civilizing mission as you say you are.

Yet they did, even so, try to interfere, and they didn't have the advantage you do, of a public opinion ripe for reform. And as for sentiment, don't you have freshly killed beef on your table, and bacon and eggs for breakfast? I am coming to the conclusion, John, that the only thing that rouses British wrath is a threat to British rule, which is based on no moral principle but superior arms. You act savagely against rebellion, as you did against the mutineers and the countryside in '57. So in the end you are no different from the Portuguese or the Dutch, crude conquerors, only you absolve yourselves of your guilt – which you have and the others don't – by hanging your indifference to important issues on rational pegs.'

My father got up and from a tall glass-doored cupboard he produced one of his *sati* files.

'Listen to this,' he said. 'This is Lord Amherst, Governor General, in his minute dated 18 March 1827, before abolition. He says that though he is not "insensible to the enormity of the evil", "I cannot believe it possible, that burning or burying alive widows will long survive the advancement which every year brings with its useful and rational learning." Such a nice leisurely view, unlike bacon and eggs, which must be had for breakfast this very day. And here's Bentinck, in the very sentence he was recommending abolition, on 8 November 1829: "In venturing to be the first to deviate from this practice, it becomes me to shew, that nothing has been yielded to feeling, but that reason, and reason alone, has governed the decision." Doesn't that amaze you, John? It is not because it is a monstrous inhuman act which prevents a decent man from sleeping at night, that Lord Bentinck finally put pen to paper, but because sweet reason finally prevailed.'

'Reason was the highest value for those men,' said Mr Timmons.

'Well, perhaps. But what was needed was a crusade with all its passion and fever. Generations of lawyers will uphold generations of laws but the old evils will go on into the twentieth and twenty-first centuries because no torch has been lit, and because *you*, who have the opportunity, don't seize the moment and break the back of evil when you have the chance. It is because *sati* still goes on that the new restrictions amounting to surrender have come in. Now a *sati* isn't interfered with if the widow has no dependents. She must not be pregnant. And she must die of her own free will! And if she is "unclean" as they say, at the time, she must wait until afterward, and be sacrificed along with some possession or part of her husband's body, his turban, his sword, his bones.'

How literally true it was. Travellers since the Greeks had seen *satis* performed. I found more recent accounts in my father's files, one written only two evenings after the episode it described in a letter to the editor of the *Bombay Courier* dated 29 September 1823:

The unfortunate Brahminee of her own accord had ascended the funeral pile of her husband's bones (for he had died at a distance), but finding the torture of the fire more than she could bear, by a violent struggle she threw herself from the flames, and tottering to a short distance, fell down; some gentlemen who were present immediately plunged her into the river, which was close by and thereby saved her from being much burnt. She retained her senses completely and complained of the badness of the pile, which she said consumed her so slowly that she could not bear it, but expressed her willingness to try again, if they would improve it; they would not do so and the poor creature shrank with dread from the flames which were now burning most intensely, and refused to go on. When the inhuman relatives saw this, they took her by the head and heels and threw her into the fire, and held her there till they were driven away by the heat; they also took up large blocks of wood with which they struck her, in order to deprive her of her senses, but she again made her escape, and without any help ran directly into the river. The people of her house followed her here and tried to drown her by pressing her under water, but a gentleman who was present rescued her from them, and she immediately ran

into his arms and cried to him to save her. I arrived at
the ground as they were bringing her this second time
from the river, and I cannot describe to you the horror
I felt on seeing the mangled condition she was in;
almost every inch of her body had been burnt off, her
legs and thighs, her arms and back, were completely
raw; her breasts were dreadfully torn and the skin
hanging from them in threads; the skin and nails of her
fingers had peeled wholly off, and were hanging to the
backs of her hands. In fact, Sir, I never saw or ever
read of so entire a picture of misery as this poor woman
displayed. She seemed to dread again being taken to
the fire and called out to the 'Ocha Sahib', as she feelingly
denominated them, to save her. Her friends seemed no
longer inclined to force her; and one of her relations at
our instigation sat down beside her and gave her some
clothes, and told her they would not. We had her sent
to the hospital where every medical assistance was
immediately given her, but without hope of her recovery.
She lingered in the most excruciating pain for about
twenty hours and then died.

The letter was signed 'A Decided Enemy to Suttees'. There
was another account I read with equal horror and fascination
from a 'List of Hindoo Widows Immolated' dated 1 December
1822. The widow was twenty-six years old and her name was
Comor. Her husband, Neerbhoy Singh, had died in service.
The account explained that her

husband's circumstances in life were such as to place the
widow beyond all fear of want had she chosen to remain
in life, but having received authentic accounts of her
husband's death at Rajmahal, she determined to burn
herself, and ascended the pile accordingly, having in her
lap the turban and inkstand of the deceased.
Intelligence of what was about to occur having been
brought to the magistrate, he immediately repaired to
the scene of action, and, after having spent some hours

in ineffectual endeavours to dissuade the widow from her purpose, at length permitted her nearest of kin to light the pile. The widow behaved with the utmost calmness and composure as long as the attacks of the flames were confined to her lower extremities, but when they reached her breast and face the torture seemingly became intolerable, and her fortitude gave way; by a violent exertion she disengaged herself from the faggots with which she was encumbered, and springing from the pile fell down nearly insensible at the feet of the magistrate, who had remained standing beside it. In a few moments, however, she revived, when the magistrate again seized the opportunity of again urging her to abandon her design, and renewed his promise of maintaining and protecting her in future if she could consent to quit the spot. This attempt was as unsuccessful as the former had been; so far from yielding to the magistrate's entreaties, the widow exclaimed vehemently against his interference, insisted on being allowed to go back into the fire, and breaking from his hold attempted to regain her position on the pile, by climbing up the logs of which it was composed, and which were by that time burning with the greatest fury. The magistrate finding that her resolution to complete the ceremony was unconquerable, and being of the opinion that any further opposition to her will might, under the existing regulations be considered as illegal and improper, permitted some of her relations whose assistance she invocated with loud cries, to lift her again into the flames which speedily consumed her to ashes.

It may be deemed worthy of remark, that this victim of superstition appeared firmly impressed with the idea of the present being the third time of her soul's incarnation. In answer to the magistrate's remonstrances and entreaties, she assured him that self-cremation was not at all terrible, or even new to her, as she had performed that rite before at Benares and at Canonge; and added

that she knew perfectly well what would be her
sufferings on the pile, and in what manner she would be
recompensed for them hereafter.

There were times when arithmetic, algebra and composition
were absurdities, and my very thoughts trembled at what had
happened up and down this land, as I sat in the glass-eyed
presence of stags and bison with Mr Timmons' broad back in
front of me. His 'friend and discussant', my father called Mr
Timmons.

'There's no such word as "discussant" in the dictionary,'
laughed Mr Timmons.

'There is now,' retorted my father. 'Do you suppose a
language travels thousands of miles and gets transplanted
without changing?'

Arguments about the powerlessness of law and reason
against custom were only part of their evening talk. I spent
more time listening than I did at my books. I felt mentally
well prepared for all that lay before me, especially, after I had
finished college, the voyage across the ocean to another stage
of learning.

The year I was nineteen, in my last year in college, was a
particularly bad year for our section of the coast. Such a spate
of calamities arrived all in a heap that people began to ask if
fate had turned against us. It was no good my father telling
the barber, Babulal, who came to shave him that there was a
scientific explanation for everything. And if there was bad
luck, it was bad luck, not fate. 'Cattle will die if there is a
severe drought like this one, but drought is not a curse. It is
caused by lack of rain.' Babulal, concentrating on the fine
blade against my father's jaw, replied, 'And what makes lack
of rain?' He slipped the blade a fraction further down, just
below the ear. I had watched this ritual for years, my father
on a mat under the mango tree, Babulal squatting on his heels
beside him. He seemed to have the planes and angles of my
father's face printed on his subconscious. He could have
shaved him with as minute a precision blindfolded, his skill as
old as the potter's wheel. 'It rains more, or less,' said my

father, 'depending on certain conditions of cloud or atmosphere.' Babulal sat back on his heels. 'And what causes those?' he demanded. At the beginning of all reasons, he said, there was definitely a Reason which chose to bless or to punish. Can you doubt it, he asked, when so many have perished and the crop failed? It is clear we are cursed.

About that time we began hearing of an old man in the nearest village who remembered his past births and had visions of the future. He would go into speechless trances for hours, or into babbling ecstasies that people would come miles to watch, when he would prophesy that this or that would come to pass. And when one or two of his prophecies came true, the village, and all the villages around, bestowed a sanctity on his babble, conferring an apocalyptic vision on him.

Half of life is made up of things we don't understand and there is nothing unusual about that. Only recently a nine-year-old girl born in a town fifty-three miles from ours said she remembered her previous lifetime and was brought back to our town by her parents. She guided them to the house of her previous incarnation where, she said, she had died of smallpox when she was six years old. The man and wife living in that house confirmed they had lost a daughter in the epidemic nine years earlier. The child then led her new parents to a tree under which she said she and her former brothers had buried a doll. They dug and there it still was. Such events are verifiable and the newspapers report them. So it was not remarkable that the old man's audiences grew. But, no one knows quite when, another man began to make an appearance in the crowds of visitors around the old one. He was either a local or from a neighbouring village – they cluster close in our sandy region – but nobody would have noticed him at all if he had not taken it upon himself to interpret the old seer's fancies, even if they were no more than inarticulate gurgles and gargles. And this is the strangest part of all, no one thought to ask him how he understood, what did he possess that others didn't, and what was he to the seer that he should appoint himself his go-between with the public? He wore a long red slash of colour down his forehead, more conspicuous than the normal *tilak*. He fingered beads, and when he was not officiating as interpreter, he prayed out loud with unnecessary zeal. Soon he was a reigning personality in his own right. I have never been able to discover whether he was truly learned and really recited the *shastras*, or whether the symbols he flaunted – the red slash down his forehead, the sacred thread on his bare chest – had persuaded people of his authority. But recite he did, strings of words and quotations no one had heard before. One, I am told, was actually from the Puranas: 'The *sati* lives with her husband in the unbroken felicity of *swarga* for thirty-three millions of years at the end of which period she is reborn in a noble family, and reunited to the same well-beloved lord.' It is clear he was trying to convey, and he was succeeding, that recent calamities were our punishment for abandoning old traditions.

Times of crisis produce such men, the ones with ready answers. They come forward out of obscurity to say Follow me and I will put things right. Only give me the power and I will put you on the road to salvation. And sometimes they emerge, as this one did, out of another man's reputation, not their own. But no one noticed that either after a while, or asked, Whence have you come, what are you doing here, and if you belong here, what in any case gives you the right to lead us? No one doubted him when he said respite and rescue were at hand, all would be well if the old ways were embraced again.

My father, on receiving information one morning that a woman had been burned by her relatives there, left immediately for the village. The people had been in an ecstasy of revival, he was told. The young widow had gone to her death half-stunned, whether by fear or potions no one was sure, but she hardly knew what was happening. Informers – the eyes and ears of the go-between, now considered the holy man's chief disciple – were everywhere, and no one cared to speak freely about the event. The village seemed to be waiting for its next victim.

'It is grotesque,' said my father on his return, 'to think this is happening in 1905.'

This was the material of his nightmares and he was deeply depressed. Since Mr Timmons' departure for England on leave he had no one to discuss it with but he wrote down all he knew of the case. I heard him tell my mother that in such a highly charged atmosphere as he had seen, this would not be an isolated event.

My mother was devout. I do not know if she was devout by nature or by habit, but it was her way of life to get up very early in the morning, to have a cold bath, winter and summer, to pray, and to fast for my father's health and long life. She was a good wife, I used to think. But now I believe all wives are good because they have little choice. The nuns in nunneries are good. Little children in their cradles are good. The Hindu wife is a Hindu wife and can be nothing else. And it is not until we can take the goodness of women less for granted that we shall learn to value it. It is only looking back that I see her as a person, not the personification of an image. She worked so tirelessly. There was never a moment when I saw her doing nothing. And each of her acts was an essential household act that meant food, clothing, succour for us all, family, servants and animals. I do not have to wonder whom I have loved most. From the beginning it was her. I respected my father and wanted to be like him. I married a girl I hardly knew. In time I grew fond of her and she of me. But my mother was touched by a special mystery. I saw her grow from one era into another, to span centuries of progress in her lifetime. My father did that, too, but he had help – the support of his family and society in getting an education, making a career, becoming influential in his generation. She who had never heard of the Enlightenment or the French Revolution or the theories of different philosophers or what industrial change was doing to economies, she who had almost never left home, achieved all this of her own being. It meant she was fearless, venturing forth willingly into realms of imagination she knew nothing of. She reminded me of flocks of migratory birds that fly thousands of miles, yet people see only their arrival, not the leagues they have travelled, the storms they have braved, the skies and seas and spaces they have spanned. It also meant her pieties had meaning, for in striving to keep up with the world she found herself in, she gave up nothing precious of the world she had known. The candles of her private shrines stayed lit.

How small she looked when I compared her to Mrs Timmons though I had never seen them side by side. I used to see Mrs Timmons in her carriage at our school sometimes, or in the shops. Her size seemed to have something to do with her long heavy skirts, the emphatic fullness of her bosom, the parasol she held above her abundant, elaborately arranged hair. It was also connected with the space her carriage occupied, the movements of the servant who climbed down from his seat on the box beside the coachman to open the door for her with a flourish and to close it with a slight bow that was not so much a bow to Mrs Timmons as the majesty her husband represented in our small state. My mother looked little, slight and contained. The sari she wore stayed close to her body in contrast with the voluminous skirts, the mutton-chop sleeves, the neck ruffles of Mrs Timmons. My mother's feet were often bare in the house. Her hair lay flat against her head, drawn neatly back in a bun. She did not smile much as Mrs Timmons did, only when there was something to smile about. Her expressions were not social expressions. She had little patience with nonsense, and that was what she considered the old man's babbling. His prediction of my father's death worried her not at all. If she had been ordinarily conventional she would have become nervous and taken steps to ward off evil. But she was not one bit superstitious. She had too much firm faith for that. She did believe in astrology, a science that went by certain rules. It was the future predicted on the basis of the latitude and the time, to the minute, of birth, and the position of the constellations at that minute. With that data accurate prediction is possible, yet even an astrologer will never say 'Death will come at such-and-such a time.' He will say it is likely, those are dangerous times, and he will prescribe remedies that, God willing, will lessen or avert the calamity. The old man did not read horoscopes or know astrology. Nor did he practise the occult. He did not belong to any school or practise any discipline. He had his own hit-and-miss brand of clairvoyance, an inner sight for which there is no explanation. So his prediction of my father's death did not disturb my mother's sleep. She had his horoscope and went by it. But I can no longer ignore the supernatural since the day my father suddenly died, at the age of fifty, in apparent good health, as the clock's hands reached the hour and the minute of the prediction. What is not wildly improbable – the earth is round, machines will fly – until the future makes it fact?

My mother was as silent through the rites of washing his body as though she had lost her voice for ever. It was my father's relatives who wept noisily. Her very appearance with its whole inviolable grief seemed to excite more demonstration from them. My uncle's wife was the one who took a brick and broke the bangles my mother was wearing. It looked a brutal thing to do when she could have let her remove them as she did every night, slipping them carefully off her wrists and placing them on a shelf near her bed. She never took off the diamonds she wore in her ears and her nose because a married woman must be adorned at all times. My aunt took these from her with scant courtesy as though my mother would have held on to them otherwise, and then she shouted for a servant to bring a brick and broke the glass bangles leaving the shards lying where they were. I picked them up when no one was looking, wrapped them in my handkerchief and put them into the pocket of my *kurta*, to throw them away later. I never did. I have them still. At the time I did not want to go far from my mother. She looked like a ghost in her white sari, but she sat erect, in the cross-legged posture of work and prayer, not in the huddle of the weeping widow. Nor did she weep. Each time she looked at me it was to signal me to be calm, too, in preparation for the solemn rite it would be my duty to perform at my father's cremation, the breaking of his skull bones before the fire was lit. Both her energies and mine met over the heads of the people gathered there to brace me for my task. In the crowd that had collected to lament a family's penultimate loss, I saw faces both familiar and new from the villages around, faces that had travelled through strange byways since the old man's visions began. Yet all these were people who had known my father well and had a right to be there. What struck me was the number of relatives present, people who had hardly made an appearance in my father's lifetime, who did not approve of his ways, now here to stake their claims. In the feeding of relatives, the rolling and unrolling of their beddings, looking after their servants and horses, not until the third night after the funeral did it dawn on me through some fragment of conversation I had overheard, that my mother had no inheritance she could lay claim to because my father had left no will, and I was not yet of age. She was entitled only to maintenance by her husband's family. Everything he possessed passed to his brother until I came of age in two years' time. She and I would have to live with him. This house would be sold. Everything in it would become my uncle's property until I was twenty-one. But I guessed from the way they were behaving that there would be trouble ahead. Would they relinquish money and assets they had controlled for two years? My uncle had little sympathy for my father's ideas. I did not believe he would honour his wishes, and his dearest wish had been that I should go to England on completing my studies here. On that third day after the funeral, when my father's ashes had been collected and stored in an urn, my mother called me to her and told me of her fears.

'What shall we do?' she asked.

In another woman the question might have been a pleading one. But she looked alert in every fibre of her being. We were in the garden, out of earshot of our relations, under the tree where my father had had his shave every day, conspirators in our own home. Ordinarily I would have gone to Mr Timmons' house for his advice and he would have known exactly what to do, but he was not back from his leave yet.

'Fetch someone who knows the law,' my mother said, 'you must know someone your father trusted.' Then she changed her mind. 'No, don't bring him here.' We were both so unused to conspiracy we had to stumble and grope towards our next step. In the end it was obvious that the man we needed was my father's clerk.

I climbed the ancient wooden stairs to his house. His wife opened the door to my knock and was overcome with shyness. She let me into a room with two string cots and two low stools. A baby crawled on the floor playing with bits of old newspaper. An oil lamp burned feebly in a niche in the wall, casting its long shadows across the room. She scooped up the baby and vanished before the clerk came in to say, alarmed, 'Why did you not send for me?' I explained my mission. My mother needed a document containing the main provisions of what would have been my father's last will and testament. He understood my mother's need at once, but his language was poor, he said, and he was not much educated. Yes, he could draft some kind of document, but would it be exactly right? And even if it ensured that my inheritance came back to me in two years' time, the money could be frittered away or invested beyond my reach by then. And in any case, what could make my uncle give it up at all?

'We can try to make sure there are no withdrawals or investments without dual authority,' said the clerk at last, 'but only if someone besides your uncle has guardianship of it.'

We both thought of Mr Timmons and the clerk said he would draft the document and keep it with him until Mr Timmon's return. Some of the strain left my mother when I told her it was being done. The larger crowd that had come for the funeral had left, but the house was still full of relations and the running of it was not my mother's any more. They behaved, in fact, as if she were not there, and their callous indifference seemed strangely and incongruously to make her the centre of their attention, as a big hole in the middle of a canvas will constantly draw one's eyes to it. I have seen a painting in an art gallery in England of a group of men with a high round circular window in the stone wall behind them. The painting is severe and undecorated but the textures are palpable. The wall is visibly rough stone, as their clothes are obviously thick and woollen besides being black, and their squarish black hats are made of something stiffer than felt.

They are sitting at a table and one is as conscious of the massive shapes beneath the folds of their garments as of the oily gleam of the table's wood. The only light on the canvas pours sharply from the circular window on to their naked faces, but in the dark background one can see the cowled heads of monks. I suppose the painting represents some actual incident. It has all the hallmarks of the particular, as of some moment in history recaptured. What I remember vividly is the intentness of those faces, almost garishly lit and unnaturally focused on one person in their midst whose lowered eyelids half cover his eyes. It comes back to me as I write. It has much in common with the focus on my mother and what was happening at our house. When all the ceremonies were over, my mother said I should go back to college and miss no more classes. I would have refused if she had tried to send me away out of town, but my classes were in the same town and I need never be away from her for more than a few hours at a time.

I felt the emptiness of the house as I approached it at noon one day after I had attended morning classes. There was not a soul about. Even my mother, who did not go out at all these days, was not anywhere to be found. I flung my books into a cupboard in my room and walked disconsolately about the garden. Then, still unsettled, I took my horse from the stable and rode over to the Timmons' to find out from the servants when they would be back. Their ship would dock at Bombay in one week's time, the head servant told me, and they would be here three or four days after that. The marigolds grew too profusely in their beds now that Mrs Timmons was not here to pick them regularly or to supervise their pruning. She would sometimes send a basket of them to our house for my mother to use at her worship. Now they were untidily packed into the beds facing the front steps of the porch where I stood, and did I imagine it, or did the whole garden have a straggling, unkempt air? A restlessness filled me, made as much of anguish for my living mother as grief for my dead father. My own future was uncertain now in spite of the legal document the clerk would prepare. It might or might not protect my future, but either way my mother would have no relief. She had years before her and if I went away, I would be absent for several of them, leaving her without any emotional support. I would have sat right down on the steps of the Timmons' house in the middle of the warm afternoon and wept hot tears if the stillness around me, accentuated by the sound of bees on the marigolds, had not brought me back to the impossible utter stillness at home. No house is ever that silent, as though every single person in it has gone on a journey. I had an instant's forewarning of disaster. I travelled miles in that instant of blinding pain and fury. My next connected thoughts and actions took me where I knew I had to go. When I got to the river bank where we had cremated my father a new pyre was blazing where the old one had been. I saw her fling her arms wildly in the air, then wrap them about her breasts before she subsided like a wax doll into the flames. Madness propelled me forward and made a demon of me. I leapt upon my uncle and threw off the men who tried to stop me. Two of them wrestled with me as I forced them nearer the edge of the pyre, until we were on the narrow parapet and they were afraid to use their full strength on me for fear of falling into the flames themselves. I was half in the fire myself, and if the scorching heat was singeing my clothes I did not feel it. In a working corner of my brain I had but one object, to take at least one victim of my own, a life for a life. I drove one of the men backwards towards the fire, heard his dreadful unending howls as the fire leapt towards him. I sprang on the other, forced him to the ground and fell on to his chest, my thumbs pressed into his throat. To this day I don't know who he was, or if I killed him, or what happened to the first one. They were not men but the powers of darkness. If I killed either of them, my mother's slayers must have disposed of their bodies without a trace, not to call attention to their own crime. They had all gone when I opened my eyes. My clothes were charred, the skin of my hands and arms torn and blackened with soot. I turned painfully on to my side. The fire was glowing softly in the evening light, and an evening breeze lifted its embers and ashes and blew them towards me.

My uncle kept out of my way until he left for his own home. He was afraid of me, and it was obvious that he did not feel equal to sorting out the business of my father's estate yet. When they had gone I sat crouched in my room with the doors and windows shut, refusing food, until my father's clerk, hearing of their departure, came and banged on the door until I let him enter. He made me drink hot tea and sat on the ground opposite me, gravely saying nothing. He went away and came back the next day and so I got through one day at a time. Many days later I heard Mr Timmons' voice along with the clerk's in the next room. Mr Timmons was repeating again and again how appalled he was, the clerk saying, 'The boy is unhinged, sir, I do not know what to do with him. I would take him home but I would never be able to care for him in this state.' And then I was in Mr Timmons' house, curtains of some heavy glazed material looped with white cord in the room where I found myself. Between them white transparent gauze blotted out the exact details of the garden. Thick carpet swallowed sound. And mercifully no one spoke a single word to me as I lay in bed. Mrs Timmons would come and look at the food on my tray, arrange flowers in a vase in my room, go away again. Her coming and going may have lasted weeks. I distinctly remember the first words she said to me: 'This downpour has absolutely ruined my roses,' as if we had been carrying on a long conversation before that. The sentence connected me with a distant normal past, when rain fell and gardens grew, words exchanged with her long ago. At the same time it put me squarely in the present. It had rained. The monsoon was here. Another season had begun. Mrs Timmons' vowels and consonants, the ruin of her roses, and even their absolute ruin beckoned to me as a beacon from another world. Out of the void in me something rose and prepared to meet it. About six weeks later they put me on a ship to England. It was left to Mr Timmons to try to find out why my mother had committed *sati*. My uncle told him she had insisted on it as part of a bargain that would ensure my inheritance and even before I came into it, my education abroad. I have no reason to believe he spoke the truth, for how could she have imagined I would begin a new life in a new world with that knowledge locked in me? How could I arise a phoenix from her ashes, and did she not join me to those who killed her, or at least make me the reason why she died? But of course it is a lie. She who had embraced my father's world and his ideas was too offensive a reminder of them.

That was ten years ago. The world is at war as I wrote at the start and some changes are expected in India. We have been promised political reforms. I believe in a gradual progress towards self-government. But underneath there will be the subterranean layers of ourselves we cannot escape. I can look back now and reconstruct as though I had actually been there, the scene as it must have happened. A procession of them took her from the house, past familiar scenery, knowing where they were taking her. They helped her to climb the funeral pyre, bedded her down solicitously on the stacked wood where so lately her husband's corpse had lain, and then stepped back to a great safe distance as the flames leapt up, to watch her dance with death. Afterwards they walked back the way they had come, through the same meadows, watched by the same men ploughing the fields behind the same oxen, to eat and sleep as though nothing had happened. And who knows, perhaps the men behind ploughs watching them pass also knew where they were taking her, to a high caste death as arcane and commonplace, after all, as the horizontal furrows their ploughs made. Yet the question remains: what kind of society is it that demands human sacrifice to appease the blood thirst of what kind of gods?

So I cannot believe in Hinduism, whatever Hinduism might be. Not because of such evils as *sati*, but because evil is not explained. If the universe is an illusion, and eternity is a split second, and there are eternities of life after life to come, then in terms of the cosmos my mother's agony is nothing. And all suffering is nothing. But it is that twitch of time in the cosmos when I saw her there, when I would have given my life to drag her out of the fire, and killed those about me who had consigned her to it, that I want explained. And if evil has led us to where we stand then the ground beneath our feet, as my father used to say, is far from firm.

I put the manuscript down. My eyes ached. I felt shaken. Illumination seems to come to me in the dark. When I switched off my bedside lamp I saw a world revealed, but strangely enough it was not the evil in it I saw. On a narrow parapet enclosing a funeral pyre I saw a boy of nineteen balancing dangerously, unconscious of the danger to himself, as he fought savagely to kill his mother's murderers. Not all of us are passive before cruelty and depravity. He had not been. Nor the boy in Connaught Place who had struggled desperately all the way to the police van. Nor even Rose's beggar, undaunted by his armlessness, slipping and slithering from his tormentor's grasp while those with arms and legs walked mutely into captivity. And I fell asleep to dream of heroisms whose company I was scarcely fit to keep.

TWELVE

Her most vivid recollection of the day she heard the words 'Quit India' was Minnie's excited phone call after breakfast.

'Rose, have you heard, Robert and his Danish Beauties were Germans all the time! Would you believe it, there's spies all around!'

'And there we were that night talking about the war with them listening all over the place,' said Rose.

'You never can tell, can you? It's a relief to know they've been interned.'

But it was Mona who made that August memorable. This time Rose was just sitting down to breakfast when the smell of burning timber reached her in the dining room. Ram had already left for the shop but she had had a headache and had slept late. The house was so full of wood, wide old wooden beams, walnut furniture, carved chestnut mantelpieces, that Rose panicked and, calling out to Kumar, ran from room to room. She flung open the door to Mona's room and smoke smothering the frail sweet scent of incense filled her nostrils. Mona kept her prayer accessories on a low table. One brass oil lamp, well lit, was on it. Its pair had fallen over near the wall panelling behind the table and could have started the fire without her realizing it. And then Rose saw her grievous mistake. Mona sat cross-legged, her eyes closed, a band of flame advancing up her cotton sari, consuming it soundlessly while she submitted to the inevitable like a woman in disciplined childbirth, her short agonized gasps barely audible. Rose dragged the cover off her bed and with Kumar's help wrapped it round Mona's struggling body and got her out of the room. Lalaji suddenly appeared and took charge, instructing the servants how to put out the fire while he telephoned the doctor. Mona's neck and left arm were a gruesome sight and she was badly shocked but she refused to go to hospital. Released from the discipline of dying she moaned and cried until she was sedated and drifted into sleep.

'She was saying her prayers when the *diya* fell over and her sari caught fire,' Rose heard Lalaji tell the doctor. 'She didn't realize.'

He looked over the doctor's shoulder at Rose and they sealed their wordless pact. It could have been the explanation, but Rose and he both knew it was not. Yet why had Mona done this now, after all these years, unless she had lived under a curse of dying? Rose's death wish for her, mechanical as the drip of a tap, had goaded and maddened as drop after drop does, wearing her down. Rose sat in front of her long delayed breakfast telling herself she was carrying fancy too far, only there was no denying that houses breathe in and out, sighs sink into walls and walls exhale them. Houses positively reek of human happiness and human grief. Any normal person would perish with the weight of feeling a house holds, yet hate could become too heavy for even a house. It was dangerous to hate.

'I don't think I want breakfast after all, Kumar,' said Rose.

'No, memsahib.' He took her untouched plate away without a word.

Rose kept looking down where the plate had been. By her own Christian principles, what right had she here? She and Mona would never have been twinned in anguish but for her, Rose, aggressor and tormentor. If one person had to die so that another might live, she was the guilty one. Only she felt no guilt for truly loving. If, as Zafar's faith so awe-inspiringly said, 'There is no God but God', then love, too, is always and only love. In the ten years she had spent here nothing had changed that. But nothing could change other facts as awe-inspiring, of guilt, responsibility, occupation. Nothing could drive those demons out.

It had taken a long time to locate Ram who had had errands in town. By the time he arrived home the crisis was over, Mona in bed and asleep, her burned neck and arm loosely bandaged. He fussed a bit when Rose would not go back to the shop with him. After he'd gone she found herself haunting the corridor outside Lalaji's room before making up her mind to enter. As though by long habit, she left her shoes outside, and sat down on the floor facing him across his low desk, as she did in the bazaar shop. It was the first time she had done it here.

'I feel so miserable, I don't know what to say.'

'You saved a life today,' said Lalaji.

'It's my fault, I'm responsible –'

'You are responsible for saving a life,' he repeated.

For some reason she would never understand Rose said, using words she never would have used, 'But it was my duty.'

Lalaji said with uncharacteristic fervour, 'May God bless and protect you all your days, for you are a good woman.'

Rose shook her head, bewildered. That's just what I'm not, she wanted to say. You can't think how I've hated her, what frightful deaths I've wished on her, how I've wanted to pack up and leave this wretched situation because of her. If there's a fire, you jump in and rescue a person if you can, that's all. What's it to do with goodness and badness? But she sat there, her ordinary duty transformed into Duty, herself into a live exhibit of Dharma, the austere morality he lived by.

'I have wronged you,' he said, 'I have judged you harshly for no fault of yours. I owe you an apology.'

Rose was overwhelmed. Monuments of stone and steel do not apologize. If he had not been so forbiddingly unapproachable she would have hugged him for being so generous, though it still did not absolve her. That was Mona's act of grace, and like all her acts it triumphantly invaded every nook and cranny of their lives. The catastrophe welded her to Rose. Like an army released from combat and too spent to fight again, she became involved in complicated manoeuvres for an immediate truce in preparation for the journey to long-term harmony. The servants sensed the transition and reacted to it. During Mona's convalescence the house lay quiet but as soon as she was up even its corridors and verandahs, not particularly personal places, took wing and alighted again amid a resonance of laughter and chatter. Mona recovered was as adamant and uninhibited as Mona wronged and injured. Her 'We are sisters!' had the rich round ring of 'We are comrades!' As they became acquainted a new chapter opened, backwards into the past before Rose's startled eyes, a Mona chapter of Ram's life, as succulent as any he could have known, and one that had produced his only child, leaving Rose to puzzle afresh at how Ram could possibly have had that look in *his* eyes at the chocolate shop counter, when he had all this waiting for him at home. They entered the fourth September of the war as a family. An odd sort of family, but unquestionably one.

'Rose-ji, poor Dev is failing in arithmetic. He has such a bad teacher at school. Please speak to himself about a private tutor for him.''

And ten-year-old Dev who called his mother Mama, and Rose Mummy, ran up and down between the upper and lower floors, saved the trip of going to another house, streets or cities away, to visit one of his separated parents.

'Don't mind me asking, Rose, but we've known each other so long,' said Minnie confidentially, at Tuesday coffee, 'and don't go misunderstanding.'

'I won't, Minnie.'

'D'you suppose Ram still, you know, treats her as his wife, which she is, of course, but you know what I mean.'

Did he or didn't he? Rose, recalling how Mona's silk petticoat clung to her narrow hips as she stood in front of the long mirror in her room to put her sari on, a touch of wildness to the huge hazel eyes under arched black brows, the indescribable glow of her melting-pot skin, imagined a procession of slim, wild, ada-mant, golden Monas behind that one and as many expressions.

'How would I know?' she replied.

'I hope I haven't upset you, Rose.'

''Course not, only how would I know?'

Minnie went into peals of laughter.

'You *are* a card. Not know? 'Course you'd know. If Dick had been to another woman I'd know, let me tell you. Oh, not right away, but eventually. It'd have to come out in the end. How could it stay hidden?'

Dick, well Dick would feel guilty, and anyone would know from ten miles away what Dick had been up to. It was different in Cythera. Ram never bothered to hide anything. If she had asked him, he'd have told her. But she didn't particularly want to say, By the way, Ram, do you still? in case he did.

'Men!' said Minnie. 'They're not very different out here from the days when a Sultan of Turkey – Turkey, wasn't it, some empire or the other – made a bundle of all his wives and dumped them into the Bosphorus because he was tired of them.'

'He did, did he?' said Rose, bemused and far away. 'Oh well.'

'I do admire you. You've got character, you have.'

Rose lifted a languid hand to brush a stray curl from her forehead. If this at last was Nirvana, it was a nice quiet place to be.

Without her new-found confidence she could not have faced the news of her parents' death, most of their row of houses reduced to rubble when a bomb came down, surely by accident, in a neighbourhood where there were no munitions works, nothing of military importance. The most piteous part of it was Mum and Dad's unrealized future, their savings and planning for the time that never came, from the last war to this. But years later Rose saw the symptoms of a more piteous malady in Dev. He had nothing in his head except the present. There's no more to him than that, she thought, no dreams at all. Even – especially – the mad have dreams. He hasn't even the saving grace of natural, harmless madness. Locked up in the present like in a cell, he's a lunatic of another kind, cut off from continuity before or behind. And the planning and sighing of Mum and Dad fell into its rightful place, where dreams should be, in people's hearts and heads.

Mona and Lalaji took the loss of her parents intimately and fiercely as their own personal loss. Rose would never have got through that harrowing time without them, especially Mona, whose hidden golden wildness broke into spoken loving lament. Unhampered by Ram's subtleties she ordered the household to revolve around Rose and a religious ceremony for her peace of mind. But, said Rose feebly, if the ceremony is for me, why should you be the one to spend the day fasting? Mona, categorical as ever, had replied, If we're a family, then we're a family. She starved herself all day with the energy of one for whom a fast is a positive act, breaking it at sundown with a horrible concoction

consisting of smoking hot milk and soggy *jelabies*. Dividing the
mourning up into its proper and strangely comforting parts, she
brought it to an end one day by clearing the path for healing
recollection. Rose-ji, tell me what your parents were like, how
did you live, was your hair always this colour, were you *born*
with it so bright and red? Who, after all, are you, Rose-ji, tell
me everything from the beginning, we have lost too much time.
And they met once again, though it was really the first time,
over the reconstruction of Rose's childhood.

They began to go out together to places that would have been
of no interest to Rose and Ram's social circle. Mona with her
fascination for religious themes took Rose to a shadow play of
the Mahabharata. On raised ground where jugglers and acrobats
usually performed, a sheet had been stretched on a wide frame
and the play started to a rousing drumbeat. The balladeer sat
with musicians below the screen, singing the saga of Draupadi,
wife of the five Pandavas, who two thousand years ago had
gambled her away to their kinsmen, the Kauravas, in a game
of dice. Rose's 'Now what are they saying?' got whispered
translations from Mona, though not much translation was
needed. Even the traffic hooting noisily on the road behind them
did not break the spell of those giant shadows on the screen or
the rise and fall of the music in Rose's blood as Draupadi was
dragged into the hall of her new owners to have her sari torn
off her in front of them. She dropped to her knees, a tiny helpless
figure in profile on the vast screen, dwarfed by sentries armed
with bows and arrows around her. (She is praying to God for
help, explained Mona as the sari went on and on unwinding.)
The music spiralled joyfully and the musicians' voices joined the
balladeer's:

> *Ten thousand elephants will lie exhausted*
> *Before this ten-yard sari grows less*
> *Thousands of enemies are helpless*
> *Before one whose protector is Raghubir.*

(Another name for God, whispered Mona.) Rose could hear the
roll and crash of drums all the way home. God's protection

occupied her these days. God had saved the King, not her parents. Some people were for saving, others were not. God had saved Draupadi, not Sita. 'Do you believe in God?' she asked Mona, the sort of question women and children ask each other, but one she need not have asked Mona.

Historians might not see it that way, Ram and Keshav had paid no attention to her that day long ago, but it was exactly what happened. There had been that unthinkable development – mutiny in the army. First the Japanese had marched from victory to victory. Then soldiers of Britain's Indian army taken prisoner in the jungle had joined their captors and broken away to become an Indian National Army and fight on the Japanese side. And after the war, more of the same, with a lightning naval mutiny in Bombay. When that sort of thing started happening, and it started with the fall of Singapore and the Japanese making white men pull rickshaws there, the British knew it was time to go. The INA was put on trial after the war, with Indian national leaders defending them as patriots but, as Rose had known, it was a storm signal the Government understood. The British don't leave their homes even when the skies are black with bombers and they certainly wouldn't stroll away one summer day from their empire without good reason. But when Gandhi said Do or Die and people who had just marched in processions began to burn bridges and derail trains and do other businesslike things that couldn't be ignored, there was reason to worry, with the war going disastrously too. Rose had kept quiet when Keshav, visiting them in Lahore, had talked politics to Ram. But what on earth were they talking about? England hadn't occupied territories to give English lessons. Empire was for profit. She loved to hear Keshav talk about British fair play and British justice, but it was the urges underneath that decided matters. Ram's falling for her and marrying her had not changed the fact that Ram's whole family, including his first wife, stayed together. She had been ill with unhappiness over it, Mona worse, and it had made no difference. 'I wasn't born today,' Ram had told her often enough, 'I can't behave as if I were. I can't start life with you on a clean slate as if I had no past. I told you I had a wife

and a child and you accepted it.' She had. She had even accepted
the future he had not told her about, and not gone away when
they became another sort of threesome. Stronger urges made
them both do as they did, so she was certain the British wouldn't
leave until *they* decided the game was up, and it would never be
up until they saw doom spelled out in a language they understood.
When it was, nothing would induce them to stay. An island race
needed no second warning of danger. But she had busied herself
giving Ram and Keshav lunch and they had not asked her opinion
again. Not that she had one really, it was just instinct.

The war had spelled other dangers to Lalaji. Bit by bit he had
transferred most of his assets and the bulk of the business down
to Delhi so that Partition, when it came, did not disturb their
fortunes greatly, and by that time it was all Ram's. His father
died quietly in his bed one night with the clockwork precision
he had lived by. As the date of Partition approached as inexorably
as a countdown, he had refused to be pulled up by the roots
across another frontier. He told them as the killings and pillage
mounted in Lahore, he'd made one transition, village to city, in
his lifetime. It was enough. He would not make the leap to
another country. He would never leave his home. And he hadn't.
His death had come calculatedly early, giving them time, at
Zafar's insistence, to pack up and move to his house before the
streets became impassable, and live with his family until he could
arrange safe passage for them to Delhi. Even Ram's father's
mortal remains had given them little trouble. His vegetarian
body, so light and disposable, seemed ready for quick, hygienic
dispersal among the elements. And at the time so much permanence was dissolving around them that his death took on a
historical significance, a loss they always equated afterwards
with the loss of provinces, rivers and a natural not a political
frontier, ending at Afghanistan. His death was the end of the old
days and they spent their own last days in the beleaguered
city in Zafar's home recalling the past, with piece after piece
of it sinking out of sight as they talked. And who was happy?
Certainly not Zafar, who did not stay in Pakistan. He remained
in Lahore, his home for generations, and Pakistan came up
around it.

Because Lalaji, the villager, had had his wits about him, Rose and Ram could sip gin and lime at the Delhi Gymkhana Club a few Sundays after Partition, driving to the Club past straggling hutments put up for the ragged, bloodstained knots and bundles that turned out at close range to be people, sights to make her heart leap into her throat and stop there, squeezing it tight. A little delayed by ambush, butchery and rape, columns of them kept arriving at the refugee camps, while at the Club it was refugee stories that grew like anglers' tales.

'I tell you,' said the whiskered chatterbox, turning round in his basket chair beside the swimming pool to tell it again to a brand new audience – 'I tell you I leapt up and caught the wing of the plane with the tips of my fingers as it took off from the ground, the last plane to leave Lahore before the bloodbath.' Well, something like it was what he said, thought Rose. Every story of the exodus was more hair-raising than the last. They had somersaulted, cartwheeled and leap-frogged out of Lahore, clutching the wing of the last plane, balancing on the wheel of the last vehicle, suspended by the tips of their fingers and travelling on the tips of their toes in swashbuckling hair's-breadth escapes from knives, axes and other humble home-made implements of fratricide. Escapes as various and ingenious as the mind of man could devise had lifted them in a single giant stride over a boundary sprung up from nowhere, from one Club to another, past herds and hordes trekking the tortured miles on foot. And freedom, just a few midnights old, wasn't the song of the Gymkhana Club's displaced persons at all. It was revenge. They had left their towns and cities behind. A lying, cheating government ruled Delhi, made up of jailbirds who didn't know property from a hole in the wall, didn't grasp that property had been looted or destroyed, and cared less for land ownership with their threats of abolishing *zemindari*. They cared so little for rupees, annas and pies that they were handing five hundred and fifty million rupees to Pakistan because a mahatma who should have been minding his ashram instead of meddling in politics said so. Bitter violent talk was a Club luxury. The hutment refugees were too busy staying alive. So it hardly surprised Rose when a Hindu who wasn't even a Punjabi, who had lost neither a city, a house, a bank account, nor a piece of land, a relative or even a memory, assassinated Gandhi.

For the Club refugees the old days, the good life, caste, class and solvency lay across the border. There were nothing but question marks ahead. What could you expect of this bunch of jailbirds? There will be no Pakistan, this bunch had said, and Pakistan was on their heads besides being lodged in their livers. Two, not one helpings of it. Stay in your homes, nothing will happen to you, they had said, and a vengeance to make the sacking of Delhi by Nadir Shah look tame, had descended on Lahore. Pandit Nehru had reacted in instinctive anger when a refugee had raised his hand to catch his daughter's *dupatta*, but look what had happened to their women. Their women, well-fed lionesses blinking into their beer, were getting sleepy and befuddled with exploits unravelling like knitting around them. As the sun rose higher in the sky and began its descent they urged their darling-jis to wrap it up now and move to the dining-room buffet before the best cuts of meat got finished. And none of them guessed, how could they, that soon, in place of good, honest, ordinary money and all the nice things it could buy, there would be a fearful appetite for it that no amount of it would satisfy, a genie escaped from its bottle after Partition, never to return. In another fifteen or twenty years most of them would be lifted from mere prosperity to bloated lashings of it, more than they had ever dreamed of on the other side of the border in simpler times, since people dreamed of so many other things besides money in those days. And business would be connected with tables, some of it done over, and most of it under them.

Soon enough third-gimlet talk at the Gymkhana Club about the jailbirds who ruled the country became, Panditji? What a man, what character, what integrity, what ability, what democracy! What refinement such as never-before-seen! Wishful memory sprouted forests of antennae. Relationships, anecdotes, encounters with Panditji popped up like jack-in-the-boxes.

'Panditji? Our families have known each other from way back, what do you know, Guddo, you weren't there, I am speaking of don't I remember him riding to the Congress session in Lahore in 1929 on a white horse, what a prince among men, Harrow, Cambridge and Kashmiri Brahmin, don't I remember the day. And my grandfather remembers that Panditji's father was present at my cousin-brother's wedding, what an aristocrat!'

'Panditji's mother came from Lahore. Don't I remember the beauty, the culture, the complexion!'

'Panditji was, I happened to be there too, at a convention in Austria in 1938.'

Or in Geneva or Ceylon or Kuala Lumpur.

One rememberer had stood with him in an air-raid shelter the day the fascist bombs rained down on Barcelona and another rememberer's uncle had been in jail with him in 1932, in the same barrack, what's more, omitting to explain that uncle had been in jail for embezzlement though in the same barrack. It seemed a minor detail beside the rage of remembering.

'Don't I remember Panditji pulling a bottle of sherry out of the top drawer of his desk in his office in the South Block.'

Ram had put his foot down. 'You don't remember that because everyone knows he doesn't drink.'

'He pulled it out and offered me a glass, don't I remember. He's a sport, I tell you, doesn't believe in all this prohibition rubbish. Don't I know the man? He knows how to live, learned about living from his father who knew Sir Harcourt Butler.'

And Rose herself couldn't know that post-Partition Sunday on the green grass of the Club's garden, as Ram's long, elegant fingers twined round his gimlet glass, that in the very instant she was thinking nothing will ever shake Ram to the core again – even Partition hasn't shaken him – Nemesis, by his side all along, fashioned by his own loins, was lolling by the swimming pool demolishing sandwiches and summoning a bearer in a peevish voice to order more Rainbow Delight ice-cream. Dev, a beneficiary of Partition, straddled two homes, ruled two little kingdoms. For it had taken a continental convulsion to divide Ram's family, and Mona now had a flat of her own and reigned over a large circle of family and friends not as a discarded but an honourably retired wife.

Mona in her new incarnation blossomed into bridge and spent hours poring over Dev's horoscope with an astrologer recommended by Ram's elder sister's mother-in-law whose home was in Delhi. And it appeared that Dev had a remarkable horoscope, the kind only leaders of men had. Even if the poor boy, due to bad teachers, was failing in mathematics and a few other subjects, look what lay before him, Rose-ji, she kept pointing out, and with so much disturbance and disruption because of Partition, what could be expected but failure at studies? But the astrologer had said – and she would go on to elaborate what the astrologer had said.

THIRTEEN

For Papa the seesaw stopped at Independence. He worked harder than ever but with the energy of a whole, not a divided man. Things fell together for him though it was a fallen-apart world we became free in. The split atom, haunting other pulpits and literatures and consciousnesses, spared ours. We saw no End staring us in the face. We were just beginning.

> At the stroke of the midnight hour, while the world sleeps, India will awake to life and freedom.

We were Not Guilty of Hiroshima, Nagasaki, or sending Jews in cattle cars to gas ovens. We could afford to remind ourselves of a past others were trying to forget, and we joined ours seamlessly to the present. The civil service was part of the join. So were English, Parliament, Commonwealth and the Word of Lord Jesus Christ. And Byculla Soufflé and Tipsy Trifle. It was a time when irresistible forces and immovable objects curtsied politely to each other and stepped aside to let enormous changes take place without a sound. *Zemindari* was abolished and culti-vators became land-owners. Maharajas with nothing to rule became businessmen, diplomats and politicians. And everything, from soap and fertilizer to refrigerators, bicycles, radios and cars, became Indian. My mother sighing, 'What a beautiful Alfa Romeo you had the year you joined the ICS' or 'I wish we had a lovely Chevrolet instead of this tin-pot Hindustan-Ambassador' was met by a severe look from Papa who had become quite stern now that he was not on a seesaw and not feeling sheepish about the government he was serving. 'But other countries were under foreign rule, too, and they –' 'Never mind other countries,' said Papa. 'This is India.' Yes, it had been for quite a while, agreed my mother dryly, but how would it hurt us to have smart foreign cars and Elizabeth Arden's orange flower cream? Paper explained in great detail how it would hurt us, bearing 'we' and 'policy' and the 'socialistic pattern of society' aloft with pride.

I don't understand this 'tic', said my mother. Either we are socialist, and I don't know why we are, or we aren't, but what is this 'tic'? The 'tic' was the balance, the compromise, the mixedness of the economy that let a private and a public sector flourish side by side. Well, tic or no tic, she complained, Indian glass has got bumps and bubbles in it, so when you go to London for one of your conferences for heaven's sake get me a decent set for my dinner parties, these Indian glasses will have to do for every day. But how were the bumps and bubbles going to straighten out unless we patronized Indian industry, demanded my father, unless this yearning for foreign luxuries stopped? The luxuries stopped even if the yearning didn't. And he was right. The bumps straightened out and everything else under the sun became Indian too, including millionaires.

The amount of money little nobodies were making, much more than Papa had after years in the ICS, was something you wouldn't believe, Mama said. The dry-cleaner she dealt with, a funny little dark fellow, had made enough to have a vulgar Punjabi sort of reception for his daughter's wedding, and the poor girl so dark too, no amount of money could alter that. And with untouchables behaving like everyone else, getting into airline jobs and other branches of government service and all over the place on quotas, really the craze for equality had gone quite far enough, where was the need to go on showing off about it? When Lal Bahadur Shastri became Prime Minister – *the* most ridiculous development, said Mama, look at his height! – she and Bhabi-jān couldn't help observing how the Delhi secretariat was filling up with Kayasths. At least one could hold up one's head with a distinguished-looking Kashmiri Brahmin Prime Minister, but here was this shrimp who was a Kayasth as well, and filling up the secretariat with Kayasths.

It did seem to me that with the old order changing and Papa opening and blossoming, Mama was closing, petal by petal, along with Bhabi-jān, whose mouth was a thin straight line by the time Shastri became Prime Minister. It was after Shastri, when the removal of poverty had been item one on the agenda for some years, that it gave me a shock to discover a beggar covered with sores standing right outside my office building, where beggars never stand, his bony arm stretched timelessly out to whom it may concern, while I wrapped my fine Indian cotton sari more tightly around me, got behind the wheel of my Indian car and drove home. Republic Days had come and gone, with caparisoned elephants and camels, smiling school children and folk dancers, MIG–21s screaming across the sky, tanks dipping their muzzles in salute to the President, all Made in India, and so was the beggar, made before the MIGs and the tanks, and still a beggar. In fact we had both new and hereditary poverty staring through the tall glass doors of five-star buildings. But managers, politicians and bureaucrats like me all got into our cars and hurried away to our next engagement unlike the Buddha who took a thornier path after the sights he saw outside his palace, and after him no one until Gandhi.

There was good reason to be disturbed as even I, desk-bound though I was, realized. Something was wrong if the fat of the land had settled high up instead of melting and trickling down, if poverty had grown and multiplied, and there was no use calling out police reserves to fire on processions protesting about the state of affairs. The all too visible police wielding tear gas and truncheons brought imperious rule and empresses to mind, waking me up to the fact that the democracy of Pandit Nehru, who had been dead ten years, was in deep trouble. But I think we sensed trouble much earlier, Papa and I, the day I came down the steps of my office building in August 1969 to get into his car to go home with him for Kiran's birthday lunch. Fourteen banks had been nationalized the day before, which was probably a good thing if it was going to mean more credit for the rural population and break the moneylenders' hold, and that is as much thought as I had given to the news as I came out, looked around for Papa, and saw his car quite a distance away near the gate. He was fifty-two, still six years from retirement, but he kept telling us he was living on borrowed time. His own father, a man haunted by the tragedy of his mother's cruel death, had died at forty-three, and his grandfather suddenly, mysteriously, at the age of fifty. Papa indicated his helplessness to drive up closer to the portico because the whole area reserved as a car park for those of us who worked in the building, as well as the driveway leading to it, was clogged with taxis. It was incredible that they had been allowed to collect and camp there.

I threaded through them towards Papa who had his hands raised in a 'What's going on?' gesture when we saw Ravi Kachru come bounding out of the building looking, as Papa said afterwards, like a joyful Alsatian. He sprang on to the bonnet of one of the taxis and seated himself there with his right arm draped casually along the roof and, in a voice resonant as bells, asked the assembled taxi drivers to raise three *zindabads* for the nation's supreme leader. Leader is one of our commoner words. All politicians are *netas*, and so are students, trade unionists and anyone else who has made a three-minute speech starting '*Bhaiyon aur behenon*'. With *netas* commoner than city grass, supreme *neta* shouldn't have raised much dust, yet we knew when we heard it that an alien note had been struck, as unexpected as the sight of a civil servant taking time off to make political hoop-la from the bonnet of a taxi. Papa could not have been more astounded if the President himself had bounded out of Rashtrapati Bhavan, jumped on a tricycle and started hawking ice-cream cones, only that would have been merely eccentric. This was prophetic. I was not the stickler for proprieties my father was. I was willing to exchange parliamentary modes and manners for another sort if they made for better communication, but I didn't like the look of it either, and we found ourselves united in our discomfort.

Ravi launched into a speech hailing bank nationalization, and the Supremo's victory it signified over vested interests and the enemies of the people, all those reactionaries who had been holding the country back all these years. This Papa definitely took objection to, having contributed to several spectacular successes himself while Ravi was still in short pants. But I couldn't hear his grumbling comment because lusty cheers and more Long Lives rose when Ravi announced loans at scrappy interest rates for Delhi's taxi drivers. Papa, who had been about to drive away in suppressed fury when the country's progress was maligned, changed his mind, reversed out of the gate and parked outside where we could listen to the rest of the glad tidings. But that seemed to be all. So rural credit would not get all the honours, but never mind, taxi drivers would be better off too. And what was more, they were going to become a new militant constituency (or one of, if Ravi and other zealous bureaucrats were handing out pieces of cake in other parts of the city as well), because now he was calling on them to serve the Supremo with the same undying loyalty their ancestors had given to clan chieftains of old, that they themselves had given (or if they hadn't they should have) to the Supremo's father, and in no time at all would be giving to her son, all of this mixed with the 12,000 rupee low-interest loan getting wild cheers. After all, said Ravi, his voice throbbing with controlled emotion, what were the Government, the Cabinet, the Ministers, the States, the municipalities? They were there to do Her bidding. What was the country? It was She, who like the many-armed goddess would be ever victorious against those who were plotting to dethrone her.

On the way to his house Papa told me the brief story of the three wells, which is 'Well, well, well', looking gloomier than I had ever seen him look, and really despondent for the first time since Independence. This was a democracy, he said, only because we believed it was, and felt morally responsible about keeping it one. Two decades of parliamentary democracy would go up like a Divali cracker if this nonsense were allowed to go on. But who was going to disallow it when rallies to hail the Supremo began to be held by the Supremo herself at the roundabout outside her own house, the Supremo's rally being the first compulsory stop on any bus route, and all roads leading to the rally. Very soon, lawyers and judges, carried away by the popular upsurge hailing bank nationalization, joined the frolic at the roundabout with roses in their fists which they were careful to deliver personally to a close aide of the Supremo before going off to their chambers to make sure that fundamental rights didn't get in the way of socio-economic justice. My main thought about all this that day was that the upsurge inaugurating the Supremo-to-people line looked suspiciously like a Kachru-to-Supremo line. I said so to Papa, adding wistfully that we might be judging too hastily, and some really revolutionary changes might be ahead. If this is a sign of revolutionary change, said Papa, my name is Abdul the Bulbul Emir.

Since Oxford Kachru and I had met less and less. I had been in Delhi on limited assignments and had otherwise worked entirely in my State. Kachru had asked for and got coveted Delhi postings, one running into the other, on the plea of his mother, her age, her health and her widowhood, though happily Bhabi-jān was in splendid health after Shastri, and had been a widow for more years than anyone could remember. Unkind critics said he was better known at seminars and conferences abroad than at home. We had little to say to each other when we met, partly because he was so good at social chit-chat and I was so lacking, but mostly because he and I, long ago, had been present at a creation, after which social chit-chat seemed rather pointless. The break had been hard on me but drifting apart afterwards had come naturally. Was I jealous of him, I wonder, buried in my State while he flew to conferences and acquired foreign gloss and gilt? I honestly don't think I was. He was welcome to his jaunts. For me this was the world's most interesting country with life's biggest challenges to be met. The rut I was in was my kind of rut. And then I had become the kind of woman who, highly concentrated on the subject in hand, is supposed to have 'a man's mind' and who disappoints the flirtatious and flippant. At an official dinner the night before populism burst upon us, the handsome member of a trade delegation from Hungary, seated next to me, had sadly remarked, 'But you are too serry-oos, too serry-oos.' A woman's brown eyes must melt and sparkle at the dessert stage of conversation, her hardness must soften and infinitesimal, exciting twinkles and half-hinted messages must shoot and dart from her pores, from the angle of her head, from her up and her down glances. We had spent all day bargaining about the list and cost of traditional Indian items for export and discussing a change-over from rupee trade to international currencies. To get from that to sinking softness over dessert was not a journey it interested me to make, since I found my work more rewarding. I couldn't ask to be excused while I stepped into my seductive garb. It was there all the time, or it wasn't. So I made no concessions to those who didn't want me to be 'serry-oos'.

Papa and I kept our impressions of the bank nationalization rally to ourselves at lunch until Neel, a private enterprise man, remarked what an inspired idea it was, making Papa remark it was as old as independence, when the Imperial Bank was nationalized to serve the goals of socialism, and there was nothing much to be gained by today's fireworks display except fireworks. A few years later Neel would exclaim with the same boyish gusto how fortunate that the radical furore was over and the country on the right track again with Madam getting the advice of her conservative son. Neel wasn't hopelessly confused. He was just playing Follow the Leader. In this game you don't worry if the leader, like the legendary courtesan, is all things to all men. You just get on with producing flashlights, which is what Neel was doing, and putting away the profits (some in hard cash for the leader) and be thankful you can still drink Scotch and not awful Indian whisky. Kiran, who thought of marriage as a shaky detente that would collapse at the first sign of disagreement, added her heartfelt tributes to bank nationalization, and since we were on the subject Papa came out with the shock Ravi's rabble-rousing performance had given him, making my mother smile at all of us babes in the wood and say, her petals opening and her eyes dancing, that she didn't know about bank nationa-lization, or what Ravi thought about it, but didn't we know and hadn't we heard that he had just got engaged to the youngest daughter of the second cousin of the Prime Minister's mother? It was as if someone had tilted a checkerboard and all the loose marbles had rolled into their slots, fitting snugly into them. My mother described the utterly sensational suitability of the match, not only the caste, community, features, complexion, height and width of it, but the Relationship. Ravi was on his way. Oh Sonali, if only! But then she sensibly stopped and went on to say that *his* mother was delirious with delight. Bhabi-jān had been thanking the Lord for the past three years that we had a Kashmiri

Brahmin Prime Minister again after that shrimp of a Kayasth,
and now here was her only child, the light of her life, so close
to the heart of power.

Anyone would have thought that the Supremo's mother's
second cousin's youngest daughter was not all that close to the
heart of power, and Ravi Kachru was, after all, still only on the
bonnet of a taxi and not yet at the dizzy heights, but that would
only have shown how slow and stupid Anyone was. Bhabi-jān
obviously saw ahead, oh, far ahead. Or didn't one need to look
ahead or behind, only to the ever-present, all-powerful bond of
blood, the mystical kith-and-kinness that held us in thrall and
would make us naturals, pushovers, for a dynastic succession?
What a match! said Kiran, her eyes starrier than I'd ever seen
them. I must say it's really something! What's so *something*
about it, I demanded in exasperation. Sonali, you are so anti-
Kashmiri, said Kiran, sweet and mild, you're always trying to
pull down your own community. Now, now girls, said Neel,
beaming with pleasure at the thought of being so close to the
person who was so close to the heart of power. Good old Ravi,
this calls for a celebration, we should have him over. Whatever
for, I demanded hotly across the *koftas*. If Ravi K had been
about to marry a raving beauty no one had ever heard of, or
an unknown triple MA whose family came from Gola Ganj in
Lucknow, or Delhi's Sitaram Bazaar, or Agra or Allahabad or
Kanpur or any one of the places where the tribe settled when
it left the Kashmir Valley, would you people have set cannons
booming to mark the event? But the vicarious thrill of Ravi's
match placing his future children tenth in the line of succession,
as it were, made lunch more than a birthday rejoicing. Though
this was long before a ruling family and succession became taken
for granted, the sweet gold saffron rice we ended the meal with
steamed deliciously, aromatically and prophetically on the table,
symbol of jubilation to come when, if not we ourselves around
this table, our tribe would capture the throne of Delhi.

I went to Kachru's office after lunch to congratulate him on
his engagement. It was an unimportant personal event Bhabi-jān
had been very keen on, he said modestly, compared with the
dramatic turn the country had taken with bank nationalization,

and certainly his wife disappeared unimportantly into the anonymity of good wives and no more was heard about her by the outside world, while the dramatic turn became more and more dramatic. He was excited and restless, and at his fluent best. In spite of myself I was affected by his longing to be up and doing once again.

'But why did you have to talk such rot about many-armed goddesses?' I said.

'Populism means using symbols the people understand. What's wrong with it?'

'And her father, and her son, a regular Holy Trinity?'

He shrugged impatiently. 'Why not? We believe in Family.'

'We believed in *sati* too. We've got to stop believing in some things. Bank nationalization is taking us in one direction and family worship in another. Which way are we going? How can you combine the two? How can you be a socialist and believe in family rule?'

'But, but, but, Sonali. Is that all you can think of at this historic moment? Are you going to be one of the sceptics or one of us?'

I suppose only the slow-witted like me were having trouble reconciling family rule with the Communist Manifesto, Kachru's last cloudless commitment, or did 'us' now cover both? To me it looked more as if the Tsar had nationalized banking in old Mother Russia and left everything else, especially Tsardom, exactly as it was.

'Well,' I said, 'I hope you'll be very happy.'

He accompanied me to the door. 'Bhabi-jān is very pleased. She's been so keen on it.'

I went out of curiosity to hear JP speak the night before he was arrested and the emergency launched. It was the first time I had ever heard him. Crowds are always big in Delhi and we are used to political spectaculars, with terylene trousers, nylon shirts and free food thrown in to bring people by the free truckload to cheer long boring speeches. This, the biggest crowd I had ever seen, had brought itself there. If JP was public enemy No. One, inciting the army to revolt and the people to lawlessness and disorder, as the emergency declaration later said, then the government was stark staring mad. I was listening to questions I had asked myself. Why were the poor still poor? Why were there so many more of them? Why had the fat got stuck high up instead of trickling down? Why? Why? Why? I was listening to a Socratic soliloquy. It didn't strike me until JP's arrest that that had been the point of the hemlock. Teaching the virtuous life when virtue is in short supply is treason. And yes, behind him on the dais a huge banner blazoned the Hindi poet Dinkar's words: 'Vacate the throne for the people are coming', conceived, as every school child knew, for the struggle against the British, but treason enough now for another aspirant to imperial power.

On the morning of 26 June I came to see Papa in this very room, now mine. When the door shut behind me I thought I was in an empty room, but Papa was in it all right, still as a statue. I asked him, 'Did you ever think such a thing could happen in India?' And he replied, 'No, never.' In the hour or so since the radio had told us about the declaration of an emergency, our voices had automatically sunk to whispers. In Nazi Germany, Papa said, people used to muffle their telephones with blankets as a precaution against listening devices, but now technology was far, far beyond such precautions. For good or evil we were dwarfed and midgeted by it. There was nothing anyone could do now, no barricades, no open defiance, that could not be wiped out in minutes by the armour of a modern state, or controlled by its invisible armour of surveillance. I went to hear JP last evening, I whispered. Papa nodded silently. I knew he must be thinking of the fiery young patriot of 1942 who had called on steel workers to strike and been jailed for obstructing Britain's war effort. Perhaps also of the young idol on his white horse who had led Indians in a pledge of independence on a river bank in Lahore over a decade earlier. And earlier still, the man in the loincloth who had urged, Let's free ourselves without the barrel of a gun, let's soil our hands with untouchable work to free our souls of the canker of caste, and no power on earth shall withstand us afterwards. Papa was thinking of battles for freedom fought and won and all that sacrifice now come to this. He didn't say a word. But I knew, as biographers do, even when they write about people dead and gone for hundreds of years, what went on just then in his mind as he sat turned to a statue. He had come to some kind of decision at a boundary he could not cross, as Uncle Ram's father must have – so Rose often said – when he told his family, I've come this far, I won't go any further because I don't want to learn the language of this particular future.

Kiran came in with a servant bearing coffee and asked, 'I suppose it will be all right for Mama and me to go out shopping today? D'you think the shops will be open?' Papa lifted his bowed head, smiled at her, said there would certainly be business as usual, and she left us to make a list. Later we heard them drive away, and much later, when the day was half over, tyres on gravel announced their return. I only blame Papa that in all those hours we were alone together he gave me no advice. He could have said, You should resign. When the Constitution becomes null and void by the act of a dictator, and the armour of a modern state confronts you, *satyagraha* is the only way to keep your self-respect. But he was so deep in his own decision-making, it is hardly surprising he had forgotten for once about me and the advice he would ordinarily have given me in a crisis. People think of 'to lie down and die' as giving up. But in his own last decision, his only unambiguous and unalterable one, I saw him at his strong and positive best, refusing to compromise with dictatorship, even one that he, now a retired civil servant, had no duty to serve. What galled him most, and this he did talk about, was that history would now be revised and rewritten. All dictatorships meddled with history. I can see that he had to die when he did, but his death left me desperately alone when I faced dismissal, and now I was alone again with Rose's problem. The bank manager might have paid more attention to Papa, and I wished it was Papa, not me, facing him across his desk, waiting for his reaction to my information about Dev's forged cheques.

'Are you sure about this?' the bank manager asked.

'Mr Ram Surya has been paralysed with a stroke for months. The last cheque he signed was in January this year. The account is a joint one with his wife, so no one but his wife should be presenting cheques. Any cheque with his signature is a forgery.'

The manager looked deadly serious until I told him the forger's name. Between looking down at the cheque in his hand and up at me his face registered the arrival and assimilation of conquerors, the need to lie low, the story of survival. And a veil, opaque and patternless, came down over it. By this time the money oozing out of Uncle Ram's and Rose's joint account was like blood draining from a wound, and I was determined to stop it, whatever excuses he made. But the bank manager was an honest man. He didn't pretend, as The Professor and The Lawyer had, that all was well. He said quietly, I am a small man, you will forgive me but these are not normal times, I think you should go to someone higher up. I came out of the bank and stood in front of the roundabout surrounded by double-storeyed government buildings, the low high-rise of Delhi. It was the end of September, the rains were over, and in the hierarchy of high, higher, highest the only higher-up it would do any good to see was Kachru, only I couldn't abide the thought of being seen with Kachru in a public place and still less did I want to meet him in a private place. With all my heart I loathed asking him a favour, but who else was there, and he *had* offered help if I needed any. Once I had made the decision I felt less burdened. There is this to be said about pinnacles of power, that if you know somebody at the pinnacle, your problem gets solved in a jiffy.

FOURTEEN

This evening the beggar was sitting on a small jutting boulder behind the tomb and Rose realized she had not yet asked about his arms and legs though whenever he was there they exchanged a greeting, followed by her standard question, had he been given a drink of water at the well, and his standard reply that he had. Then she would deliver her customary warning, Be careful when you go to the well, *khabardar*, don't go too near, and she would rock her body from side to side like an oversize armless doll to show him how treacherous the well could be for someone like him without the balance whole arms provide, which of course he knew, but she looked so funny imitating his mutilation, it gave them both a laugh. The other day she had been about to ask him about himself when Nishi came tearing out of the house to join her. But usually she was alone and it was episodes of the past pushing and plucking at her like children demanding her attention that kept her from finding out more about him. She had heard that when you're going to die your whole life passes before your eyes. But here she was very much alive and this kept happening. Could she be anticipating her widowhood, reliving their life together for Ram because she was no longer sure he could do this for himself?

Rose who had seen little of Mona when they lived under the same roof, visited her regularly when Partition landed them all in Delhi, and was welcomed with a genuine warmth that also had much to do, she could not help suspecting, with her child-lessness.

'What's being fried at this hour, Mona?' The smell of bubbling hot oil was all over the flat.

'Dev must have chips at tea-time. What can I do, Rose-ji?'

'Dev didn't come to the shop today. If he isn't regular about coming he'll never learn the work, and Ram's got so much to do with the business expanding so fast.'

'His mind is not on it, poor boy. We must start looking for a girl for him.'

'He's only twenty, Mona. He ought to get down to work first.'

'What is twenty, a mere child.'

'A mere child doesn't need marriage.'

'Don't mock me, Rose-ji. You have English ideas. It is different among us. You know our ways. My sister-in-law's daughter is only sixteen but already so well developed, they have started looking for a boy for her.'

By that reckoning Mona, girlishly slim and graceful as ever, a shade too thin now, had never been ready for marriage at all. But marriage was the land of Oz, Rose's years in India had taught her, it filled you out if you were thin, and thinned you out if you were fat. It was an all-purpose cure for sex mania and sloth, impotence and imbecility. If you were good, it made you better, if you were bad, it transformed you, and if you were a kleptomaniac you stopped filching things. Mona knew a concrete case, the dreadful child of their neighbours in Lahore, who used to pinch loose change and cigarettes whenever he came with his parents to call, and was now a model husband.

'Do you know who I would love for a daughter-in-law, Rose-ji? The elder daughter of Keshav Ranade, ICS. Out of the two of them she is fairer-skinned. But I have heard her mother wants a Kashmiri boy for her.'

'Kiran is a lovely girl,' Rose agreed.

'Isn't she?' Mona's eyes shone. 'Chiselled features, good height and snow-fair. I have set my heart on her, I tell you. Why is her mother so stuck on a Kashmiri boy when her own husband is not a Kashmiri? You and himself could put in a word to her, couldn't you? I would not ask himself this with my own mouth, but we are sisters and I can talk to you.'

'It would do no good, Mona. Kiran's mother rules the roost in that household.'

'What about the younger daughter then? She wears glasses and she is not so snow-fair but it doesn't matter. A few months of rubbing her with lemon juice and curd would make a lot of difference. Her features are all right. And it's a well spoken of family. Of course we are not Brahmins like them but since Partition that might not matter so much.'

'Sonali is her father's little pet, very bright little thing she is too. She'll make up her own mind.'

Mona looked crestfallen.

'But since Partition there are so many families you know here in Delhi and in Bombay. There must be any number of girls to choose from,' said Rose.

But the difficulty was, Rose discovered, that Dev wasn't turning out to be too much of a catch. He would come into money, of course, but parents seemed to want sons-in-law with company careers, and the best catches were the Civil Service and the Foreign Service. And really, how could she say this to a doting mother, but Dev seemed to be making a career of wolfing down sandwiches and ice-cream by the Club pool when he was not at the cinema or fooling around at the home of some retarded acquaintance. He was not exactly retarded himself, he could look sharp enough when he wanted to, but the astrologer must be as mad as a hatter forecasting a glorious future for him. Rose had never heard anything so daft. It was queer, she thought long afterwards, how her solid reliable instincts had failed her utterly with Dev. It may have been because she and Ram had never been so busy in their lives, being invited to diplomatic parties and cocktails with Lieutenant-Generals, and having fashion shows with their own designs and materials at the shop for Delhi's top drawer, a mixture now of dowager maharanis, dry cleaners and Indian company boxwallahs. She worried constantly and was positively certain now that she was the wrong wife for Ram, who needed someone with a proper vocabulary, and a la-di-da accent that curled at the top and uncurled at the bottom, and fashionable flatness beside him to advertise the elegance he sold. She didn't have the refinement, she never would, and she was getting fat. At a time when she would have liked to settle down to a comfortable, quiet, unambitious life with Ram, private life seemed to have ended for ever. A competitive business had Ram by the throat and social life was overflowing with Madam This and Monsoor That, names she couldn't pronounce, of people who disappeared off their horizon as soon as she learned to pronounce them. There were no real friends you could ring up and drop in on for a chat about nothing special like in the old days. Minnie and Dick were back in England after an Indian posting that had got much prolonged by the war, and she missed Minnie badly.

Ram needed his new clientele for his business, and he was in his element in their Delhi social circle. But she wished he wouldn't carry on the way he did with his 'Allow me' and his fussy manners, trailing bits of Persian poetry after him like ribbons come undone. It was beginning to irritate her, but the diplomatic wives lapped it up and he was looking deeply into the eyes of serried ranks of them over lunches, cocktails and dinners. They had taken to entertaining at a five-star hotel when they had a pleasant apartment of their own. Ram ruled out the apartment. It wasn't a posh enough setting. 'The foreigners I do business with are used to the best hotels around the world, and they're enormously rich. There's no comparison between the standard of living in their countries and ours.' So foreigners had to have bacon wrapped around chestnuts on hotel toothpicks instead of Kumar's home-made eats. It seemed such a waste of time trying to impress foreign Joneses who, by the time you'd had a heart attack making a dent, had graduated to a rarer variety of canapé. Rose thought nostalgically of Lalaji, nobody's replica and never wanting to be, doing a furious turnover in business at floor level in the bazaar, everybody else down on the floor with him and not a canapé in sight.

But what troubled her most was the sugar-coated glaze Ram had dropped over Dev. 'My son' had to be spoken in a holy whisper. Never mind if he hijacked cars for fun, boys will be boys and they were returned to their owners in the end, weren't they? And if he helped himself to money from the till, well, after all, it was going to be his one day and Ram had spoken to him about it and he wouldn't do it again without asking. And when Dev and his picture-going, ice-cream guzzling gang took to abducting girls from Miranda House at the university and taking them to a private room at the Ashoka for a lark, these little escapades were part of growing up. We had the little Anglo-

Indian girls from the railway colony to do our growing up with, said Ram with a sigh. Little beauties some of them were too. Young men now have a real problem. A man has to get his experience somewhere. You shouldn't be hard on poor Dev, Rose. Sometimes Rose wished Dev would rob a bank, do something criminal the police would have to deal with. All these little teenage pranks when he wasn't a teenager alarmed her. But Ram and Mona were a Gibraltar of parenthood, as deaf, dumb and unbreachable as the rock where poor Dev was concerned. He will come out of this, Rose-ji, great heights of fame and glory are forecast for him. All my eye and Betty Martin, thought Rose, but Mona was entitled to her dreams. Don't we all live one foot in fantasy, and try to make that foot more desperately real than the other? Who was Rose, a failed womb, to advise breeders of children? But she had the lurking suspicion that Dev's delinquencies had their approval. He was a fun-and-games man and companion hijacker to the highest in the land. This was no ordinary delinquents' club, so there was nothing for his parents to worry about. He could rob as many banks as he liked.

'Rose-ji, I need your help. Please come this evening.'

Ordinary investigation and overture to get him married having failed dismally, they were now down to advertising. Together Rose and Mona composed an advertisement for the Sunday *Hindustan Times* to say that Mona was inviting correspondence from parents of fair-skinned daughters with (returnable) photos and (returnable) horoscopes.

'Though I think we ought to say that horoscopes will be no bar,' said Mona anxiously, '*if* everything else – height, colour, temperament, etc. – is all right. With Dev's horoscope so good, the girl's horoscope doesn't matter.'

In the advertisement they drafted, Dev turned out to be handsome, wheat-coloured, educated and well-settled. But there was a lacuna readers would notice, Rose observed. She had been through old columns of the *Hindustan Times* carefully. Well-settled in what? Usually the ad said Canada-returned medico, or earning four-figure salary as research chemist, or possessor of green card. Ad readers wanted details. One could have one's own idea of handsomeness but calling a person educated meant listing degrees. But if there weren't any, better leave that vague too and hope for the best.

'Now for the girl,' said Mona. 'We want a beautiful, home-loving girl of good disposition, with domestic virtues, and excellent social background. She must be snow-fair, of course, and we had better put that down too though what else can beautiful mean? Shall we say virgin? Nobody says it nowadays.' She hunted for virgins through the old columns they had collected and couldn't find any. 'That means virgin may be taken for granted,' she concluded.

'What about caste?' asked Rose.

'We should say caste no bar, like horoscope no bar. It's not as if untouchables will be applying, or other low castes. And caste is not so strict nowadays, we should be more broadminded except for untouchables.'

The fact was that by this time the options were narrowing and no flood either of virgins or non-virgins, or even the luckless legion of dark-skinned marriageables had sent in their credentials for the scrutiny of Dev's family. But the dropping of crucial qualifications did bring some answers. Rose and Mona went through those mentioning an affectionate nature and height in centimetres behind the photo. But Mona was so particular about chiselled features, the length and shape of nose and eyes and other anatomical details that they were not much further along. It was only when they advertised 'dowry no bar' that a sudden spurt of parents of pale girls began to pass through Mona's portals in carefully casual visits, and if encouraged, brought the girls next time. And Dev was nearly twenty-seven when a bride was snared.

'Rose-ji, please come to tea this evening,' came Mona's familiar summons over the telephone.

'I have found her,' she said when Rose arrived. 'She is coming with her parents. They used to be well-to-do in Lahore, now they have practically nothing, poor things. But it is a respectable family, the same caste as us, and the girl, though not the right height, is chiselled and snow-fair. So I thought you should meet your daughter-in-law to be.'

A statement that would have sounded outlandish years ago in Lahore, an idea she had coped none too successfully with, fell softly with the ring of reality on Rose's ears. Impulsively she took Mona's hands in hers and kissed her on both cheeks. I must show her how delighted I am, became genuine delight.

'Congratulations to both of us! But Mona you look all worn out.'

Mona's skin had a sallow tinge that had nothing to do with the long, exhausting search for a snow-fair bride for Dev, though she may have been overdoing the fasting and praying.

'Has Dev met her?'

'How would he know what's good for him, poor boy? It is for his elders to decide. He will meet her after you have met the parents and the girl today, and when you have told himself about it, and got his approval. One thing at a time.'

They sat in a circle of chairs, having tea and *jelabies* – a shrivelled, tired, little man who looked as if a puff of breeze would blow him over the *jelabies*, his speechless wife, and a doll-faced girl in a canary-yellow sari with a canary's soft chirp and twitter – and made disconnected conversation.

Rose took the news to Ram who welcomed it absentmindedly and set a date for a party to announce it to diplomats, Lieutenant-Generals and foreign Joneses. He was too preoccupied to listen much when she spoke of Mona's health. He spent a lot of time these days listening earnestly to the woes of the First Secretary to the Belgian embassy's wife, whose husband didn't understand her or any of their six children. Platonic stuff, Rose supposed, but the misunderstood creature's breasts were all over the place, in and out of the shop, resting on counters along with Benares brocade, suspended over cups of coffee and five-star pastries, and wobbling out of evening gowns, amiable mountains that made sensible conversation impossible.

'Rose, you've put on too much weight. Join a Figurette and lose some,' Ram suggested.

'I'm not joining any Figurette. In two years' time I'll be fifty years old.'

Ram was sensitive about age. He was meticulous about

touching up his hair and his new moustache, leaving a speckle of patrician silver at his temples.

'It's not a matter of age, but of looking your best.'

'I've already looked my best, and this is the best I can look now. And if you don't like it, there's Janet What's-her-name.'

'Oh come now, my dear,' he said, pleased, 'there's no need to be jealous of Jeanette. She's just a charming –'

'Misunderstood, top-heavy little creature,' finished Rose, putting Ram in an even better mood.

The weight question came up now and then, whenever a visit from Zafar and the wife of his new stage in life was expected. Bugs-Bunny, as Zafar playfully called his American bride because of her two adorable front teeth, was twenty-five, had a film-star's figure and had even had bit parts in films, and Rose would no more have tried competing with her than a bullock cart with a rocket.

'Ram, I do wish you'd drop in on Mona. You haven't for such a long time and she's not looking at all well. You could persuade her to see a doctor, which is more than I've been able to do.'

He promised he would and turned round from the mirror to ask Rose about the girl Mona had chosen.

'She's tiny,' reflected Rose, 'a sweet, tiny thing. Such a slip of a girl. I don't know how she's ever going to handle Dev.'

'Oh, Dev will be all right once he's married and settled.'

And having spoken the falsest words in human history, Ram finished dressing – these days it took him longer than it took her – and they left to spend the evening with someone-or-the-other whose name she'd forgotten.

The wedding day was set by the astrologer for the coming winter but Mona did not last until then. The cancer consuming her had done its job before winter came. Only the husk of Mona was left on her bed as Ram and Rose stood on either side of it. Mona's hazel eyes, remote and drugged with pain, sought Rose's. 'Our daughter-in-law,' she brought out with an effort, 'you will look after her, won't you, Rose-ji?' Rose nodded dumbly, tears scalding her cheeks, Mona's brittle-boned hand held fast in hers. 'In our family she must never want for anything,' Mona whispered. Ram tried to reassure her but she wasn't

listening to him. She was looking at Rose. 'She's yours now.'
And Rose stepped into the shoes Mona had vacated, a desolate
place she no longer wanted for herself. As Mona slipped away,
she fell clumsily to her knees beside the bed and wept into the
blankets until Ram helped her up, put an arm around her shaking
shoulders and led her away.

Delhi's early morning streets blurred past Rose's aching eyes
in the taxi going home hours later. Wrapped in the chill of Mona's
death, she recalled the distant nights of Mona's living sorrow
and the house in Lahore that had held them both, reconciling
them at last to each other. Not quite what Ram's English poet
had called 'A way we both shall understand' – but strange how
within those walls they had adventured over hills and woods into
another pasture, into friendship, and one fine morning, into love.

FIFTEEN

When the police came a second time Kishori Lal did not so much as glance up from the newsless newspaper he was reading. One passing look from the doorway would show them that even the toilet rolls and the smallest soap dishes had conspicuous price tags on them, and while he was going to all that bother, he had also put Madam (She Stood Between Order And Chaos in bold capitals underneath) sent by Nishi up on the wall behind his desk and hung a saffron garland made of cloth rosettes around her picture, which he had found in his clothes cupboard at home, left over from the Hindu revivalist RSS rally he had attended about a year ago. Only fools rotted in jail, he had a shop to take care of. The one who looked like the boss, a fine-looking specimen, sturdy and lithe, must have been a Haryana policeman brought in to help the police in Delhi, though the newspapers said there was no trouble of any kind and Madam had told a foreign journalist never had the police had so little work, there wasn't a thing for them to do. She could be right, because if this fine-looking Hariyanvi could stand staring at rolls of toilet paper with prices clearly marked on them, he couldn't have much to do. Well, leisure was a good thing. Kishori Lal remembered the poem from Government College days starting What is this life if, praising leisure. The Hariyanvi was tapping his fine-looking calf with a baton. But the three or four with him weren't even doing that. And it struck KL, as his friends called him, that there was nothing so menacing as these splendid policemen so visibly enjoying their leisure on the threshold of his shop.

'You will come with us,' said the boss, not will you, having finished surveying the shelves and tapping his calf.

KL was so surprised he gaped. 'Be so good as to tell me why?' he asked cautiously.

'Up, old man. We haven't got time to argue. Orders is orders.'

Yes, they were Hariyanvi. Familiar Delhi policemen normally on this beat wouldn't be so rude even if they had an arrest to make. Decidedly not. It was well known how they went in through the front door of Nanaji Deshmukh's house countless times, saluted smartly, and told him to escape out of the back door, until in spite of all their efforts not to arrest him, he went and got himself caught. The police are our brothers, the anti-Madam student movement in Bihar had chanted, we have no quarrel with them. So Central police had had to be sent for to do what the State police wouldn't, *lathi*-charge and tear-gas the students and pack them off to jail. It took an outsider to cut up rough, and these outsiders had had to be imported from Haryana, the neighbouring state whose Chief Minister's loyalty to Madam and her son had made headlines before the emergency and was still being tempestuously proved every day. When the other three or four came into the shop they turned out to be three, showing, as Madam had said, how the police presence could be grossly exaggerated. One of them jerked Kishori up by the back of his neck and, no one would believe this, handcuffed him. Another pulled out his desk drawers and turned them upside down and the third did his blitzkrieg through the shelves again. It was quite obvious they had nothing better to do. But even if this was how they spent a holiday, it still made no sense. Behind a row of red and orange polythene buckets and basins collecting thick Delhi dust the third found a wooden stick and a shorter stave, picked these up and brandished them. From their excited Hariyanvi chitchat it would seem they had discovered an ammunition dump. KL was pushed and prodded out on to the pavement towards a waiting van, the doors of his shop left wide open, while his servant, strolling back from his lunch across the road, stood thunderstruck in the middle of a yawn with his striped pyjamas flapping in the breeze as the van took off. Kishori Lal sat blankly inside because he still wasn't believing it.

A long drive took him, not to the neighbourhood *thana*, but much further away. When he got down he was in Daryaganj, a stone's throw from the upper floor nursing home where four of his children had been born. That place is in your horoscope, his mother had told him, every time you turn around you're in Daryaganj again. And here he was again, this time without a nine-months-pregnant wife, and Madam's police force was finding it hard to call five an illegal crowd and disband it in a street where crowds were a permanent fixture and cows and calves staggered against cycle rickshaws.

The policemen inside the *thana* were drinking tea. Yes, Madam knew her police force and it really had very little to do, bringing odds and ends like him in. That and the obvious good humour of the tea-drinkers to whom he was delivered before the others went away to enjoy their leisure again should have struck him as a favourable sign, but it didn't. You are so-and-so, declared the head tea drinker. After all these years KL hadn't got ranks in the army, navy, air force and police force sorted out, since uniformed authority had not impinged much if at all on his life. He said he was. You are a member of the RSS! Certainly not, he replied. The head tea man gestured towards the wooden stick and stave, the dust and fluff of the ages still clinging to them, and shoved a crumpled scrap of paper at him he had forgotten he had, from one of his desk drawers probably, a notice of the same RSS rally he had attended a year earlier, where he'd been given the saffron garland now on Madam. But he denied he was a member of the RSS because of course he was not a member. And the only reason he denied it so vigorously was that he not only wasn't, but never could have brought himself to be. Shelves could be untidy and shops in a mess, but minds definitely could not. He wished to explain with strict accuracy, in the manner of the history researcher he might have become if Partition had not hit him, that he belonged to the Jan Sangh party as a matter of principle and not because he was a Hindu, because in any case he was an atheist. The Partition would have made him a Jan Sanghi regardless of if he'd been born Christian, Sikh or Zoroastrian. The RSS didn't interest him at all. If it had, why wouldn't he have joined it when he joined everything on earth he could? Joining himself to organizations gave him weight and anchorage, boulders against another blast. But the head tea man didn't give him a chance to say any of it. He, no one would believe this, called him a liar and slapped KL's face, knocking him off balance so that he reeled and clutched the corner of the table for support. It is only because I am five feet four inches tall and weigh one hundred and twenty pounds that it feels like a hard slap, KL told himself, otherwise it is not a heavy blow, but Aren't these yours? The stick and stave were thrust at him. Of course they weren't 'his' in the sense that his fountain pen and his watch were his, though he had certainly swung them around at that rally doing exercises and singing songs praising the geography of India early one morning about a year ago. Well then, said the head, you are a saboteur, part of a conspiracy to overthrow the government, and shovelled him into the lock-up.

The bicycle thief in the lock-up introduced himself and told him to confess to whatever they were accusing him of. They are so busy arresting this one and that one that they can't be bothered with common criminals like us, just say you did it and tell your friends to hand them some money and they'll let you out. They had a fascinating chat about the techniques of bicycle lifting, and the fun the thief had had taking bicycles apart and putting them together as he'd seen the cycle mechanic in his village do. In his father's day there had been a long trek on foot, or a tedious journey by bullock cart, to the main road. But in his own childhood bicycles had come along with people getting from here to there in the space of All India Radio's Your Favourite Song programme on the transistor which was also new. It takes very little to be happy, said the thief, a good road connecting the village to the main road, a bicycle to travel it on, with a transistor hung on the handle and Lata Mangeshkar hitting the high notes, and frankly I'm happy, I've seen progress with my own eyes. He said he had so many stolen bicycles lying around now he was thinking of going into bicycle manufacture, dismantling the parts of Hero, Avro and Hercules and reassembling them in a new construct named after his best friend, a scholarly restaurant owner near Jama Masjid called Hafiz Mian. A secular state needed a Muslim bicycle. KL was charmed by the idea and mentally made notes to tell his university friends about it when they were released from jail, giving them a concrete example of how secularity had entered the very marrow of the nation. The Jan Sangh would have to gather these new liberals into its vote count. And the future reminded him that tomorrow he would have to say yes, he was a saboteur and he was sorry, and sign a paper supporting the emergency and go. His fool servant would have locked up the shop, that much sense he had, but it was hardly good for business to have a padlock on the shop all the days of the week, and established customers finding they had to go somewhere else for sponges and mops, and once the word got round he'd been in the lock-up, people would be frightened to come. Luck had not blessed his business ventures, he wasn't cut out for business in any case so he couldn't afford another disaster.

A disgusting place this lock-up. He didn't mind the cramped closed quarter with no window to the outside world, the darkness, the flies or the mice. He minded the stink from the adjacent toilet over the knee high partition filling the air with its festering fumes. He had been sitting leaning against the wall, holding his nose, facing the bicycle thief holding his, until after some considerable time and adenoidal talk with their noses held, the thief was taken out and he was left alone. The light in the lock-up, though so weak, was at least a light, like street lights used to be, dim and yellow, intimate-looking, making street corners mysterious places, and the road ahead adventure, before fluorescent lighting and highway robbers on motorcycles took over. And before both those, kerosene and lamplighters. He'd seen it all, lived through many changes. It was already ten years since he'd set up the shop of bathroom accessories, after two other ventures had failed. He remembered explaining why to his friend at Delhi University who was a professor of Sanskrit besides other distinctions, and who had asked him, why in heaven's name *bathroom* accessories? There was a reason for it. Religious leaders used allegory, spoke in parables, why shouldn't business? Flush toilets had completed the crusade against untouchability Mahatma Gandhi had started. There too, as with lights, the community had travelled far, from out in the fields to wooden commodes transported long distances on mule-back for sahibs on tour who couldn't squat in fields, to flush toilets. But Gandhi's commandment, Carry your own excreta and no nonsense about it, got it going. Yes, revolution had many forms and faces, no doubt about it. The mahatma had made them carry their own shit and bury it neatly, sanitarily in the ground, and those who had carried other people's stink for generations and been pariahs got new names and became God's children. I like to think of myself as an honorary, transmuted, transposed and transfigured Harijan, he told his Brahmin professor friend. I am carrying out the commandment as it relates to our time.

The pallid bulb in the lock-up neither wavered nor winked. It had a lowly endurance that would keep it lit when powerful bulbs had flashed heroic displays of light and fused and gone. He wondered if it was daytime or night, and how long since the bicycle thief had been taken away. His watch had stopped but it was still on his wrist, his pen was in his pocket, and this not to be believed episode would be over in the morning or the evening, whenever the present cycle of day or night ended. He would genuflect before Madam's image, confess errors past and to come, and go home to put an extra garland on Madam and welcome his customers. Selling bathroom equipment, he had told his professor friend, was a solemn joke, as no doubt the Partition was from some cosmic perspective, blasting people like him off their feet and into the air and making the Jan Sangh the only political party for him. So, having become a Hindu twice over, once by birth and once by politics, he had neatly crowned the exercise by making a profession of bathroom requirements, his answer to the 'Chi-chi-chi don't touch' of his non-flush-toilet youth before untouchables became children of God and were still cleaning potties. He remembered his mother shouting a warning, 'Chi-chi-chi move away, son, the sweeper woman is coming, how can she get past you without touching you?' and later watching the same woman squatting at the garden tap, tranquilly washing out his sister's menstrual rags, pounding, scrubbing, drying them till they lay folded in their place in his sister's cupboard, smelling of sunshine like the rest of the laundry, only that was touchable so the *dhobi* had washed it. Then came Kotex and the end of rag-washing under the separate tap. And so on. The passage of time. Well that was the gist of it really, he told his friend. Hinduism needs antidotes. Gandhi had picked up excreta and he, Kishori Lal, had assembled the paraphernalia needed for potties and their environs. Well, what is that double-sized *tilak* doing on your forehead if you're an honorary Harijan, his friend wanted to know. In the cosmos, said KL, who knows, maybe Harijans wear *tilaks* and Brahmins clean transportable potties, and the age of the flush toilet is yet and for ever to come so that ancient injustices can be put right meanwhile and balances restored.

The floor became hard and uncomfortable but curiously the stench from the clogged toilet across the knee-high partition assailed his nostrils with less fury and he realized why untouchability had lasted for centuries. The nose became less sensitive. Ears could take just so much noise and then would blank out with pierced drums or deafness. Eyes would smart and burn when tried too far. His lean behind ached and stiffened and the floor felt as though he sat naked on it, but noses, it seemed, carried on. He dozed and woke by turns. When he heard his own soft snoring he knew he had fallen into a deeper doze and then that he was dreaming of a public meeting. He of all people was addressing it, though he had never addressed one in his life. In the language of the newsless newspapers describing the meetings of Madam, he was standing before a boundless sea or an uncrossable ocean – depending on which Hindi newspaper you read, for the Hindi press had more interesting variations on the theme – and he, not Madam, stood on the dais constructed at great cost, lifted his eyes over the sea, and it was his voice that spoke. And it said, *'Bhaiyon aur behenon'* – 'Brothers and Sisters,' a conventional enough opening. What is more, he could see each brother and each sister. For instance, the first sixty-five rows on the left were Muslims. He could recognize them as his ancestors had spotted the Mussulman at a glance, knowing in a trice even in profile or three-quarter view the dreaded cow killers, the idol smashers, the ravagers of temples, and hearing till the sound died down the pounding and thudding of their horses' hoofs back over the mountain tracks, leaving sword-spilled blood and carnage behind them in the plains. KL recognized them, too, but now as part of the same unified sea. Or one might say it was all one donkey-load of laundry, the proudest and humblest garments side by side, the menstrual rags as clean and sweet-smelling as the rest. He could identify every item. Over on the right were the Sikhs, Buddhists, Jains and Zoroastrians, and on the opposite side the Protestant and Catholic Christians and the Cochin Jews. Equally identifiable in their infinity, taking up most of the sea, were the castes and sub-castes and sub-sub-castes, as well as the untouchables and unapproachables of his own religion, not to mention the rows of agnostics, atheists and pessimists, who were not just godless like himself but hopeless.

Comradeship overwhelmed him as he looked upon these, his people, all collected in the same sea, looking up, amazingly, at him. His reedy voice was picked up and carried by powerful microphones paid for by profiteers, blackmarketeers and smugglers, but never mind, the message was the thing. Yet instead of making the proper grand vague and general speech which the party that had put up the mikes and the dais and truck-loaded all these people there for expected, why did he say what he did? 'Do you or do you not,' he questioned the multitude with a researcher's precision, leaving out all the flim-flam, 'need food for your families?' And unhesitatingly the sea roared back, 'We do.' 'Do you or do you not need clothes for your bodies?' he asked again, and 'Yes, we do,' came the answer tossed back on waves of voices. 'Do you or do you not need shelter?' 'Yes, oh yes,' was seaborne on the wind. 'Then,' said KL, 'in return for all these blessings, do you agree that you shall do as you're told and if you do not, the name of your lodging shall be Delhi Central Jail?' 'No-o-o-o' came the cry from each individual heart. It came from the left and the right and the middle. It was astonishing. It was something the anthropologists and sociologists and leading lights of departments for the study of developing societies would have given their eye teeth to hear, the unanimity of that cry. And just to make sure he asked the question once more on the smugglers' excellent mike and back came the ringing 'No-o-o'. Then KL raised his arms and spread them wide in benediction over the sea, telling his people they deserved to be for ever free and would remain so. They became quite delirious with joy, carrying him upon their shoulders up and down the lanes and alleys in the ocean, then making a chair of their arms for him to sit on. He was so light that the chair of human arms could bounce him up and down while the ocean of voices cheered, and hands caught at his hand or his foot or his *kurta* as he passed, to touch so heroic a maker of promises. The chant of 'free-dom, free-dom' rose and fell around him. In the heaving and tossing of the ocean his elbow got sharply hit and he woke. Kishori Lal examined his elbow, and now the stench assailed his nostrils again, making him clutch at his empty, heaving stomach, but the cries of the crowd still resounded in his ears and a mugful of tea stood just inside the door. So, morning. He would briskly confess his sins and go. Time was getting on. But when the lock-up was opened, he didn't know when, and he stumbled out dirty and worn in front of the tea drinkers who were drinking tea again, jolly as ever, he suddenly remembered, as one does irrelevantly sometimes, how the Germans treated Russian prisoners during the war, differently, very differently from other Allied prisoners. And standing before the chief tea drinker he knew without a doubt that Madam was a German and he was a Russian. And now he started to believe it was happening.

SIXTEEN

They were in London the summer after Dev's wedding principally because Marcella had suggested in one of her long letters that it would be best for Ram to make personal contacts before establishing an outlet abroad for his Indian fashions. Naturally one of the directors of Harrods was Marcella's cousin. And she had done better than marry a lord. She had married a man who'd made a fortune in the construction business, an impossibly good-looking husband who called her My darling as if he meant it, a fit companion for Marcella's hair which still looked washed and dried by the light of a crescent moon. This was the trip before the one that made London look like a parade of broad, naked, miniskirted thighs of all ages. England was still, as far as thighs were concerned, as it had been, though perhaps not in other ways, and it took the naked thighs to flourish all the other changes, but at the time the music, jokes and films seemed the familiar sort, and formality was still part of life. Marcella's drawing room was very formal, a well-arranged miniature woodland of flowering plants against the opulence of very familiar, softly glistening gold fabric. Yards of material selected by Ram had come from RamRose, New Delhi, for it. And Marcella in it looked like a glistening gold horse, long-limbed, ageless, mythical, in a narrow cylindrical sheath. Ram and she in the drawing room they had thought up between them, with Rose and Brian there too, of course, looked wreathed in the peace and contentment of every known hunger satisfied, which was what an affair should lead to, to correspondence and friendship, and Marcella's husband who had a century for a hobby, talking entertainingly through ice-cold martinis, saddle of lamb and strawberries about Baroque and Rococo and the difference between the two, and why one style followed another. Brian's hobby, instead of covering one century from start to finish, went from the middle of one to the middle of the next. Baroque and Rococo would both have been double Dutch to Rose, but the way he explained them made sense, that everyone had got a bit fed up with Louis XIV and his grand overpowering Versailles and wanted some littleness around for a change. All good stories fascinated, and Brian was such a good storyteller. Apart from calling each other their darling they looked so luminously at each other. There was a solid base there. Marcella might look like moonbeams but she understood marriages had to be made of asbestos cement if they were going to last, as obviously this one had and would. And how do I feel about Marcella at this long distant point in time from when it all began, wondered Rose, eyeing the luscious strawberries for which Brian darling had just passed her the cream when Marcella darling raised her glass of champagne for a tiny toast to the four of them. Rose drank to it with pleasure and got back to wondering how she felt about the affair, which for her had been a state of mind surrounded by a mosquito net, a foreign moon drilling through her forehead, propeller-driven insects jarring her ears, and at last a step on the stair that was Ram returning, and her falling asleep exhausted when she knew that wherever he'd been, he was back. The affair had begun with an absolute right to begin, and just as inevitably it had ended because like the empire it had to. It had been connected with the coming and going of ships through the Suez, the meetings and partings of races, relationships passionately begun but punctually ended when clocks struck and ships sailed. Both its beginning and ending had had a meaning she understood. How could she have prevented it, or have felt anything but helpless before the inevitability of it? But now with acute anguish long past, she could admire this gossamer creature who alone in all the world had ever turned Ram upside down and inside out, drink her champagne and enjoy her husband's Baroque and Rococo.

London had been too rushed, Ram working under a lamp even when they got back to the hotel late at night, up before her making calculations on a pad with his morning tea. Rose had walked her feet off going to art galleries with him, and because

Brian's Baroque and Rococo talk had been so interesting, she had gone with him and Ram and Marcella to a Rococo exhibition. Her delight was swift and spontaneous as she stepped into the rosily glowing salon with its ivory-light porcelain, gold and silver and tapestry, and its furniture on tiptoe like ballerinas. Slender columns on either side of a door had scrolled curled tops, and mirrors had scrolled curly frames. Everything was scaled down, like Brian had explained, artificiality stripped away, tradition cut down to size. The difference, Rose thought, between Ram and Marcella, then and now. Sweeping passion come down to a lovely, friendly, family-size intimacy, the dainty decorativeness of once big things. You could stand back and enjoy it instead of being swept under. But it was Ram's London, all this. Her own had been simpler, buried in the blitz, along with her parents, two of the sixty thousand and five hundred civilians cold figures said had been killed in air raids. I'll get the figures for you if you like, Ram had told her, but why go into all that, my dear, you'll only upset yourself. Yet it somehow helped to hang their incomprehensible deaths on to a peg of reality. Not just two people she dearly loved had perished, sixty thousand four hundred and ninety-eight others had been evilly killed in a massacre from the sky.

She had gone to her old neighbourhood, walked past a new row of houses and been glad of the damage repaired, but there was not a brick or a pebble now to connect her with her past. As she stood on the pavement nausea and giddiness assailed her, streets and council houses vanished and she stood on a faint smudged pencil line high above a chasm between two crags at the mercy of a rising wind, feeling as they must have felt as they waited to be destroyed. She put her hands up to her head and squeezed it hard. A scream raked through her, sticking at bones, dissolving in cartilage, locking her terror into her body. 'You all right?' A man going by with a wheelbarrow stopped to ask. She smiled shakily, 'Just got a bit of a headache that's all. Must be this wind.' He looked up at the calm, clear sky and back at her, his eyes blue and kind. 'You've got a bit of fever, I'd say. Better get home and wrap up.' Rose put a hand up to her cheek and it was cool, cold. She'd come years too late for a keepsake, a scrap of road sign or a bit of twisted metal from the bomb blast, to remind her that she and her family had lived here. She turned round and started walking back towards the bus stop. The man with the wheelbarrow, engaged in some repair work across the road, watched her, raising a hand to her and nodding when she reached it and joined the queue, as though he had guided her there through a dangerous void. Kind as he had been, it was too late to talk of personal loss with a stranger who had probably dealt with more rubble than that of Rose's past. How, except as Ram's father had done, by dying fastidiously, sensibly and precisely at the correct time, did one avoid calamities that wiped the past away or come to terms with them? The bus arrived, received her into its known and limited shape and went on. Does it matter if no one knows I sat here, thought Rose, once I get down? I know that I, Rose, sat here, lived down that road in London, until I was twenty. And though the buildings have been blasted away, it doesn't mean Rose-until-twenty never existed. But being here in this bus was not, of course, the end of the story. For a time would come when she wouldn't be here and then there would really be nothing, not a scrap of metal or a pebble or a child to mark her passage, nothing at all. The hotel dining room set with pale pink satin-like linen crowned with pink carnations for the lunchtime buffet had the preserved look of a stage setting. It would look the same when she was no longer here for lunch. There would be no proof she ever had been.

'I think I've finally got everything in order here,' said Ram one night, which like every night was late.

Rose had soaked her feet in hot water, put cream on her face and got into bed, ready to drop off, when he said, 'If you're not too sleepy, there's something I'd like to talk about,' and went on without a pause to say he had been thinking about it and he was convinced they needed to live separately for a time. She woke herself up enough to say why don't we talk about it in the morning? It was not possible at this time of night to deal with another baroque sort of phase which instinct told her this might well be. Ram had had a distracted air since Mona's death. She would never forget the post-Marcella heavy gloom blotting out the shop and everything in it. Tragedy took to Ram like bandages to a mummy, wrapped him round and round till he couldn't move a muscle, much less think a thought or handle a crisis, and whatever soul's agony was bothering him now could wait till after a good breakfast tomorrow. But tomorrow, he said, he would have to start winding up his business talks and making arrangements for their departure, and once they were home, he would be involved in setting up the new venture, so this was the best time. Rose sat up in bed and waited, her face shining with dry-skin cream.

He needed, he said, to think about his life and get himself together. It would be a separation, not a divorce, and she would have everything she wanted. He had to be by himself. For his new phase, she thought, new phases being connected with old phases, his with Mona's death last year, and the marriage of their son, Dev, a few months ago. It doesn't make sense at our ages, she wanted to say, only Ram hated age. And Ram must be talking sense since he never talked nonsense.

'Is it Marcella?' she asked, knowing it couldn't be.

'How could it be? She's happily married,' said Ram, 'so it isn't, in the way you mean.'

What it was all about, apparently, was that he wanted to keep himself free (and pure?) so that he and Marcella could evolve the perfect *companionship*. An affair, Rose had called it all this time, but if it had been *the* affair, the classic original on which all others would in future be patterned, it obviously could not just tail off into letter-writing and material for the drawing room. This visit had to take them further, make him a worshipper at her shrine, down on his knees, prostrate before her image. From the pantheon it had come to this. And this was the other thing, Marcella and Brian would be cosy together all the time. It was Ram who would be lighting the candles and burning the incense, putting on the hair shirt and keeping the vows. And of course he and Marcella must have discussed it, woven it into their calculations and plans for the new boutique at Harrods.

She and I have so much in common, Ram was saying, as though he'd made a remarkable discovery, it needs to be kept alive. There's so much of the intellect to link us. I don't know

if you can understand this, he said, but there is a type of
encounter that keeps growing. He quoted:

> She turned away, but with the autumn weather
> Compelled my imagination many days,
> Many days and many hours:
> Her hair over her arms and her arms full of flowers.
>
> Sometimes these cogitations still amaze
> The troubled midnight and the noon's repose.

Nobody has ever said it better than Eliot. There is a quality of
relationship, Rose dear – Yes, I know, said Rose abruptly. He
looked a little hurt but continued, Well then, that's all right. I
knew you would understand. Now that we've talked about it
there's nothing for you to fret about, he concluded gently –
always the gentleman – his plans for his intellectual love of
Marcella placing Rose on the pencil line between high crags
again, the void falling away below. The crags melted away but
in the warm sunshine of a street no longer familiar, she was
standing where her home had once been. When Ram shook her
awake to stop her cries she told him of her visit to it. 'Oh, my
dear, how dreadful for you.' And before she entered the next
instalment of her tormenting dream they lay awake for a little
while, side by side in the warmth of the hotel's double bed,
hardly a sound from the London night beyond the white ruffled
curtains, Rose grateful for contained spaces that brought safety
and comfort, like the bus, like this bed.

In the morning, no longer able to share Ram's good breakfast,
Rose was finally able to persuade Sonali to come down from
Oxford and have lunch with her. Sonali was subdued through
the meal and upstairs in the bedroom afterwards she wept, Oh
Rose, Oh Rose, and couldn't get another word out. You'd feel
better if you talked, said Rose. I know, and especially to you,
howled Sonali, it's just that it's all over between me and Ravi. I
know now that a perfect relationship is the only kind one
shouldn't have, she said, it's the only kind that goes to pieces
at the drop of a hat. But who dropped the hat, Rose demanded.

It seems they both had, but the actual break had come because they couldn't agree on step three and step four of the Marxist process, whatever that was, and especially what happened to artists and writers and thinkers at that point, and Sonali recovered herself enough to explain painstakingly what ought to happen but didn't at stage four of the revolution. But there's no revolution round the corner that you need fall out over, Rose said, why not stay together until you come to the crunch? That's what I felt, but he's so rigid, so bossy, so selfish, if I married him I'd have to agree with him all the time. Of course we aren't going to get married and I don't think he loves me any more, but I am, oh, I still am in love with him, oh Rose!

'Now then, blow your nose, ducks. Did you say he's stopped loving you all of a sudden because of step three and step four?' Sonali looked up, puzzled, through her tear-bright eyes. 'Well, yes, I suppose so.' She plumped up the cushions she had been wailing into, smoothed her skirt and obediently blew her nose. 'Well, yes, that's it in a nutshell, I never thought of it that way.'

Other people's reasons like the Almighty being weird and inscrutable, there was no more to be said about it. They went to Kensington Gardens, fed ducks, watched children sail paper boats. And while we're sitting here on a bench, the two of us, thought Rose, in another part of the city Ram is making plans to take him and me ever so gently apart, and Ravi, terrified by the trueness of love, or just trueness, is using Karl Marx as a getaway. Not enough red blood in his veins. She'd never seen anyone look so much like Marcella's pale dry sherry. Sonali was down on her knees in the grass, rescuing a boat caught in a clump of reeds, and returning it to its small frantic owner, and Rose envied her her youth, energy and indignation.

In an old bookshop later that afternoon where Sonali was pursuing second-hand books on Marxism, Rose found, quite by accident among a boxful of picture postcards and pamphlets, 'L'Embarquement pour l'île de Cythère' by Jean-Antoine Watteau, 1684–1721. The pamphlet below it explained about its style and composition. The voyage was a quest, it said, and Cythera a paradise, an impossible dream, towards which pilgrims journey but never arrive. She picked up the postcard and looked searchingly at it. Sonali, looking at it over Rose's shoulder, shuddered and said 'Ugh!'

'I think it's very pretty,' said Rose, always at a loss for words to match her feelings. They were there in her head, like tunes she knew but couldn't carry.

'Oh, artistically yes. But all that powdered hair and rouge, aristocrats dressed up and romping around pretending to be peasants, living in a little dream world. Ugh! No wonder they ended up on the guillotine, and nothing less would have woken them up from their silly fantasies.'

'Poor young man, he didn't live very long,' remarked Rose, turning the postcard over in her hand.

'Which one?'

'The one who painted this.'

'Oh, didn't he? Well, Rococo, the style, went out with the French Revolution anyway. How could all that mythical nonsense survive the blast?'

But here it still was in a bookshop in the hand of Rose, and in the salon she had visited with Brian, enshrined for ever. She was struck by the wistfulness of the scene she held. To be dressed in regal satin splendour in a wonderland whose very trees looked enchanted, waiting to set sail for an island they were never going to see, with those beautiful fairy ships anchored nearby to make it seem the trip was real! The Revolution might have finished Rococo, but had it destroyed myths as Sonali said? Myths were the most indestructible of all things. They're what we're made of, Sonali's father so often said, and there was more than history to prove it, there was Marcella.

After going so manfully about her Marxist book-shopping, Sonali collapsed again without warning back at the hotel and said she couldn't face one single more day of her term. Rose would not have had the slightest idea what to do with the child if the phone had not rung and, only a miracle would explain it, it was Ravi ringing Sonali from the lobby, sounding as woebegone. Sonali sat up rapturous.

'He's on his way up. Now go along and have dinner with him,' instructed Rose.

'You come too,' insisted Sonali, and Rose was glad she went.

Ram was later than usual that evening, and it was restoring being with those two, intercepting their shining glances, children playing at love, who didn't know how dangerous a game it was. With an intensity that surprised her, she hoped that whatever had gone wrong with the stages of the revolution would be put right.

SEVENTEEN

Now look here, my good fellow, KL felt like assuring his interrogator, it's not only that I am *not* a revolutionary – researchers turned shopkeepers never are – but that I never had *time* to be one. How could the question arise? One major upheaval in a lifetime is quite enough, and have you, my good fellow, ever had to earn five dowries? To be a great public figure – and what else is a revolutionary in his service of the masses – he has to stop being a private one, and let someone else bother about the school bills and the dowries. But then KL's back and legs felt the stinging slash of the corded whip and he subsided, stupefied, to the ground. The monologue proceeded in his head after he was back in his cell, and he kept trying to explain, because everything depended upon his making them understand this very obvious point. Thank heavens whips were not what one calls torture. Ordinary village schoolmasters used whips and he was grateful now he had had plenty used on him. This much he had so far been able to stand, though he was not a schoolboy and this was not a schoolmaster's whip. But the domain of true torture lay ahead. Amnesty International's accounts of it proved there was an everyman's library of torture now, classic, illustrated, itemized editions of it passed from country to country, ideology to ideology, knowledge freely shared. Governments dipped into the same glittering treasure store. That treasure KL decidedly did not want the benefit of, upside-down hangings, rods up anuses, lighted cigarettes held to tender organs, and more, much more. So it was necessary to explain that he didn't believe in overthrow and violence and if they would only listen they would understand that this was a ghastly mistake made by overzealous Haryana policemen who wanted to impress Madam with their Chief Minister's loyalty.

Of course I believe in social change, he had tried to tell his interrogator, peaceful change, but how can a nobody, an insect like me, bring even that about all by myself when national figures who have spent their lives trying, haven't succeeded? He was thinking of the crowds JP had talked to at the universities just before the emergency, asking them to raise their hands in a pledge not to accept dowry. The whole concourse of every university had raised its hands, but when JP had said thoughtfully, Aren't you being hypocrites? Aren't you going to go back, you boys, every one of you, and say I want a motorcycle, I want a sofa set, I want a refrigerator, *in addition* to the rest of the dowry? Aren't you going to make big demands on your prospective in-laws for a house, a car, a trip abroad, if you can squeeze it out, well, aren't you, there was a stunned silence. No shouted denials, no pleas, nothing. Because that was exactly what that sneaky lot were going to do, slyly practise what they preached against, one message for the public platform and another for the private, like their elders before them, and JP had seen through and through them. KL had been one of dozens of people waiting for a word with JP after the meeting, at the Gandhi Peace Foundation where he was staying, and had said, when his turn came, 'Excuse me, I don't see how we are ever going to abolish dowry unless – forgive me for making such a very unorthodox suggestion – unless we stop arranging marriages. It is Arrangements that become money matters, contracts, you give me this, I'll give you that. But if two people marry because they are *fond* of each other, then what need would there be of dowry?' JP had smiled and said it was a new approach, and maybe the one we should propound. JP and KL, calling each other by their initials, then had a few minutes of refreshing conversation in which KL, emboldened, had said that Madam, using her para-military organizations so freely on peaceful demonstrations, seemed headed for authoritarian rule, and JP had replied with sadness, Yes, I cannot understand it, her father was a great democrat, a hero, an elder brother to me, she is like my daughter. But then of course his daughter's civil servants had pulled JP out of bed in the night and taken him to jail, and the whole ghastly misunderstanding, landing KL here in this cell, had begun. But look here, my good fellow, he was just starting his feverish round of explanation again, when the other prisoner, his age disguised by dirt and unshavenness, woke up and groaned, the first sound KL had heard him utter, and KL realized it was a young groan.

He was probably younger than KL's youngest son, so calling him 'son', he asked him what he was here for – as if any of them knew. For his membership of the Marxist party, the boy said, and described his acrobatic arrest. The police had been through Nehru University with a sieve and a fine tooth comb and taken vanfuls of Marxist prisoners. But him they hadn't been able to find until one day, when he thought they'd finished combing the campus, he had returned to his hostel-room and they pounced on him. He had dashed out of his room and down the corridor. Two policemen had caught him and lifted him above their heads, and, said the boy, I must have looked like a rotating windmill, the way I was wheeling and thrashing above their heads. Going through the doorway for which I was too wide, my arms and legs got banged and smashed but still they didn't put me down. When they hauled me into the police car, I was still kicking and my leg was sticking out of the window and nearly got cut off when it hit the gate as we went through. I promise you I made a noise those policemen's grandmothers will hear on their deathbeds. When they let me out of the van at the jail entrance and told me to walk in ahead of them, I knew it must be the end, with a bullet in my back like the Naxalites in Bengal got three years ago, bang, bang, bang as they walked in. But they didn't mow me down. And you, he asked, how did they bring you? KL described his own comparatively sedate arrest while the boy held his nearly broken leg and put his head down on his knees. Why, oh why did you let them catch you, KL asked uselessly. I never knew I was in any danger, he replied. I had joined the Naxalites years ago, but it never worked and I left them and got down to my studies.

KL realized how pitifully little he knew about the political scene with its glut of political parties and even two Communist parties. One, the CPI, was, he knew, Moscow-backed and now a satellite of Madam's party, but the independent Marxist party opposed her, and apart from the fact that plenty of them had been gunned down along with Naxalites so that Madam's party could win the Bengal election three years ago, he really didn't know much about them. Well, jail is a great chance for education and writing books, as Pandit Nehru had found, only that was a different sort of jail, with pencil and paper provided and light coming in through a window. Still, KL would have to make the best of it, and he did. The youngster told him he had sincerely tried to make a revolution years earlier and then given it up temporarily because he had got discouraged and decided to get on with his studies. It hadn't worked because the strategy had been all wrong. You couldn't start with the peasants. He had, in effect, said over and over again to that village in eastern Bihar, Hey you, friend, brother, comrade, come on, let's go, what are we waiting for? And the men had paid not the slightest attention because they were, one and all, staring up at the sky, waiting not for revolution but for the monsoon. And if I'd hung around there long enough, said the youngster, and the rains had come and gone, then they would have been waiting for the harvest, and after that for the next planting. I would have been hanging around there for the rest of my life. It was different for the Chinese. They'd been through years of civil war, then outside war, and they were thoroughly shaken up and unsettled, so Mao was a stabilizing factor almost, something known and dependable in the chaos, and he could organize them. And then Mao was *Mao*, you know what I mean? Yes, nodded KL, just like Mahatma Gandhi. The youngster laughed, amused but not derisive, what do you mean like that bourgeois pacifist goat's-milk drinker? And KL said I mean that before you were born, when the day of India's independence arrived, a reporter came to the Mahatma for a message, and was told, My life is my message, and everyone knew it was, like Mao's life. The youngster admitted, Oh, I see. Well, yes in that sense. Then he cried because his leg was throbbing and KL did not dare ask him what else the police or the jail had done to it for fear of the answer, and an additional anxiety his own brain would not be able to absorb.

The youngster stopped crying, raised his head from his knees and looked so forlorn beneath the dirt on his face – since they were both supposed to be plotting to overthrow, the authorities had decided to demoralize them by not letting them wash or shave – that KL reached out a timid hand, patted his untidy head and made the very curious remark that never mind, son, you'll get back to making revolution when this is over, which was not only a silly thing for a shopkeeper to say but also ridiculous to imagine with things as they were. There was a fiery path of pain where his own back and legs had felt the lash and one leg refused to move at his bidding. In a way he supposed his beatings were a sign of hope. Prison hadn't yet become a planned routine, scientifically organized to receive teachers, students and shopkeepers. The government was merely authoritarian, not totalitarian, so prison ways were still experimental, and naturally jailers improvised, invented, took inspirational leaps and bounds. They were only trying to make better careers for themselves. It would be time to worry when one day passed exactly like another in jail, with no beatings and badgerings.

After the gritty food neither of them was able to get down their gullets, and neither had the money to bribe the warden to bring some from outside, the youngster started talking again. Have you ever been to the United States? he asked. KL gave a weak titter. Where did the boy think that kind of money was coming from? The boy said he had, which enabled KL to docket him in the conscience-stricken affluent class. He had been there to university, that's what had made him want to become a Naxalite, but that was a different story. In the United States they had these laughter programmes on television when after every few remarks the actors made, there was loud taped laughter from an invisible audience. Whether you, sitting in your room, watching and listening, felt like laughing or not, there was this loud hilarious laughter, which had given him an idea for a play of his own. Shall I describe it to you, he asked, and since neither of them had another engagement, he went ahead. First of all the dictator's chariot arrives. Chariot? asked KL, isn't that rather old-fashioned, or are you setting your play in olden times? I don't know if this will appeal to you, said the boy, but I am making this a surrealist play which you probably won't understand, but the chariot turns into a car and then into a jet plane and through all of this the dictator is arriving, and he steps down to trumpets and fanfare and all the rest, and then instead of a big Heil So-and-so going up, there's this loud taped laughter, a huge barrage of it, that's all, then silence. Next he/she – and by the way one half of the dictator is a he and the other half is a she – this not a sexist play – tells about what he/she is going to do for the people. Politicians are such bullshitters and this one starts bullshitting. And after every few sentences when he/she stops for applause, there's this loud hilarious Ha! Ha! Ha! instead. And soon you have everyone bloated with laughter, falling over themselves with jollification, and they can't stop laughing while he/she is getting enraged and baffled because every time he/she says 'I shall banish poverty' or 'Watch me remove disparities', there's this colossal raucous cackle. What do you think of it? Assuredly it is a good play, KL said, once I know the story in-between. I'll think of that later, said the boy and fell asleep. When they were let out for their exercise into the yard, there was no else there they could contaminate with their revolutionary ideas. And probably Madam's other Russian prisoners were let out in driblets like that too. KL tottered around the yard a few times, anxious to be cooperative, while the boy who could not manage it, sat, and they were put back into their cell almost before their eyes had become adjusted to the outside light. By now KL could hardly concentrate on his monologue, his mind was on the boy, fallen on one side, with his leg drawn up. Useless tears came to KL's eyes and crawled uselessly down his filthy face.

There was not a life that might not have been different, he thought. Suppose Spinoza had confined himself to grinding lenses, he, KL would have lost many spell-binding hours of philosophy. Suppose Hitler had remained a house painter, or Madam had not been an only child, driven to furious doll-sized encounters with enemies, and suppose Madam's son had stayed a hijacker of cars and not become leader of a cultural revolution, suppose, suppose. Suppose he, KL had taken his wife's advice. I don't like black money any more than you do, she had said, but now that you've fathered all these children, we've got to live somehow, and black money is not something to make such a fuss about. Her brother had sold a car for 40,000 and taken a receipt for 20,000, with the other twenty sensibly put away where the taxmen didn't get to it. And the same with rents. Landlords charged 2,000 but took receipts for 1,000 and the rest went into gold and silver bars or into trunks under beds instead of into tax returns, and who was any the wiser? The best people were doing it, and she named some of the very best people who were, and a very impressive list it was, so why couldn't he? Jail gave you time to think of matters like that. Why didn't I become a blackmarketeer when I had the chance? It's black money to you but it would give us the money to join the club where the girls would find better matches. Why must you be so selfish, so atheistically arrogant, always showing off, Kishori Lal? Oh yes, she called him by his name. Though she catered to formality by calling him 'him', or 'As I was saying-ji' if people they didn't know were around, she thought nothing of bawling Kishori Lal when they were by themselves, and he liked her spirit. If he had any criticism of her, it was her religious faddism. Otherwise, from the beginning of their marriage she had never put on an act. And, as she had once told him, after eight pregnancies followed by eight rousing deliveries, four of which had made her famous at the nursing home in Daryaganj, there wasn't an ounce of demureness, real or feigned, left in her, nor could be in any living woman – it was different with those moronic heroines in Hindi movies – and she could hardly go mincing around like a blushing bride pretending she didn't know his name, and calling him 'As I was saying' when she knew him and he knew her down to the last bump on their respective vertebrae. Had it been selfishness, or honesty, arrogance or stupidity that he had not taken her advice? He didn't know what it had been, only that with his cursed tidy-mindedness, there was nothing for him to do but pay his taxes. Joining the forty-per-cent-over-the-table and sixty-under club would not have worked for him, just as the peasant revolution had been such a miserable failure for the boy. The boy was whimpering in his sleep and KL moved close to him to pat his shoulder and mutter soothingly. The scripture that I don't believe in doesn't deserve my belief, he told himself. The Bhagavad Gita said, the Lord speaking, 'Whenever there is decay of righteousness . . . I am born from age to age.' From age to age. But righteousness had decayed and rotted. And there was no sign of renewal or rescue that KL could see.

EIGHTEEN

Rose liked to think the separation hadn't worked, that Ram had lived too long with two women to live without any, that intellectual love needed a more earthy sort nearby to keep it going, but she couldn't be certain about any of this, or how intellectual Ram's two trips to England without her during this time had been, or whether the separation would have lasted much longer than it did, to the end of their days, if Ram had not bought a site outside Delhi when the area was converted from a rural zone to plots for sale, and decided to build a house, bringing the family together on the project. There had never been anything monastic about him, but then, how well did she know Ram? She had not suspected he was a nationalist, however hidden, but apparently there was that side to him, judging by his wartime letters to Marcella. Maybe he was a hidden monk all the time, not seeking separation from Rose so much as a rest from domesticity. But in these little exercises and displays – an exercise of sheer male prerogative, Sonali had called it when Rose had told her about it – something important gets lost and one is too tired to go hunting for it again. If Sita, for example, had been taken back by Rama after her ordeal by fire, if Rama had conceded, All right, my dear, you've been faithful, you'll do, you may stay with me in the palace, wouldn't she some time later have flung out at him during one of their quarrels. Why the hell did you have to put me through that grisly experience? And when Rose's Ram decided they should get together again, with no reconciliation or new start – since they had been in friendly touch all along – she wanted to give Ram a furious shaking and ask him what he meant by his bland assumption that they would go on exactly as before, as though there had been no break in their married life and she hadn't been put on the shelf like a pumpkin while he went off to sigh for Cinderella. When he came back it was with a plot of land, a blueprint and an architect, and not a word about why everything should swing back to normal only because he said so.

It had been so humiliating to have Zafar and Bugs Bunny arrive on a delegation from Pakistan during the separation and see her and Ram separately. Zafar had lost his attractive lounging indolence, having become a high political personage. It took more imagination than Rose could muster to see Zafar serving a military government, the Chocolate Soldier was more his style. Bugs, a begum of consequence in the regime, fitted into it much better, she was so like a military regime herself, and as condescending as if she, Rose, were a flatfooted old bag. Bugs signalled Zafar when Rose got slightly tiddly on gin and lime, and the signal might have been strung up in neon lights across the Intercontinental bar where they insisted on taking her, so clearly did it say And you used to call her the rosebud! Equally clearly Rose caught Zafar's unmilitary return message, Oh but she was! Bugs being Bugs could not contain her curiosity about the separation very long. 'It's crazy, isn't it? It would make some sense if this Marcella person was getting a divorce and if they were going to get married, but will somebody tell me what *this* arrangement is all about?'

'Now, bunny,' said Zafar, putting a warning hand on her wrist which she smacked off at once, 'Rose might prefer not to talk about it.'

'If she doesn't want to talk about it she'll say so,' said Bugs crisply, 'and don't treat me like I was two years old.'

'All right, you're nearly three,' said Zafar indulgently, getting a sergeant-major scowl from Bugs.

Glamorous autocratic Bugs with her legs and her latest everything was really rather a simple Simon, Rose decided, wandered into an antique jigsaw puzzle, Indo-Pakistan, only unlike Rose, Bugs would jump up and march away from it, not go deeper and deeper into the puzzle. She would never sit down long enough to learn a little about it, she was so impatient. It was not nice to smack away a courtly hand in full view of passersby. No, she wouldn't wait for the centuries to move aside and make a hospitable space for her, as they had for Rose.

'You don't have to take this lying down,' dictated Bugs, 'it's positively prehistoric.'

And after Bugs had finished outlining what a woman should do in such a situation, in which Bugs herself would never allow any man to put her, no siree, Rose came to a revelation about herself, if revelations are what have been inside you all along but a hit on the head makes them come out in a big flash.

'The only thing I couldn't bear in any circumstances would be a divorce,' she said, stopping Bugs dead in her talkative tracks. 'I could never bear to lose Ram.'

'I don't believe it,' Bugs said, recovering. 'I just don't believe it after the way he's treating you. Any man who treats a woman like that –'

But Ram was not any man. How had the evening gone when they had dined with Ram, Rose wondered, trying to picture it but not altogether succeeding. She could see Bugs as clear as troops on parade and Zafar clearly enough, guess at their conversation and their jokes, but Ram faded into transparency when she tried. It was like watching a play with three characters on-stage, one of them totally transparent and the scenery showing right through him. The one she had known the longest and best was fundamentally no better known, yet no less magnetic or mysterious than on the day in the chocolate shop. Almost he wasn't a person. He was a pull, luring her out from behind the counter, and she had never looked back. He was a piece in a complicated jigsaw puzzle. There was not a shred of simplicity about Ram. Instead of being plain Mr Wu, he was, as the song went, the husband of the wife of Mr Wu. And actually Zafar, though he'd tried to simplify himself so absurdly by becoming a Pakistani, with Islam for a nationality instead of a religion, wasn't simple either and never could be, and was just as much the husband of the wife of Mr Wu. As the evening wore on and they moved up to the exorbitant restaurant for dinner, Zafar's simplicity started to slip off and one by one his many selves encased him again, subtly altering his posture and his smile, darkening his glances, the shadowy transformation dissolving

Bugs' brisk assurance, unnerving her, until she was querulous
with questions, 'But when did this *happen?*' or 'I didn't know you
believed that', or 'How come you never *mentioned* it before?'
She didn't realize, poor young Bugs, that Zafar had lived the
better part of a lifetime before he met her, that the present is
the merest flicker between the long long time past and the
things that haven't yet happened but most assuredly will, in the
clockless dateless membrane that holds them all. Bugs was
nearly in tears by the end of the evening, one would have
thought jealous, if anyone so young and glamorous could be
jealous of a flatfooted old bag – except when Zafar uncannily
transformed Rose for one crystal instant into some shimmering
other with the remark, And how are things in Cythera? Even
Rose's blue eyes becoming puddles of tears that smudged her
mascara couldn't spoil the electric effect of that remark. But just
as Bugs was going to demand, 'Will somebody tell me what this
is all *about?*' Rose became a middle-aged woman again and Bugs'
jangled nerves relaxed. Was that the sort of thing that had
happened when they had dined with Ram? What else had happened to Ram during the five years of their friendly separation
while he had worked his intellectual love for Marcella out of his
system, or faced the fact that he never could and came home?

It was during the building of the house that Rose had discovered the tomb for herself. Thirteenth century, when Delhi
was in the hands of Turkish adventurers, built for one of the
sultans or a relation, said Ram. What a pity the archaeology
department did not see to its upkeep, the architect remarked.
It was going to rack and ruin, but what a fabulous view of it the
bedroom windows had, an unexpected bonus of building on this
site, they agreed, before they went back to discussing where
the electric fixtures should go, while Rose, shielding her face
from the sun with an old newspaper, walked out through the
black wrought-iron gates guarded by a muscular Gurkha sentry,
a rifle slung over his shoulder, and out to the tomb which seemed
to swell like an elephant's temples as she approached it as though
introducing itself. Without meaning to, she entered and the
temperature dropped degrees with the suddenness of a curtain
falling. She could see why. Massive walls and a great dome kept

the sun out, trapping its rays mid-wall and softening their intensity. The high hollow monument was furred with moss and mildew, cool, so pleasantly cool that she spread the newspaper she was carrying on the ground and sat down on it. The glitter of tiny teeth and eyes, or a mineral sparkle, winked at her. A frog leapt lightly past. She breathed the damp intermingled smell of lime and clay, so different from the scent of herbs and grasses outside. The newspaper was hardly a comfortable seat and she felt tempted to ask herself why she was sitting on it, but the question seemed a much older one, going all the way back to an ocean voyage in 1932 and not the short walk from Ram's new house, that had brought her here. There must be a reason why we are born, why we live, she mused, and it is peculiar not to know it even yet, though smaller questions have got answered. The song from the revival of the old musical they had seen in London on their last visit together came back to her. 'Why was I born? Why am I living? What do I get? What am I giving?' All questions, but one question seemed to answer another, as perhaps the songwriter meant it to, and if so, there was no more than that to understand. She sat very still and after a while she could hear the stillness. Time passing, she had called the seashell sound of which silences are composed when she was a child. Now she knew time didn't pass. It was present, all of it, all the time.

Rose was not sure whether she or the beggar had discovered the tomb first when she found him one day, looking like a magnified spider, talking to himself, recounting out loud the splendours of his life in the tomb. After that they shared it. On Mona's once a week beggar-feeding days Rose had never seen an entirely whole one among them. There was always something major or minor missing or mutilated, always a beggar at the corner of her eye, or the street, a usual enough sight. In fact it was Nishi's penetrating scream the first time this one appeared at the kitchen door, and Nishi's gasp, 'Is it human?' after she had controlled herself, that made Rose look examiningly at him. But as she did so she saw reflected in the beggar's eyes the bright blur of colour, the dazzle of ornaments that was Nishi, saw their mutual violent recoil from each other, and told Nishi to stop screaming at once. It was just a poor beggar, Rose said, he had to eat somewhere, and he was going to eat here. Kumar or she herself would feed him. After that she imagined his journeys to the house. Fortunately crossing the main road was not dangerous. It was a country road with very little traffic on it. Once across, there was the circular drive leading to the house, planted with long lean trees, imposing enough by day and ominous by night, towering over him as he propelled himself up the drive. He could neither walk upright nor on all fours because his arms ended at his elbows and his legs right-angled at his knees. But those stumpy arms and twisted feet had become competent tools perfected with use, she could tell from the rapid roachlike crawl she had watched once or twice and pictured afterwards, for most of the time she saw him sitting in the tomb or near the wall beyond it where he got a bit of social life and a drink of water when the construction workers or surrounding villagers came to fill their vessels.

Rose could have been getting away from clouds of building dust and Ram's long confabulations with the architect and the contractor when she first walked into the tomb, but that, she knew, was not the reason because she had kept walking away from the house after it was built, furnished and moved into. She had watched the whole process with a detachment new to her, watched Nishi's violent excitement, Nishi far removed from sharing clothes and a bed with sisters, to a mansion she would be mistress of one day. And Dev, master-to-be, still not settled into any occupation, supervising the building of a bomb shelter in the basement. No, a strong room for valuables, importantly handling bushels of money before he had earned any. Nishi's transports had reminded Rose of the starling trying to fly out of her bedroom window that flew up to the ceiling instead, and flew round and round in an ecstasy of anguished anticipation before it got away. Rose herself had not been able to join in the house-building euphoria. Between Ram and herself there had been a five-year spell of amnesia, when, their day-to-day contact cut off, they had moved in unconnected worlds. There was a stale and tired edge to him on his return. Was it because of what Marcella wrote? Marcella not writing? Or Dev still prankish in

his thirties? Or the people he was trying to interest in giving
Dev work?

'We have to meet these people, Rose. No one can do business
without connections of this kind.'

'Your father did.'

'My father did business in simpler times, when he wasn't
harassed by so many restrictions and didn't have to finance
politicians.'

And when money was the result of doing some work, thought
Rose, not a wishfulfilling genie out of a bottle.

'But why do you need that pious old hypocrite? Everyone
knows he's a crook.'

'We can't be other people's conscience-keepers. I have Dev
to consider.'

'What exactly are you talking to the Minister about?'

'All sorts of things,' said Ram vaguely, 'I want to fix Dev up
in something.'

So the groundwork had been done by Ram, though afterwards
Nishi had met Ravi Kachru on an inaugural flight to London, and
he had tied up the ends so to speak, getting a lock, stock
and barrel Happyola factory for Dev, making him into a New
Enterprenner with a wave of his wand when Dev hadn't enter-
prennered anything in his life and never would if he lived to be
one hundred and one years old. By that time Ram had had his
stroke. Still, Ram had done his best to get the Industries
Minister interested in Dev. All the poor boy needed, Ram kept
saying, was an opportunity to prove himself. Sometimes it
seemed to Rose the only sane person around was the beggar.
She thought about the journey shaped like an inverted question
mark he made with such skill, first the straight bit from the tomb
across the road, then the curved bit up the circular drive to the
kitchen garden. Once from her bedroom window she had seen
him caught in the glare of a car's powerful headlights and had
held her breath until the car passed him, while he, she was
convinced, had sent an impassive glance upward to the window
to reassure her he was safe.

NINETEEN

I hadn't realized how hard it would be to reach Kachru. Joint Secretary is in Paris until the 25th, I was told. When I rang after the 25th Joint Secretary had returned from Paris, but had had to leave almost immediately for Indonesia. I left my telephone number each time and the PA knew my name, but Kachru did not return my call. After Jakarta Joint Secretary must have held classes in other capitals, to explain how Left adventurist and Right reactionary conspiracies had been foiled, and the stability that could now be handed on to blood relations to safeguard. I went to see Rose, taking her some money. I don't want to buy anything, she said apologetically, I only want to know I've got some in my handbag. It's so uncomfortable having to ask Nishi for every *paisa*. I'm being such a nuisance to you, Sonali.

I took Rose out once or twice, to the cinema and lunch at our house, but she seemed to have lost her natural verve and bounce. It frightened me. People like Rose have inextinguishable fountains of optimism. This wasn't like her at all. She was not meant to feel lonely or grow old like the rest of us, like me, already so much older than her at thirty-eight. There are people one fastens one's faith on because they are young and questing and keep the courage of laughter. Rose was one of them. I couldn't bear to lose these qualities in her. The long drive out to see her and back, past the Qutab Minar, built when Turkish tribesmen were sultans of Delhi, gave me plenty to think about and helped to explain why she had that quenched look. It's what happens to ordinary life when power is arbitrary, as power always has been on this prize Gangetic plain, except for the last twenty-eight years when elected governments ruled it. Our joint life span, Papa's and mine, had seen the beginning, and now

. ..

perhaps the end, of a gentler order, a political springtime inter-rupted before it had come into full bloom. Otherwise, power had been power. The old myths meant to convey this. The god hurls a thunderbolt and it rains. He frowns his displeasure and his adversary is reduced to ashes. He comes to Draupadi's aid and her sari stays on her though several strong men are trying to pull it off. Prahlad in the legend embraces a fiery pillar and remains unscathed. It all depends on whether you are on the right side of power and omnipotence. Sita wasn't and it was banishment to the wilderness for her. Smiles and frowns become the law of the land when power is arbitrary and there is no appeal against smiles and frowns. It was sobering to imagine how many little victims the snapping jaws of the emergency were claiming in the course of an ordinary working day, how many big and small tyrants one act of whimsy had created.

I had to admit Rose would probably have had difficulties with Dev anyway, with Uncle Ram no longer master of the house except in name, and Dev so resentful of her. He might have taken over Uncle Ram's chequebook and account as a right and refused to give her any money even if Rose hadn't annoyed him by talking too much and hearing too much and saying the wrong thing at parties. But the emergency making him a VIP close to the throne and guarding a royal secret shaped like foreign car parts had given Dev a bullying power and confidence he never would have had. He was behaving abominably and no one, except Kachru who had put him there, could do a thing about it. It made me think of the considerable way each of us had come, Dev from petty criminal and dunce to VIP, Rose from one culture to another, me from being first in the competitive exam to swift oblivion, but Kachru furthest of all since the days when he and I had danced for joy of it around the pond reviving under the riches of rain, with vistas and highways stretching endlessly ahead of us. Rose and Dev and I had been brought where we were by other people, but Kachru's journey had been his own, a vista deliberately forsaken and forgotten every time he took a turn. And every turn took him inwards into a maze.

When, allowing time for several more flights to foreign capi-tals, no phone call came from Kachru's office, I tried once again and this time I got through to him. He sounded amazed and delighted, my voice his dream of many moons, vibrant chords of discovery in his own, like a spadeful of earth turned over and lo and behold violets! Sonali! Tell me what I can do for you! So at last I made an appointment with him. Kiran who heard me make it said, If that's Ravi, ask him to come and spend an evening with us, Sonali, we haven't seen him in an age. I handed her the telephone. Back in my room a tremendous relief exactly like tiredness flooded me. My whole body trembled with it. I let myself go limp and relaxed for the first time since Rose had brought me her problem, or since my illness, or since my dismissal, or since Papa's death, I didn't know which. All of it had come fast and furiously at me, each shock or sadness part of the one before it, soldered to the one after it. When had I last felt healthy and normal, Papa's 'star of my eyes', with a star of my own to follow? But to come back to the present, as we are constantly forced to, that supposedly being where we are, life is a very personal affair. All the other victims were still where the emergency had placed them, but I could breathe more easily because there was a solution in sight for Rose.

The next few days were full of cheerful bustle. Kiran was busy around the house getting it ready for the dinner and gambling party she always gave on Divali night. I was glad she used *diyas* instead of electrically lighting the house with coloured bulbs as some of Neel's co-entrepreneurs were doing nowadays at company expense, though it is no more incongruous, I suppose, than electrically lit Christmas trees and great shopping binges to commemorate a refugee birth in a manger, less so in fact, since the return of Rama to Ayodhya had been royal and triumphant and splurging must have been the order of the day. But I much preferred *diyas*, mustard oil and home-made wicks, all ancient as Divali itself, symbols of the continuity that Papa used to say broke through every other frame of reference, continuation in human affairs being so important to him. As I sat and rolled wicks for the dozens of *diyas* we would light in a few days, I thought of a celebration years ago at the restaurant Rose took Ravi Kachru and me to the night he had turned up at her hotel in London.

It was early for dinner and there were only a few people besides ourselves. Rose said to me, 'Well, ducks, what are you going to eat?' while Ravi and I pretended to study menus and tried hard to contain our private ecstasy within the decorum expected of those who are nearly twenty-two. We'd torn and mended our relationship a good few times. If it had been a strip of cloth to spread out between us, or to cover the table with, it would have looked lumpily darned and patched by sweaty fingers, and it wouldn't have mattered in the down-to-earth normality of Rose's presence. I had never minded showing her my bruises. She was the kind of person who put a relationship like a tablecloth to use and didn't mind it looking messy and darned and might have been suspicious of one that wasn't.

I can tell you it's a relief, Rose said, being in a restaurant where I can read the menu and understand what it's about, good old English food written in English and not those French squiggles I can't make head or tail of. And for goodness' sake, she told the waiter, bring us some beer. I'm that sick of vintages and vineyards and what year which grape and his baby brother was born. She rapped the table energetically, And what's wrong, may I ask, with good plain English cooking? Plenty, said Ravi, it's awful. It makes cabbage taste like wet flannel and everything tastes cooked to death. Aha, so you're in the plot too, she said, the light of war in her blue eyes. Like it or not, you're going to get a decent roast beef dinner tonight, feller-me-lad, and if your Brahmin grandmother turns in her ashes you'll have to put it right with her afterwards, that's all. It's time we had some food we can pronounce as well as eat. Last night we were out at one of these Frenchified places and Marcella started poking her nose into the order after we'd finished ordering. Who's Marcella? we chorused. An old flame of your Uncle Ram's. Or I should say, continued Rose with unabashed belligerence, what you might call a steady flame that's blazing like a ruddy beacon these days, never mind if Marcella's a bit long in the tooth same as the rest of us. What your Uncle Ram says is he's attached to her in-tel-lec-tually. It's all up there in the head, he says, they're just chums. Oh! said Ravi and I, wrenched out of ourselves, Uncle Ram said that? And, she went on, you two great in-tel-lec-tuals sitting here at this table can tell me if anything that's just up in the head can last more than two minutes all by itself without a bit of workaday attachment thrown in, because a bit of that is what's going on, if you ask me. But let me tell you what happened last night. We'd finished ordering dinner and quite a ballet dance that was. Then Marcella pokes her nose in to say that the lobster is five degrees fresher than the crab and the sauce on it will have a dash less of this and a smidgeon more of that which is to say it's more goor-may to the taste. And because her ladyship says so, we all change our order around. You couldn't call it showing off because Marcella doesn't show off. She's the queen bee and she doesn't need to. It's just that she knows better. *They*, all that lot, know better. They know best and it's no good arguing. Everyone else has to listen and do as they're told. You can't say what's all this fuss about bloomin' lobster and crab and what's wrong with having a side of English beef, oh no fear, because their accents are dancing the light fantastic, tripping over syllables, and with a bit of French thrown in with the crab and the lobster it's like lace tacked on to the crown jewels. You can't say, Look here, Marcella my girl, get off your high horse, because she's not *on* a high horse, that's really *her*, and that's how it's been since the world began. Rose's promising diatribe had trickled down into a drop or two of pure perplexity, and Ravi and I, roused and uplifted in support of her, ready to join our wrath with hers, suddenly had nothing to join it with. We looked at each other and at Rose's puzzled expression, and the three of us were rocking and gasping with laughter, making a vast amount of noise. No one who Knew Better or Best was with us to tell us to behave ourselves. When the waiter set down our beers with a cheery That's right now, enjoy yourselves, we knew we were on our own, free and equal, at liberty to break rules and dance jigs. Rose, you are such a *Rose*, I cried, getting up to dance one and to kiss her resoundingly, there's not a single person in the whole world like you. And Rose, I said accusingly, why haven't you ever told me about this Marcella person before? Because there's nothing to tell, ducks. Like I said, it's the way things have been arranged since time began. There's some that do the ordering and others that take orders. Well, here's to change then, said Ravi, raising his glass. Some things never change, said Rose flatly.

The night Kachru came over we sat in my room, not the drawing room, before dinner. How nice you've made it, said Kiran doubtfully, ever so many books, and Neel lowered himself into a lotus position on the carpet to show how relaxed and undismayed he was by the Indian whisky I was serving. Mama joined us since it was 'only Ravi and not a party', having banished herself from parties after Papa's death. Kachru was full of his foreign travels and they with questions about it. I had to interrupt to tell him Dev was withdrawing his father's money with forged cheques which the bank manager of the nationalized bank now knew were forged but he needed permission from a higher-up authority to take action.

'You're the only one who can put a stop to it,' I appealed to Kachru.

Kiran was the first to react.

'None of us can have any conception of what Dev has been through. It must have been a traumatic experience for a child to see his mother so badly treated.'

'At least her life wasn't torn up by the roots when Uncle Ram married again,' I said.

'You've never been married, Sonali, and you've never had a child. You wouldn't understand.'

The argument to end all argument. It's a common enough belief, too, that one must go through each human experience oneself to 'understand' it. We'd all be run ragged by the end of our days. There would never be any crossing age, sex or race barriers and precious little average sympathy to hand around. Nor need Jesus Christ have bothered getting himself crucified for mankind if salvation depends on our nailing ourselves to individual crosses every Good Friday.

'Dev has had too much spoiling,' I said. 'You know it as well as I do.'

'To make up for the dreadfulness his father exposed him to, I'm sure,' insisted Kiran. 'Don't forget he was growing up in a household that drove his mother to suicide.'

'It was Rose who saved her.'

'Can't you see how galling it must have been to be saved by the person who had driven her to it in the first place?'

'Mona wouldn't have waited ten years to try and kill herself if Rose had been the reason. I don't believe Rose's presence made much difference to Mona's relationship with Uncle Ram. Papa said it was when he started his affair with that English-woman the whole of Lahore was raving about that he gave Mona up and she got so desperate.'

'Poor Mona,' said Kiran. 'Uncle Ram's behaviour was enough to drive any woman up a wall, and she was such a simple, unsophisticated, religious woman.'

'I didn't know them as well as your father,' reminisced Mama, 'but it struck me the very first time I went to their house I'd never seen anything so pathetic as that poor, lost, lonely, little boy. I don't know how he can ever forgive Rose or forget what her arrival did to his mother.'

'But he'd only just been born when she arrived,' I pointed out. 'As far as he was concerned she had always been there.'

'That's what I mean,' said Mama and sighed. 'Once when Bhabi-jān and I were in Lahore together we attended a *kirtan* Mona was having. She was very devout. I've known orthodox wives with westernized husbands, but nothing like what went on in that house. It was really the limit. Why Ram had to have a cocktail party the same day I can't imagine, but you could hear literally every word said and every drink poured. I don't know how the poor woman bore it. I wanted to get up and leave, but Bhabi-jān convinced me we must stay and support Mona. Bhabi-jān is such a marvel, such strength of character. I know her presence gave Mona enormous confidence. She even put that boring Arya-Samaj pundit of Mona's in his place. He would go on and on with his anecdotes and explanations, simply loved the sound of his own voice. Bhabi-jān told him to get on with the reciting and not waste everybody's time with his long-winded explanations. Arya Samajis are great bores, always wanting everyone to understand the scriptures. Scriptures are just meant to be chanted.'

'Considering what he's been through Dev has come out of it remarkably well,' commended Neel.

'Yes, he has,' Kiran agreed, 'and it's all working out. I can remember his mother telling Mama years ago about the political career the astrologer had predicted for him.'

Neel said astrology couldn't be ruled out. Any science dealing with human behaviour couldn't be cent per cent accurate, but the accuracy of predictions by reliable astrologers was incredible. He and Mama gave strings of incredible examples.

'I'd say on the whole Rose has done very well for herself,' Neel said, 'considering her origins and so forth. It's hard to see why Uncle Ram got hitched up with her. Of course in those days only the landlady's daughter or that class of person was available but why did he have to marry her? She's probably been nothing but an embarrassment to him since. I've felt sorry for him at times.'

'Say what you like, breeding counts,' said Mama.

'I wish she wouldn't dye her hair that frightful scarlet,' said Kiran.

Negotiations between governments can be trying when there isn't much common ground between them, but I had never felt as sorely tried negotiating for my government as I did now. I was talking about forgery and they were talking about astrology and hair dye. But worse, there was an arctic waste between us, a loveless no-man's-land. What I saw across it was kith and kin arrayed against me. There was no rock-solid basis for fraternity here, blood tie or no blood tie. Then it's only some blood and tribal ties they believe in, not others, I told myself. Or it may have nothing to do with blood or belief, and any victorious army would find them hanging out flags and bunting. The one I had appealed to hadn't spoken. He stood by the empty fireplace, one arm along the mantelpiece, his face in profile. My imagination automatically clothed him in the diaphanous robe and turban of the Moghul courtier, a jewelled dagger in his belt, a rose in his hand, for only the costume of courtiership had changed through two empires and freedom's short aftermath. But the robe, the dagger, the rose, the studied elegance did not disguise the life I thought I saw caught breathless in a maze, scrambling and

stumbling through turning twisting alleys, each hoped-for opening a dead end and no destination in sight because a maze has
no destination. I don't know whether my face betrayed my
misery for Rose, or a queer compassion for him, but when after
an interminable time Kachru in his tweed jacket turned to look
at me, there was a directness in his glance I had not seen since
the Isis and the hurdles facing the millennium. He said quietly,
as if not a word had been spoken between my plea and his
answer, 'I'll see what I can do, Sonali.'

Neel and Kiran, supported by Mama, objected vigorously. It
was downright meddling to interfere in another family's private
affairs. It was also politically unwise. And it was certainly quite
unnecessary, Rose having done so well for herself considering
her origins.

'After all, what more does she want?' asked Mama, bewildered. 'She's been living in comfort for years.'

'People can be so ungrateful,' concluded Kiran.

But at that moment there were only two of us in the room,
one with the look of a man getting ready to take a halting step
that meant he might be learning to walk again.

TWENTY

The wall above their beds looked sprayed in blood and the obscene splatter framed in teak. Nishi bent forward in her chair, oppressed by the sight. Her mother had telephoned an hour ago with the news that her father had been in jail for a week, and for the past hour Nishi had been unable to move, rooted to the chair facing the blood splatter with the telephone beside it. She had never more than glanced at the painting before. The shop servant had got word of the arrest to the family but soon afterwards their telephone had been disconnected and the neighbours had not been friendly about letting her mother use theirs. Then the electricity had been cut off, the gas cylinder had taken days to arrive, and she'd had to buy a kerosene stove and queue up for kerosene to get food cooked, and finally she'd had to trundle two miles by scooter to get to a friendly telephone. Nishi unbent her back a little when Dev came in, recognizing him by his shoes. It was so long in any case since she had looked him in the face, if she ever had, though she knew Daddyji's and Rose's faces by heart.

'I've asked Ravi to lunch tomorrow,' Dev said, 'but don't expect too much. He may not want to use his influence in this case and I wouldn't blame him.'

'Why shouldn't he want to? My father hasn't broken any law.' She kept her eyes on the floor. Even so the elderly slope of Dev's stomach appeared at the rim of her vision.

'Your father's an old fool, joining the wrong party and mixing with the wrong people. He's been asking for trouble and he's got it.'

Silence, constraint, dignity, Nishi counselled herself, watching the shoes walk the length of the carpet, stop under the splatter, return.

'If he's lucky enough to get released, he'll have to mend his ways –'

'Stop!' commanded Nishi in a voice like the savage scream she remembered at the end of her last indescribable effort before her body was delivered of her two children, the crowning of the only two acts of her life there had been no stopping until their bitter end. Except for these she had always known pity and reprieve.

The shoes obeyed but their owner said sharply, 'Pull yourself together.'

Her selves lay torn in jagged halves on the delivery table, under the masked indifferent scrutiny of strangers and their implements, near glass cupboards lined with bottled tumours, skulls, forceps and scalpels. It was night and a scientific light fell mercilessly on her exposed and wounded flesh, her cry deranging no one but herself. Their announcement of motherhood revived fresh raw protest which they took to be the exhausted end of gruelling labour, not knowing even when they heard it the terror of those sent out to fight and die for causes they didn't believe in. A stranger laid the child she hadn't wanted, and next year the second child she did not want, like trophies beside her and took them away to the trophy room when she shut her eyes pretending sleep or death. She'll be all right in the morning, it's been a hard labour, she heard them say. By morning, bathed and bandaged, the blood of battle washed away, barbed-wire stitches buried deep in sewn flesh, her voice mid-octave again, a wall shutting out the memory of the night's violence had implacably, invisibly encircled her. Through slitted battlements, safely out of reach, she could smile and nod at telegrams, gifts and flowers. There, see, Mummy's fit as a fiddle this morning, all ready to become a Mummy. Grappling with her selves was simple if she kept her inner and outer selves apart. Pulling them together showed her the world as it was, and her single will, defiant, disobedient and distraught, confronted it.

Lunch next day was as big and heavy as the hour they spent consuming it. She took no interest in Dev's conversation, it was better that way, concentrating on meat, spinach and passing the chutney instead of how responsible the newspapers had become, no longer carping and criticizing as they used to, how well the debate to amend the Constitution was going with the opposition in jail, and once it was amended Madam's son could be brought up to front rank leadership and the car he's trying to make could finally hit the road.

'I 'adn't 'eard there's a car,' said Rose, betraying the gins she'd had before lunch, ''ow's a car that's not there going to 'it the road?'

Dev continued, ignoring her. 'Once a few models are ready Madam should nationalize the project. Then the public sector will be responsible for it. After all, it's meant to be a people's car.'

'Sounds like the emperor's new clothes to me,' said Rose. 'First of all there's no car, and then you nationalize the one there isn't. And in all these years wot you're saying is there isn't even a model.'

'Mummy, why don't you have some more spinach?' said Nishi.

'What do you think, Ravi? Doesn't the project need to be nationalized? Then the government can get French or Italian or Japanese collaboration and produce the car in no time.'

Ravi mumbled something about the licence being one to produce an Indian car of private manufacture and Nishi saw her husband's head jerk up, scenting a change in the wind.

'That's right,' agreed Rose. 'Either you're an enterprenner or you're not, and if 'e is, wot's all the fuss about? 'Oo was supposed to be producing this famous car anyway, 'im or the Japanese?'

Dev scraped his chair back noisily and stood up, followed by Ravi, who came round to Nishi's side of the table to say that Madam was on tour in the South and he could make no promises, but he would do the best he could for her father. When the men had gone, Nishi and Rose stayed aimlessly on, with no earthly purpose in sight but to watch the dining table brushed clean of crumbs and cleared of tablecloth, dishes and cutlery. After the servants had departed, the sun slanting on a bowl of apples and oranges, warming the table's wood, and their arms upon it, reminded Rose of similar sunlit silences, smiling currents of air replacing the harshness of heat as the season changed and she waited day after day for mail to arrive with news that her parents were safe, and after one letter for the next. The long agony of suspense, unlike other agonies, got mixed with shapes and textures outside one's self. Her frantic fears during London's wartime bombardment must be indelibly stamped on the streets and buildings, trees and stones of Lahore, the bazaar she had frequented, the cubicle where Mr Parameshwar Singh's soapy shampoo had trickled into her eyes. Bomb shelters hadn't helped much in the end. What use were underground shelters and why had Ram built one here for valuables, she asked Nishi. Why not keep them in a safe upstairs, or in a bank? Nishi's fog of depression cleared and she answered alertly, 'They couldn't be kept in a bank, Mummy, because they're going to Mauritius soon to be put in a bank there. Daddy-ji might have built the vault for valuables but Dev keeps stacks of money down there, the deposit money collected from dummy companies and dealers who are going to exhibit the car when some models are ready.'

'If they aren't ready, wot's so much money doing down there already, and wot's Mauritius got to do with it?'

'They'll be ready one of these days. The parts keep arriving and they're stored down there too. They come straight from the airport without clearing customs.' Nishi jumped up and left the room with the suddenness of a sprite.

Ram's money, though not in Mauritius, might as well be, Rose sighed. Religion must have helped Mona during her trials, or why would she have hung on to it as she did? As they had driven home together after the shadow play, Draupadi's honour unsullied, Rose had said enviously to her, I wish *I* had something certain to hang on to. I don't know what you mean by certain, Rose-ji, Mona had said, but it's questions we're all hanging on to, not answers. Will this happen or won't it? Will my son come first in his class? Will he marry a nice girl when he grows up? I don't know how it is with Christian prayers, Rose-ji, but among us questions aren't answered quick quick quick because time is not only clock time, and they have to work out in their own time. I don't get you, said Rose. I also did not until I heard this story, said Mona and told it. Once a teacher asked his young disciple to fetch him a glass of water and the young man went off to get it, but on the way he met a beautiful girl whom he fell in love with and married. They lived happily together, had three children and cultivated their fields. Before long floods came, and later drought, and they had to work very hard to recover from these calamities, but finally all was well again. Their children were growing fast and in good health, and the whole family was prospering when one day the teacher arrived in the village, looking for his disciple, and said to him, 'Where is that glass of water, my son? I have been waiting half an hour for it.' So! said Mona, wrapping her shawl around her, collecting her handbag and packets of peanuts and spun sugar candy she had bought for Dev, as their car arrived at the gates of the house. She shouted to the *chowkidar* who was hurrying to open the gates he had latched against cows to look smart about it and not take all night. What does it mean then, persisted Rose, was it a dream the disciple was having, or didn't the teacher realize how much time had passed? Or *what*? But Mona stepped out of the car and into the little earthquake of commotion her arrival had stirred. If that kind of question was all I had to hang on to, mused Rose, trailing Mona into the house, not knowing what had actually happened from what had supposedly happened, I'd be less certain of anything than I am now.

Rose left the dining table reluctantly and wandered out on to the front verandah, the same soft seducing sunlight announcing the season of chrysanthemums and bumble bees on roses, of garden radishes and celery, and sat down in a basket chair to enjoy the sun on her feet. It had crept up with clock time into her lap while she slept and woke to see Ravi come out of the house and ask if he could join her. It seemed to Rose half a life-time had passed since he had raised his glass in a toast, 'Here's to change.' Or it may have been only half an hour since that glass of beer according to some calculations. Or hardly that, so distinctly did she recall the communion the three of them had shared that evening over English roast beef.

'How's your mother?' she asked, that being a more relevant question to ask a pale specimen, looking as much as ever in need of a good healthy tan, than how's your wife.

'Fit as a fiddle.'

'Bhabi-jān means brother's wife, doesn't it? I suppose it's the custom in your community to call your mother your sister-in-law.' Punjabis often used relationships instead of names, and Kashmiris, who were supposed to be more subtle, probably used non-existent relationships to call each other by to show how much more sophisticated they were than anyone else. And after forty-three years here she wouldn't put any custom past any community.

'Not exactly,' Ravi laughed, 'though I did call my father Bhai-ji, which means brother. I must have copied what I heard others in the family calling them.'

Or maybe he'd actually thought of himself as his father's brother, or of his father and mother as brother and sister. Maybe they'd kept their relationship a secret from him. Quite possible with what she'd seen of sleeping arrangements in joint families, men's beds lined up on one verandah, women's on another, as if they didn't know each other when obviously they must have done plenty of verandah-swopping in the dark, judging by the swarms of children all over the house. The Mr Wu theme had endless variations. Lord, it was confusing.

'Sonali's put you to a bit of trouble for me,' she said.

'That's what I came to tell you about. I've had a long talk with Dev. He's very angry with me for mentioning it. He says the money is his. I can't persuade him to stop forging cheques.'

The information gave her a nasty jolt.

'We're talking about forging cheques, not having another drink,' said Rose. 'It's against the law.'

'I know,' said Ravi.

'And the bank manager who knows they're forged has to go on letting them be cashed.'

'It's one of the banks that made huge loans for The Car,' said Ravi.

'And the emergency is supposed to be putting crooks into jail?'

'Yes,' said Ravi.

'There's something wrong somewhere.'

'I'm afraid so,' he admitted. 'It's got beyond me.'

Any muddle is possible, she thought, in a set-up where you keep calling your mother your sister-in-law.

'If you couldn't persuade Dev, you being so important in the set-up, nobody can,' she said.

'I'm dreadfully sorry, Rose. You were right when you once said some things never change.'

But it was other changes, the established order she had been talking of at the time, not pickpockets, highway robbers and bandits getting away scot free. And, of course, where one's own affairs were concerned, one kept foolishly expecting some magician (since the Almighty didn't always oblige) to wave his wand and put things right. She had counted on Ravi Kachru's wand.

'I don't know why I didn't see this coming,' she said. 'If only I didn't have to spend the rest of my days under Dev's roof, but where can I go with him holding on to the money?'

'You wouldn't want to, with Uncle Ram here.'

'No, not while he's here. But how long's he here for?' And the rigid circumscribed dial of clock time took over, its minutes relentlessly replacing each other.

'I wish I could have helped,' said Ravi.

Rose became severe. 'You could've helped by not starting this rigmarole.'

It was why she forgot to thank him or to feel surprised that it had got beyond him, as he said. He should have known it would when he started it.

She was walking by the tomb several days later when Nishi came flying out to say her father was going to be released in an hour's time. Rose decided to go to the jail with her and suggested they bring him back with them for the night. Back with us for the night, Nishi repeated, high and clear. I'll go and get a cardigan, I'll be down in a jiffy, said Rose, and the end of the sentence re-echoed in Nishi's light accents. Nerves took some people that way, repeating the ends of other people's sentences, but Nishi's nerviness had never taken this form, and she looked so cool and collected, it was bizarre her chiming 'in a jiffy' after Rose.

Steeling herself to feel nothing as the car drove through the prison gates under the arch announcing it was a prison, Nishi walked calmly into the superintendent's office where Ravi had told her to go, but the sight of the wizened man waiting in a small dirty heap on a corner of the bench against one wall sent her into a frenzy of tears for his entire past and not just the last fortnight. Not often, if ever, had a diamond ring that size attracted and reflected the weak voltage permitted in the superintendent's office, and he half rose from his chair in alarm to reassure the rich sobbing visitor, but when the memsahib motioned him to leave her alone he sent for a glass of water for her instead.

Rose went to the bench. 'Well, KL, I've seen you in some rum spots, but I never thought I'd be visiting you in one like this!' KL gave a ghostly imitation of a chuckle but it improved with a little practice as Rose and he talked about *jelabies* dipped in hot milk, Mona's favourite soggy concoction to break a fast with, which apparently was what KL missed most in jail. Nishi still standing, abruptly stopped crying when she heard her father say he would have to go on missing *jelabies*. He couldn't go home with them as there was a young prisoner with him in his cell whom he couldn't leave. Nishi would have to get the boy released as well and they would leave together. Rose discovered it was a student with a leg that may or may not be fractured but needed immediate medical attention. We'll make arrangements for him, she offered with a confidence she was far from feeling, but KL made no move to get up. I have this fear, he patiently explained, of the gates clanging shut behind me and the boy remaining here, perhaps for years, so I can't go till he can come too.

Nishi, Rose could see, had not accepted the fact of his refusal. She had a fixed stormy look in her eyes. Tell him, she shrilly instructed Rose, he will have to come with us. He must be mad to think we're going to leave him here. Rose turned interpreter again, only she was speaking his language, not Nishi's, hearing her parents' obstinate refusal to leave London, bombs or no bombs, other people were sticking it out, weren't they? And Lalaji refusing to crawl on his belly along that stretch of road, knowing full well they would tie him to a flogging frame and thrash him within an inch of his life if he didn't. There was a core of obstinacy nothing could budge. But she tried to persuade KL to go home with them.

'What about your shop?' Nishi demanded.

He looked mystified. He might never have heard of shops. It took him seconds to realize and register 'shop'. His face cleared.

'Oh yes,' he said. 'Your mother will have to take charge of it until I come. She must already have done so. Your mother is a very capable woman.'

Nishi recalled her mother announcing his arrest, and packing the announcement with news of the telephone, electricity, gas cylinder, neighbours, and two-mile trip to a friendly telephone. All that breathtaking activity and the food to cook besides. In contrast Nishi had sat numb and torpid on a chair and looked or avoided looking at the splatter. Well, capable or not was hardly the point. It was beyond comprehension that her father had forgotten the shop and now was dismissing it as a trifle for her mother to look after. She felt sick and faint at what they must have done to him to make him forget the most important thing in his life, leaving his mind to wander like this, talking irrelevant nonsense to Rose about Germans and Russians and the treatment of prisoners in World War II.

'My wife will look after the shop better than me,' he ended, and added in polite dismissal, 'Come back, if you please, with another release order for the boy.'

He might as well have said, Make arrangements to have thousands of people released, it was that impossible and unrealistic. You can take it from me, he was going on, the boy has been involved in no violence or law-breaking. He wasn't preparing to overthrow anything when they put him in jail, practically breaking his leg on the way. He was getting on with his studies. But who's going to take it from you? Nishi burst out. Her father looked acutely embarrassed at her behaviour. 'Mrs Rose,' he appealed, 'kindly explain my predicament to my daughter.'

'I understand how you feel,' Rose assured him, 'but we're so anxious about you, we can't leave you here.'

'That is precisely how I feel about the boy,' he promptly replied.

KL took off his bifocals, wiped them carefully on his soiled *kurta* and put them on again. Rose looked like a being from another happier planet, her solid white bulk, her large white face bland, benign and comforting in their obvious good will. She came from clean sheets, plentiful food and fresh air. The sight of her refreshed him but it was not a lifeline. He had no desire to grasp it and go. His pull was the other way, to the cell. Strange things happen in prison cells. Aurobindo, a bomb-throwing terrorist, had had a religious vision, set up an ashram and become a spiritual leader, and though KL was no spiritual leader and never would be, and didn't believe in religion and never would, he had found the person he would have been had ill fortune not turned him to failure after failure in business. He was meant to be a teacher, to touch the minds and spirits of the young, to pass something of himself along that they could carry with them all their days, and it had taken a prison cell to illuminate that long buried dream and invest his life with its true meaning. At least a corner of this mission could be accomplished if not the whole of it.

I'll force him to come, thought Nishi, realizing how idiotic that was, with him and Rose a great distance away in earnest conversation, leaning towards each other, nodding and murmuring as if she were not there. She turned away to sit on the chair against the opposite wall but she could hear him say, sounding touched in the head, that he and the boy were working on a play – in their minds because there was no pencil and paper – and only as therapy for the boy as it took his thoughts off his pain. The boy had the makings of a real student, the kind to whom studies mattered, that's why he had come back to them. Then their voices dropped lower and Nishi could hear no more, but she saw Rose walk over to the superintendent, and her father get up to leave, moving with a limp. It was too late during their hurried leave-taking to ask him why he was limping, and concentrating tenaciously on his release she forgot about Rose on the drive home.

It was peculiar about Dev, Rose thought, sitting with the stiff gin and lime she felt in need of on her return. Dev had been in existence since her arrival in India, in fact since she and Ram had first met. Ram's father had cabled the news of his birth to London: Eight pound boy born fifteenth nine eleven p.m. mother and son doing well eagerly awaiting your return Father. They had returned to a house with Dev in it and were married on the raised verandah outside his nursery. Yet he had not become actual for her until she had seen him running around the garden, though he had been growing in the house all the time. And then again she had hardly realized he was there all the years he was poor Dev, failing exams, eating stacks of chicken sandwiches by the Gymkhana swimming pool and getting into boyish scrapes with scions of the best families. Even when she was helping Mona make out ads for a bride for him she had not quite grasped the reality of Dev. But like his flesh and blood appearance in the garden in Lahore, the emergency had placed him foursquare in her attention, blocking doorways, materializing unexpectedly at the end of a corridor, coming out of his room at the identical moment that she was coming out of hers, and, soon after Ram was stricken, taking stealthy possession of her joint account with Ram. Still not quite an actual person, if that meant human give-and-take. As a very young child he had backed away from her, back, back, till he bumped into something, turned and ran. Now the process was reversed. He came towards her, or if not that, he stayed where he was, wider, fleshier, a presence that yielded nothing to being there, did not smile, talk, say offhandedly, Nice day, isn't it, or What are we having for lunch today, or anything at all. His face and manners were blank and neutral, but sometimes behind closed doors she heard him say, 'She was my father's keep, so why shouldn't I control her account?' or 'She nearly killed my mother' or 'She lorded it over the house, bossed the show when it was my mother's house.' On the other hand, thought Rose, *did* she hear his voice saying all this behind closed doors? Was this what Dev thought and felt about her? Or was she listening to a voice in herself? In normal houses sound travels freely, feelings go back and forth, up and down stairs, in and out of rooms, and fade out eventually like notes of music. There had not been time enough in this house, as time and houses go, for feelings to bloom and fade. Instead locked doors held captive sentences she could not be sure she had heard, yet how could she have made them up? How could one imagine someone saying about one's self, 'One of these days I'm going to break her neck?'

What is truth and what isn't, and must truth have evidence? She could sometimes feel the back of her neck grow tense, her ankles drag, putting words like ambush into her mind, forbidding her to move in any direction, which was surely evidence of a kind. And there were the locked and barred sounds and sentences unable to escape, rattling at closed doors to get out into open air and open talk. So much locked and barred, she hadn't had the remotest idea that car parts and bundles of car dealers' money were accumulating in the basement, a car growing in this house as a child had grown in the other. The secrecy more than anything told her how much she had irretrievably lost, how alone she was. She cradled her glass of gin in the palm of her hand, half of it already warm and consoling inside her, and tried to imagine life in this house when Ram's symbolic presence wasn't in it any more. A cold breeze from the window – it was so much cooler out here than in the city – had made Divali seem upon them for weeks when it had been only yesterday. It had been the first Divali since Ram's stroke, the festival of lights commemorating the other Rama's return to his kingdom after fourteen years of exile and war. A short sharp memory from her own first Divali came troublingly back. Mona was kneeling on the verandah below to light a *diya*, her hand curving around it to protect it from the night breeze. Suddenly she had looked up at Rose on the balcony and their glances had interlocked, driving Rose back instinctively into the shadow for asylum, making her the intruder Mona believed she was. Kumar had found her shivering behind a pillar and said, 'Coming to see the Divali lights, memsahib?'

'What is Divali?' Rose had asked.

'It is the beginning of winter,' he replied.

Why hadn't he said it was the return and enthronement of Rama, a festival of rejoicing, of lights and feasting and gambling? The beginning of winter and another exile was what it had been for Sita.

When Kumar came in to tidy her room, remove the coverlet

from her bed and pour her another drink, she told him about the jail visit, and how the only good it had accomplished was an end to the brutal treatment Nishi's poor father had been getting. She had told the superintendent that since his release order had come from the highest, the beatings must stop, a point the superintendent had understood at once. Obviously a mistaken arrest, he had said, these mistakes were most regrettable. He would see about proper food and bath water and get the doctor to examine the cellmate of the prisoner who was so highly connected and about to be released. Indeed it only needed a word from the highest to get the cellmate out, too. These cells were needed for more prisoners, such a turnover as they had never had.

When Rose entered the drawing room Nishi thought, Oh dear, she's had too much to drink and she's going to be difficult like when Mr Neuman came to dinner and Ravi came to lunch. She wished she hadn't asked Leila and Pritam that evening, but Leila had insisted they talk about the Protestant phase of vasectomy. We can't sit on our laurels, she had said throatily into the telephone. Rose had the ponderous walk drinking gave her. When Kumar came in to ask her as usual if she wanted to feed the beggar, Nishi heard her say, No you do it, I'm too tired tonight, but tell him I'll see him tomorrow.

'There's a certain taste that likes a sweet snippet to eat with a liqueur,' Pritam was elaborating. 'Champagne is served at the end of a meal with the sweet, so why shouldn't a morsel of some kind be served with liqueurs? We're trying to work out a biscuit of the right kind, thin, crisp, with fillings to suit various liqueurs.'

'You won't get much of a market for that,' said Rose. ''Ow many people serve liqueurs?' and that confirmed Nishi's suspicion. Drink brought out her Cockney, and there was bound to be trouble. It was all Nishi could do to keep her attention on the problem Leila was having with the video films she and Pritam were getting from abroad. The servants were allowed to watch the Hindi movie on TV every Sunday so they expected to be allowed to watch these, but she would have to put a stop to it because of the love scenes being so embarrassing for them.

'Wot do you mean embarrassing?' Rose enquired.

'After all, auntie, they aren't used to it.'

Rose reared up in her chair. 'They're used to rape, aren't they, so a bit of love-making on the screen can't be very 'ard for them to get used to.'

'Now Mummy, really –' began Nishi.

'Don't now Mummy me. If you and I get raped the militia is out looking for the rascal. But their kind nobody bothers about.'

'I don't know where you get your information,' said Dev, diverted from the thinness and flavour of the coming biscuit.

'From them as it 'appens to.'

He had told her the last time she had chatted with him near the well that when his wife disappeared he had gone searching for her. He thought the police had grabbed her. They had rumbled into the village in trucks like an army, sprung out, and occupied it. The landowner who owned most of the cultivable land in the village, and whom they worked for, had sent for the police at harvest time to make sure they didn't get off with their full share of the crop, and didn't try any land-grabbing tricks as were going on in the area and could be catching. Feet marching in unison, scythes on shoulders, and songs being sung in the fields had made him jittery. The police had plundered the stored grain, helped themselves to cows and hens, smashed cooking vessels and set huts on fire if there was any resistance. They had made free and easy with the women, so lots of them had run away. His neighbour said he had seen five women fleeing together towards Bakhadda. He found them, with eight police-men. Two of the men lay on their sides chewing blades of grass. The rest were in a circle with one woman in the centre. Through the shrubbery he saw the tip of a *lathi* raise the woman's sari above her waist, poke and prod her and turn her round and round like a marionette. Another *lathi* joined the first. She was the only one still clothed and standing. The others lay like overlapping corpses on the ground. He had vomited into the bushes but stayed crouched until he heard the clank of chains and saw the women being led away naked, each shackled by an ankle to the one in front. But his wife was not among them. He was still roaming the low hills wild-eyed, looking for her, when the villagers straggled back to their homes from their hiding places and sent a party to search for him. After the crop had been harvested and the police had gone he heard his wife had been taken along with some others to one of those brick-kiln-pig-hole places along the Ganges. Rose saw the harsh outlines and features of four faces and realized she had, without planning to, said it aloud.

'I can't see any of it 'appening to you and me, can you?' she ended. 'So wot's the 'arm if they see a bit of kissing on the screen? Less embarrassing than wot they see in real life, I'd say.'

The composition of the biscuit was resumed while Nishi prayed Leila wouldn't get on to Protestant vasectomy. This wasn't the night for it with Rose in this mood, and in her anxiety to prevent it she blundered into the only other subject she could think of. 'I hope your car isn't giving any more trouble, Leila?' Rose pounced. 'Car? Wot's all this about storing car parts underground 'ere in the basement, Dev? Wot's so secret about it and why can't it be made on the ground like other cars?'

A fleeting fury replaced Dev's neutral mask, and Daddy-ji's absence settled like cold grey ashes around Nishi's heart.

Rose hadn't had so much to drink that she, now aware of Dev every waking minute, hadn't noticed his expression too. It had alarmed her and she made up her mind to warn the beggar to keep out of sight as much as possible, what with the youth camp armed to the teeth and Nishi and the biscuit woman hell bent on sterilizing everything in sight.

The next evening after her hour with Ram she went walking as usual. The beggar, generally airing himself near the well, was nowhere to be seen. He'd probably cottoned on to the dangers himself. She would have to talk to Nishi about money matters, ask her to arrange whatever meagre settlement Dev was willing to make. It wouldn't do to let matters drag on. Once Ram was gone, and it could happen tomorrow, she'd be entirely at Dev's mercy, having to beg for every penny. Ram's breathing body induced a restraint that would snap when life left it, when the body itself no longer lay upstairs, a mute but august reminder of who was master of the house.

She entered the tomb. The in-between weather made it

neither cosily warm nor comfortably cool. Today's warning of coolness to come revealed it for what it was, a tomb, with the remains of a thirteenth-century Turkish sultan interred in the soil below. No picnic spot this, as Lodi Garden was, adjoining a main thoroughfare, with the blue domes of the Lodi kings' tombs glistening in the sun amid the domestic neatness of flower beds and morning and evening walkers. This was a desolate place. The building of a house and a Happyola factory had not made it less so. They looked unnatural, popped up out of sandy, stony desolation. Scattered, stunted shrubs and thrusting clumps of sweet-smelling grass only heightened the feeling of distance from anywhere, making them ghost relics of bygone gardens, or had the Turk dynasties been too busy making war on the infidel, building towers of victory and mosques and tombs, to bother with gardening and government as the Moghuls and British had done? The silence of the tomb enclosed her and as her eyes adjusted to the darkness, she saw the friendly wink of minerals and distinguished the shape of the beggar in the corner, only because she knew so well what he looked like, otherwise he blended into the wall. He lay asleep and she decided not to disturb the poor fellow.

Rose sat down to think things over, her legs folding more easily under her since the practice begun with Lalaji and continued with diminishing discomfort ever since. The first time she had come here, the house had still been under construction. Strings of consequences had followed from the house Jack had built, beginning with the malt that lay in it. And Ram's was not so different. Sonali had told her a rural area had been converted against expert advice into private plots. A separated family had moved in, Ram coming back to her for no other reason than bricks and mortar, and someone having to live in the spaces they boxed in. And now it was unfeelingly owned and possessed as only bricks and mortar could be by Ram's son who in ordinary circumstances could never have been the threat to her peace of mind he had become. A factory the rules didn't allow had been built to make a drink no one needed, and hide car parts that shouldn't have been arriving. All of it convinced her fate had taken several stupid, blundering turns, or rather that silly preventable disasters could hardly be called fate. And even if that's what it was – the powers who were supposed to know better sometimes being as vicious as they were, e.g. their barbarous treatment of Sita – of course it had to be fought. But was she the one to start fighting it at sixty-three, when all her life, or ever since meeting Ram, she had been in the clutches of a necessity she didn't understand?

The last resistance of Rose's English legs eased and she found herself as relaxed as a yogi in her cross-legged posture, her thoughts beautifully clear. It came to her she'd been in the grip of no fate at all. She had been beckoned by curiosity, lured and compelled by mystery, come halfway round the world following the unknown. Scientists and explorers had done it before her and would go on doing it after. She was here because she wanted to be, and only her doubts and fears had disabled her. For that matter, even Mona, most accepting of creatures, had not accepted fate. And then another obvious fact leapt at Rose. Mona had never been accepting. She had wept and raged, summoned the whole rousing melodrama of religion to her aid, held her world and everyone she loved in it in a close embrace, never letting go, fate or no fate. Rose heard her bright contagious laughter, her loud protesting tears, the tigerish appetite for joy and grief named Mona that had rocked the Lahore house to its foundations. Around Rose insistent voices whispered it wasn't too late to tackle Dev, to try for justice, make scenes for it, and Mona's urgent voice was among them. Rose-ji, get up and deal with my son, your son now. Why did you sit here doing nothing all this while? She was on her knees in the act of getting up when a cloth came down over her head, arms pinned hers down, and she heard a thick satisfied grunt as she lost consciousness.

TWENTY-ONE

Rose's body was found in the well two days after Divali. Dev was at the front door seeing a batch of callers off and receiving another when I arrived to take my place among the mourners in the drawing room. There was no need to make statements at the front door either to arrivers or leave-takers, but I heard him murmur how avoidable this tragedy had been. Rose had drunk too much, walked out of the house after dinner, unsteady on her feet, gone to the well, fallen in. In the drawing room the heavy hush of Rose's friends contrasted with the excited talk in the ante-room I had passed of those who had come to congratulate Dev on his appointment as Cabinet Minister, that morning, and the political rejoicing of the youth camp outside. One youth, aged thirty-five or forty, *lungi* clad, stragglyhaired, had his arms straight up in the air, his eyes rolling white, while his body twitched and lurched to the rhythm of the *bhangra* and a circle of loose-limbed dancers revolved around him.

I went to the chair beside Nishi, the only empty one in the room. The bereavement was mine, not Nishi's. Far from finding formal words of condolence or squeezing so much as a single tear out of my dry unslept eyes, I felt a freezing, baffling anger I couldn't explain. I needed the facts, but mature conversation was something I didn't expect from Nishi. Not that I had ever had much to do with her. As a hostess she gave the impression of a puppet, wire-pulled and master-minded, trotting out conventional, feather-light responses. Imprisoned inside those delicate bird bones I suspected 'Nishi' was a creature no one knew, in recoil from experiences too painful to assimilate, and I pitied her. But at the moment this doll in mechanical mourning filled me with horror, her mouth and eyes forming busy o's and ah's in a stream of soft incessant chatter. I had expected the ritual recital, with a certain amount of repetition, of what had happened and how, but not quite this. 'I suppose she couldn't bear it any more. I used to see her sitting in Daddy-ji's room, looking at him, waiting for him to recognize her, whispering Ram Ram Ram to herself like a prayer. She was getting into a desperate state about his not improving. I suppose she couldn't bear it any more. Any more,' mouthed Nishi, winding down before taking up the toneless narrative again, 'She couldn't bear it –' My hand closed around her wrist and Nishi stopped. She turned to look dreamily at me. 'Will you stay,' she whispered, 'and go through her things? Will you look after that side of it?'

I went upstairs. So Rose had walked out of the house in desperation in the dead of night, not being able to bear it any more, and jumped into the well. Or been drunk and fallen accidentally into it. Unsteady on her feet, Dev had said, as I stood on the doorstep, before I was even inside the house. Yet it was very noticeable how steady Rose was on her feet when she had had a drink or two, taking care to put her feet heavily on the ground in a slow, measured way. 'Ram says I walk as if I were flat-footed,' she used to joke. Nothing unsteady about her walk, especially if she had had one too many. And then there was the matter of her drinking. If a searchlight were trained on that habit, it would light up the blazing truths she tactlessly tumbled out with, revelations far from pleasant to behold as they lay naked on the drawing room carpet, or had to be swallowed with the *roganjosh* at dinner. Rose drunk usually meant Rose making merry with freedom of speech, hitting nails squarely on their ugly heads. Desperation there must have been with Rose drinking, but was it Rose's? Within minutes of my arrival fables had arisen and become eternal verities. My murdered great-grandmother's relatives had said she had sacrificed herself – which even a goat has too much sense to do – on the altar of *sati*. They had built a shrine on the guilt-soaked spot to commemorate the martyrdom of the last woman to perform the noble act in the entire region. A place of pilgrimage, no less, with nothing but a document at the bottom of my father's trunk to prove it had been murder. I was in a rage as I got down to sorting Rose's possessions, dark tides of blood around me ending in monuments and shrines.

Here in this house the revision of history had begun and there would be no end to the lies. In no rational world could Dev have become a Cabinet Minister and by no stretch of the imagination could Rose have taken her own life. She did her walking before dinner, not late at night in the pitch dark. Why would she have crossed a road without a street light on it, stumbled along the stony ground on the other side, gone way out past the tomb, past the rowdy youth camp, and thrown herself into a well she was constantly warning the beggar about? It was plain she had been killed and plainer still that Rose's killers would never be brought to justice. They would live out their comfortable lives and die patriotic citizens. I had not been able to stay a forger's hand. A murder protected by the ramparts of political power put it much further beyond the reach of justice. I asked Kumar whether he had seen any signs of desperation in Rose and he said none. She had been depressed since sahib's illness but she still joked and laughed. He added in a subdued voice while he lined up Rose's suitcases and cartons that I should speak to the beggar before going home. He hung around there near the well, and the well was where her body had been found.

I spent all day in Rose's room. Everything she owned was in it. To concentrate her whole being there, with not a stray cushion or an ashtray of hers anywhere else in the house, showed what a desert the rest of the house must have seemed to her. Now it was a desert to me. Even if I had been hungry I couldn't have brought myself to eat lunch with accessories to murder. Kumar brought me some food on a tray and took it away untouched. I told him I didn't need him, but he waited in the corridor outside, and after a while came in again to help me sort and pack. I had been wrong. We needed each other. He began lifting dresses off hangers, taking clothes from drawers and laying them on her bed. Her life had ended abruptly but so had the use of these garments. What use would ample dresses belonging to an Englishwoman be to anyone? She had no relatives I knew of who would want even a souvenir kept for them. Only these piles of clothes, shoes, trinkets and snapshot albums remained to show Rose had been here. It was an ending terrible in its finality. In Kumar's haggard presence I sat on her bed on top of her dresses and cried as I had cried my heart out to Rose years ago in her hotel room in London.

Through my tears I saw the picture postcard she had bought that day, clipped to her dressing table mirror. I hadn't noticed it when I had come here after the Happyola ceremony and several times since to give her what support I could, but there was so much of life right under my nose it had taken me so long to notice, I could easily have missed a postcard staring me in the face. 'L'Embarquement pour l'île de Cythère.' I had scoffed at the operatic make-believe of it, but now, all these years later when I did not have my own consuming love affair on my mind, the landscape worked its spell on me with its impossible trees, its charmed foliage, its invitation to fantasy. The poignance of the embarkation for Cythera reached out to me as it must have to the dreaming, yearning heart of Rose, and I cried bitterly, till Kumar begged me agitatedly to stop, glancing at the door from time to time as though we were traitors to the household and would be caught red-handed in treason if we did not take care. I unclipped the postcard from the mirror and put it in my handbag. I couldn't think of a lovelier remembrance of Rose.

I went into Uncle Ram's sickroom. The nurse got up to leave but I told her not to disturb herself. All I wanted was to tell Uncle Ram about Rose's death. I did not think Dev had made the effort, and Nishi had enough to do keeping herself on the rails. I called his name again and again. There was not a flicker from him, not even the feeble sign of awareness Rose used to say she saw. It might as well have been a corpse on the bed. His coma was complete. Had he, her own husband, known the woman who had passed through his life? The nurse took me for a relative as I stood beside the bed with my face in my hands and started to weep all over again. Then I determinedly stopped, and went back to her room to pack away the belongings no one would ever use again.

It was hard to shut out the fiendish possibilities my mind kept supplying about the manner of her death. But after a while I found myself calmed and soothed as I handled her clothes. Kumar

and I managed conversation between us, rallying ourselves with
the friendly feel of possessions we'd seen her use. We had
known her a long time, I through all the ages and stages of my
life, as one knows brightness, warmth and the comfort of
everyday things.

'Sonali,' I heard my father say, his hand holding mine, 'come
and meet Rose.'

I was seven years old, looking up at a being from another
world, the most dazzlingly red and white creature I had ever
seen.

'Is that her name or is she one?' I asked precociously, showing
off in the company of my proud father.

'That's enough of being ready with answers,' Mama ticked
me off.

But Papa replied, 'It is her name, and she is one, too,' making
Rose blush with pleasure as he quoted:

> *And then and then came Spring, and rose-in-hand*
> *My threadbare penitence apieces tore.*

I sat on Papa's lap entranced, busying myself with my favourite
occupation of staring at the grown-ups, taking in the scene
around me, most of all this vision on the sofa beside me. Uncle
Ram and Mama sat in chairs across from us, poised, perfect and
complete in themselves. I could almost see a circle around each
chair that in children's games is the boundary you never cross.
But Papa and Rose looked uncertain, their smiles hesitant, with
an expectancy about them only the love of others could fulfil. I
wanted to fling myself on each of them in turn and say reassur-
ingly, here's lots of love from your loving Sonali.

'I'm not sure what that means, Keshav,' said Rose.

'It means I've repented of repenting, of apologizing for being
what I am, doing the job I do. If a seesaw is what I've chosen
to live on, I'll live on it and make the best of it. But it was you,
Rose, who came along and made me see it was a seesaw I was
on and that I was neither doomed nor dying!'

Rose said delightedly, 'Well, I never! It's only because I was

on one too.' And she went on with her twinkling talk, unaware
of the legacy she'd handed on in her lifetime.

I looked about me at the suitcases I had packed, the blankets,
sheets and curtains, also Rose's, lying folded on her bed, the
uncurtained window a rectangle veiled in grey light, and below
and beyond, the tomb, reminding me I had to see the beggar
before I left. Kumar came out to the car with me. When I got
in and rolled the glass down, his hands grasped the open window
fiercely as if he meant to keep the car from moving. 'What can
I say?' he cried out, his turn now, tears streaking his sunken
cheeks. I covered his hand with mine. 'Say nothing,' I said
firmly, never surer of my advice. As against justice for the dead
which would never be done, there was no need to imperil the
employment and security of the living. 'She would want you to
be safe.'

I drove out through the gates past the well. I had been here
before, generations before, and I felt the enfolding chill of a
death I knew to be murder. I followed my great-grandmother's
instincts when she led her son away from the house, away from
watchers and listeners, to the privacy of the garden. Seventy
years later and hundreds of miles distant from the scene of that
earlier crime I parked my car under a tree on a Delhi road, out
of sight of the youth camp now being dismantled. My grey shawl
draping me blended me into the evening, and I returned on foot
to the well, a solitary walker from one of the few houses in the
area. The beggar was nowhere to be seen. Nor was anyone
else. I walked in Rose's footsteps to the tomb. When he's not
around outside, he's usually in the tomb, she had once told me,
it's his home, he hasn't got any other. Inside I could see nothing
until my eyes grew accustomed to the gloom. After a while I
saw him, part of the moss-covered wall, curved foetus-like
against it, and I called out softly saying I had a message for him.
He woke with a frightened jerk and came towards me shivering
and muttering, moving with his sideways crawl. I sat down
facing him and I knew what Rose had meant when she said, A
man should at least be able to wipe away his own tears. Helpless
as he was, I felt as helpless, not knowing whether I should reach
out and wipe them with my handkerchief. Social etiquette does

not cover these situations. But I was glad I could tell him about
the artificial hands I had arranged for him and that I would take
him in a day or two to get them fitted. After he had learned to
use them he would be taught a trade. He had been waiting for
the news, and now that I had come, he said, his voice teary and
rasping, he couldn't stay here any more, not after what he had
seen, a youth camp tough suffocating her with a sack descending
over her head, another pinioning her arms, both of them carrying
her out, where else but to the well where her body was found?
If those two ever recalled seeing him here in the tomb, a
witness, they would come for him. But didn't she come walking
in the early evening, I brought out with difficulty, before it was
properly dark? How could they have carried her body all the
way to the well? Weren't they afraid they'd be seen? Who was
there to be afraid of? asked the beggar. It is their *raj* around
here. They do what they like. That's why you must take me
with you.

We came out into a deeper dark, he covering the ground
towards my car almost as rapidly as I did myself, both of us in
a frantic hurry now to get away. 'I'll help you in,' I offered, but
he clambered agilely on to the back seat, refusing help, a
confident candidate for a new future with artificial hands.

'How did you lose your hands?' I asked, getting behind the
wheel.

As we left the tomb far behind us, I could sense the change
in him, the almost leisurely way he said, 'They were chopped
off the second year of the police occupation of our village at
harvest time.'

The second, I asked? So he told me about the first. The
following year he and the other sharecroppers had joined the
movement the surrounding villages had begun. He would never
forget how elated they had felt, and how safe, all of them
together. They had cut the rice, tied up their share of it and
brought it home. The word had spread and more villagers had
taken home their share of the harvest. It had gone off smoothly
and they had decided to do it every year, but that was just what
two of them, chosen as random examples, were prevented from
doing. They lay in the landlord's backyard covered in each

other's blood before they were dragged along the ground and dumped in a thicket outside, face down in the mud. Nor had his village ever tried it again after that, he didn't know about the surrounding ones.

We were driving past pleasant drifts of woodsmoke and tidy stacks of rice husk ready for burning. It was too late for my painful shock to mitigate a fearsome tragedy, but not too late for me to wonder when the saga of peaceful change I had been serving from behind my desk had become a saga of another kind, with citizens broken on the wheel for remembering their rights.

'Were you able to do nothing?' I asked.

'What can a person like myself do? It is their *raj*.'

They, them, the ruling class on one side, the ruled on the other. Power had changed hands but what else had changed where he lived? If ever there had been an emergency, it was this.

'There are laws to protect tenants. Didn't you put your sharecropping arrangements on the land record? Wasn't there some evidence of it?'

'It's the landlord's *raj* in my village, record or no record.'

'Didn't any political party help you to get your due?'

'They are all landlords at heart.'

There are events that make peaceful change and progress sound like macabre jokes. Like my great-grandfather's my very thoughts trembled at what happened up and down this land.

'How did you come all the way from Bihar?' I asked.

He was talkative, a man who did not get much chance to practise talking.

'On a train with my elder brother and eleven others recruited as migrant labour for a farm not far from here by one Divan Singh – except myself of course. My brother brought me because he refused to leave me behind. He thought I would lose my reason sitting in the village. Why cart a useless non-earning carcass hundreds of miles, I told him, but he wouldn't listen. You can beg, he said.'

He had tried cultivating the beggar's whine in Connaught Place, lifting an elbow towards the empty tin tied to one ankle.

But New Delhi's population had walked past him with its face rigidly averted. Some sights were way beyond pity. Finally with his brother's help he had found shelter in the tomb, and afterwards the memsahib had appeared out of nowhere to provide food and protection.

'Your brother has a kind heart.'

'He is my brother.'

Brotherhood. Family. The nurture that had brought him and me where we were.

'The memsahib's kinsmen must be coming for the last rites.'

'I don't think she has any.'

'No brothers? No sisters? No relatives?' he asked in dismay.

Except ourselves, I could have said.

'What a calamity to have no one of your own flesh and blood to lay your body to rest.'

But Rose had transcended those things, blood, race, distance. I wondered how I could have felt there was nothing to show for her ever having been here. I had not looked at the faces of Nishi's callers, those whose paths Rose had crossed – I wouldn't have known the man in my car but for her – and if streets and sidewalks could have spoken, the places here and across the border she had made hers. No, it was no calamity, I said, in fact just the opposite. There had to be a special grace and favour reserved for people like her who loved and cherished strangers.

After Rose's burial I drove out every afternoon to Tughlakabad and wore myself out tramping the fields, trying to come to terms with the evil of concealed, unreported murder as much as with the terrible way Rose had died, and the wilderness of loss that now included Rose. The jagged, unresolved edges of a disastrous year dovetailed at home into ginger-fried new green peas, the first of the season, and fragrant sugar-and-spiced Kashmiri tea Mama liked to make as soon as the cold weather came. She would be waiting for me with both on a *takht* on the back verandah, her way of loving. She told me she had gone to the market herself early one morning to buy the peas, to avoid the avalanche of Punjabis who arrived later, and didn't know an old pea from a new one, poor dears, so it didn't matter which they got. I was brushed by the same butterfly touch of concern from

Kiran and Neel in my new orphaned state. It made me feel lulled and held, if not yet healed. Kachru was there with Mama on the third or fourth day after the funeral, eating her peas and drinking her tea, and I heard Mama say as I came in from my outing, 'What a blow to Bhabi-jān.' His intervention for Rose had been most unwise, as she had known it would be, and now it seemed that Kachru, no longer chief explainer of the emergency, was just a Joint Secretary who would soon be shunted out of Delhi. 'Oh my God, what a blow to Bhabi-jān!' Mama repeated as I took a cup of tea from her. 'Tell her I'll come and see her tomorrow.'

'I'm sorry your speaking to Dev has got you into trouble,' I said. 'I feel responsible.'

'Things have slipped out of control. There are no rules and regulations any more. I never realized it would come to this.'

He lapsed into silence, unusual for him.

Mama said, 'Well, I must go indoors, it's getting too chilly for me out here.' She patted my head, drew her silky brown shawl more snugly around her and tucked her feet into her bedroom slippers. The screen door swung shut behind her. Kachru and I sat leaning against the bolster on the *takht*, as we had at his house or mine in another place and time. Good food is childhood's food. And nothing in the world could have so warmed me or sounded so funny as Mama's outrageous Kashmiriness outwitting the Punjabis over peas, while they, unknown to her, probably went home chortling over carrots.

'I want you to know I kept my word,' said Kachru. 'I did my best for Rose. I tried to help.'

'I was sure you had."

'I did it for you. I wanted to do at least one thing for you.'

'Why – suddenly?' I asked.

'There was something in your face, testing me, that night. I've always failed your tests. I wanted to measure up for once. You've always been so "burning bright".'

'I thought *you* were, sometimes about the wrong things.'

'I may have been, on my soapbox, about one theory or another. But you were – are – in yourself. Burning brightness is an inner quality.'

'Was it the blinding glare that put you off?' I asked lightly.

He gave it serious thought. 'You were too brave for me. You set impossible stardards.'

'It's your own standards you didn't meet,' I protested.

He fell silent again and we watched a smoky haze envelop the small compound.

'I had to think of Bhabi-jān,' he said at last. 'One can't always do as one wants.'

An unlikely ending to dreams of changing the world, I thought, with Marxism foundering not on the fourth stage of the revolution but on Bhabi-jān. Only the cloudless commitment, like the perfect relationship, could be knocked sideways with a feather. It was doubts and uncertainties that kept things alive and kicking.

'It's too late now, but if we had our time over again, I'd work it out differently,' he said quietly. 'I spoke to Dev because I loved you dearly. I suppose I always have.'

As ever I saw life the wrong way round. Bimmie's wedding had cured me of marriage, and the saint had been a blob. This admission of waste, of years gone and opportunity lost, filled me with a sweet relief. Isolated from all that had happened outside our private creation it had the wonder for me of broken ends mending, of Kachru becoming Ravi again, of friendship resuming, of love having been really love and not a mistake he had been trying to forget.

'I loved you too,' I said, and it was true and always would be of the uncorrupted offerings we freely make to others at times of our lives.

'But would you have it over again?'

It had been a jewel of a time. It belonged in its young and shining setting, in the past. It wasn't mine any more to remake. And I was free of it. Most of all I was free.

'I've never been so happy or so unhappy as I was then,' I told him, an honest answer.

He was dejected about his transfer and his fall from grace, matters we could discuss now that we could talk.

He got up to go and I slipped my arm through his. Kiran was on the porch as we came out. 'Ravi, I've just heard about your transfer. How dreadful for Bhabi-jān!' Ravi's hand tightened on mine and the ghost of absent Rose between us made us shake with secret laughter as I went out with him to his car to see him off. Bhabijān was sure to start a campaign to restore her son to royal favour and he would probably let himself be restored, but we had shared for a minute the absurdity of it all, and I knew there would be times and ways we still could recapture our private past, have it, more gently, over again.

The day after his visit Mama told me when I returned from my walk, 'A Mrs Carlyle rang for you. She's staying at the Ashoka.'

The name meant nothing to me until her voice on the telephone said, 'This is Marcella Carlyle, a friend of friends,' and asked if I would have lunch with her and her husband at their hotel the next day. There was a matter they would so like to discuss with me.

I went straight up to their table in the Peacock Room. I had no problem distinguishing them. Her face was the face on tapestries it took months to embroider in the Middle Ages. Its features had a clarity and purity human features don't often retain. All it needed was the medieval gown and headdress, sleek hounds and horses, chivalrous attendants and a flower-strewn foreground to make it a priceless Gothic heirloom. Brian, handsome, but more like you and me, no chivalric or stained glass magic about him, was on his feet greeting me.

'How good of you to come, my dear,' said Marcella. 'I feel I know you. Rose and Ram spoke so fondly of you. We'll order lunch first and then talk.'

I left the ordering to her. Rose was right. She had done it for centuries.

'We came to India to see how Ram was. We had had such garbled accounts about his condition, I felt we really must come and see him for ourselves. We wanted to discuss a new project Brian has in mind. You know Brian's passion is the mid-seventeenth to the mid-eighteenth century.'

'No, I didn't.'

'He's decided to retire from his business and devote all his time to it, haven't you, darling, and to extend his interest to that marvellously creative era outside Europe as well. I've persuaded him to start with India.'

'It's very curious to be a stranger to a country Marcella adores,' said Brian. 'I'm eager to close the gap. You will help us, won't you?'

'We wanted Ram to join our venture,' said Marcella. 'There was almost nothing he didn't know about the decorative arts of the period. But when we went to the house yesterday we heard about Rose's fatal accident and saw the state Ram is in. It was the most awful shock.'

Brian laid a sympathetic hand over hers and she rewarded him with a grateful glance. The food arrived and Marcella started eating and talking at the same time with a quicksilver delicacy that created the illusion she was merely gently gossiping, except that the food kept disappearing off her plate. It was an accomplishment I had never seen before. Brian was discussing a meagre wine list with the waiter.

'What we'd like is research assistance – a picture of the century, as it were – and then you'd have to help us set up an exhibition perhaps at the end of next year at a gallery Brian is opening in London this coming spring. Ram always spoke of you as being so exceptionally bright. Did you know I met your father at his house more than once?'

'I have no training in art. I was a civil servant until I was thrown out, soon after the emergency began. I'm no use at anything else.'

'It's much too soon to decide that,' said Marcella. 'When a career ends one should try one's hand at another. Famous detectives grow marrows. Statesmen open pubs. In your case you're so young you could take off in any direction you liked. This will have as much to do with history as with art, and that, I'm told, was your subject. I promise you it will be interesting.'

'It sounds wonderful, only I –'

'I took an art course when I was young,' continued Marcella, as a bottle of wine arrived in a bucket of ice. 'Like all the other girls in the class I had my little notebook and pencil with me and as soon as the instructor started showing slides we opened our notebooks and got busy copying down every word he said. He put us right in no time. "Young ladies," he said, "close your books and open your eyes." I've found it the only prescription for understanding art ever since. Or, I daresay, life. Is that the wine, darling?'

The waiter whispered to Brian that wine was not to be served to Indian nationals in public places.

'How quite extraordinary!' exclaimed Marcella musically. 'But this will have to be an exception because our guest will be joining us in a glass of wine.'

We raised our glasses to each other and to the exhibition.

'We're counting on you,' said Brian.

'But why me? You must know everyone there is to know here, artists, historians, officials and experts.'

'Oh, of course, my dear,' said Marcella, 'but they're all so busy with the emergency, and no one wanting to set a foot wrong. And frankly, I don't think we can do better than rope you in.'

'We shall be travelling for a fortnight. Think it over and give us your answer when we get back. Then we can sort out the details,' said Brian, taking my answer for granted.

'And after all it needn't be a lifelong commitment,' said Marcella gaily. 'If you find you don't enjoy it, you can always do something else later, when the emergency is over.'

'Over?'

A word can start the rumour of a rainbow. Until she said it I hadn't realized the emergency could ever be over, or that my future hadn't come to an end on a steamy day in July this year.

'Meanwhile you'll find working with Brian quite an experience,' she assured me. 'You two are going to be a most successful combine.'

Marcella had made an excellent choice of food and Brian's wine was the best the hotel had to offer. I was hungry and I felt dangerously on the brink of enjoyment, no notebooks or desks to impede me, and my eyes wide open. I looked at Marcella, a translucence about her that belied her strength. A flame is both. So was the civilization that had produced her, matchless in the Western world for its unbroken continuity.

That afternoon I did not go walking. I went straight home and took a history book off my shelves, opened it and started to read:

The seventeenth century was the great age of the Mughal Empire. Akbar had reintegrated northern and central India and given it a Persian form. His successors maintained his work until the empire extended nearly to Cape Comorin and the Persian dress seemed the natural garb of India. India presented an impressive picture to the world and created the modern legend of wealth and power which lasted well into the nineteenth century. India was the land of the 'Great Mogul'. For the first time since classical days India was open to detailed and skilled European observation. She ceased to be a legend about which tales could be spun with little relation to the facts . . . India had become real to Europe.

I turned the pages and read on:

. . . there was a general recognition that a great power existed in India embracing a developed civilization with great attainments in letters and the arts, with polished manners and a complicated social life. India occupied in the mind of seventeenth-century Europe something of the place taken in the eighteenth century by China. The picture of India derived from classical sources was at last replaced by a contemporary one.

I went on reading. I read for two weeks. Dutch and English travellers, said my historian, had been accurate observers. The Italian, Manucci, who had come as a boy and stayed till he died, about 1718, was full of anecdotes though not so strong on facts. Sir Thomas Roe had been James I's ambassador to the court of Jehangir. The French jeweller, Tavernier, had valued the Peacock Throne. The French doctor, François Bernier, spent nine years at the Moghul court, his accounts informing the French minister, Colbert, and all Europe about Aurangzeb's savage war of succession and the society of his time. And there were encyclopaedic accounts of Moghul administration, beginning with

Abu'l Fazl's monument to Akbar's reign. There were contemporary Indian histories and the personal documents and correspondence of the emperors. There was, in fact, a mountain of work
to do, producing a picture of Brian's century, which thank
goodness was such a well-documented one.

I went to work. Immersed in the past, I was preparing all the
while for the future beyond Brian's century and his exhibition.
Marcella had reminded me of it, made a gift of it to me. Though
it was really Rose's legacy again, the paths that had crossed
hers now crossing mine, reminding me I was young and alive,
with my own century stretched out before me, waiting to be
lived.

GLOSSARY OF INDIAN WORDS

Angrezi bahu – English daughter-in-law
Arya Samaj – a society founded in 1875 that attacked orthodox Hindu
   customs and ritual, and promoted religious reform, social uplift and
   education
ashram – a community founded for an ascetic or religious purpose
Bhabi-jān – sister-in-law
bhangra – a dance popular in the Punjab
Bhaiyon aur Behenon – brothers and sisters
chaman – homemade cheese
chappati – unleavened bread
chota peg – a small whisky
chowkidar – watchman
dal – lentils
dharma – duty, religion
dhobi – laundryman
diya – earthen lamp
dupatta – long scarf
hai hai! – a lament
Hindu-Muslim ek ho – Hindus and Muslims, unite
ICS – Indian Civil Service
Inquilab Zindabad – Long Live Revolution
Ishvar-Allah tere nam – Ishvar and Allah are thy names
Sab ko sammati de bhagvan – All in God's eyes are one
jelabies – a syrup-filled sweetmeat
jungli – wild, undisciplined, uncivilized
katori – a small bowl
Kayasth – the name of a caste usually associated with bureaucratic
   occupations
khabardar – be careful
kirtan – prayer meeting
koftas – meatballs
kurta – long loose shirt

lathi – rod (steel-tipped when used by the police)

lungi – a length of cloth worn wrapped around the waist, reaching to the ankles

mitha bhatta – sweet rice

neta – leader

nivar – bands of cloth webbing

Oof toba toba! – an exclamation of shock, regret, condemnation

Panditji – the name (title) by which Jawaharlal Nehru was known

raj – rule

Rashtrapati Bhawan – the official residence of the President of India

RSS – a Hindu revival organization

roganjosh – a meat dish

samosa – a pastry filled with meat or vegetables

sati (suttee) – a woman who is cremated alive on her husband's funeral pyre

satyagraha – fight for truth, the name by which Mahatma Gandhi's civil disobedience campaigns were known

shastras – scriptures

shikar – hunt

swarga – heaven

takht – divan

thali – round tray on which food is served

thana – police station

tilak – caste mark worn on the forehead

tonga – two-wheeled horse-drawn vehicle

zemindari – feudal system of landownership

zindabad – long live

WILLIAM McILVANNEY

DOCHERTY

Winner of the 1975 Whitbread Award for Fiction

An unforgettable evocation of a Scottish mining community

Docherty: survivor of an impoverished life of hardship in the Scottish town of Graithnock. Conn: the son in whom Docherty invests all hope for a far different future. High Street: the heart of the squalor and degradation of the mining community. Their home. Docherty may dream of escape, but in his tough, uncompromising and fiercely guarded world he emerges as an unelected leader of indomitable strength. And though he may resist it, his son too is entrenched in a society whose traditions and fellowship exercise a relentless grip on any who have known it . . .

'An intense, witty and beautifully wrought novel . . . marvellously rendered'

Daily Telegraph

'He has a hard muscular quality to his writing. Some of his phrases hammer against you like a collier's pick. And he cares for them too'

The Times

IRMGARD KEUN

AFTER MIDNIGHT

'And now I feel like crying, because I really do *not* understand, and I don't think I will when I'm older, either'

Nineteen-year-old Susanne is not political. She is an ordinary, fairly carefree teenager who lives with her brother Algin, a writer. But her life is increasingly disrupted by the pressures of the Nazi regime. Queues of people form as informers flock to denounce their neighbours. Someone has invented a divining rod to detect Jews. Algin's books are banned and finally her boyfriend is arrested for 'talking like a communist'.

First published in 1937 in Amsterdam, and written in the natural, often surprisingly humorous, prose of a young girl, AFTER MIDNIGHT paints a terrifying picture of Germany under the Third Reich.

'I cannot think of anything else that conjures up so powerfully the atmosphere of a nation turned insane . . . one of those pieces of fiction that illuminate fact'

Sunday Telegraph

'Keun effectively conveys a sense of the inevitable helplessness of the individual . . . it feels truthful. A worthwhile new translation'

Sunday Times

Current and forthcoming titles from Sceptre

WILLIAM McILVANNEY

DOCHERTY

IRMGARD KEUN

AFTER MIDNIGHT

BERNARD LEVIN

HANNIBAL'S FOOTSTEPS

CONDUCTED TOUR

LAURENCE OLIVIER

CONFESSIONS OF AN ACTOR

LYALL WATSON

DREAMS OF DRAGONS

BOOKS OF DISTINCTION